THE CR(EE

Ben Cheetham

Cover design by Ivan Cakic (cakamuradesigns.com)

If you want to find out more about the author and his
books, you can do so at bencheetham.com

By the pricking of my thumbs,
Something wicked this way comes.

SECOND WITCH, MACBETH.

1

'The Dark History of Nursery Rhymes' Lily typed into her laptop. Puffing her cheeks, she stared vacantly at the screen. Why should she care about the history of nursery rhymes? What was the point of knowing that 'Mary Mary Quite Contrary' was really about Queen Mary I burning protestant women at the stake? Or that, according to some nerdy professor, 'Jack and Jill' were actually King Louis XVI and his wife Marie Antoinette on their way to be guillotined? How would any of this help her get a job after she finished school?

She scrolled down to a cartoonish image of a rosy-cheeked woman in a frilly maid's hat. With her head, arms and legs poking out of holes carved into a giant pumpkin, the woman resembled a criminal in the stocks. A stick-thin man in a black suit and yellow waistcoat was sat on the pumpkin. Sad, angry eyes squinted out of his beaky face.

Lily read the bizarre picture's title aloud. "Peter, Peter Pumpkin Eater."

Music suddenly blared from downstairs. Bunching her eyebrows, Lily got off her bed and went to the landing. The twanging of a guitar reverberated through the house, accompanied by a husky voice. She knew the song well. Every year on their anniversary, her parents danced along to it in each other's arms. Or, at least, they used to.

Lily began to descend the stairs, tiptoeing even though the music was loud enough to cover her footsteps. She stooped to peer between the angle where the bannister met the hallway ceiling. Just beyond an open door, her dad was slumped in an armchair. He had a tumbler of amber liquid in one hand and a bottle in the other. She frowned. The bottle was almost empty.

A framed photo was propped on the arm of the chair. A younger, decidedly slimmer version of her dad stared back at him from the photo, alongside a dainty bride in an off-the-shoulder lacy white dress. A calligraphy caption underscored the photo – 'Peter & Hazel, 13th of July, 2006'. Lily knew the date off by heart. It was the same as her birthday.

The newlyweds' heads were tilted together, touching at the temples. Peter's short blonde hair contrasted with Hazel's long black curls. Stilettos just about raised her up to his height. A gossamer train trailed down her slender body, pooling at her heels. Her dark eyes were set wide apart in a face as pale and delicate as a Tudor portrait. The groom was grinning like the proverbial cat that got the cream. Lily couldn't remember the last time she'd seen him smiling like that.

Peter raised the tumbler to his mouth, his eyes narrowing to ugly slits. Lily's stomach tied itself into a knot. She could almost hear the thoughts squirming through his mind – thoughts even more poisonous than the alcohol he was pouring down his throat.

She quietly took out her phone and messaged her mum 'Dad's drinking again'.

The music cut off mid-song. Lifting her gaze, Lily found herself looking into eyes that were the same opal blue as her own. Father and daughter stared at each other uncertainly, almost as if they were strangers. His lips curving into a strange happy-sad smile, Peter beckoned to Lily.

With a hint of reluctance in her step, she made her way to the living room. She halted in the doorway.

"Here's Daddy's little princess," said Peter, his words slurring into one another.

A flicker of irritation crossed Lily's face. He knew how much she hated being called that. Seemingly too drunk to notice the stony stare his term of endearment elicited, he beckoned again.

Lily hesitated for a telling moment before moving closer. This time, Peter's eyes betrayed a glimmer of hurt. His smile remained intact as he reached out to stroke her knuckles with his thumb. "Remember how I used to do this when you couldn't sleep?"

She nodded. There had been a time when he sat at her bedside every night playing her knuckles like piano keys for as long as it took – sometimes minutes, sometimes hours – to soothe her off to sleep.

"Your mum didn't approve," he continued. "She used to say I was making a rod for my own back. But I didn't mind. To be honest, I was sad when you stopped needing my help to go to sleep."

Peter heaved a sigh as if the sadness had never gone away. Lily shifted her feet uneasily, watching his thumb move back and forth.

His smile vanished. Tightening his grip, he tugged her towards him. "You know I'd never hurt you, don't you, Lily?"

Her nose wrinkled as his whisky breath stung her nostrils. She gave an unconvincing little nod.

Peter's drink sloshed over the rim of his glass as he prodded his chest. "I'm not a bad person."

His eyes implored Lily to agree with his words. She blinked away from them.

He released another sigh that seemed to come from the depths of his lungs. His hand dropped from Lily to the bottle. He refilled his glass, drained it, then let his head fall back against the chair. His eyelids closed slowly over glazed pupils. A faint singsong voice trickled from his lips.

Lily's mousy brown hair curtained her face as she leaned in to hear what he was saying.

"Peter, Peter, pumpkin eater, had a wife and couldn't keep her. He put her in a pumpkin shell, and there he kept her very well."

Her big blue eyes grew even bigger. She'd never heard that nasty little rhyme before today. Now she'd come across it twice in the space of a few minutes. Was it merely a weird coincidence or was there another explanation? Had her dad been eavesdropping on her? The way he'd been acting lately, she wouldn't have put it past him. As he repeated the rhyme, an unsettlingly comical image came to mind of her mum imprisoned in a giant pumpkin with him perched on top of it.

Lily flinched backwards as her dad's eyelids snapped apart. He peered up at her, his dilated pupils swimming with disorientation. His lips spread into the same happy-sad smile. "Here's Daddy's little princess," he said as if their earlier conversation hadn't taken place.

With worried eyes, Lily watched him struggling to sit up. The heavy drinking of the past few months had exacted a visible toll. The whites of his eyes were a jaundiced yellow. Networks of spidery red veins crisscrossed his cheeks and nose.

Lily was suddenly struck by the strongest feeling that the man in front of her wasn't her dad. He was an imposter. Her real dad – the one she idolised – had been kidnapped and replaced with a paranoid alcoholic doppelgänger.

As if reading her mind, Peter said forlornly, "I'm sorry, Lily. I know I've not been myself." He hooked a finger at his scalp as if trying to dig out a tick. "I keep having these thoughts."

Lily felt compelled to ask the obvious question. "What

thoughts?"

"Bad thoughts. The–" Peter's voice cracked with shame. "The worst you can imagine."

Lily wasn't sure she really wanted to know what the 'bad thoughts' were. All she truly wanted was for things to go back to how they'd been before the drinking started.

A confused, lost look haunted Peter's eyes. "Why can't I stop feeling this way?"

"Maybe…" Lily chewed her lips, screwing up the nerve to continue. "Maybe it would help if you stopped drinking."

"Stopped drinking?" Peter echoed as if he'd never heard anything so absurd. He tapped the whisky bottle. "This is the only thing I can trust to be there when I need it."

"That's not true, Dad. You can trust me."

"Can I?" Peter cocked a bleary eye at Lily. "What were you doing on the stairs?"

"I was…" she faltered, blinking guiltily.

"You were messaging your mum," he finished for her. He screwed his mouth into a smile that made him look like he was about to cry. "Don't feel bad, Lily. It's not your fault. It's just life. Eventually, everyone lets you down."

Her face crumpled like a paper bag at his words.

He reached out as if to stroke the creases from her forehead, but drew his hand back. "What the hell's the matter with me? I shouldn't be talking to you like this." He shook his head. "This isn't me. This isn't who I am." As if to prove he meant what he said, he snatched up the whisky bottle and made to upend its contents over the carpet. Before a single drop was spilled, though, he turned the bottle back upright. He stared at it abjectly. "It's funny how we take things for granted until they're gone." His tone suggested it was anything but funny. "I just want what we had. I want us to be a happy family, but–" He broke off at the jangle of keys in the front door.

"Hello?" a concerned voice called out. "Lily?"

"In here, Mum."

Heels clicked rapidly along the hallway. Hazel's pale face appeared in the doorway. A relieved smile lifted her glossy lips as she met Lily's gaze. It faded as she looked at her husband.

Peter directed a suspicious squint at her high-heels and figure-hugging suit. "Well, don't you look nice." His lips twisted on the word 'nice' like it was an accusation. "Where've you been all dressed up like that?"

Hazel heaved the sigh of someone aware that anything they said would incur anger. "Do we have to do this, Peter? It's been a long day. I'm tired. All I want to do is–"

"I don't care what you want," he cut in. "*I want* to know where you've been. It's almost eight o'clock. You finished work hours ago."

"I told you I'd probably have to work late."

Peter furrowed his forehead as if he was sifting through old memories. "No you didn't."

"*Yes I did.*" Hazel's mane of black hair bounced on her shoulders as she strode forwards to snatch the whisky bottle from him. "This is why you can't remember a word I said."

Scowling like a petulant child, Peter made a grab for the bottle.

Hazel lifted it beyond his reach. He started to stand up, but dropped back into the armchair as if the effort was too much for him.

Hazel gave him a look that was equal parts pity and despair. She turned to Lily. "Have you eaten?"

Before Lily could respond, Peter bellowed, "Don't you dare turn your back on me!"

He lunged to grab Hazel's wrist. She grimaced as he yanked her around to face him.

"Let go of her," demanded Lily.

Peter glared at her. "This is none of your business, Lily. Go to your room."

She remained where she was, her gaze alternating between her parents.

Hazel smiled reassuringly, putting her free hand on Lily's shoulder and ushering her towards the door. "Go on. Do as your dad says."

Dragging her feet, Lily headed for the stairs. Halfway up them, she paused to look at her parents. Her mum wafted her onwards before closing the door. Lily stared at it as if trying to drill through the wood with her eyes.

"I want to know where you've been!" Peter shouted.

Like a startled rabbit, Lily bolted to her room. As more shouts rang out, she threw herself onto her bed and squeezed a pillow over her ears. Confusion pounded in her temples. Why was her dad doing this? Why was he ruining everything?

A loud crash shook the walls as if something heavy had fallen over.

"Mum!" Lily cried out, springing to her feet.

More crashes vibrated through the floor as she darted from her room. Once again, she stopped halfway down the stairs. A silence like a restraining hand was emanating from the living room. She didn't move, didn't even breathe as the door opened.

2

"You know where I've been." A tremor forced its way into Hazel's voice as she pleaded, "Please, Peter, don't do this. Think about Lily. Think about what effect this is having on her."

A sneer twisted Peter's lips. "Perhaps you should have thought about that before you did this to us."

She flung her arms wide in exasperation. "Did what? What exactly is it you think I've done?"

"Don't play the innocent with me, Hazel. I saw you with *him*." A look of pure hatred warped Peter's features almost beyond recognition. "You were laughing and touching his hand."

She gave a bewildered shake of her head. "I've no idea who you're talking about."

Peter snorted as if to say, *Yeah right.* "How long has it been going on?"

"Nothing's going on!" Hazel scrunched a handful of her hair like she wanted to tear it out. "I'm not having an affair." She shook the whisky bottle at Peter. "This stuff's rotting your brain. It's making you paranoid."

Heaving himself to his feet, he spat out, "Stop gaslighting me. Who is he? What's his name?"

Hazel retreated from him. "What can I say to you, Peter? What can I do to convince you that you're wrong?"

His bloodshot eyes bulged as more questions poured from him. "Where do you meet up? Has he been to this house? Have you screwed him in our bed?"

The walls of Hazel's composure came crashing down. "Ok, you got me! Yes, I've screwed him in our bed. I've screwed him everywhere and in every way you can imagine. Is that what you wanted to hear? Are you satisfied now?"

Peter swayed back on his heels, slack-jawed. After a dumbfounded moment, he mumbled, "Do... Do you love him?"

Tilting her face upwards, Hazel exhaled a silent *argh*. She met Peter's gaze. "God, you're such an idiot." The insult was tinged with sadness. "I love you, Peter, but I..." She took a deep breath to fortify her resolve. "I can't go on like this. I want a divorce."

"A divorce?" He spoke slowly as if deciphering a secret code. "You're leaving me?"

"I'm doing what needs to be done." Hazel's tone was brutally matter-of-fact. "This is on you, Peter. Not me. Whatever's going on in your head, I can't have it around Lily."

He pressed his fingertips to his temples as if he had a splitting headache. "I can't help it." His voice hitched. "Oh Christ, why won't it stop?" His tearful eyes begged Hazel. "Make it stop."

She sighed heavily. "I've told you the truth, Peter. I don't know what else I can do."

There was a moment of silence. Then, as if an idea had struck him, Peter said, "Give me your phone."

Hazel frowned. "Why?"

"You're always tapping away on that thing. I want to know who you're messaging." Peter held out an upturned palm. "Give it to me."

"No." Hazel's tone was final.

They faced each other like duellists. As if responding to a silent signal, Peter lunged forwards. He braced an arm across Hazel's chest, pinning her to the door. His free hand groped at her pockets.

She rammed the whisky bottle into his belly. Air whistling through his teeth, he staggered backwards.

Hazel gasped in dismay as Peter triumphantly held up her phone. He prodded at its screen. His lips curled into a grim smile. "Well, well, fancy that. You've changed the pin. What's the new pin?"

Hazel met the question with icy silence.

"If you don't give me the pin, I'll–" Peter began in a menacing murmur.

"You'll what?" Hazel cut him off. Her voice took on a taunting edge. "Are you going to hit me?"

"Don't push me, Hazel. I'm warning you."

"Come on then, Peter, show me what a big man you are." She thrust out her chin, practically daring him to take a swing at her. He bared his teeth, but did nothing else. She nodded as if to say, *That's what I thought.* "I refuse to let you control me any longer, Peter. It's over. Our marriage is over."

"No it isn't." Peter shook his head so hard that spittle sprayed from his mouth. "We're not getting divorced."

"That's not your choice to make."

Like a toddler throwing a tantrum, Peter flung the phone at the floor and stamped on it.

"Oh, that's very mature of you." Hazel's voice was dripping with sarcasm.

Peter spun away from her. His neck muscles stood out like ropes as he picked up the television and hurled it against the wall. He glared at Hazel. "Go on, say something else. See what happens."

She took a slow breath, composing her face into a calm mask. "I'm not afraid of you, Peter."

His lower lip wobbled as if he was about to cry, but then his rage came surging back. "Lying whore!"

As the words erupted from him, Peter launched himself at Hazel. His fingers closed like a vice around her slim neck. She gasped as they dug deep into her flesh. Pushing his face close to hers, he hissed, "I'll put you in a pumpkin shell."

Mouth agape, she fought for breath. It was like trying to suck air through a pinhole. As Peter's thumbs gouged her windpipe, blobs of white light danced across her vision.

Her eyes popping halfway out of their sockets, Hazel jerked up the bottle and brought it arcing down. It hit Peter's head with a hollow clunk. His grip loosened, but only for an instant.

Hazel's spasming throat emitted a high-pitched, strangely musical whistle. The blobs of light were spreading like spilled ink, blotting out everything else. With a burst of desperate strength, she swung the bottle again. It connected flush with the crown of Peter's head and flew out of her hand. This time, his hands flinched away from her throat and he reeled backwards. She fell to her knees, choking and gasping.

Peter's feet snagged on the hearth rug. Arms windmilling, he toppled over. His head crunched sickeningly against the tiled hearth. He reared up into a sitting position. His pupils were dilated and glazed over. He felt at the back of his head. When he drew his fingers away, they were glistening with blood. He looked up at Hazel with a sort of dazed lucidity as if seeing her clearly for the first time in ages. "Hazel, I... I..."

Stammering off into silence, he slumped sideways. Suddenly, his breath was coming in short, sharp gasps.

"Peter?" Hazel croaked like she had laryngitis. She crawled to him on her hands and knees. His face was a ghastly grey and his lips were turning blue. His nostrils contracted a few more times, then stopped as abruptly as if an air pump had been switched off.

She warily touched her fingertips to his throat. There was no pulse to be found. "Peter? Peter?"

Her words met with a silence that sent shivers down her spine.

She clutched the mantlepiece, hauled herself to her feet and teetered to the door. Upon opening it, she found herself staring into Lily's wide eyes.

Lily clapped a hand to her mouth at the sight of the red welts on her mum's neck. She craned her head to look past her. Hazel quickly stepped into the hallway and closed the door behind herself.

"Where's Dad?" Lily asked through her fingers.

"I need–" Hazel's hoarse voice failed her. She cleared her throat. "I need your phone."

Lily handed it over.

Hazel dialled 999. "Please send an ambulance," she told the emergency operator. "It's my husband. I think he's dead."

Dead. The word hit Lily like a brick dropped from a high place. She sagged forwards, her fingers sliding up over her eyes.

"I had to do it, Lily," said Hazel. "He was going to kill me. Look at me, Lily. Tell me you believe me."

Lily kept her hands over her eyes. Clammy fingers encircled her wrists, squeezing gently at first, then harder and harder.

"Tell me, Lily. Please, tell me. Please, please..."

3

Six months later...

Lily was hunched over her laptop on the bedroom floor. A floppy-brimmed sunhat shadowed her face as if she'd just come into the house and not thought to take it off.

She skimmed over an article entitled 'Fulham Woman Killed Abusive Husband in Self-Defence'. Fragments of sentences jumped out at her – 'Peter Knight had been drinking heavily... accused his wife of being unfaithful... bruising on her throat... ruled that she was protecting herself and her fifteen-year-old daughter...'.

Chewing her upper lip, Lily scrolled down to the reader comments. The first read simply 'She's a liar'. She progressed through the comments, biting her lip harder with each negative one and skipping the positive ones – 'She's guilty as sin', 'She should be locked up forever', 'Bet she's slept with half of Fulham', 'I hope her husband's ghost haunts her for the rest of her life'.

Lily's shoulders lifted as if cold fingers had touched the nape of her neck. A soft knocking drew her attention to the door. Her hand darted out to flip the laptop shut as her mum entered the room.

Hazel's eyes narrowed a fraction. "What are you up to?"

"Nothing." Lily's reply was revealingly quick.

Arching an eyebrow, Hazel bent down to reach for the

laptop. Lily kept her palm on it. Mother and daughter locked eyes. After a brief battle of wills, Lily conceded defeat with a sigh and moved her hand.

Hazel lifted the screen. Upon seeing the comments, she gave a sighing shake of her head. "Why are you doing this to yourself, Lily?"

Lily shrugged somewhat sheepishly. "I want to know what people think about us."

"Who cares what these idiots think?" Hazel's tone softened. "There'll always be haters. We can't change that. The best way to deal with their kind is to ignore them."

"That's easy for you to say," Lily muttered dejectedly from under the brim of her sunhat. "I can't get away from the haters at school. And my friends treat me like I've got the plague or something."

"Do you want me to call the school and–"

"No," Lily interrupted, horrified by the suggestion. "You'll only make it worse."

Hazel squatted down to look her in the eyes. "I know it doesn't feel like it right now, but things will change. They always–" She broke off, exhaling sharply as Lily lowered her head further. "Will you take off that damn hat? I'm sick of the sight of it."

Afraid her mum might try to snatch it away, Lily darted a hand to the sunhat.

Hazel let slip another sigh, then summoned up a small smile. "I'm sorry, Lily." She spoke as softly as a vet soothing a traumatised animal. "It's just I hate to see you hiding away your beautiful hair."

"My hair's not beautiful. Dad ruined it like he ruined everything else." Lily's mouth twisted as if she was trying to force down something bitter. "Why did he do this to us?"

"He was ill. He didn't know what he was doing."

Hazel's compassion only exacerbated Lily's resentment. "Are you sure about that? Sometimes I think he enjoyed making our lives a misery."

"Your dad loved you very much."

The brim of Lily's hat fluttered as she shook her head. "The only thing he loved was whisky."

"That's not true. Yes, he lost his way, but–"

"But what?" Lily interrupted incredulously. "How can you defend him after what he did?"

"Because…" Hazel's eyes grew distant as she tried to find the words to explain. "Because the man I fell in love with was the kindest, most gentle–"

"Then why did he change?" Lily cut her off again. "Why did he start drinking?"

Deep creases etched themselves into Hazel's forehead. "The truth is, I don't know. We'll probably never know. None of this makes any sense and we just have to live with that."

Lily swiped the words away with a flick of her hand. "No we don't. There has to be a reason."

"I wish I had answers for you, Lily." Hazel's lips lifted into a smile touched by sadness. "Life can be senselessly cruel. Sometimes things happen that make you think, *What's the point? I may as well just give up.* But then something else comes along out of the blue. Something that makes you wonder if there's a higher power looking out for you after all."

As if to illustrate her words, Hazel pulled a folded-up sheet of paper from the back pocket of her jeans.

Lily eyed it curiously. "What's that?"

Hazel handed it to her. "Read it."

"The UK Deed Poll Service, London," Lily read out. "This

change of name deed is made by I, the undersigned, Hazel Wylde of Fulham, London, formerly known as Hazel Knight." Her gaze rose to her mum. "You've changed your surname?"

Hazel nodded. "And yours too. You're now Lily Wylde."

"You never said anything about this."

"I wanted it to be a surprise. Wylde was my mum's maiden name. Do you like it?"

"Wylde, Wylde," Lily murmured, testing how the name felt on her tongue. She shrugged. "It's ok. Why didn't you go back to your maiden name?"

"I felt like a complete change. A new beginning, if you like."

Lily made an unconvinced noise in the back of her throat. "It won't be a new beginning, though, will it? People around here will still know who we are."

"Which brings me to my next piece of good news. Do you know what synchronicity is?"

"No."

"Have you ever dreamt about something happening, then it actually happens? Or have you ever thought about a song, then it comes on the radio?"

Peter, Peter pumpkin eater, had a wife and couldn't keep her.

A tingle crawled over Lily's scalp as her dad's singsong voice echoed in her mind. "Yes."

"Well that's synchronicity. Some people say it's just coincidence. Personally, I think there's more to it. To me, it feels like… like messages from the universe." Hazel paused dramatically before continuing, "I had a call from a solicitor today about an Emily Wylde."

"Who's Emily Wylde?"

"She was my mum's older sister."

Lily's eyebrows lifted, then drew together. "That would

make her my great-aunt. How come I've never heard of her before?"

"Because I'd never heard of her before, either. Don't ask me why. Maybe my mum and her had a falling out. I don't suppose the 'why' matters now that both sisters have passed away."

"Emily's dead?"

Hazel nodded. "Her body was found in her house. Apparently, she'd been dead for weeks."

"That's really sad. I take it she lived alone."

"Emily never married or had children. In fact, we're her only surviving relatives."

Lily lowered her gaze, thinking about what it would be like to be so alone in the world that you could drop dead and no one would even notice. "She was our only surviving relative too." Her voice was a morose monotone. "Now there's just us left."

"Unless my mum had other siblings she didn't tell me about."

"The solicitor would have tracked them down."

"I suppose so."

Lily stared gloomily at the floor. "I don't see how this is good news. It would have been nice to have a great-aunt."

"Yes, it would have been, but..." Hazel let out a guilty little laugh. "I feel terrible saying this, but Aunt Emily's death might be the best thing that could have happened to us right now."

Curiosity sparked in Lily's eyes. "What do you mean? Was she rich?"

"No, she wasn't rich. Quite the opposite. She did have one thing of worth, though – her house."

Lily's eyes widened. "Are you saying we've inherited a house?"

"That's exactly what I'm saying."

"Oh my god. Where is it? How big is it?"

Hazel smiled at the flurry of excited questions. "It's a little cottage in a village called Midwood."

"Where's Midwood?"

"It's in the New Forest. It's supposed to be a beautiful area. Do you fancy taking a trip down there?"

Lily gave a noncommittal shrug. "If the body wasn't found for weeks, wouldn't it have rotted and made a mess?"

"Emily died the best part of a year ago. I'm sure the place has been cleaned up since then. Even if it hasn't, I still want to see it." Hazel encouraged Lily with a gentle nudge. "Come on, at the very least it'll be interesting. You might even enjoy it."

Enjoy it. The words jabbed at Lily like a taunt. Sometimes she wondered whether she'd ever really enjoy anything again. "How long are we going there for?"

"Just the day. For now."

Lily's eyes narrowed as if she suspected she was being baited. "For now?"

"Ok, Lily, hear me out. This is going to sound a bit... umm... out there." Hazel pointed to the Deed Poll certificate. "What if this and Aunt Emily's death are our messages from the universe?"

Lily rolled her eyes as if to say, *Are you serious?*

"Don't give me that look," Hazel continued. "All I'm saying is, we should be open to the possibility that someone or something is trying to guide us in the right direction. I mean, how many people get a chance like this? We could sell this house and–"

"Whoa, wait a second. Are you talking about moving to the cottage?"

"If we like it enough, why not? I could give up my job. You

could make a whole new set of friends." Hazel motioned to their surroundings. "We could put all of this behind us."

Lily's silence suggested she wasn't sure she was ready to 'put all of this behind' her.

Hazel's voice dropped to a tender murmur. "I'm not suggesting you should forget about your dad. He'll always be a part of you. Who knows, maybe this is his doing. Maybe he's trying to help us get on with our lives."

Lily's lips curled into a crooked smile. "He couldn't help anyone when he was alive. So how can he help us now?"

Frowning faintly at Lily's sneering tone, Hazel steered the conversation back to more tangible matters. "The solicitor sent me a photo of the cottage."

She brought up a photo on her phone of a thatched cottage nestled amidst overgrown grass and tall trees. The cottage didn't appear to possess a single straight angle. A pair of precariously leaning chimneys bookended its sagging roof. Crooked black beams zigzagged across the white rendered walls. Wonky windows peeked out from under a deep overhang of mouldy thatch. A mossy porch shadowed a plank door with rusty iron braces at the top and bottom. The house had a distorted look as if the image was skewed off to one side.

Hazel pointed to a boarded-up window on the ground floor. "That must be where the police broke in."

Lily shuddered at the thought of entering a house to check for a dead body.

"The place needs a bit of work," Hazel observed.

Lily met her mum's understatement with an arched eyebrow. "It looks like a witch's house from a fairytale."

Hazel chuckled. "It's funny you should say that..."

4

L ily stared at the passing landscape from under her sunhat, blankly watching mile after mile of woodland sweep by. For half-an-hour, dense forest had flanked the road. Spindly pines and stout oaks towered over ghostly birches and gnarled hollies. Barrel-chested chestnut and bay ponies could occasionally be glimpsed grazing on the sun-dappled forest floor. Sandy tracks branched off the road, leading to carparks and cottages, or simply trailing away into the trees.

Hazel was humming along to the radio. Unseasonably warm April sun flickered through her open window, bringing a faint flush to her porcelain skin. Lily glanced across at her. She seemed lighter somehow, as if a burden had been lifted from her shoulders.

Hazel flashed Lily a smile. "Not much further now. It's exciting, isn't it?"

Lily gave a slight shrug. She felt strangely flat. It was nice to get away from the city, but the thought of leaving it behind forever for this seemingly endless expanse of green was underwhelming to say the least. What was there to do out here? There were no shopping centres or cafes. There were barely even any houses. They might as well be considering moving to the Moon.

She kept her thoughts to herself. It was the first time her mum had been excited about anything since... well, since she couldn't remember when. The last thing she wanted to do was spoil her mood.

"So it doesn't bother you?" Hazel asked.

"What doesn't bother me?"

"The history of your Great-Aunt Emily's house."

"You mean that a witch was once supposed to have lived there? No, it doesn't bother me at all. I think it's pretty cool."

Hazel's smile broadened. "I suppose it is 'pretty cool'."

"I found some stuff online about what happened."

"What did happen?"

"I thought you knew."

"All I know is what the solicitor told me – the cottage dates to the seventeenth century and a wicked old witch used to live there."

"A wicked old witch?" Lily squinted at her mum, unsure whether to be amused or irritated. "We're not talking about some fairytale. Her name was Mary Long. She was a widow who was accused of witchcraft and burned alive."

Hazel wrinkled her nose as if she'd caught a whiff of burning flesh. "That's awful. What else did you find out?"

"Not much. Only that Mary was executed in 1690 on a hill near Midwood. Oh, and apparently the tree she was tied to is still there."

"I find that hard to believe."

"Me too. Hey, maybe we should go check it out."

Hazel laughed. "I'll give it a miss, thanks."

The car swept around a corner, passing a sign that proclaimed 'Welcome to Midwood'. Lily lifted the brim of her hat with a finger as the forest gave way to a grassy common. "Wow, it's like a postcard!"

Rows of higgledy-piggledy cottages were nestled amidst well-kept little gardens. Daffodils carpeted a village green. A sign depicting a tree speckled with red berries hung over the door of an olde-worlde timber-framed pub. 'The Rowan Tree' was emblazoned on it in gold leaf lettering.

"I bet that's supposed to be the same tree I was talking about." Lily tapped at her mobile phone. "It says here rowans are also known as the Witch Tree. People used to think they protected against witchcraft."

"Some around here probably still think that," Hazel said with a chuckle.

At the centre of the village was a short row of shops that looked like it had been there forever.

Beyond the shops, a man as fat as the proverbial pig was slouched on a bench in the shadow of a church tower. Scruffy curls of brown hair tumbled down the sides of his round red face. His mountain of a belly pushed against some sort of burgundy robe as he watched the car go by.

"I wonder if that's the vicar," said Hazel.

"Whoever he is, he needs to go on a serious diet."

Lily's gaze travelled along a flagstone path flanked by gravestones to the weathered grey stone church. Next to the graveyard, wrought-iron railings enclosed a little primary school. A dozen or so children were milling around the playground. A few more houses were strung out alongside the road. Then the car was back amongst the trees.

"Is that it?" Lily asked as if maybe they'd missed something.

Hazel couldn't help but smile at her nonplussed tone. "I said it was a small village."

The sat nav announced that they'd reached their destination. Frowning, Hazel pulled over and peered into the trees. There were no houses or indeed buildings of any type to be seen. "Perhaps we should ask someone in the village for—"

"Hey, what's that?" Lily interrupted as something black

darted across her field of vision and disappeared into the undergrowth up ahead. "Did you see that?"

"No."

"Something ran across the road. It could have been a black cat."

"Was it wearing a pointy hat?"

With a roll of her eyes, Lily gave a sarcastic, "Ha, ha."

"Sorry, I couldn't resist." Hazel craned her neck, squinting. "Is that a driveway?"

She pulled the car towards a tangle of brambles blocking the entrance to a narrow track.

"There's a sign," said Lily, pointing to a swatch of wood visible through the undergrowth.

They got out of the car. Lily gingerly moved aside a prickly stem. With a fingertip, she traced the lettering carved into the wood. "B...L...A–"

"Blackmoss Cottage," Hazel finished for her. "This is it."

"Are you sure? It doesn't look like anyone's used this track in ages."

"I'm sure."

They returned to the car. The sign toppled over as Hazel nudged the bumper through the brambles. Overhanging branches tapped a tune on the car's roof as the track rose gently into the trees. Shadows clustered beneath the canopy, chased away here and there by shafts of sunlight. A deep bed of leaves on the forest floor gave off an earthy aroma. Clumps of red-and-white-spotted toadstools flourished in the cool, damp air. The place had a muted, almost otherworldly feel.

"I wonder if the cottage is made of gingerbread," Lily said dryly.

Hazel chuckled. "I hope so. I'm hungry."

The bumpy track snaked its way deeper into the forest. Lily looked over her shoulder. All she could see were trees, trees and more trees. Midwood suddenly seemed a long way away. "I don't suppose there's any internet out here?"

"I very much doubt it."

Lily shook her head. "No way am I living somewhere with no Wi-Fi."

Hazel laughed. "It'd do you good to get away from your phone and all the other screens you spend half your life staring into."

"Oh yes, I'm sure it would do me the world of good." Lily's voice was laced with sarcasm. "But why stop there? Why not get rid of all electricals?"

"That sounds like a great idea. We'll live off the land. You can go foraging for mushrooms while I gather wood to cook them." Hazel's tone was deadpan, but there was a teasing gleam in her eyes.

Lily let out an unamused sigh.

"Come on, give me a smile." Hazel playfully dug her long fingernails into Lily's ribs.

Lily's lips twitched upwards.

"Is that supposed to be a smile? Surely you can do better than–" Hazel broke off, hitting the brake pedal hard enough to jolt herself forwards against her seatbelt.

"Why did you–" Lily started to ask, but she too fell silent as her gaze came to rest on the scrawny creature in front of the car.

"Is that what you saw run across the road?" Hazel asked.

"Yeah, I think so."

The dog looked like a cross between a Labrador and a Border Collie. Except for a white flash on its chest, its fur was coal-black. Batlike ears were standing to attention on its broad, flat head. Its feet were planted in the middle of the track as if it had no intention of letting the car pass.

Hazel scanned the trees on either side. "I don't see an owner."

"It could be a stray." Lily eyed the dog's prominent ribs and the sharp ridge of its spine. "It's really skinny."

"Yes, the poor thing's in a bit of a sorry state."

Lily grabbed a Tupperware box from the backseat. She peeled apart a sandwich, extracted a slice of ham, then got out of the car.

"Careful, Lily," Hazel cautioned as the dog bared its teeth. "Don't get too close."

Lily's heart was beating fast, but she managed to keep her voice steady. "It's ok, I'm not going to hurt you."

She tossed a scrap of ham to the dog. Keeping its amber eyes on Lily, the wary animal sniffed at the meat. Its tongue flicked out to lick it up.

"Do you want some more?" Lily threw another scrap, which the dog caught in midair and eagerly devoured. She edged nearer. The dog recoiled onto its haunches, fur bristling.

Lily stopped. "Ok, ok, I won't come any–" She flinched into silence as the dog sprang up with a snarl and prowled forwards.

She half-turned to make a run for the car, but a voice rang out from behind her. "Don't you dare growl at my daughter, you ungrateful mutt."

Like a scolded child, the dog immediately fell silent. It retreated with its tail tucked between its legs as Hazel strode forwards.

"Sit," she commanded.

The dog did as it was told. Its bloodshot eyes followed Hazel's every movement as she took the ham from Lily and held out her hand.

Now it was Lily's turn to caution, "Careful, Mum." But even as the words left her mouth, the dog dipped its head to snaffle up the ham.

Hazel stroked its back. "Good boy."

The dog wagged its tail, stirring up puffs of dust. Hazel reached for the leather collar buckled around its neck and read out the inscription on the silver tag, "Sam. Blackmoss Cottage."

Lily's eyes widened. "This is Emily's dog?"

"*Was* Emily's dog," Hazel corrected. She picked bits of leaves out of Sam's fur. "Looks like he's been living in the woods."

The dog eyeballed Lily as she took a step towards him. "Hello, Sam." She glanced at her mum. "Is it ok to stroke him?"

"Yes, just go slowly."

Lily stroked Sam tentatively at first, then with growing confidence. She ran her fingers through the soft white fur on his chest. She smiled and squirmed as his rough tongue licked the ham's salty residue from her hand. "You're still hungry, aren't you? I'll get you something else to eat." She fetched the rest of the ham from the sandwiches and giggled as Sam ate it out of her cupped palm. "His tongue tickles."

Hazel smiled. She'd almost forgotten what Lily's laugh sounded like.

Lily looked hopefully at her mum. "Is he ours now?"

The question prompted a reticent, "Erm."

"Who else is going to look after him?" Lily persisted. "And besides, if we live out here, we'll need a guard dog."

Hazel's smile rose higher at Lily's sudden change of tune. "Tell you what, let's have a think about it while we look around the house." She patted Sam's thick ruff of neck fur. "Maybe there's some dog food there for you."

They returned to the car. Sam stared after them with his head tilted. Hazel opened the backdoor and beckoned to him. "Come on, Sam, get in."

He darted forwards to spring onto the backseat. He thrust his head between the front seats and nuzzled Lily's cheek.

"Ugh, your breath stinks," she exclaimed.

Laughing, Hazel got behind the steering-wheel. "I think you've made your first new friend."

5

After a short distance, a wide, flat circle of grass opened up. Lily blinked as the car emerged into bright sunshine. Two enormous Buddleias in early bloom flanked the clearing's entrance. Their purple flowers were teeming with bees and butterflies. Sparrows, blackbirds and bluetits fluttered to-and-fro, filling the air with their warbling songs.

The cottage squatted like an off-white mushroom at the clearing's centre. Its flaky walls were draped with ivy. Sunlight bounced at all angles off its uneven windows, making it seem like they were illuminated from within. Long beards of greenish-black moss dangled from the gutters. The thatching was crusted with bird droppings from nests that balanced like bedraggled wigs atop the sooty chimneys. The gabled porch sagged as if it was too tired to hold itself up.

Hazel pointed to the moss. "That must be where the name comes from."

"It looks like horrible stuff."

They exited the car. Lily opened the backdoor and Sam hopped out. He stared at the house with dolefully big eyes. "He looks sad," said Lily. She patted him. "Don't be sad, Sam. We're here to look after you now."

Sam stuck close to their heels as they waded through tall grass towards the front door. "At least there are no holes in the roof," Hazel observed.

"Oh great. So we won't get wet when it rains. That's alright then."

Hazel frowned at Lily's sarcasm. "Don't be so down on the place before we've even seen inside. Who knows, we might be pleasantly surprised?"

"Ouch!" Lily exclaimed, stubbing her toe against something. She pushed aside the grass with her sandaled foot. A bed of rich dark soil was mounded up within a rectangle of wooden planks. The soil was riddled with weeds, from amongst which sprouted a bell-shaped violet flower fringed by ragged green leaves.

Hazel pointed out several other raised beds populated by more of the bell-shaped flowers and a host of scraggly herb plants. "Looks like Emily was into growing her own. I fancy giving it a go myself."

"That's *if* we decide to live here," stressed Lily. "And you've never been into gardening."

"Only because I've never had the time before, but if I'm not working..." Hazel trailed off, leaving the obvious unsaid.

"Can you really afford to not work and do up this place?"

"Honestly, I don't know." Excitement bubbled up in Hazel's voice. "But right now I don't care whether I can afford it. I'm just looking forward to a new challenge."

She took a rust-flecked iron key from her pocket, caught hold of Lily's hand and drew her towards the door.

Faded paintings adorned the dirty-white rendering around the doorframe. Dark brown rectangles alternated with lighter brown circles, diamonds and stars. The shapes were decorated with white spots and squiggly lines.

"What are these supposed to be?" Lily wondered. She traced the outline of a rectangle that enclosed a vertical row of three dots. "This looks like a domino."

Hazel studied the shapes for a moment, then her eyes lit up

with amusement. "They're not dominos."

"Then what are they?"

"Can't you guess, my sweet Gretel?" Hazel teased. "They're gingerbread biscuits." She gave a delighted little clap. "Oh I love it. Aunt Emily must have had a wicked sense of humour."

Grinning like a child on Christmas morning, Hazel inserted the key into the lock and turned it. There was an instant of resistance, then a *clunk*. The hinges squealed as the heavy old door swung inwards. It pushed against a long curtain on a brass rail. She swished the curtain aside and stepped into a low-ceilinged, flagstone floor hallway. A galaxy of dust particles floated in the sunlight streaming over her shoulders. At the far end of the hallway, a steep flight of worn wooden stairs led up into gloom. A pair of plank doors with lever latches faced each other at the foot of the stairs. Several half-melted candles occupied black iron brackets on the bumpy white walls.

Lily glanced at a frilly lightshade dangling from the ceiling. She flicked a brass switch on the wall. Nothing happened. "The electricity's not on." She sniffed the air. "It smells like..." she wrinkled her nose uncertainly, "like apples?"

"You're right. It does have a cidery smell." Hazel looked down as Sam snuffled and whined. "Can you smell it too? Does it remind you of Emily?"

Sam quietened down as Lily stroked his head.

Hazel gestured to the doors. "Which shall we try first?"

Before Lily could reply, Sam padded forwards to paw at the left-hand door. Exchanging an amused glance with Lily, Hazel moved to open the door. It led into a living-room with a black-beamed ceiling and a dusty parquet floor. A scorched metal teapot dangled on a chain over a pile of ashes in a stone fireplace. Gurning Toby jugs were lined up on the mantlepiece. A poker, brush, tongs and shovel hung on a stand next to a wicker basket full of kindling. A high-backed armchair faced the fireplace. Beside it was a small table with a teacup and saucer in the centre of its round top.

Lily approached a piano with an open music sheet on its easel and tapped a couple of keys. The tinkling notes fell dead in the damp, musty air. Hazel crossed the room to open a pair of curtains. Light seeped through the deeply recessed window, slinking across a dead-fly-speckled sill.

Another basket lay overturned on a shabby sofa beneath the window. Balls of wool and knitting needles were scattered over the floor.

Lily peered into the teacup. It was half-full of murky liquid. "It's like Emily was here just a minute ago." A glimmer of unease showed in her eyes as she looked at the armchair. A large dark stain discoloured the threadbare material. She imagined Emily's corpse sitting there for weeks, gradually turning as greenish-black as the moss on the roof. She reached out to touch the chair, but drew her hand back with a shudder. "That thing would *have* to go."

"Don't worry. We'd buy all new furniture."

Sam rolled his eyes towards the ceiling, snuffling as if he'd caught a scent. Three bouquets of dried flowers were hanging upside down from hooks on the cobwebby beams. Their petals were the same pale violet as the flowers in the garden. Lily rose onto tiptoes to sniff the bouquets. "Ugh, they stink!" she exclaimed, pinching her nostrils.

"I think they smell quite nice."

"Only if you like the smell of rotten stuff." Lily's gaze slid back to the armchair.

Hazel swiftly changed the topic. "Do you think Emily liked dogs?"

There was a wry edge to her voice. Dozens of paintings of black dogs covered the walls. Amongst other breeds, there were stocky terriers, wiry greyhounds, floppy-eared spaniels, bright-eyed sheepdogs and regal Labradors. The quality of the artwork varied from finely detailed to childishly simplistic. A plaque on each frame was inscribed with a name and date.

Lily read out the name of a diminutive Jack Russell. "Midget, 1912." Next came a bulldog that was so fat it didn't appear to have any legs. "Roly, 1956." Then a doe-eyed whippet. "Sad Bill, 1833." The portraits weren't arranged in chronological order. Indeed, much like the windows, they seemed to be positioned randomly on the walls.

"What's the earliest date you can find?"

Lily scanned over the portraits. Her gaze stopped on a cracked oil painting of some sort of long-legged hound with tatty ears and a whip-thin upright tail. "Doubting Tom, 1690. He must have been Mary Long's dog."

Hazel pointed to a watercolour of a healthier-looking version of Sam. "This is the most recent one – Sam, 2016. So Sam must be at least seven."

"Do you think it's like a tradition or something that there's always a black dog living here?"

"I'd say so, yes."

Lily's voice dropped conspiratorially low. "It seems a bit *witchy* to me."

Hazel laughed. "So all these dogs are what? Witches' familiars? Wouldn't that mean Emily was a witch too?"

"I suppose so. Do you think she was a witch?"

"From what I can tell, Emily was just an old woman who preferred to keep herself to herself. That's probably all Mary was too." Hazel glanced at her wristwatch. "Come on, let's finish looking around. I want to get back to Fulham before dark."

Sam trailed after them to the second door. It opened into a

good-sized kitchen with windows at both ends. Broken glass glinted on the flagstones below the boarded-up front window. Mismatched crockery was stacked on a dark wood Welsh Dresser. Petals from a vase of dead flowers were scattered across an ancient-looking trestle table. Uneven shelves lined the walls, crammed with jars and bottles of what looked to be homemade preserves and wine. Cooking utensils dangled from hooks on the ceiling beams. At one end of the wooden work surface was a deep farmhouse sink. At the other was a monolithic Rayburn stove, burnt brown around the edges of its oven doors. A dog basket padded with a patchwork blanket was positioned snuggly beside the stove.

Sam nosed his way between Lily and Hazel, got into the basket and stood there as if uncertain what to do next. He made big eyes at them.

"Poor Sam," Lily soothed, stroking his velvety ears.

Hazel bent to open the oven. "What do you think? You could probably fit a small child or two in there."

"Ha, ha," mouthed Lily.

Hazel drew aside a floor-length curtain, revealing a walk-in pantry. Canned and boxed food was stored alongside baskets of withered fruit and vegetables. The floor was cluttered with mismatched wellies, scuffed leather shoes, an ironing board, clothes rack, vacuum cleaner and other household items.

"I don't see a broomstick," said Hazel.

Lily gave an unamused roll of her eyes.

"You're in luck," Hazel said to Sam, picking a tin of dog food off a shelf.

The dog's tail windmilled as Hazel peeled the lid off the tin and emptied its contents into an earthenware bowl by his basket. He set about devouring the chunks of jellied meat. Pipes clanked and banged as Hazel turned on a tap. Cloudy water sputtered into the sink. She waited for it to clear, then filled a bowl and put it on the floor. Her gaze travelled approvingly around the kitchen. "I bet it's really cosy in here when the stove's on."

She took out another key and opened the backdoor. A faintly visible path led through hordes of dandelions to a rickety old shed. Rows of overgrown canes, a few stumpy fruit trees, a collapsed chicken coop and a greenhouse missing most of its panes provided further evidence of Emily's self-sufficiency. Logs were piled high against the cottage's rear wall. An axe was embedded in a tree stump.

Lily pointed to a rusty metal box with wires and pipes sticking out all over the place. "What's that?"

"An electricity generator. The cottage isn't on the mains."

They turned at the sound of Sam hopping back into his bed. He curled up on the blanket and began methodically cleaning himself.

He stayed put as Hazel and Lily returned to the hallway and climbed the creaking stairs to a small windowless landing. Lily shone her phone at a tapestry on the wall at the top of the stairs. Its scarlet embroidery depicted three identical naked women, their soft-featured faces aligned vertically, one above the other, their hair flowing into a single long mane. The lowermost woman was covering her mouth with both hands. The middle woman's hands were masking the uppermost woman's eyes. The uppermost woman's palms were pressed against the ears of the middle woman.

"I wonder what it means," said Lily.

"They look like they're protecting each other."

Lily photographed the tapestry, then turned her attention to the landing's three doors. The nearest led to a bedroom with a ceiling so low that Hazel's pinned-up hair brushed against the mildew-spotted plaster. The ceiling sloped down to a little window overlooking the front garden. An iron bedstead draped in a patchwork quilt took up most of the floorspace. At the foot of the bed was a brick fireplace, flanked by a big old wardrobe and a dressing table. Unlabelled lotion bottles were scattered like bowling pins across the dresser. A picture frame above the mantelpiece contained what appeared to be pressings of the moss the cottage was named after.

Hazel opened the wardrobe. A sparse selection of well-worn jumpers, blouses and long skirts was hanging inside. The clothes gave off the same fruity, acidic aroma as the dried flowers.

Lily pinched her nose again. "That smell's giving me a headache."

She approached a bedside table and wiped the dust off what looked to be a wooden jewellery box inlaid with mother-of-pearl. She turned a small key and the box clicked open. Its red velvet-lined interior contained a black iron circlet with a hinge and a lockable clasp. The circlet was edged with sharp metal teeth. It was just about big enough to fit around her slender neck. She showed it to her mum. "I've changed my mind. Emily wasn't a witch, she was a dominatrix."

Hazel feathered a finger along the circlet's serrations. "It looks like a mediaeval torture device." She closed the box and took it away from Lily. "I think I'd better put this somewhere safe. You never know, it might be worth something."

Lily pushed her lips out doubtfully. She returned to the landing. The neighbouring door opened into a little bathroom with a yellow-stained bath, sink and toilet. Mould speckled the tiled walls. Scuff marks and tears marred the linoleum floor. A frayed towel hung on a ring by the sink.

Lily sniffed at a waxy-looking greenish lump crusted to a soap dish. "Ugh! It has the same disgusting smell."

There was a toothbrush in a glass on the window ledge, but no toothpaste. Nor was there mouthwash, shampoo, bubble bath, deodorant or any of the other toiletries Lily took for granted. "How could Emily live like this?"

"Maybe she liked it this way," Hazel mused. She opened a mirrored wall cabinet that contained tweezers, nail scissors, a hair brush, a pumice stone and the like. "It doesn't seem to have done her any harm. I don't see any medication."

Lily treated her mum to a sceptical frown. "If you want to live some kind of back-to-nature lifestyle, go for it. But I need my shampoo and conditioner and–"

"So do I," Hazel interrupted with a chuckle. "I have no intention of giving up my creature comforts, but I do think it would do us good to lead a simpler life."

"Are you trying to put me off living here?"

Laughing and shaking her head, Hazel headed for the last door. It led to a room facing onto the back garden. A swan-necked treadle sewing machine and a three-legged stool basked in sunlight by the window. Spools of cotton thread, boxes of sewing needles, rolls of fabric and other sewing paraphernalia were neatly stored on shelves. Several more patchwork quilts were folded on the floorboards. Hazel ran her fingers over their almost seamless stitching. "Emily was obviously a talented seamstress. I wonder if she sold this stuff. You know, I used to be a pretty good seamstress myself."

"Really?"

"Uh-huh. I made all the curtains and cushions for the first flat your dad and I…" Hazel fell silent as a pained look crossed Lily's face. Reaching for Lily's hand, she said softly, "I think we've seen everything we need to see."

They went back downstairs. As if he knew they were leaving, Sam emerged from the kitchen and stared at them. His strangely human eyes seemed to say, *Please take me with you.*

"Oh you really know how to lay it on thick, don't you?" said Hazel. "You and Lily should get on like a house on fire."

The comment drew a delighted look from Lily. "Does that mean we can keep him?"

Conceding defeat with a sigh, Hazel nodded. Her sigh turned into a smile as Lily exclaimed, "Yay!" and bent to ruffle Sam's fur. "Did you hear that, Sam? You're coming to live with us."

Sam's otter-like tail whacked the flagstones as if he understood every word.

"We'd better get his things," said Hazel.

They gathered together Sam's bed, bowls and the rest of the canned dog food. Hazel unscrewed the lid from a jar labelled 'Gooseberry Jam'. She dipped a finger into the pale green gloop and tasted it. "Mmm, delicious. We can't let this go to waste." She put the jar into a basket and picked out a dozen more to go with it.

They carried the bits and bobs to the porch. Sam looked over his shoulder as Hazel closed the door.

"Don't worry, Sam, we'll be back here soon enough," she told him. She glanced at Lily as if to ask, *Won't we?*

Lily backed away from the cottage, eyeing it like someone trying to decide what they thought about a painting. The thatched roof gave off a mellow golden glow in the afternoon sun. A crow was basking on one of the chimneys. The place exuded a feeling of contented neglect.

Hazel inhaled deeply through her nose. "The air smells so good here. Wouldn't it be wonderful to breathe this air every day?"

Lily smiled at her mum's not-so-subtle attempt to sell the move to her.

"It's so peaceful too," Hazel continued. "There's no traffic, no sirens, no roadworks–"

"No Wi-Fi," put in Lily.

Hazel laughed. "That'll be top of my to-do list."

Lily's gaze traversed the encircling trees. Could she really be happy here, cut off from the wider world? Or would she go out of her mind with boredom?

"I could definitely live here happily ever after," Hazel said as if replying to Lily's thoughts.

Lily's gaze came full circle to her mum and Sam. They stared back at her with matching expectant expressions. Her dad's whisky-slurred voice resurfaced from the depths of her mind – *I just want what we had. I want us to be a happy family.*

"Yes," she blurted out, then blinked as if surprised by her own voice.

"Yes what?"

"Yes, I'll move here."

Breaking into a broad smile, Hazel stepped forwards to plant a kiss on Lily's forehead. "I can't tell you how happy it makes me to hear you say that."

"You might not be so happy when I'm moaning at you about being bored."

"Trust me, Lily, you won't have a chance to be bored. There'll be too many jobs for you to do." Hazel ticked them off on her fingers. "Chopping wood, picking mushrooms, making smelly green soap–"

"That's not funny, Mum. I've still got a headache from that smell."

"Don't you worry. By the time I'm done with it, this place will smell brand new."

They loaded up the car. Sam clambered into his bed on the backseat. As they drove away, he stared at the cottage, whining plaintively. Lily shushed and stroked him. When a bend in the track hid the cottage from view, he settled down, resting his jaw on his paws and letting out a long sigh.

As if infected by Sam's mood, a heavy feeling descended over

Lily. The thought of returning to Fulham and everything that went with it – the awful memories, the judging looks – was almost too much to bear. She, too, heaved a sigh.

"You ok?" Hazel asked.

"Just processing. It's a lot to take in."

Hazel nodded as if to say, *I know what you mean.* They passed through Midwood in silence. The school playground was deserted. The fat man had vacated the bench.

'What does three women covering their eyes, ears and mouth mean?' Lily typed into her phone's search bar. She followed a link to 'The three wise monkeys proverb'. "I think the tapestry means hear no evil, see no evil, speak no evil. It says here it can be interpreted in two ways – either to avoid doing evil or turn a blind eye to it."

"I think it means be good or else."

"Or else what?"

"Or else the wicked witch of Blackmoss Cottage will get you."

Hazel let out a fake evil laugh. Lily puffed her cheeks. "One more witch joke and I'm definitely not living there."

Hazel made a mouth-zipped gesture.

6

Hazel watched the last cardboard box being loaded into the removal van. Only half-a-dozen small pieces of furniture were scattered amongst the boxes. As she'd told Lily, she wanted to take as few memories with them as possible.

She turned to call upstairs, "Lily."

Lily appeared at the top of the stairs with the seemingly glued-on sunhat pulled down low over her head. Concern flickered in Hazel's eyes. Dark smudges under Lily's eyes spoke of many long hours spent with her head buried in textbooks. Only the day before, she'd sat her final exam. But rather than being happy, or even just relieved, she'd returned from school exuding apathy. Not for the first time, Hazel wondered about the zeal with which Lily had thrown herself into revising. Had it simply been about getting good grades? Or had it been more about distracting herself from everything else in her life?

As usual, Sam wasn't far behind Lily. The dog had undergone a remarkable transformation – his coat was shiny and sleek, his ribs were no longer visible and his clear eyes seemed to smile out of his face.

Hazel's concern gave way to a grateful smile. In the months since coming to live with them, Sam had been Lily's constant companion. He spent every night curled up on the end of her bed. He'd forced her to take revision breaks by pawing at her whenever he wanted a walk. The sound of Lily laughing as she played with him never failed to lift Hazel's spirits.

"Time to go," said Hazel.

Lily started down the stairs. She hesitated, a knot forming between her eyebrows as she looked into the living room.

"Come on," Hazel urged, striving to keep her tone light. "Let's get this show on the road."

Lily remained stock still, her eyes fixed on the hearth. She gave a little start as Sam nuzzled her hand. Lowering her head like someone fleeing the scene of a crime, she hurried from the house and ducked into her mum's car.

The backseat was crammed with bags and suitcases, except for a space reserved for Sam's bed. Hazel opened the door for him to jump in, then she got behind the steering-wheel. "Ok." A tremor of excitement ran through her voice. "Here we go."

Lily stared at her lap as her mum started the engine and pulled away from the house. She felt like if she saw one of her friends, she might just burst into tears.

"Can you believe it?" Hazel piped up after a couple of miles. "Can you believe we're actually doing it?"

"Yes and no," came the flat answer.

Hazel glanced at Lily. "What does that mean?"

Lily shrugged. If a fortune teller had told her a year ago that her mum would kill her dad, then they'd move to a cottage in the middle of nowhere, she would have laughed and asked for her money back.

Hazel pursed her lips as if reading Lily's face and realising that silence was, indeed, the only sensible response to the events that had brought them to this juncture.

They left behind the sprawling outskirts of London. A big blue sky beckoned them westwards. Hazel didn't bother with the sat nav. Since last making the journey with Lily, she'd visited the cottage half-a-dozen times to ensure the renovations were going to plan.

"I can't wait for you to see the cottage," said Hazel. "You'll hardly recognise the place."

Lily tuned out as her mum rambled on about the repairs that still needed doing and the difficulty she'd had finding a master thatcher to patch up the roof. A peculiar sense of dislocation settled over her. It was as if she'd left part of herself behind in their old house. She rested her head back against the seat. Her eyelids drifted down as the motion of the car lulled her to sleep.

Peter, Peter pumpkin eater... Peter, Peter...

Her dad's words circled in her mind like a trapped bird searching for a way out.

I keep having these thoughts... Bad thoughts... The worst you can imagine...

Lily blinked awake. They were on a quiet road bordered by trees whose branches swayed in a brisk breeze.

"Hey there sleepyhead," said Hazel.

"Where are we?"

"We're not far from Midwood."

Lily rubbed her eyes. "I can't believe I've slept for almost the entire journey."

"You must have needed it."

"I suppose I am tired from these last few weeks."

"You and me both. Well now we've got all summer to relax and get to know our new home."

"What's to get to know? The cottage is even smaller than our old house."

"I don't just mean the cottage." Hazel swept her hand at the forest. "I mean all of this. There's so much to explore." She reached back to ruffle Sam's fur. "You'll show us around, won't you, Sam?"

He responded with an enthusiastic *woof!*

Hazel laughed. "I swear that dog understands every word we say."

The 'Welcome to Midwood' sign came into view. Lily squinted as the car passed from the dappled shade of the forest into the full glare of the midday sun. The main street was sleepily quiet.

"We'd better pick up something for lunch," said Hazel, pulling over by the shops.

Before getting out of the car, Lily looked in the sun-visor mirror and tucked several loose strands of hair under her hat. Hazel wound down a window enough for Sam to poke his nose out. They headed for 'Midwood Post Office & General Store'. In the shop window, a sprig of green leaves with red berries hung alongside community notices and adverts for local services. A bell tinkled as Hazel opened the door.

A bottle blonde just barely hanging on to her looks peered over the till. Her gaze followed them along the narrow aisles. They filled a basket and took it to the till. The shop assistant gave them a buck-toothed smile. "Lovely weather, isn't it?"

Hazel smiled at the pleasantry. "Yes, it is."

The woman set about scanning and bagging their basket's contents. She glanced out of the window at their jam-packed car. "Are you here on holiday?"

"No. Actually, we're moving to the area. We're on the way to our new house."

"Oh really. Whereabouts?"

"Do you know Blackmoss Cottage?"

The woman's eyebrows rose high enough to touch her fringe. "You mean Emily Wylde's cottage?"

"That's right. Emily was my aunt. I'm Hazel Knight–" Hazel broke off and quickly corrected her slip of the tongue. "Sorry, I mean Wylde. Knight was my married name."

"I'm Susan Cooper." Susan paused as if expecting them to recognise the name. Seeing their blank expressions, she continued, "I'm surprised Emily never mentioned me."

"We weren't close to her."

"Oh I see. Well, your aunt used to make blankets and I sold them for her. She came by here at the end of every month to pick up her earnings and supply me with new stock. When I didn't see her last July..." Susan faltered. A hint of shame flickered across her heavily made-up face.

Last July. The words echoed in Lily's head. That was about the time Dad's drinking had begun to get out of control. She thought back to the birthday party her parents had thrown for her and a few of her friends. Dad had got drunk and started yelling and screaming for no apparent reason. A couple of her friends had ended up in tears. Even now, the memory of it made her cringe.

Susan heaved a sigh. "At first, I just assumed Emily was under the weather or something. But after a week or two, I started to get worried. That's when I called the police. The constable that found her told me she'd been dead for at least a month. I hate the thought of her being left there all that time to..." She trailed off as if she couldn't bring herself to say it.

"To rot," Lily put in bluntly.

Susan gawped at her, seemingly too taken aback to speak.

"This is my daughter, Lily," said Hazel.

Susan pushed out another toothy smile. "Where are you moving from?"

"Fulham," said Lily, drawing a faint frown from her mum.

"I had heard Emily's cottage was being renovated," confessed Susan. "I wondered who was moving in. Is it just the two of you?"

"Yes, just us," Hazel answered quickly as if she wanted to

beat Lily to replying.

"What did Emily look like?" asked Lily.

"We never met her," Hazel explained.

"You wouldn't soon forget her if you had," said Susan. "She was small. Tiny in fact." She gestured to Hazel. "She had hair like yours, except it was white at the tip. Like she'd dipped it in paint. I used to wonder whether she'd suffered some sort of shock. They say a nasty shock can turn your hair white overnight."

Like a reflex action, Lily lifted a hand to press her hat to her head.

"If you don't mind me asking, how come you never met Emily?" said Susan.

Hazel responded with a polite little smile. "She was estranged from her family. There's really not much else to tell."

"Do you believe in witchcraft?" Lily asked.

The question elicited a curious look from Susan. "Why do you ask?"

Lily pointed to the branch in the window.

Susan let out a giggle of comprehension. "Oh that. It's an old tradition around here to put rowan in your window. Do you know anything about Midwood's history?"

"Lily's been reading about Mary Long," said Hazel.

"Is the tree where she was burned really still standing?" Lily asked.

"Yes." Susan pointed out of the window to a blunt green hilltop a mile or two away. "It's in Dead Woman's Ditch. Near the top of Chapman Hill."

"Dead Woman's Ditch," Hazel echoed. "That's an, err... ominous name."

"It's not actually a ditch." Susan drew a circle in the air. "It's a manmade grass bank. It's been there a lot longer than the tree. No one really knows who built it or why. It's a lovely walk up there, although the tree isn't much to look at. It's half-dead. God knows how it's survived this long." She leaned closer to Lily, lowering her voice like someone telling a spooky campfire tale. "There's a hollow at the base of the tree. The story goes that while Mary was burning, Doubting Tom ran into the hollow and that was the last anyone ever saw of him."

"Doubting Tom was Mary's dog, wasn't he?"

"Yes, except he wasn't actually a dog. He was a demon disguised as a dog. Legend has it that if you put your arm in the hollow and say his name three times, he'll bite your hand. But only if you have a pure soul."

"Why only if you have a pure soul?"

"Because Doubting Tom's always hungry for pure souls. He feeds on the blood of his victims, then lets them drink his milk."

Lily's forehead rippled in confusion. "But if he's a he, how can he produce milk?"

"Ah well you see, he has a secret nipple, put there by the Devil himself. The deal is, you get Doubting Tom's milk and the Devil gets your soul."

"That doesn't sound like a very good deal to me," Hazel remarked dryly.

Susan wagged a long pink fingernail. "But this isn't just any old milk. This is magic milk. It lets you see things." She put on an eerie voice. "Things from the other side. And it adds years to your life." She let slip another girlish giggle. "I wouldn't say no to it myself."

"Have you tried summoning Doubting Tom?" Lily asked.

"Yes, when I was about your age. All the kids around here have. It's a... what do you call it?"

"A rite of passage?" said Hazel.

"That's the one. Come to think of it, that was the last time I went up Chapman Hill. Not that I'm scared of bumping into Doubting Tom. It just... well, it doesn't feel right going up there considering what my ancestors did to Mary. My great-great-great-something-or-other-grandad was one of the three men who accused her of being a witch. Another was an ancestor of Toby and Carl's. Toby Spencer, the butcher that is, and his brother Carl, the landlord of The Rowan Tree."

"Who was the third man?" Lily asked.

"Baron Walter Chapman. He was lord of the manor at Chapman Hall back then and a strict Puritan to boot. He was convinced a coven of witches used to meet up in the forest near the village." Susan's voice dropped again as if she was imparting some sinister secret. "Rumour has it there are still covens around here."

Lily frowned, unsure whether to be intrigued or perturbed. "Seriously?"

Susan's bright red lips curved into a smile at the effect of her words. "Yes, but I wouldn't worry. It's just gossip. If there's one thing people around here like to do, it's gossip. My mum used to say, *You can't break wind in this village without everyone knowing about it.*"

As if that was her cue to end the conversation, Hazel took out her purse to pay. "Well it was nice to meet you, Susan."

"Nice to meet you, too, and welcome to our beautiful village. I'm sure you'll love it here."

With carrier bags in hand, Lily and Hazel headed towards the door. "Just a heads up, I wouldn't mention Mary Long or witches in general to the Spencer brothers," Susan cheerily called after them. "They can be a bit touchy about that sort of thing."

7

"She seems nice," Lily remarked as the shop door jangled shut.

"Hmm." Hazel sounded far from convinced. "If you ask me, she's a nosey cow."

Lily's eyes widened a little. Her mum never usually bad-mouthed anyone. She wondered what Susan had said to annoy her.

Sam pressed his mouth against the car window, smearing it with slobber. As Hazel opened the backdoor, he jumped out, panting and whining. "Sorry for taking so long, Sam." Her apology turned into a rebuke as the dog cocked a hind leg in front of the General Store. "No Sam. Stop that."

Lily dodged aside as a rivulet of urine coursed towards her. Sam shook out the last few drops before trotting back to the car. Hazel and Lily exchanged a glance, then swiftly got into the car. Lily's hat caught on the doorframe and fell to the ground. Her brown hair unfurled around her shoulders. A streak of white, like a badger's stripe, stretched from root to tip down one side of her long fringe. She snatched up the hat and stuffed it back onto her head.

"I don't know why your hair bothers you so much," said Hazel. "I think it's beautiful."

"I *hate* it."

"So dye it."

Lily exhaled sharply. "What would be the point? It would

just keep growing back."

Taking the hint, Hazel changed the topic. "How long do you think it'll take to get around the village that we're moving into Blackmoss Cottage? Five minutes?"

Lily raised a cynical eyebrow. "More like about thirty seconds."

Hazel started the engine, but hesitated to pull away. Her gaze lingered on a giant of a man emerging from the butchers. As he stooped to avoid hitting his head on the doorframe, a bald spot gleamed through his slicked back brown hair. His barrel chest flexing against a blue-and-white striped apron, he put out a sandwich-board chalked with 'HIGHEST QUALITY NEW SEASON'S LAMB FROM CHAPMAN HALL'.

"God, look at the size of him," said Hazel, watching the man plant a cigarette in his downturned lips. He squinted as he lifted a lighter to the cigarette.

"Toby Spencer, I presume," said Lily.

"What an ugly brute. I wouldn't want *that* on top of me." Hazel shuddered as if imagining just such a thing.

Lily chuckled uncertainly, somewhat taken aback by the comment. She wondered at her mum's newfound willingness to speak her mind. Was this a *new* her for their *new* life? Or perhaps it was the real her that had been repressed by marriage.

Lily pointed out two sprigs of rowan dangling above the cuts of meat in the shop window. "Do you think that's just for show or what?"

"I don't know, but it looks pretty. Maybe we should get some for our windows."

The suggestion elicited a flat laugh from Lily.

Hazel's gaze returned to the hulking butcher. She sized him up for a few more seconds, then put the car into gear and accelerated away.

A corpulent figure splayed across the bench in front of the church caught Lily's attention. "Look, there's that guy again."

The obese man was swaddled in the same shapeless robe. He was munching on a chocolate bar as contentedly as a pig with a turnip. He paused to watch the passing car.

"What a weirdo," said Lily, rubbernecking at him like he was an exhibit in a freak show.

"Don't be so cruel," Hazel reprimanded.

"Says the person who just called the shopkeeper a nosey cow and the butcher an ugly brute."

Hazel's lips lifted into the crooked smile of someone who'd been caught out. "I suppose that is a bit hypocritical." Her smile faded. "I hope I'm wrong about Susan Cooper. Between me letting slip our old name and you mentioning Fulham, it wouldn't take much for her to find out about us."

Lily's stomach clenched at the possibility.

"Hazel Wylde, Hazel Wylde..." Hazel repeated her name multiple times, hammering it into her brain.

They entered the corridor of trees at the far side of Midwood. Occasional glimpses of Chapman Hill could be seen through the foliage. At that distance, the sheep dotting its slopes looked like they were pinned in place.

"How long do you think it would take to walk from the cottage to Dead Woman's Ditch?" Lily asked.

Hazel gave her a knowing glance. "Don't get any daft ideas."

"What do you mean?"

Hazel tilted her head at Lily's butter-wouldn't-melt expression. "Don't play the innocent with me, Lily. I can read you like a book. You'll give yourself nightmares if you try to summon Doubting Tom."

Lily snorted. "Give me a break. I've got plenty of things to have nightmares about, but demon dogs aren't one of them."

Sadness clouded Hazel's eyes. She couldn't argue with those words.

Her gaze strayed from the road to a carpet of wildflowers. As she took in a riot of daisies, buttercups and dandelions, her sadness drained away. Surely if there was a place to rediscover a sense of wonder, this was it.

The cottage track came into view. The brambles and rotten sign had been replaced by a farm-style gate with a sign that announced 'Private Road. Access to Blackmoss Cottage only'.

"What do you think?" Hazel asked.

Lily shrugged. "I kind of preferred the old sign."

The comment drew an eye-roll from Hazel. "Open the gate, will you?"

Their progression along the track was a lot smoother than before. The worst of the potholes had been filled in with gravel. The encroaching branches had been trimmed. Sam thrust his head between the front seats, trembling in anticipation.

Lily stroked him. "Someone's happy to be back here."

The car emerged into the sunny clearing where Blackmoss Cottage hid from the world. Lily couldn't contain a, "Wow!" She took in the scene with wide eyes. "It looks amazing."

Hazel beamed at her reaction.

The grass had been cut to a pale, dry-looking stubble. Plumes of purple flowers sprouted from a row of raised beds. A new shed stood proudly in place of the old one.

Hazel parked in a gravelled area, from which stone slabs led to the front door. The kitchen window had been repaired. The ivy had been stripped from the walls and a spotless coat of creamy paint sparkled in the sun. Likewise, the moss had been cleared from the gutters and roof. The new thatching was as neat as freshly trimmed hair. Mushroom-shaped terracotta pots crowned the repointed chimneys.

Lily let Sam out of the car. He sprinted along the path, barking delightedly. Hazel and Lily laughed as he ran in circles on the lawn, so happy he didn't know what to do with himself.

Hazel put an arm around Lily's shoulders as they approached the house. Not a breath of wind penetrated the clearing. The warm air was buzzing with bees, dragonflies, wasps and a multitude of other insects.

"This place is crawling," said Lily.

"I know." Hazel inhaled deeply. "Everything's so alive here."

A sickly-sweet scent drew Lily's eyes to the bell-shaped flowers. Clusters of pale green berries nestled amongst the frills of leaves. She thought about the deliciously sour jam they'd taken from the cottage's kitchen. "Are they gooseberries?"

"No, gooseberries grow on bushes. I have no idea what these are. They're pretty, don't you think?"

"Yes, but they smell awful."

"Forget them. What do you think of that?" Hazel pointed to the paintings of gingerbread biscuits around the door. They, too, had been treated to a touch up.

Lily ran her fingers over a biscuit that glistened as if it had just come out of the oven. "They make me want some actual gingerbread."

Hazel unlocked the front door. It swung open soundlessly. Sam darted into the house, his claws skittering on the flagstones as he plunged under the new door-curtain. He was halfway up the stairs before Hazel could draw the curtain aside. With a flourish, she motioned for Lily to come into the hallway.

Nothing much had changed, except the dirty grey plaster

walls were now a pristine white and the stairs glinted with new varnish. The half-melted candles still occupied the iron brackets. The smooth-worn flagstone floor remained in situ.

Lily sniffed the air. "The smell's gone." She flipped the light switch to no effect. "Still no electricity?"

"Ah well, here's the thing. The old generator was kaput and the new one hasn't arrived yet. So for now, we'll have to make do with those." Hazel motioned to the candles. "It'll be fun. We can make-believe that we're living in the seventeenth century."

Lily replied with a groan.

"It should only be for a few days," Hazel assured her, heading for the living room.

Lily trailed after her. The parquet floor had been polished to a lustrous sheen. A new three-piece-suite and deep pile rug gave the room a welcoming feel. The Toby jugs and dried flowers were gone. The portraits chronicling the dogs that had lived there were still present. As were the piano and coffee-table.

Lily pointed to a small black box on the windowsill. "Is that what I think it is?"

"Yes, it's a router. And let me tell you, it wasn't cheap to have the cabling installed. It's battery powered, so the Wi-Fi should work just fine."

"It's a shame I won't be able to use it once my phone runs out of charge."

Hazel sighed. "I'm doing my best here, Lily."

Lily glanced upwards at a series of soft thuds from above. "It sounds like Sam's having a good nose around."

"Maybe he's looking for Emily."

Sadness crept over Lily's features as she thought about Sam searching for someone he would never find. She headed for the stairs. He was mooching down them with his head hanging low. She stroked him. "You still miss Emily, don't you?"

His ears pricking at the name, he lifted his big eyes to Lily.

"Are you hungry?" she asked. "Let's see if there's anything for you to eat."

He followed her into the kitchen. It was the most changed part of the house so far. The grubby old cupboards and worksurfaces had been replaced with shiny, modern ones. A fresh coat of enamel gleamed on the Rayburn and farmhouse sink. The Welsh Dresser, along with its collection of mismatched crockery, remained in place, but a solid wood dining table and four matching chairs had taken the trestle table's spot. The pantry now had a door. The overall impression was a pleasant blend of old-meets-new.

"This is my favourite room," said Hazel. She proudly opened a cupboard, revealing an integrated fridge-freezer. "There's also a dishwasher, microwave, washing machine and anything else we could possibly need."

"Except without electricity all this stuff's useless," Lily couldn't resist pointing out.

"Not this old girl." Hazel patted the Rayburn. "And I've had a back boiler installed so we can use this to heat the house and water."

"Great. So we'll be spending half our lives chopping wood."

"Look on the bright side, Lily. Just think how fit you'll get from all that chopping."

Lily shot her mum an unamused glance. Prompted by a soft whine from Sam, she opened the pantry door. The shelves had been emptied of everything except the homemade preserves and wine. "There's no dog food."

Hazel clicked her tongue. "I meant to buy some at the store. I'll have to nip back into the village later." She filled a bowl with water and set it down on the flagstones. "Sorry, Sam. This will have to do for now."

As Sam lapped up the water, Hazel and Lily went upstairs. The 'Hear no evil. See no evil. Speak no evil.' tapestry still adorned the landing wall.

Hazel opened the back bedroom door, releasing a smell of new woollen carpet. The walls had been painted in Lily's favourite pastel green. Instead of the sewing machine and shelves, the room was furnished with a set of pine bedroom furniture.

"Do you like it?" Hazel asked.

Smiling at her mum's slightly nervous question, Lily nodded. "It's nice."

Hazel gave Lily's hand a pleased squeeze.

Lily checked out the remaining rooms. The bathroom had been gutted. Everything in there was sparkling white and chrome. Emily's former bedroom had been replastered and painted white. The treadle sewing machine occupied a previously empty corner. Apart from that, the room was unchanged.

Lily's gaze passed over the big old wardrobe, framed moss pressings and patchwork quilt before landing on the pearl-inlaid box atop the bedside table. She unlocked and opened it. A faint line etched itself between her eyebrows at the sight of the serrated circlet. "I thought you were getting rid of all this junk."

"I happen to like this 'junk'. I get the feeling there are a lot of happy memories attached to it."

Lily's frown deepened. "I suppose we need all the happy memories we can get, even if they belong to someone else."

An uncomfortable silence followed. Displaying his usual sixth sense for when he was needed, Sam trotted into the room. As he nuzzled Lily's hand, her frown melted away. Hazel gave him a grateful smile.

The rumble of an approaching vehicle drew their attention to the window. "Sounds like the removal van's here," said Hazel, turning to head downstairs.

Lily stared at the circlet for a moment more before closing the box and following her.

8

Wiping sweat from her forehead, Hazel dropped onto a chair at the kitchen table. Her gaze lingered on the cardboard boxes cluttering the room. She puffed her cheeks at the thought of unpacking them. "Thanks," she said as Lily handed her a sandwich.

Lily took a bite of her own sandwich. She tossed Sam a chunk of cheese. He gobbled it up and whined for more.

"I'd better go and get some dog food," said Hazel. "What are you going to do?"

"Sam could do with a walk."

"Ok, but don't go too far. We've got *a lot* to do." Hazel rose and weaved her way through the boxes. She paused in the doorway to give Lily a grateful smile. "Thank you."

"What for?"

"For giving this place a chance."

Lily watched from the window as her mum got into the car and drove away. The engine noise dwindled to nothing. She turned to survey the kitchen, struck by how utterly quiet it was. If there was any such thing as deafening silence, this was it.

"Come on, Sam, walkies." She spoke more loudly than necessary as if to push back the silence.

With Sam at her heels, she made her way to the front door. She locked it behind her with a brass copy of the rusty old key.

Eyeing the trees, she wondered out loud, "Which way should we go?"

As if in answer to her question, Sam scampered towards the back garden. Her eyes sparkled with amusement. "Ok, Sam, you lead the way."

Leaves twirled down from the apple trees, landing on Lily's sunhat as she followed him across the lawn. She passed a glittering new greenhouse with plant pots and bags of compost stacked on its floor.

Sam headed for an archway formed by the interlaced branches of two old oaks. A dirt path led between the trees, rising steadily into the forest. Sam stopped and glanced back as if seeking Lily's permission to continue.

"Go on," she said. "Just don't get us lost."

He barked and broke into a run. The forest exhaled its cool, earthy breath into Lily's face as she quickened her pace to keep up with him. She blinked as the path passed through pools of bright sunlight.

"Wait, Sam," she called out as the dog leaped over a tree that had fallen across the path.

He took no notice, seemingly carried away by the excitement of being back on his home turf. Branches scratched Lily's ankles as she too hurdled the fallen tree. Bracken crowded in on either side as the path dwindled to little more than an animal track. She glanced over her shoulder. The cottage had long since disappeared from view. Her gaze returned to Sam, who was now just a vague shape darting through the undergrowth. She shouted him again with the same result. Beads of sweat trickled down her face as she strove not to lose sight of him.

"Sam, you're going to get me in trouble," she muttered, thinking about her mum's instruction not to go too far.

The path levelled out, broadening into an avenue of stubby,

densely packed trees with serrated oval leaves. Lily shrank aside as a black branch armed with long, straight thorns reached out to prick her wrist. Bobbing and weaving to avoid the thorns, she scurried onwards. The avenue was so straight that she wondered if it was natural.

After about fifty metres, the double row of trees flared into a circle of daisy-starred grass with a patch of scorched earth at its centre. Sam was sniffing at the ashes. He looked at Lily as she remonstrated breathlessly, "That was really naughty, Sam. Next time, I'm going to put you on a lead."

Her harsh tone evaporated as he responded with an apologetic whimper. "Ok, Ok." She ruffled his fur. "I know you're just excited to be back here."

The afternoon sun beat down on Lily as she scuffed a sandal at the ashes. "Did you used to come here with Emily? Is this where she met up with her coven?"

She chuckled at her little quip. She flinched into silence as a golden-brown pheasant burst from the undergrowth. Wings whirring frantically, it rocketed off through the trees.

"No, Sam. No," Lily exclaimed as the dog sprang away in pursuit. He plunged into a thicket of bracken, startling several more pheasants into flight.

Lily waded after him, parting the bracken with her hands. After a short distance, she stopped to listen. A crunch of undergrowth drew her attention. She spotted him through a tuft of swaying fronds. His nose was pushed against the ground as if he was following a scent.

She ran towards him as fast as the dense bracken would permit. Within a few strides, she lost sight of him again.

"Sam! Sam!"

There was a note of anxiety in her voice. All around her, there were trees as far as the eye could see. Feeling completely disorientated, she imagined herself wandering in circles as lost as Hansel and Gretel. An echoing bark rang out. She headed towards where it seemed to come from. The ground began to rise, getting steeper with every step. Her leg muscles burned, unaccustomed to such strenuous exertion.

She pushed through a curtain of leaves into dazzling sunlight. Shielding her eyes, she saw that she was high up on the slopes of Chapman Hill. Beyond a barbed wire fence, pastures of grass, gorse and heather undulated towards the rounded summit. Sheep and lambs speckled the hillside. Maybe half-a-mile to her left, a manor house was nestled amidst broad lawns towards the head of a valley. Ranks of chimneys lined its roof. Tall windows glittered in its grey stone façade. To one side of the house was a walled garden and what appeared to be a cluster of barns.

A guttural cawing broke out like an argument. Lily squinted up at a quartet of crows perched in the treetops. The birds took flight. Sunlight flickered through their fingerlike wingtips as they soared towards the hilltop. A flash of movement from beneath their flight path caught her eye. Sam emerged from a grassy gully, scattering sheep and lambs in all directions. As he zigzagged after them, their distressed bleats echoed across the slope.

Lily ducked under the barbed wire to resume her pursuit. She instinctively threw herself flat on the grass as a thunderous *bang* reverberated through the air. High overhead, the crows reeled and swirled as if they were being buffeted by gale-force winds.

A boy about her age came striding around the lee of the hill. The butt of a double-barrelled shotgun was pressed into his shoulder. Lily's heart kicked at her ribcage as he took aim at Sam.

Seemingly sensing he was in danger, the dog turned to stare at the boy.

"Don't shoot!" Lily cried out. The brim of her sunhat flapped as she jumped up and sprinted towards Sam.

The boy lowered his gun as she came between him and his target. Sam peered up at her with his tongue lolling over slobber-flecked jowls and his flanks heaving like a hard-ridden racehorse. She dropped to her haunches and wrapped a protective arm around his neck.

"Are you stupid?" a cut-glass voice demanded to know.

The boy marched towards them, an angry red flush rising from under the collar of his waxed jacket. Pale blue eyes glowered from beneath the peak of a tweed flat-cap. He stopped in his tracks as Sam bared his teeth and growled. He eyed the dog warily, his fingers flexing on the gun.

"I said, are you stupid?" he asked again. "I could have shot you."

Lily whipped out her phone. "If you hurt my dog, I'll call the police."

"Go ahead. I'd be well within my rights to shoot him for worrying the sheep." The boy pointed to the manor house. "Do you know what that is?"

"Chapman Hall?"

"That's right and I'm Jude Chapman."

Lily bit down on an urge to tell him she couldn't care less who he was. Sam emitted another rumbling growl. She felt a twinge of satisfaction as Jude retreated a step.

"You'd better keep him under control," he warned.

"Or what?"

"Or he'll end up like that." Jude indicated the ground nearby.

Lily's face scrunched into an appalled frown. A crow was splayed out on the grass, its wings shredded to bloody ribbons. She let out a jaded sigh that suddenly made her seem older than her years. "Why do people like you get a kick out of hurting things?"

"*People like me?*" Realisation dawned on Jude's face. "You're not from around here, are you? Where are you from?"

"None of your business."

Jude pushed out his lips in thought. "From your accent, I'd say London." He smirked at Lily's silence. "I'm right, aren't I? Well since you're a townie, I'll explain how things work around here."

"Don't bother. I'm not interested."

"Firstly, I don't get a kick out of hurting things," Jude continued as if she hadn't spoken. "I'm shooting crows because they attack the lambs. Secondly, all of this belongs to my family." He made a sweeping motion with the shotgun. "We usually prosecute trespassers, but…" He gave Lily a once-over, taking in her sandals, baggy floral trousers, clashing striped blouse and floppy sunhat, "seeing as you're obviously not quite all there, I'll let you off just this once."

"Oh thank you, milord." Lily's voice was laced with sarcasm. "I'm so grateful."

Jude gave a humourless laugh. "You're hilarious."

And you're an arrogant toff, Lily resisted the temptation to fire back. Keeping a tight hold of Sam's collar, she stood up and started towards the woods.

"Not that way," said Jude. "We have pheasants in the woods. I don't want you disturbing them." He pointed to the hilltop. "There's a public footpath up there."

"But that's not the way I need to go."

Jude's almost femininely plump lips curled upwards. "And that's my problem why?"

It was on the tip of Lily's tongue to tell him she was from Blackmoss Cottage. She pressed her lips together. She didn't want him knowing they were neighbours. What if he came to the cottage to complain about Sam? No way was she going to risk this idiot ruining the first day in their new home. This move meant too much to her mum.

Heaving a sigh, Lily set off towards the humpbacked summit. "God, what a creep," she said to Sam.

He barked and lunged forwards, yanking her shoulder. Several wildly flapping crows launched themselves from a clump of heather.

Lily flinched at another ear-splitting *boom*. One crow fell to the grass with a soft thud. Feathers seesawed down around Lily as she pivoted to glare at Jude. Her jaw clenched at the sight of his smug face. She hadn't realised it was possible to dislike someone so much in such a short space of time. God, she wanted to tell him where to shove his gun.

Sam jerked forwards again, almost pulling her over. His jaws clamped around the dead crow.

"Drop it," Lily commanded.

He sank his teeth deeper into the carcass. Lily grimaced at the snap of breaking bones. "Alright, keep it. Eat it and make yourself sick for all I care. Let's just get out of here before that idiot shoots *us*."

They resumed their ascent. The crow's wings dangled from Sam's mouth, dragging over the ground. Lily's step faltered as she saw what the birds had been gathered around. The contorted body of a lamb was lying amidst the heather. She swallowed queasily. The lamb's eye sockets were black hollows. Blood ringed them like mascara. The torn remnants of its tongue were protruding from its mouth. Its ears were mutilated stumps.

Lily retreated a startled step as the lamb's legs twitched and it emitted a feeble bleat. Caught between curiosity and horror, she looked on as the lamb lifted its head and peered around sightlessly.

"What are you waiting for?" Jude called out. "Get moving."

Lily wrenched her eyes away from the grisly sight. "There's an injured lamb here."

As Jude started towards the spot, Lily hurried on her way. The lamb was clearly beyond help. For mercy's sake, it would have to be put out of its misery. No way was she hanging around to watch Jude finish off the poor little thing.

Hunching her shoulders in anticipation of another gunshot, Lily made for a gap in a hedgerow. Despite herself, she couldn't resist peeking over her shoulder. Jude was on his knees by the lamb. Sunlight glinted on a knife in his hand. She quickly looked away as the blade plunged downwards.

Her gaze traversed a footpath that skirted along the hilltop before looping down towards the vast expanse of trees. She couldn't see Blackmoss Cottage, but she had a rough idea of its location in relation to Midwood. Returning via the public footpath would add a good mile to what was already an unexpectedly long excursion.

She scrolled down her phone's short list of contacts to 'Mum'. The call went straight to voicemail. Doubtless, her mum had no signal.

"Oh how I love the countryside," she told Sam sarcastically. She took in the view for a moment more. A sea of green stretched away to a hazy blue horizon. "I suppose it is beautiful," she conceded before turning to head for the footpath.

Sam suddenly swerved in the opposite direction.

"No," Lily said sternly. "We're not going that way."

He gave another arm-jarring pull. She opened her mouth to reprimand him, but closed it as she saw what he was straining towards. Not far away, a grass bank curved along the rim of a wide shelf cut into the hillside. Curiosity gleamed in Lily's eyes. The top of the embankment seemed unnaturally flat.

She nibbled her lower lip for a moment. Then, as if absolving herself of responsibility, she said, "Ok, Sam, have it your own way," and let him tow her towards the earthwork.

9

T he embankment was about two metres tall with steeply sloping sides. Lily's gaze followed its curve to an opening wide enough to admit one person at a time. The earthwork enclosed a circular, shallow depression about twenty metres in diameter. A gnarled, leafless skeleton of a tree stood at its centre. At two-thirds of its height, the trunk was girdled by a tangle of twigs that resembled a massive nest. Clusters of scarlet berries crowned the treetop.

"It looks like it's in pain," Lily remarked.

Sam pulled her towards the tree. At its base, on the side facing away from the hill, the trunk split into a hollow. As if laying an offering at an altar, Sam set the dead crow down in front of the aperture. Lily poked her head inside the tree. What looked to be a burrow – from the size of it, possibly dug by a badger or a fox – sloped down into darkness. She switched on her phone's torch. The pale light didn't reach the bottom of the root-veined tunnel.

A musty smell tickled her nostrils. Did it have a smoky tinge? Or was she merely imagining it?

At a flapping of wings, she withdrew her head from the hollow. A crow swooped down from the blue to land in the tree, closely followed by several more. Fluttering their wings to keep their balance, the crows pecked at the berries and swallowed them whole.

Lily wondered if they were the same birds Jude had shot at. Would he pursue them here? She glanced around uneasily, half-expecting another gunshot to ring out. The only sound, though, was that of the crows squabbling. They jabbed their bristly beaks at each other and the berries, celebrating with boisterous caws whenever they plucked another juicy red prize from the branches.

Lily's gaze fell to Sam as he nosed the dead crow into the hollow. She tightened her grip on his collar, fearing he might try to crawl down the burrow. Instead, he folded his rear legs under himself and rested his head on his front paws.

She peered into the hollow again. The darkness stared back, black as a crow's eyes. "What do you think? Should I try to summon Doubting Tom?" she asked Sam.

He rolled his eyes up at her. As if she saw a challenge in them, she said, "I'm not scared. I don't even believe in that stuff."

So why do it? she asked herself. She recalled what Susan Cooper had said – *This is magic milk. It lets you see things. Things from the other side.*

Lily's thoughts turned to her dad. What if it was true? What if she could see him again, maybe even speak to him? She could ask him why. Why did you do this to us?

She almost laughed at the absurdity of the idea, but her eyes remained fixed on the darkness. For a moment, she remained stock still. Then she thrust her arm into the hollow. The dead crow's feathers tickled her wrist as she called out, "Doubting Tom, Doubting Tom, Doubting Tom!"

The hollow swallowed up her voice. Her racing heart made a lie of her claim that she wasn't scared. Ten seconds passed. Twenty. Nothing moved in the darkness. No demon dog sank its teeth into her. She withdrew her arm and displayed it to Sam as if it was evidence. "See. I told you. It's just a story to frighten kids." Her dismissive tone couldn't conceal a trace of relief.

"No it's not and you shouldn't have done that."

Lily gave such a start that her hat fell off. She whirled around to find out where the voice had come from. A boy was sitting cross-legged by the earthwork's entrance, watching her intently through black-rimmed glasses that were half-hidden by a mop of brown hair.

"How long have you been there?" Lily demanded to know.

"Long enough to see what you did." The boy unfolded his lanky legs and stood up. He was wearing frayed cut-off jeans and hiking boots. A leather satchel was slung across his hairless chest.

"So what? I was only messing around."

The boy shuffled into the enclosure, dragging his feet as if he couldn't be bothered to lift them. His right hand was inside the satchel. "You shouldn't mess around with that kind of thing."

"Why not?" Lily eyed the satchel suspiciously. She wished Sam would growl, but the dog merely turned his head to eyeball the boy. "What's going to happen?"

The boy scratched his dimpled chin, mulling over the question. "I don't know."

"Well I do. Absolutely nothing. That's what. All the kids around here try to call Doubting Tom, but he's never once appeared."

"I'm from around here and I haven't tried to call him. I'm not about to risk my soul being taken by a demon. That's what Doubting Tom is, you know. He's a demon sent by the Devil to collect souls."

Lily gave a tight-lipped smile. "Thanks for the warning." With a shake of her head, she spoke as much to herself as to the boy. "Is everyone around here crazy?"

A smile played at the edges of his mouth. "Where are you from?"

Lily responded with a vague gesture in the cottage's direction. "I live down there with my mum."

"The only house in that part of the woods is Blackmoss Cottage."

"That's where I live."

"Emily Wylde lives at Blackmoss Cottage."

"Emily died."

The boy's eyes widened. With sudden surprising speed, he shuffled to within arm's reach of Lily. "When?"

She drew back slightly. "Last June. Did you know her?"

"Yes... well no, I knew of her. I never met her." The boy's voice was tinged with what sounded like regret. "So are you related to her?"

"She was my great-aunt. I'm Lily..." Lily hesitated just long enough to suggest some uncertainty, "Wylde."

"Are you sure about that?"

"What do you mean? Of course I'm sure about it." There was a defensive edge to Lily's voice.

A brief silence ensued. The boy withdrew his hand from the satchel and extended it. "Nice to meet you, Lily."

Lily hesitated to shake his hand – not simply because she was nervous, but because it had only one finger and a thumb. Where the other three fingers should have been, there were smooth bobbles of flesh not much bigger than rowan berries.

Realising she was staring, Lily quickly accepted the boy's hand. A squeamish shudder ran through her at the squishiness of the malformed fingers. She gave him a somewhat apologetic look.

He smiled unconcernedly. "I'm Tom."

Lily's contrition gave way to scepticism. "You're joking?"

"No."

She pulled her hand back, narrowing her eyes, trying to work out whether he was telling the truth.

His dusky grey eyes glimmered with amusement. "Honestly, my name's Tom. Don't look so worried. It's just a funny coincidence." He turned his attention to the dog. "And who's this?"

"That's Sam."

"Hello Sam." Tom stooped to stroke the dog. He laughed as Sam rolled over to have his tummy scratched. "Who's a good boy?"

"Not him. We were only supposed to go for a short walk, but he ran off. That's how we ended up here. He was Emily's dog. I'm wondering if she used to bring him here."

"I come up here all the time and I never saw them."

"You come here all the time? Why?"

Tom's fringe flopped over his glasses as he somewhat shyly titled his head forwards. "I like to be alone. Hardly anyone else ever comes here." He glanced at the crows. "Except for them."

Lily looked at the dark shapes. Their numbers had doubled. They were silent now, like sentinels watching over Dead Woman's Ditch. "Are they always here?"

"Yes. All year round." Tom took a sketchbook out of his satchel. He flicked through pages with photos of the old rowan sellotaped to them. In one, the branches were laden with snow. In another, they were glistening wet. The crows were ever present.

Watercolours of the tree and the surrounding area were mixed in amongst the photos. Lily leaned in for a closer look as Tom turned the page to a detailed depiction of Blackmoss Cottage and its garden. Well-tended vegetable plots were interspersed with bursts of familiar purple flowers. A little old lady was scattering seed for the hens clustered around her long patchwork skirt. Her shoulder-length hair was black at the crown and white at the tips as if she was greying in reverse. Craggy, tanned features spoke of a life spent toiling outside. Her eyes were hidden within dark hollows that reminded Lily of the mutilated lamb.

"I thought you never met Emily," she said.

"I didn't. I went to have a look at the cottage one time and she was in the garden."

"You enjoy spying on people, don't you?"

"What? I... No..." Tom stumbled over his words in his haste to explain. "I'm just interested in the cottage's–" His eyes widened as Lily broke into a grin. "You're teasing me."

She realised with a jolt of surprise that he was right. She couldn't recall the last time she'd felt relaxed enough around someone other than her mum to poke fun at them. "Sorry."

"It's alright, I'm used to it."

Tom self-consciously returned his malformed hand to the satchel. Lily cringed at the uncomfortable silence that ensued. Then it was his turn to grin, prompting her to exclaim, "Now *you're* teasing *me!*"

"Yes, but you deserved it."

Lily's smile returned. "I suppose I did."

Sam barked as if he wanted to join in on the joke. Several crows broke into flight and circled overhead, cawing loudly.

"I get the feeling they're shouting at us," said Lily.

"They are. Sometimes they sit up there insulting me for hours on end."

Lily looked at Tom to see if he was having her on again, but his face was serious. "Insulting you how?"

"They laugh at my hair, my clothes and everything else

about the way I look."

"Why would they do that?"

Tom shrugged. "Maybe I once annoyed them in some way. Never make an enemy of a crow. They hold grudges forever."

Lily tilted a curious glance at the birds. "Why do they come here?"

"Supposedly, they flocked here to feed on Mary's corpse and they've been here ever since."

"Do you believe that?"

"I suppose it could be true. Crows are very territorial. They'll fight anything that threatens their territory. I don't just mean other birds. If you hurt them, they'll remember your face. They'll tell each other about you. They might even attack you."

"Then Jude Chapman had better watch out."

Tom frowned. "You know Jude?"

"I didn't until about twenty minutes ago. He almost shot Sam."

Tom didn't seem surprised. "The Chapmans think they can do whatever they want around here. To be honest, they probably can."

Lily eyed the tree. "I guess Mary found that out the hard way three-hundred-years ago."

"Three-hundred-and-thirty-two years ago," Tom corrected. Gently, almost reverently, he ran his fingers over the scaly bark. "Did you know rowans are only supposed to live for two-hundred-years at most?"

"So this isn't the same tree?"

"Yes it is." Tom's voice rang with conviction.

"How can you be sure?"

"I..." Tom faltered, then conceded, "I can't." He lowered his

74

eyes as if embarrassed. Keeping his gaze on the ground, he said, "Did you also know that Walter Chapman said he saw Mary having sex with Doubting Tom?"

Lily wrinkled her nose. "Seriously?"

Tom was silent for a few seconds. Then, as if quoting from memory, he started slowly, "She did approach the creature on all fours like a beast, and the creature did lift its tail, and she did kiss its anus."

"Yuck! Why would she do that?"

"Osculum infame."

"Oscu-what?"

Tom repeated the Latin-sounding words. "It means 'kiss of shame'. Witches pay homage to the Devil by kissing his bum." Closing his eyes, he resumed reciting, "She did then present her bare buttocks to the creature, and it did mount her, and I did know that it was the foul Tempter himself in the guise of a black dog." He opened his eyes. "That's The Right Honourable Baron Walter Chapman's account of what he saw while out hunting on the night of May the 11th, 1690."

"He was obviously lying."

"I don't know about that. I do know that, for years, he'd been trying to buy several acres of woodland from the Longs. The problem was, Mary's husband, Bill, refused to sell. He needed the land for his pigs. Walter made another offer for it after Bill died, but Mary gave him the same answer. It was a couple of months later when he caught her having sex with Doubting Tom."

"Wow, what a lucky coincidence." Lily's tone was as dry as the July air. "Didn't it occur to anyone that he was lying?"

"Walter wasn't out hunting alone. Three men from the village were with him – Robert Cooper, Geoffrey Spencer and Thomas Hughes. They backed up his accusation."

"I've heard the first two names, but not the last one."

"Thomas Hughes was Midwood's rector. Mary fell out with him after he tried to convince her to accept Walter's offer. In revenge, she bought a dog and made sure everyone knew she'd named it after the rector."

"How is that getting revenge?"

"Because back then being called a Doubting Thomas, a man of little faith, was just about the worst insult possible. Even after Mary's death, the name stuck with Thomas Hughes. It eventually drove him to suicide. Suicide is a mortal sin, you know. That's why the rector was pretty much written out of Midwood's history."

"So he also had a reason for wanting Mary dead."

Tom nodded. "And it was his testimony that really sealed her fate. After the execution, her daughter, Agnes, was allowed to keep Blackmoss Cottage. But The Crown seized the land Walter wanted as reparation for Mary's crimes, then sold it to him for about half of what it was worth."

"God, what a bunch of creeps! They were the criminals, not Mary."

"Unless the accusations were true."

"Are you seriously suggesting Mary was a witch?"

Tom shrugged. "She was often seen foraging in the forest for strange plants."

"Oh well then, she was obviously a witch." Lily rolled her eyes.

Tom snickered. "Obviously." He squinted as the sweltering sun shifted into his eyes. "Wow, it's hot." He took a bottle of water out of his satchel. Clasping it between his thumb and only finger, he unscrewed its top.

Lily ran her tongue over her salty lips as she watched him gulp down water. Sam gave him a big-eyed stare, whimpering.

"Are you thirsty, Sam?" Tom asked. He poured some water into his palm. Sam lapped it up.

Tom offered the bottle to Lily. She accepted it and put it to her lips. The tepid water tasted slightly bitter, but she didn't care. It felt heavenly on her parched throat.

"Thanks," she said, giving back the bottle. She glanced at her phone and was surprised to see that they'd been talking for almost half-an-hour. "I have to go. My mum will be getting worried."

"My dad's the same. He's always worrying about me."

My dad's the same – the way Tom said it made Lily wonder if he had a mum. Had he lost a parent too? She gave him a searching look, wanting to ask the question, but not wanting to pry. In the weeks after her dad's death, she'd been bombarded with questions. Had your parents ever been physically violent with each other before? Do you feel safe living with your mum? Is there anything else you want to tell me? She'd been asked that last question so many times, by so many people – police, social workers, counsellors – that the mere thought of it made her want to scream.

"Well, erm, it was…" she began, but trailed off as a sensation she couldn't make sense of tingled through her. Tom's eyes were sparkling in the sun. It struck her that she'd never seen such beautiful eyes before. They were like smoky jewels. And his hair… It shone like silk. She just barely resisted a powerful urge to reach out and run her fingers through it. Her gaze slid down over his smooth, wiry abdomen.

Her cheeks reddened as she realised that she was eyeing him up like he was a piece of meat in Toby Spencer's shop. "Bye," she blurted out, grabbing Sam's collar and starting towards the enclosure's entrance.

"Lily."

She paused, half-turning, not wanting Tom to see her

blushing.

"You forgot your hat."

He held out the sunhat. Mortified, she quickly retrieved it and squished it onto her head. Her blush deepened at the gleam of understanding in Tom's eyes.

"I…" He hesitated as if gathering his courage. "I really like you hair."

Lily's heart seemed to somersault. She smiled uncertainly, needing time to process not only the compliment, but also the emotions surging within her. "Thanks," she mumbled, turning to leave.

As she exited the enclosure, she was seized by an irresistible urge to take one more look at Tom. Her head rotated as if it was being turned by an invisible hand. He waved to her. She waved back, but her eyebrows pinched into a perplexed line as she hurried on her way.

10

The moment Lily was out of the enclosure, she broke into a run like a racehorse released from the starting-gate. With Sam keeping pace at her heels, she followed the footpath to the far end of the hill's broad summit. The path snaked down towards the trees through a patchwork of grass, gorse and heather. Bees buzzed around drowsily, overloaded with pollen. A pack of sturdy brown ponies trotted across the hillside.

Lily angled her hat over her eyes. The afternoon was wearing on, but it felt hotter than ever. She was drenched with sweat. Her legs were leaden and she could feel blisters squishing on the soles of her feet.

Finally, she reached the forest. She sighed as cool shadows enfolded her. 'MIDWOOD 1½ MILES' a wooden sign beside a stile informed her.

The path descended through the trees, spotlighted by the slanting sun. Lily stopped at a stony stream that bubbled alongside the path. She splashed water on her face and neck. Sam plunged his face into the stream. She waited for him drink his fill before continuing on her way.

After another half-a-mile or so, Sam veered off the path in what Lily judged to be the direction of the cottage. She allowed him to lead the way. He scampered along, head down, tongue lolling. He wagged his tail and let out a happy whine as Blackmoss Cottage's creamy white walls came into view.

They emerged into the garden a few metres away from

where they'd exited it. The backdoor was open. Sam sprinted across the lawn and into the kitchen.

"Hello there, Sam," Lily heard her mum exclaim. Hazel appeared at the backdoor. "Where have you been?" She sounded more relieved than angry.

"Sorry, Mum. Sam..." Lily hesitated, reluctant to get the dog into trouble. "We got lost."

Hazel eyed Lily's flushed, sweaty face. "Are you ok?"

"I'm just thirsty."

Lily entered the kitchen, dodging around Sam whose face was buried in his food bowl. She gulped down a glass of water, refilled it and limped over to a chair. She carefully removed her sandals. A blister the size of half a grape bulged on one of her big toes.

Hazel winced at the sight of it. "That looks nasty."

She dug a sewing bag out of a cardboard box, sat down, lifted Lily's foot onto her lap and took aim at the blister with a needle. Lily flinched before it had even touched her.

"Don't be such a baby," said Hazel. She pricked the blister in several places and squeezed out the watery fluid. "There. All done."

"Thanks, Mum."

Hazel stroked a curl of pure white hair that had escaped from Lily's hat. "Promise me you'll be more careful in the future."

"I promise."

Hazel smiled. "Good. Now go get a shower."

Lily hobbled to the bathroom. Her shoulders hunched as the hot water hit a red patch where her neck had caught the sun. She closed her eyes, picturing Tom's tanned, sharp-featured face. Her mind's eye travelled down his lean torso. She found herself imagining what might be inside his denim shorts.

She gave a start at a knock on the door. "I've got a plaster for you," said her mum.

Lily turned off the shower, wrapped a towel around herself and opened the door. "Have we got any paracetamol? My head's killing me."

"I think so. I'll have a look."

After gingerly applying the plaster, Lily went through to her bedroom. Her bed had been made up with a brand-new duvet and pillows. She lay down, sighing as she sank into the cool, soft material. Fresh sweat was bubbling up all over her body. She towelled herself off, but within seconds she was soaking wet again. Her headache was intensifying. Her brain seemed to palpitate against her skull.

She dragged shorts and a vest over her sticky skin, pausing as she caught sight of her hair in the dressing-table mirror.

I really like your hair.

As Tom's words replayed in her mind, Lily's gaze alternated between the sunhat and her reflection. With a sudden decisive movement, she picked up the hat and tossed it behind the bed.

The smell of cooking hit her as she opened her bedroom door. Her stomach squeezed like it was being wrung out. After several deep breaths, the nausea receded.

Wiping sweat from her eyes, she made her way downstairs. Her mum was folding an omelette in a frying pan. Sam was flat out in his basket, snoring contentedly.

Hazel glanced over her shoulder, clocked the hat's absence and smiled. She pointed to a blister-strip of tablets beside a glass of water on the table.

Lily popped out a couple of paracetamol and struggled to swallow them. Her tongue felt like cotton wool. The Rayburn was pumping out heat. Even with the backdoor open, the kitchen was stiflingly warm.

Hazel plated up the omelette and put it on the table in front of Lily.

"I'm not hungry." Lily pushed the plate away. "My stomach feels funny."

Hazel touched the back of her hand to Lily's forehead. "You're burning hot. Maybe you've got a touch of heatstroke."

A loud, purposeful knock reverberated along the hallway. Lily and Hazel exchanged a slightly startled look. Sam stirred, but didn't get up to investigate.

"Who on earth could that be?" Hazel wondered.

A mixture of excitement and apprehension washed over Lily. What if it was Tom or Jude? Hazel headed into the hallway. Lily trailed along, combing her fingers through her wet hair. Surprise and curiosity took over as her mum opened the front door.

A man almost as wide as he was tall filled the doorway. Lily recognised him at once. How could she not? His enormous belly and balloon-shaped face weren't something you soon forgot. Had he walked here all the way from the bench? It appeared so from the wet curls of hair stuck to his forehead and the sweat patches on his burgundy robe.

"My name's Hugo Gready," he informed them in a snuffly, soft-spoken voice.

Lily's mouth fell open at the absurdly appropriate surname.

Hazel gave him a small, polite smile. "I'm Hazel–"

"I know both your names," Hugo interrupted as if he didn't have time for chitchat.

"Oh right, erm..." Hazel paused, taken aback, but quickly recovered her smile. "What can I do for you, Mr Gready?"

"I just wanted to introduce myself. I was a close

acquaintance of Ms Wylde."

Lily stared at Hugo's stomach. There was something almost mesmerising about the way it inflated as he breathed in to speak. Tearing her eyes away from it, she met his beady gaze. "I didn't think Emily had any friends."

He sniffed as if he had a stuffy nose. "I didn't say I was her friend. I said I was her acquaintance."

Lily was silent, unsure how to respond to the pedantic correction.

Hugo slid a podgy hand into a deep pocket in his robe and withdrew a clear plastic bag containing chunks of lumpy chocolate. "Please accept this Rocky Road." He proffered the bag solemnly as if it were a sacred gift.

Hazel accepted it. "Thank you, Mr Gready."

"Please call me Hugo."

"Thank you, Hugo. Lily loves Rocky Road, don't you?" When Lily didn't respond, Hazel threw her a prompting look.

"Yes," said Lily. "Thanks."

A silence followed her less-than-enthusiastic words. Hugo drummed his belly with his fingers, producing a hollow sound. Lily's eyes dropped back to the immense dome of flesh as if it exerted a gravitational pull on them.

"Was there anything else?" Hazel asked gently as if talking to a child.

"I'm a witch," Hugo announced with a little flourish of his hands.

There was another silence. Hazel and Lily exchanged a bemused glance.

"I thought only women could be witches," said Lily.

"That's a common misconception. Historically, most witches are female, but men can be witches too." Hugo paused contemplatively before continuing in his nit-picking way, "I suppose technically, a male practitioner of witchcraft is a warlock."

"That's erm… interesting," said Hazel.

"Are you in a coven?" Lily asked.

"Yes, I'm the magister. Or, in layman's terms, the male head of a coven." Hugo gestured vaguely towards the trees. "I had an understanding with Ms Wylde that we could use the woods every full moon for our Sabbath."

"And what do you do on the Sabbath?" Although Hazel's tone remained friendly, there was an underlying unease.

"It would perhaps be better to tell you what we don't do," Hugo answered as if prepared for the question. "We don't engage in orgiastic behaviour. We don't offer sacrifices. We don't seek to summon demons or other supernatural entities. And we don't fly around on broomsticks."

Lily's eyes narrowed a fraction. If Hugo hadn't delivered his assurances in a deadpan tone, she would have suspected he was being tongue-in-cheek.

"You won't be inconvenienced in the slightest by our presence," he continued. "Indeed, you'll never even know we're there. We endeavour not to disturb any of the forest's inhabitants, be they plant, animal or human." He took out a business card and gave it to Hazel. "If you have any further questions, feel free to get in touch."

Lily peered over her mum's shoulder at the card. 'Hugo Gready. Custom Spells For All Your Needs' was printed on it in gothic lettering, along with an email and web address. "What type of spells do you do?"

Seemingly irritated by the question, Hugo sniffed again. "To properly answer that would take all evening. There are almost infinite varieties of spells."

"Do you do curses?"

"There's no simple answer to that either. What is a curse for one person can be a blessing for another."

Lily's thoughts turned to her dad. Was his death a curse or a blessing? She felt a little stab of shame for even asking herself the question.

Hugo's gaze shifted to Hazel. "May I have your decision? Will you honour the agreement?"

She pursed her lips uncertainly. "No noise. No litter. Nothing... dodgy."

Hugo puffed his belly out to its full gargantuan extent. "You have my word as magister of the Midwood Coven."

"Ok, Hugo, I'll honour the agreement."

Lily looked at her mum as if she couldn't believe her ears.

Hugo bowed as low as his belly permitted. "In that case, I shall disturb you no more." He made a swift gesture as if he was sketching arcane symbols in the air. "May the blessings of the forest spirits be with you. May all your sorrows be left behind and may you be filled with joy and magic. This is my will." He raised his voice as if in appeal to the aforementioned spirits. "So mote it be!"

A sad, hopeful glimmer found its way into Hazel's eyes. So quietly as to be almost inaudible, she echoed, "So mote it be."

Hugo bowed to Lily, repeating, "So mote it be."

She remained pointedly silent.

"Enjoy the Rocky Road," he added, turning away. "It's the best you'll ever taste." Feet splayed like a penguin, he waddled along the garden path.

"Why did you say yes?" Lily hissed at her mum as soon as he was out of earshot.

"How could I not when he asked so nicely?"

"Well, for starters, he's a devil worshipper."

"No he isn't. He's a witch."

"What's the difference?"

"I don't really know," Hazel admitted after a moment's thought. "But he seems harmless enough to me."

Lily let out a soft snort. "*Huge-O* could crush us to death just by sitting on us."

Hazel flashed her a disapproving look. "I don't like name calling."

"Oh give me a break." With a shake of her head, Lily returned to the kitchen. She dropped onto a chair and stared at her phone.

"Hugo could have mental health problems," said Hazel, approaching the stove and putting a kettle on it.

Lily tilted an eyebrow as if to say wryly, *Do you think?* "Do you want to know when the next full moon is?" She showed her phone to her mum. The screen displayed that day's date.

"So it's tonight. So what?"

Lily pointed out of the rear window. "Someone's had a fire in the woods back there. I bet that's where Huge-O and his coven do… whatever it is they do."

"So we stay away from there tonight. I don't see the problem."

Lily's voice rang with exasperation. "They're *witches*."

"And I'm not going to judge them for that. You know what it's like to be judged, Lily. So why would you do the same to someone else?"

"I'm not judging…" Lily began to protest, but faltered. "Well maybe I am, but you have to admit, it's messed up letting witches do their thing on our land."

Hazel's lips quirked into a smile. "We could always sneak up there and spy on them. Make sure Hugo keeps his word."

Lily mulled over the suggestion, then shook her head. "What if they do have an orgy? I'd be traumatised for life from seeing Huge-O naked."

Hazel gave her a reproachful glance, then chuckled despite herself. She reached for the kettle as it started whistling.

Lily's gaze returned to her phone. She typed in Hugo's website address. A photo of him in his monkish robe amidst a moonlit glade dominated the homepage. One of his arms was raised as if saluting the Moon.

She read out the website's header, "'Hugo Gready. England's preeminent practitioner of herbal magic'."

"At least you can't accuse him of false modesty."

Lily rolled her eyes at the dry remark. "Listen to this – 'Magister Gready specialises in spells for healing, fertility, luck and love'." She hmphed. "So much for there being 'infinite varieties' of spells." A link in the menu led to a shopping page. "He's selling all sorts of junk – crystals, charms, witch balls."

"Witch balls?" Hazel laughed again. "Do they come in pairs?"

"Ha, ha," mouthed Lily. "It says here that they're glass balls full of herbs and pins. You hang them in a window or doorway to protect yourself from evil spirits and spells."

Hazel put two mugs of steaming tea on the table. She plucked a piece of Rocky Road from the plastic bag.

"You're not actually going to eat that, are you?" Lily asked.

In answer, Hazel popped the chunk into her mouth. "*Mmm. It really is the best I've ever tasted.*" She exaggeratedly licked smears of chocolate from her fingers.

Lily scrunched her face as if her mum was tucking into Sam's leftovers. Her stomach was suddenly churning. She sipped her tea to try to calm it down. The mug felt strangely heavy in her hand. She pushed back her chair. The mere effort of standing up made sweat seep from every pore. "I'm going to bed before you grow horns or something."

Hazel mimicked Hugo's theatrical hand gestures. "May you sleep well and feel better in the morning. This is my will. So mote it be."

With an unamused sigh, Lily headed for the stairs.

11

As Lily flopped onto the bed, a floaty feeling enveloped her. When she closed her eyes, the mattress seemed to dissolve into nothingness. She gripped the headboard as if to anchor herself in place, waiting for the sensation to pass. It only intensified.

She rose to open the window and tried to clear her head with several deep breaths. Birdsong flowed into the room. The sun had sunk behind the trees. A pastel blue blanket of twilight was settling over the forest. She sagged to her knees, resting her forehead against the cool wooden windowsill. Her eyelids drifted down again.

Lily, she seemed to hear someone calling from the forest. The low, velvety voice exerted a strange pull on her. She felt herself floating towards it.

Lily.

Suddenly, she was no longer in the bedroom, she was hovering above the trees. The Moon's pitted face was peeping over Chapman Hill. Like a kite being snatched away by a strong wind, she flew up the hill. The treetops and grassy slopes passed in a blur. She came to an abrupt stop above the horseshoe of Dead Woman's Ditch.

Two figures were splayed out naked on the grass, bathed in frail shafts of moonlight. The pale buttocks of the uppermost figure were thrusting between the even paler thighs of the lowermost. Crows crowded the rowan's skeletal branches, looking on like an audience at some sort of obscene show.

Lily.

The voice fell to a husky gasp, drawing her downwards. Warm tingles welled up from her groin. The closer she got to the lovers, the hotter the tingling became. Pleasure blurred into pain, sweeping through her like a wildfire.

She opened her mouth to scream, but before she could do so, she was soaring skywards again. The fire inside her was extinguished by a rush of air as she swooped back down the hillside.

The cottage's chimney pots came into view, the thatched roof, the bedroom window...

Lily's eyelashes fluttered apart. She peeled her sweaty face off the windowsill. Her hair was as sodden as if she'd been caught in a downpour.

The house was jarringly dark and quiet. She tiptoed to the bathroom, wetted a flannel with cold water and wiped herself down. Then she returned to her bedroom and sat by the window. Goosebumps broke out on her skin as the night air caressed her.

She mentally travelled along the forest path to the hidden glade. Were Hugo and his coven there right now? What if he'd lied? What if they were dancing naked whilst offering a sacrifice to the Devil?

A powerful sense of curiosity – almost a compulsion – gripped her. She had to see for herself what they were up to. After putting on black jeans and a matching hooded top, she pocketed her phone and padded to the landing. She paused to listen. Not a sound came from downstairs or her mum's bedroom.

Cringing at every creak, Lily descended the pitch-dark stairs. She groped about for her pumps. She lifted her head at the click-click of claws on flagstones. Sam's damp nose nuzzled her face. Her own nose wrinkled at his hot, meaty breath.

She eased the backdoor open. Sam tried to follow her, but she nudged him back inside. "Sorry, Sam, you can't come with me."

As Lily turned around, the Moon edged from behind a cloud. She grew wide-eyed with wonderment. The leaves of the purple flowers were shimmering like flames made of moonlight. She stood transfixed by their cold beauty for a moment before slinking along the garden path.

The phosphorescent leaves dimly lit her way. She hesitated beneath the branches of the embracing old oaks. The darkness up ahead was deeper than anything she'd ever experienced before. She knew she couldn't take another step without light. It wasn't simply that she might trip over or lose her way, it was a response to some instinct beyond her comprehension.

She switched on her phone's torch, covering it so that only a faint glow trickled between her fingers. As she crept along the path, bats flitted around. Owls hooted at each other. An occasional rustle came from the undergrowth. Every sound seemed amplified tenfold in her ears.

Her heart leapt into her throat as a knee-high black shape darted across the path and went crashing off through a clump of bracken.

Doubting Tom!

The name rang out in her mind like an alarm. What if the summons had worked? "Don't be silly," she muttered to herself. "It was just a badger or something."

She continued on her way, clambering over the fallen tree. When the track levelled out at the thorny avenue, she reluctantly switched off her phone. She pulled up her hood and padded forwards.

An orange glow flickered into view. Lily's heart jumped again. *I was right! They're here!*

The light lured her onwards like a moth to a flame. A

familiar nasal voice arose from the glade. "Let the Moon's radiance fill you. Let it guide you."

Lily dropped to her haunches. A small fire was crackling at the clearing's centre. The full moon hung overhead, haloed by wispy clouds. Eleven figures were standing in a circle. Their shapeless robes made it difficult to tell if they were men or women. Deep hoods concealed their faces. The unmistakable figure of Hugo waddled around the circle, wafting a bundle of smoking twigs.

"What does the moonlight show you?" he asked. "What do you need to hold on to? What do you need to let go of?"

The other figures fanned the smoke into their hoods. Lily caught a whiff of a pleasantly musky, minty aroma.

"Soak in the lunar energy," intoned Hugo. "Can you feel it supercharging your body and mind?"

"Yes," his fellow witches replied as one.

"Hold up your crystals so that they, too, are recharged."

Moving in synch like a dance troupe, the witches raised their hands. A constellation of crystals sparkled in the moonlight.

"Now think again of the things you need to let go of."

As if conjured by Hugo's words, the last image Lily had of her dad took shape in her mind – him being zipped into a white plastic body bag, his eyes closed, his face streaked with blood. She pressed a hand to her mouth, fearing the memory would wrench a sob from her.

"Put those thoughts into your crystals," Hugo continued. "Fill them with all your pain."

The witches clasped their crystals between their palms.

Lily felt about on the ground and found a stone. She tried to imagine the memory flowing out of her and into it.

"Good," said Hugo.

She stiffened, mistakenly thinking for an instant that he was talking to her. He did another lap of the circle. One by one, the crystals were passed to him. He bowed his head. "Let us give thanks to the spirits of the forest."

The witches joined hands. They revolved around the fire – clockwise at first, then anti-clockwise – each of them taking a turn to call something out.

"I'm thankful for being here."

"I'm thankful for the Moon."

"I'm thankful for this coven."

Lily puffed her cheeks. Talk about a disappointment. She'd been to wilder school discos. She rose and began to retrace her steps along the avenue, not taking as much care to be stealthy. A sudden silence emanated from the clearing. She stopped dead and looked over her shoulder. The witches had turned to face outwards. Hugo was a silhouetted black blob at the glade's entrance.

Lily stood like a deer in the headlights. Had they heard her?

"O spirits of the forest, we give thanks to you for letting us use this sacred place," Hugo called out.

"Thank you. Thank you. Thank you," joined in the others.

A soft breath of relief escaped Lily. She tiptoed on her way. At the fallen tree, she turned her phone back on. The stone she'd filled with her last memory of her dad looked like a grey egg. On an impulse, she hurled it into the trees as hard as she could.

She closed her eyes. How did she feel? Had anything changed?

Once again, the body bag rose like an apparition to the surface of her mind. She heaved a sigh. No, of course nothing had changed. A deadening weariness overtook her as she trudged back to the cottage.

12

A familiar meaty aroma seeped into Lily's sleep. She opened her eyes and found herself looking at Sam. He was standing over her, panting. She pinched her nostrils. "Ugh, it smells like something crawled into your mouth and died."

In response, Sam darted his tongue out to lick her face. Squirming and laughing, she pushed him away. She sat up to look at her phone. It was almost midday. The sun was flickering through the open window. Cotton ball clouds were scudding across a bright blue sky.

Sam rolled onto his back, legs splayed. He writhed in delight as Lily scratched his tummy. The instant she stopped, he whined as if to say, *More tummy scratches, please!*

"That's all you're getting for now." Lily swung her feet off the bed. As she left the room, her mum appeared at the top of the stairs.

Hazel's sleeves were rolled up as if she'd been busy. Her thick black hair was piled into a practical bun on top of her head. "Morning." Her voice was cheerfully brisk. "Or should I say afternoon? You look a lot better."

"I feel it."

Hazel smiled. "The spirits of the forest must have listened to me."

Or maybe it was the lunar energy, Lily thought wryly.

"Do you want some breakfast?" Hazel asked.

Lily's stomach grumbled hungrily at the mere thought of food. "Yes please."

Hazel started to turn, but paused and added as an afterthought, "I didn't hear anything outside last night. Did you?"

"No."

"I don't know about you, but I slept better than I have done in... well, in as long as I can remember." Hazel breathed deeply as if inhaling the silence. She placed her palm against a wall. "I'm so thankful for this house."

A faint frown disturbed Lily's forehead at the echo of the coven's ritual. Had her mum snook out to spy on the witches too? After all, it was her who'd suggested it in the first place.

Lily shrugged aside the thought. What did it matter if she had?

After a quick shower, Lily flung on shorts and a vest. The smell of cooking was drifting up the stairs. She was pleased to note that the only thing it did was make her mouth water. Sam jumped off the bed and pattered down to the kitchen behind her.

Hazel was stirring a pan on the stove. Sam ambled over and gave her a wide-eyed, begging stare. "These are scrambled eggs," she told him. "You wouldn't like them."

"Are you kidding? He'll eat anything," said Lily, plonking herself down at the table.

Her mum had indeed been busy. The floor was almost free of clutter. Empty boxes were stacked outside the open backdoor. Lily's gaze drifted past them to the treetops. She replayed the dream – flying up Chapman Hill, the naked figures grinding against each other, their moans getting louder and louder.

Her thoughts turned to Tom. She bit her lower lip. God, she wanted to see him. She wanted it so badly that it gave her an ache in her chest.

She blinked as her mum put a plate in front of her.

"You looked like you were miles away," said Hazel.

Lily responded with a sheepish half-smile, then tucked into her breakfast as if she hadn't eaten in days. Hazel looked on, taking obvious pleasure in watching Lily polish off the food.

When her plate was empty, Lily fetched her sandals from the hallway. "I'm going to take Sam for a walk."

"I'll come with you."

"There's no need. I'll be fine on my own. Trust me, I won't get lost again."

Lily clipped Sam's lead to his collar and drew him out of the backdoor.

"Stick to the paths," Hazel called after her.

"I will do."

Lily made an instant lie of her words by heading into the trees where she'd exited them the previous afternoon. Her feet were sore, but that didn't prevent her from walking fast. Sam pulled ahead of her as if he, too, was in a hurry to reach their destination.

Before long, they came to the public footpath. Lily pushed on, oblivious to the steepening slope. All she could think about was Tom – his smoky eyes peering through his tousled mop of hair, the way his waist tapered into his shorts.

Soon, yet not soon enough for Lily, they emerged from the forest. Her gaze traversed the sky, tracking where she'd flown in the dream. She squinted as the sun played hide-and-seek with fast-moving clouds.

A series of guttural cries drew her attention. A dozen or so crows were circling above the hillside. Were they on the lookout for lambs?

She powered onwards to the accompaniment of a constant plaintive bleating. It sounded like the sheep speckling the hill were warning each other about the crows.

When Lily's burning calves and breathless lungs forced her to slow down, Sam strained at his lead, practically dragging her up the hill.

"Please be there. Please be there," she said to herself as Dead Woman's Ditch came into view.

The rowan's branches jutted above the grass bank like fingers clawing at the sky. They were crowded with crows croaking, clicking and cawing in their unknowable language.

Disappointment stabbed at Lily as she entered the enclosure. Tom wasn't there. She called his name twice. She opened her mouth to do so a third time, but stopped herself. Her gaze came to rest on the hollow at the base of the tree.

The crows broke into a raucous, *Arrr! Arrr! Arrr!*

She peered up at them. Were they laughing at her? "Shut your beaks," she shouted. Like a classroom of rebuked children, they immediately fell silent.

She scuffed her sandals at the grass, unsure what to do next. After a long moment, with a sigh of reluctance, she turned to leave. At the same instant, Sam jerked in the opposite direction so powerfully that she lost hold of the lead. With it trailing between his legs, he bounded towards the rowan.

"No, Sam, come back here," Lily commanded. She wasn't in the slightest bit surprised when he ignored her. As she gave chase, the crows cawed as rowdily as a crowd cheering on a race.

Sam thrust his head into the hollow, dropped onto his belly and crawled forwards. His tail disappeared from sight as Lily reached the tree. She made a grab for the lead, but her fingers closed on air. He began scrabbling his way down the burrow. His hind paws flicked soil in her face as she dove after him.

She squeezed her eyes shut. When she opened them again, the darkness had swallowed him.

"Sam! Sam!" There was a note of panic in Lily's voice.

A bark rang out, amplified by the confined space.

Wondering if Sam was responding to her or barking at something else, Lily pulled out her phone. Its pale torch beam revealed his backend four or five metres away. "Please, Sam, come back," she pleaded as he crawled deeper.

He stopped at the edge of the torchlight. A growl rumbled in his throat.

"What is it, Sam? What..." Lily trailed off as a name whispered through her mind – *Doubting Tom*. She snorted at herself. More likely, Sam was facing off with whatever wild animal called the burrow home.

The growling intensified. Lily's heart lurched as a high-pitched yelp reverberated off the tunnel walls. Sam burst into movement, twisting from side to side in a futile attempt to turn around.

"That's it, Sam, good boy," Lily encouraged as he began inching his way backwards. Arms outstretched, she squirmed her shoulders into the burrow. Roots poked her in the ribs as she slithered forwards. Cobwebs clung to her hair. Her entire body was inside the tunnel. A wave of claustrophobia swept over her at the thought of going any deeper.

Another yelp echoed along the burrow. Lily stretched for Sam, but he was still well beyond her reach. Grabbing a thick root, she dragged herself onwards. She jerked her head up as her chin brushed against something feathery and sticky. She swallowed in disgust. It was a dead crow, minus its head and half of its body.

Sam wriggled closer to Lily. Stretching until her shoulder felt ready to dislocate, she caught hold of his tail. She pulled him along, pushing herself backwards with her other hand.

Pull, push, pull, push… The short climb seemed to go on and on. The dusty air made her throat itch. Sweat stung her eyes. As her toes hooked over the burrow's edge, she gasped with relief. One final effort was all she needed to haul herself and Sam out of the tree.

She seized his lead. "Bad–" she started to reprimand him, but the words died on her lips. His muzzle was flecked with bloody spittle. A deep gouge glistened on his nose. Scratches crisscrossed his front legs, punctuated by what looked like bite marks.

Lily cast an anxious glance at the hollow, half-expecting Sam's attacker to come charging out. She coaxed him to his feet. The crows looked on silently as she hurried towards the enclosure's entrance. She kept darting looks over her shoulder until the embankment blocked the tree from view.

Emitting a thin whine with each step, Sam limped down the hill behind her. They were nearly at the forest when he sank to the ground. Lily pleaded with him and tugged on his lead, but nothing could persuade him to move. He whimpered as she slid her hands under his chest and lifted him. Trembling from his weight, she wound her way through the trees. Every few hundred metres, she had to put him down to shake out her arms.

By the time they got to the cottage, Sam had become quiet. His silence troubled Lily just as much, if not more, than his whimpering.

"Mum!" she shouted breathlessly.

Hazel appeared from the kitchen, wide-eyed at the distressed summons. "What is it?" She ran to meet Lily and Sam in the middle of the lawn. "What's happened now?"

"Something attacked Sam."

Hazel grimaced at the sight of his injuries. "Give him to me."

Lily carefully transferred Sam into her mum's arms. Hazel

carried him to the kitchen, gently lowered him into his basket, then wetted a cloth. He lay motionless as she set about cleaning his wounds.

Lily looked on worriedly. "Is he going to be ok?"

"I think so. There's a first aid kit in the boot of the car. Fetch it, will you?"

Lily snatched up the car keys and ran from the house. When she returned, her mum was picking at the cut on Sam's nose with tweezers.

"There's something stuck in this," Hazel explained. "Got it." She held up a curved, dusky black shard. "It looks like a broken claw. What attacked him?"

"I don't know. I didn't see."

Sam trembled as Hazel rubbed antiseptic cream into the scratches. "No, Sam, don't do that," she reprimanded softly as he licked his nose.

"Do you think he needs to see a vet?"

"Only if the cuts start to look infected." Hazel bandaged Sam's front legs, then eyed Lily intently. "So come on. Let's hear the full story."

After a brief silence, Lily confessed what had happened.

Hazel gave a sighing shake of her head. "You're lucky you didn't get stuck down the burrow."

Lily shuddered at the thought of it. "What animal would attack a dog?"

"I'm not sure. Maybe a badger. Whatever it was, I don't want you taking Sam to Dead Woman's Ditch again. Do you hear?"

Lily lowered her eyes contritely. "Yes."

"Good. Now take off your clothes. I'll see if I can get the blood out of them."

As Lily stripped, Hazel filled the sink with water and

washing up liquid.

Lily picked up the black shard. It tapered to a sharp point and had a smooth, ridged texture. Her brows drawing together, she turned and went to the living-room. She leaned in to scrutinise Doubting Tom's portrait. His claws blended in with his paws.

"What are you doing?" Hazel asked from the doorway.

Lily turned to her with a guilty little start.

There was a knowing gleam in Hazel's eyes. "Please, please don't tell me you tried to summon him."

Lily's silence as good as confirmed her mum's suspicion.

Hazel tutted. "I thought you had more sense than that, Lily."

"I was only having a bit of fun." There was a petulant edge to Lily's voice. "You want me to have fun, right?"

Hazel winced as if the question had touched a sore spot. "Of course I do, but I don't call trying to summon something back from the dead fun. I call it a good way to scare yourself silly."

"I'm not scared. I don't seriously think Sam was attacked by Doubting Tom."

"Then why are you so interested in his portrait?"

"I…" Lily began, struggling to come up with an answer. She jerked her gaze towards the window as a loud bang went off outside.

Lines gathered on Hazel's brow. "That sounded like a gunshot."

They returned to the kitchen and peered out of the rear window. There was no one to be seen. Another thunderous *boom* echoed through the trees. Sam struggled to his feet, barking hoarsely.

"Stay," Hazel commanded. He obediently lay back down. She turned to Lily. "That goes for you too."

"But–"

"No buts."

Her face torn between irritation and worry, Lily watched her mum go out of the backdoor.

13

Lily frowned as she thought about Jude's smug face. Was it him out there? If so, she was going to take great pleasure in telling him to get off her property. She started towards the door, but paused as she realised she was only wearing a bra, knickers and sandals. She put her bloodstained clothes back on and ran outside.

More loud bangs shook the air. Swirls of birds were fleeing the treetops a few hundred metres from the cottage. Hazel was striding in their direction. Lily broke into a run. She caught up with her mum a short distance into the trees.

Hazel shot her an annoyed look. "I told you to stay in the house."

"Hey!" Lily shouted, passing her mum. "Stop that."

Two figures in matching flat-caps and waxed jackets emerged from behind some bushes. Both were carrying double-barrelled shotguns. Jude squinted as he took aim at a nest near the top of a tall tree. The shotgun spat out a puff of smoke. The nest exploded and twigs rained down.

"Stop that!" Lily yelled again.

Jude nonchalantly lowered his gun. Scanning Lily's bloodstained vest, he nudged his companion as if to say, *This is the one I told you about.*

"Sorry if we startled you." The man at Jude's side spoke through a bushy greying beard. Despite his friendly voice, something in his sky-blue eyes made Lily's hackles rise even further. A gleam of condescension? A hint of superiority?

"You're trespassing," she retorted.

"Well now we're even," said Jude.

Lily glared at him, thinking how much she would love to punch the stuck-up idiot right on his big nose.

As Hazel came up alongside Lily, the man's beard split into a smile. "I'm Rupert Chapman. And you must be Hazel and Lily Wylde, the new owners of Blackmoss Cottage."

Hazel returned a small smile, unfazed by Rupert's display of knowledge. "Word gets around fast."

"Yes, it does." Rupert's tone suggested he felt no need to elaborate.

"You're trespassing," Lily reiterated.

"True," conceded Rupert. "I suppose I should have dropped by and told you what we were up to."

"'*Told*'?" Hazel frowned at the presumptuous word.

"Yes, 'told'," put in Jude. "We don't need your permission to be here."

"Yes you do," Lily countered. "This is our land."

Jude smirked. "Is it? Are you certain about that?"

"Jude," Rupert said, casting a reproachful glance his way. Jude compressed his lips sullenly. Rupert's smile settled back into place as his gaze returned to Hazel. "What my son's alluding to is an old, old land dispute."

Relishing the chance to show off some knowledge of her own, Lily explained to her mum, "Walter Chapman tried to buy Mary Long's land. And when she wouldn't sell it, he accused her of being a witch and had her executed so he could steal it."

"That's a lie," Jude protested. His jaw muscles clenched as his dad gave him another silencing glance.

"You're correct and incorrect, Lily," said Rupert. "It's true my ancestors acquired the land under regrettable circumstances. However, it wasn't stolen. A fair price was paid to the Crown."

She arched an eyebrow. "Really? I heard they paid about half of what it was worth."

"A fair price was paid," Rupert repeated in the well-modulated voice of someone accustomed to being listened to. "We seem to be talking at cross-purposes here, Lily. The dispute in question arose sixty years after Mary's death. It wasn't about the legality of the sale, it was about the position of the boundary line between our properties. You see, according to the 1690 title deeds, my family owned the land up to the edge of the cottage's garden. Unfortunately, those deeds were destroyed in a fire in 1750 and a new set had to be drawn up by a local conveyancer."

"A double-dealing scumbag," said Jude.

Rupert cleared his throat at the interruption. "The new deeds restored the boundary line to its pre-1690 position. Initially, this was put down to simple incompetence. Years later, it came out that the conveyancer – one William Pickles – had been having an affair with Mary's great granddaughter. By which time, my family had long since lost a costly legal battle over the land."

A corner of Lily's mouth curled upwards. "It sounds like they got what they deserved."

"That's enough of that, Lily," Hazel admonished.

Now it was Lily's turn to seethe silently.

"That's an interesting bit of local history, Mr Chapman," said Hazel. "Maybe what happened was the universe's way of righting a wrong. I don't know. What I do know is the deeds the solicitor showed me make it very clear – this land belongs to Blackmoss Cottage."

"Which means you have no right to shoot crows here," Lily

added, unable to contain herself.

Rupert's smile slipped. "I realise it's difficult for you to understand, Lily, but sometimes these things are necessary. Crows can be very destructive. And this year they've been particularly aggressive. I've lost more livestock than ever before. The crows in this part of the forest have been allowed to breed unchecked for years." He pointed out the numerous nests dotted around the treetops. "We need to bring their numbers down."

"It sounds to me like Emily didn't allow you to shoot them," said Hazel.

"Emily was crazy," scoffed Jude.

"She was an eccentric," Rupert amended. "She'd lived here for as long as I can remember, yet in many ways she was regarded as an outsider. She simply didn't fit in. In a small community like ours, it's important to fit in. It doesn't take long to acquire a bad reputation around here. But people in these parts have *very* long memories."

Hazel's polite tone didn't waver at the veiled warning. "I'll bear that in mind."

Rupert and she locked eyes for a brief moment. A loud caw broke the silence.

"Look at the size of that thing!" Jude exclaimed.

A crow so big it could have been mistaken for a raven was perched by the ruins of the nest. It strutted along a branch, rowdily voicing its displeasure. Rupert plucked two shotgun cartridges from a leather pouch attached to his belt. As he chambered them, Hazel asked, "What do you think you're doing?"

"I thought I'd made that abundantly clear." As if for emphasis, Rupert clicked his shotgun shut and took aim. "It would be advisable to stand back and cover your ears."

Hazel didn't move. "Did you hear me give you permission to shoot on my property?"

Keeping his gun trained on the crow, Rupert levelled a steady stare at her. Once again, Hazel stared straight back.

"What are you waiting for, Dad? Shoot it," Jude urged. "If you don't, I will."

He took a cartridge from his own belt pouch. Lily stepped forwards and grabbed his wrist.

Jude's mouth fell open as if he couldn't believe she had the audacity to lay a hand on him. "Let go of me," he demanded, attempting to wrench his arm free.

Lily staggered, but managed to hold on. Jude raised the butt of his shotgun as if to slam it into her forearm.

"Jude!" Rupert's blue eyes were suddenly ablaze.

Lily felt Jude flinch. He lowered the shotgun. She released his arm and retreated a few steps, watching him closely lest he tried to chamber a cartridge again.

"Apologise at once," Rupert commanded.

"I'm sorry," mumbled Jude.

"Oh for God's sake. Is that the best you can do? That was pathetic. Pathetic!"

At the vehement reprimand, Jude gave another little start. Directing a blank stare at Lily, he repeated in a louder but equally unconvincing manner, "I'm sorry."

In response, she snatched up a stick and hurled it towards the crow. The bird spread its wide, unusually white-tipped wings. With a rasping croak, it took flight. Lily's gaze descended defiantly to Jude and Rupert.

Rupert reset his face into a precise smile. "We obviously aren't welcome here, so I'll bid you good day."

He tipped his cap to Hazel, about-faced and strode away

with the self-assurance of someone who owned the ground beneath his feet.

Jude leaned in so close to Lily that only she could hear him. "That's twice you've stopped me from pulling the trigger. There won't be a third time. Oh and by the way, it looks like a bird crapped on your head."

Lily began to lift a hand to her white-streak, but stopped herself and glowered at Jude. He, too, performed the hollow gesture of doffing his cap before following his dad.

"What a pair of–" Lily said, but broke off as a shuddering breath burst from her mum.

Hazel bent forwards, bracing her hands against her knees. Her face was sheet-white.

Fearing her mum was about to faint, Lily reached out in readiness to catch her. "Are you ok?"

"What the hell were you thinking?" Hazel snapped. "You could have gotten yourself killed."

"Jude's gun wasn't loaded."

"What if he'd pushed you over? What if you'd fallen and hit your–" Hazel faltered, unable to bring herself to finish the sentence. Tears welled in her eyes. "What happens to me if you die? You're all I have left. Do you want me to end up like Emily? Do you?"

Lily's lips moved, but no words came out. She knew her mum was right. It was crazy risking her life over a crow. It wasn't even as if the Chapmans didn't have a valid reason for wanting to shoot them. And yet...

With a despairing shake of her head, Hazel straightened and headed for the cottage.

Lily's eyes sought out Jude. As she glimpsed him through the trees, her fingers twitched into fists. Ugh! What an entitled idiot. The mere sight of him made her want to lash out.

She wondered at the strength of her feelings. Plenty of people at school had pushed her buttons, but she'd never laid a finger on them, not even when they made loud remarks in her vicinity about her mum being a murderer. What was it about Jude that triggered her anger so much?

Her thoughts turned to Tom. He would understand. He hated Jude too. He hadn't said it aloud, but she could tell. That strange, aching need to see him seized her again. It was all she could do not to call out his name.

She scrunched her face in confusion. What was wrong with her? Was it heatstroke? Or was this how it felt to be in... She shook her head. No, it wasn't possible. Was it? How could she be in love with someone she'd only met yesterday?

14

Hazel threw herself back into sorting out the house. There was something unsettlingly familiar to Lily about the way her mum bustled around arranging and rearranging ornaments, putting up light fittings, hanging pictures and curtains. It reminded her of how, after Dad died, Mum had cleaned the house until her hands were red raw.

Lily was half-tempted to join in to distract herself from thinking about Tom. No matter how many times she pushed him under the surface of her consciousness, he kept bobbing back up like a cork.

Noticing that the house had gone quiet, Lily went in search of her mum. She found her upstairs, fast asleep, wrapped in the patchwork quilt. She stared at her as if searching for signs of life. A bark came from downstairs. She turned and hurried to the kitchen.

"Shush, Sam," she hissed.

Sam was at the rear window with his front paws perched on the work surface. His bloodshot eyes were bulging. Strings of saliva swung under his jowls as he continued to bark.

Lily looked out of the window, wondering what had gotten him so riled up. Her eyes widened. There was a crow on the garden path. Its white-tipped wings identified it as the same bird she'd saved from being shot.

The crow hopped forwards, clutching something in its downturned beak. It dipped its shaggy head to place whatever it was on the ground. Spreading its wings, it sprang into the air and skimmed across the lawn before rising steeply to clear the cottage's roof.

As soon as it disappeared from view, Sam ceased barking and hobbled back to his basket.

Tom's cautionary words resurfaced in Lily's mind – *If you hurt them, they'll remember your face. They'll tell each other about you. They might even attack you.*

What if the crow thought she'd been trying to hurt it? Warily glancing skywards, Lily stepped outside and advanced along the path. Her forehead creased as she saw what the crow had left behind. It looked like a wet black marble partially encased in wax. Revulsion rippled through her as she prodded the thing. It had a sticky, fleshy texture. Was it… "Eww," she exclaimed. Yes, it *was* indeed an eyeball. A yellow-orange iris haloed an oval pupil. Had the crow plucked it from some poor lamb? Why had it brought the disgusting object here? Was it a thank you gift? If crows could remember the bad things you did to them, surely they could also remember the good things.

Lily fetched a spade from the shed, scooped up the eyeball and catapulted it into the trees.

When she re-entered the kitchen, Sam was asleep. His bandaged legs twitched like he was being zapped with electric shocks.

Hazel appeared at the hallway door, bleary-eyed. "What was all that noise about?"

"Sam was barking at a crow."

"Was it that same crow? The one with the white wings?"

"Yes. Did you see it?"

Hazel stifled a yawn. "No, but I had a feeling it would be back."

"How come?"

Hazel pursed her lips as if unsure whether she should say. "You'll only laugh at me."

"No I won't. I promise."

"I was thinking about how some religions believe we can be reincarnated as animals."

"What's that got to do–" Lily broke off with a chuckle. "Oh, I get it. You think Emily's come back as a crow."

"You said you wouldn't laugh."

"How am I supposed not to laugh at something so silly?"

"You have to admit, it's odd that a crow with feathers like Emily's hair is hanging around the garden."

"Why would Emily want to hang around here?"

Hazel mulled the question over for a moment. "Perhaps she's keeping an eye on us."

"Keeping an *eye* on us?" A frown etched itself into Lily's brow as she thought about the eyeball. "What for?"

Hazel shrugged. "Maybe she wants to make sure we look after her cottage. Or maybe she's looking out for us."

"What? You mean like a guardian angel?"

"Something like that, yes." Hazel smiled. "You know, after meeting our neighbours, I was beginning to wonder if moving here was a mistake, but now I'm sure we made the right decision."

Lily remained noncommittally silent. All she knew for sure was that she was relieved to see her mum smiling again. "Are you hungry? Do you want a sandwich?"

"That sounds good. I'll put the kettle on." Hazel checked the stove. The fuel had burnt down to glowing embers. She added some kindling and a couple of logs.

"I really hate Jude Chapman." Lily chopped a cucumber as if imagining it was part of his anatomy.

"You barely know him."

"I can't explain it, but I… I feel like I've hated him forever."

"Well I feel sorry for him. Did you hear the way his dad spoke to him? It must have made him feel about this big." Hazel held her thumb and forefinger a centimetre apart.

Lily recalled how she'd felt around her dad when he was drunk. It had been impossible to predict what would throw him into a rage – an innocuous remark, the slightest noise. In the end, the only thing she could do was avoid him and hope he left her alone. She let out a heavy sigh.

A flutter of black from outside caught her eye. The crow was back! It swooped down to land on the path. As if alerted by a silent alarm, Sam's eyes popped open. He clambered to his feet and began scratching at the backdoor.

"What is it, Sam?" Hazel asked.

"Our guardian angel's here."

Hazel peered out of the window. "Wow, look at that, what a beautiful bird."

The crow strutted closer. It had something clasped in its beak again. Lily's stomach gave a squeeze as the crow placed its new offering on the path. Was it the victim's other eyeball?

"What's she doing?" Hazel wondered.

"How do you know it's a she? Look at the size of it. It's got to be a he."

Hazel pulled Sam away from the backdoor and motioned for Lily to get hold of his collar.

"Careful," Lily cautioned as her mum opened the door.

Hazel edged towards their visitor, hands raised, palms outwards as if hoping it would recognise the universal *I-come-in-peace* gesture.

The crow opened its beak wide. Its pointed pink tongue

vibrated as it cawed.

"I think it's telling you not to come any closer," said Lily.

Bobbing its head as if to let her know she was right, the crow gave out a final harsh, *Arrr!*

At the same instant, Sam twisted his head to snap at Lily. His teeth clacked together as she snatched her hand away from his collar. He surged out of the backdoor. The crow launched itself into the air. Flapping furiously, it flew at a low trajectory towards the rear of the garden with Sam in pursuit.

"No Sam! Heel! Heel!" Hazel yelled to no effect.

The crow veered upwards to soar over the treetops. Seemingly unhindered by his injures, Sam chased it into the trees. Lily watched the crow dwindle to a black speck against the backdrop of Chapman Hill.

"That damn dog doesn't listen," said Hazel.

"Tell me about it."

"Where do you think he's going?"

Lily lifted an eyebrow as if to say, *Do you really need to ask?* "Dead Woman's Ditch. He's obsessed with the place."

"He'll end up getting injured again. Or worse. Come on, we'd better go after him."

Lily puffed her cheeks at the prospect of tramping up to Dead Woman's Ditch yet again.

"Stay here if you want to," said Hazel, putting on her trainers.

What if Tom's there this time? Lily asked herself. She cringed at the thought of introducing him to her mum, but the feeling was swiftly displaced by the desire to see him. "You need me to show you the way."

They set off, pausing halfway along the garden path to look at what the crow had deposited. A medallion of pale, wrinkled flesh glistened on the ground. "Ugh, what is that?" Lily wondered.

Hazel squatted down for a closer look. "I think it's a tongue."

"Last time it left us an eyeball."

"If she brings us some vegetables, we can make a lamb stew."

Lily rolled her eyes at the droll remark. "Will you stop calling it 'she'. It's not Emily. It's just a normal crow."

Hazel glanced at the gruesome gift. "I don't call that normal."

Lily gave the tongue a wide berth. She led her mum into the forest, heading for the public footpath. "Sam! Sam!" both of them called out.

Shadows were pooling in the creases of Chapman Hill and birds were trilling their evening songs by the time Lily and Hazel emerged from the other side of the trees. As they climbed the hill, Lily's gaze roamed all around. She wasn't only on the lookout for Sam. Her stomach was churning at the possibility of seeing Tom.

The usual scattering of ewes and lambs speckled the slopes. Their quavering bleats reverberated across the hillside as if they were mourning the dying sun.

"There's a funny atmosphere around here," said Hazel, watching the sun bleed into the horizon. "It feels like..." Her gazed traversed the hillside and landed on something. She nodded as if it had provided her with the appropriate word. "It feels like death."

"Don't be so melodrama–" Lily fell silent as she noticed what her mum was looking at. A crow's carcass was dangling upside down from a barbed wire fence. Its feet were tied together with string. It swayed gently in the breeze, wings spread as if it was about to take flight.

"At least it's not your white-winged friend," said Hazel. "It's like some sort of voodoo sign. A warning to turn back."

"I bet Jude put it there. God, I wish a crow would peck his eyes out." Taken aback by her own vehemence, Lily added a touch shamefacedly, "Sorry, I know I shouldn't wish that on anyone."

"You shouldn't," Hazel agreed. A mischievous little smile played on her lips. "Well maybe a crow could peck out just one of his eyes. It would teach him a lesson, that's for sure."

Lily smiled too, but it quickly faded. "Is it possible to hate someone at first sight?"

Hazel's eyes became misty as she reminisced, "Your dad always said he fell in love with me at first sight. I suppose if that's possible, so's the opposite."

Lily's thoughts circled back to Tom. Once again, a churning sensation that might have been love or an upset stomach took hold of her.

They resumed the climb, skirting the hilltop. Dead Woman's Ditch came into view. Hazel stopped at the earthwork's entrance, wide-eyed with curiosity. "I wonder who made this and why. I don't suppose we'll ever know."

With a strange blend of eagerness and apprehension, Lily entered the circle. As before, the place was deserted. Even the tree's branches were unoccupied. "He's not here." Her voice was indignant as if she'd been stood up on a date. She felt like she would have a screaming tantrum if she didn't see Tom soon.

Hazel pointed to the hollow. "He could be in there."

Lily briefly frowned in confusion before realising her mum was referring to Sam. She peered into the cavity from a cautious distance. It was empty. "Sam," she called out. Silence emanated from the hollow. She turned to her mum. "What do we do now?"

"I don't see what we can do other than go home and wait to

see if Sam turns up."

Lily's worried eyes returned to the tree.

"Sam will be fine," said Hazel. "He survived in the forest for months after Emily died." She put a hand on Lily's shoulder and ushered her to the enclosure's entrance.

They descended towards the sunset. The sky's redness was shading into velvety blue-blackness. A ghostly moon was rising at their backs, stretching out pale fingers to rub away the last remnants of sunlight.

When they came to the dead crow, Lily said, "Wait a moment." She untied the string from the barbed wire, laid the carcass on the grass and stared at it as if saying a silent prayer.

"We're running out of daylight," said Hazel.

They hastened on their way. Under the trees, the gloom was deep enough to conceal the path. Lily switched on her phone's torch.

It was almost fully dark by the time they got back to the cottage. Lily stopped in the same place on the garden path. Her torch revealed an assortment of fresh offerings. Another eyeball was nestled between two scraps of woolly flesh that appeared to be ears.

"My, my, our feathered friend has been busy," said Hazel.

"If the crow's been back, Sam might have come back too." Lily swept her torch across the garden. "Sam!"

She was met with silence. Heaving a defeated sigh, she trudged to the backdoor.

Warmth flowed from the stove as they entered the kitchen. Hazel set about lighting several candles. Lily dropped onto a chair and stared despondently at Sam's basket.

"Don't worry, as soon as Sam gets hungry, he'll be back," Hazel assured her.

Prompted by the words, Lily rose to fill Sam's bowl with dog food and put it outside the backdoor. She stood listening to the forest. Nothing disturbed the silence. Not a rustle of leaves. Not a flap of wings. Even the wind seemed to be holding its breath.

She looked at Sam's basket again. Her gaze lingered on his blood-stained blanket. All of a sudden, the possibility of losing something else she loved hit her so hard that a sob escaped her.

In a blink, Hazel was at her side, enfolding her in an embrace. "I know, I know," she soothed, seemingly reading Lily's mind. "Listen, if Sam doesn't come back tonight, we'll head out first thing in the morning to look for him. Ok?"

Lily nodded and swiped away her tears as if irritated by them.

"What you need is something to eat," said Hazel, guiding her to the table.

"I'm not hungry."

"If you don't eat, you won't have the energy to search for Sam tomorrow."

"What's the point?" Lily muttered. "We won't find him. Nothing ever goes right for us."

"That's not true."

"Isn't it? Name one good thing that's happened to us."

Hazel's frown suggested the answer was obvious. "We moved here."

"Yeah and look how well that's turning out." Lily heaved a sigh. "Sometimes I think we're cursed."

"Why would anyone curse us?"

"You tell me. You're the one who thinks we're being haunted by a witch."

"Haunted by a witch? What are you talking–" Hazel broke

off as realisation dawned. "Ok, Lily, firstly I never said I believe the crow is Emily. I'm just trying to keep an open mind. And secondly, Emily wasn't a witch. She was just an old lady who liked to keep herself to herself."

"I know how she felt. The more time I spend around people, the more I just want to be alone."

"You know who you sound like? Your dad."

Lily scowled. "I'm nothing like *him* and I never will be."

A troubled expression crossed Hazel's face. "Your dad was–"

"I swear to god, I'll scream if I have to hear again about what a saint Dad was," Lily interrupted. "And don't you dare tell me he was too ill to know what he was doing either."

Hazel spread her hands as if to say, *But he was.*

A cruel smirk marred Lily's lips. "Is that why you put him out of his misery like a sick animal?"

Hazel winced as if she'd pricked herself on a thorn.

Seeing her pained reaction, Lily said quickly, "I'm sorry, Mum, I didn't mean that." Her shoulders slumped as if weighed down by a heavy burden. "It's just that I'm so sick and tired of feeling like this."

Hazel reached across the table to lay her hand on Lily's. "Believe me, Lily, things are going to get better. It just takes time."

"How much time?"

Hazel's silence signalled that she didn't have an answer. She turned towards the front window at the rumble of an engine. Headlights lit up the massed ranks of trees. "Who could that be calling around at this time?"

"Maybe it's Mr Chapman."

Hazel's eyebrows gathered together like dark clouds. "It had better not be."

15

Lily grabbed a candle. "Someone might have found Sam." The flame wavered as she rushed to the front door.

"Hang on, Lily, let's see who's out there before we open the door," Hazel cautioned.

Lily drew her hand away from the handle. They went to the living room window. The engine had fallen silent. A figure was approaching the cottage. The soft light seeping out of the windows revealed a tall woman in a loose-fitting, ankle-length dress. Wavy brown hair framed her angular, middle-aged face. She plodded along with a kind of constipated expression like she was undertaking an onerous task.

Lily stated the obvious. "Sam's not with her."

Hazel glanced at the woman's rounded belly. "She looks pregnant."

There was a knock on the front door. As Lily used her candle to light the ones on the hallway walls, Hazel opened the door and looked askance at their visitor.

"I'm sorry for calling around so late." The woman was well-spoken and a touch breathy. "I'm Margaret Chapman."

"Oh, hello." There was a hint of frostiness in Hazel's voice. "What can I do for you?"

"I'm here to apologise for this afternoon's little incident."

Hazel frowned faintly at Margaret's trivialising manner. "I see. Would you like to come in?"

"Thank you." Margaret entered the house, gazing around curiously.

Hazel showed her to the living room. "We're waiting for a new generator," she explained as Lily lit yet more candles.

"Living by candlelight." Margaret smiled at Lily. "What fun."

Lily mustered up a stilted smile in return.

Hazel motioned Margaret to an armchair. Margaret lowered herself slowly onto it, supporting her stomach with one hand. Her potbelly pushed against her dress as she propped a cushion behind her back.

"When are you due?" Hazel asked, seating herself on the sofa.

"Late August." Margaret blew out a long breath. "To be honest, I can't wait to pop the little blighter out. I'm far too old for this pregnancy lark. This wasn't exactly planned."

Hazel's face softened into a smile at Margaret's frankness. "The best things never are. Would you like something to drink? Tea? Coffee?"

"Tea would be lovely."

"I'll make it," said Lily, not wanting to be left alone with Margaret.

"Can I cheekily trouble you for something sweet to go with it?" Margaret asked as Lily left the room. "I've developed an awful sweet tooth this time around. With Jude, it was cheese. Now it's cakes, biscuits, chocolate, anything sugary I can get my hands on." She patted her belly. "I'll be as big as a whale by the time this one gets here."

"Well you look–" began Hazel.

"Please don't say I look like I'm blooming," Margaret cut her off. "That's what Rupert keeps telling me and he's a terrible liar."

Hazel nodded in understanding. "I remember when I was pregnant. I was sick as a dog most days. All the well-meaning comments about me 'glowing' drove me up the wall. I can only imagine how bad-tempered I'd be if I got pregnant at our age."

Margaret's lips lifted into a half-smile as if she wasn't sure whether the remark was backhanded in some way. Her hazel-green eyes roamed the room. "This is my first time here. I understood the cottage had fallen into an awful state of disrepair."

"It needed a bit of TLC, that's for sure."

"Well it looks like you've done a wonderful job."

"Thank you."

Margaret's gaze lingered on the dog portraits. "Did you paint those?"

Hazel laughed. "No. I can't paint to save my life. We think those were painted by the owners of all the dogs that have lived here over the years. The oldest dates to 1690."

"1690," Margaret echoed. "Isn't that the year–" She fell silent as Lily returned carrying a tray with three mugs and a plate on it.

Lily put the tray on the coffee table. A frown flickered across Hazel's face as she saw what was on the plate.

Margaret smiled in thanks as Lily passed her a mug and the plate. "Ooh, this looks delicious. What is it?"

"Rocky Road," said Lily. She approached the sofa, shooting her mum a mischievous glance.

Margaret took a bite of the marshmallow-laced chocolate. "*Mmm*, this is heavenly. Who's the chef?"

"My daughter," Hazel replied before Lily could say anything. She laid a hand on Lily's wrist and gave it a squeeze that was just firm enough to be a warning.

"Well you have a genuine talent, Lily." Margaret cleared her throat as if a crumb was lodged in it. She bit off another chunk of Rocky Road and washed it down with her tea. "Jude's clueless in the kitchen. Perhaps you could come over to the house sometime and teach him how to make this."

I'd rather pull my fingernails out, thought Lily. She gazed at Margaret intently, almost as if waiting for something to happen.

Clearing her throat again, Margaret set aside the half-eaten Rocky Road. "Now," she began briskly as if it was time to get down to business. "About this afternoon. Believe you me, I'm well aware of how hot-headed Jude can be. But then again, it's understandable that feelings run high when it comes to the welfare of livestock."

"What about the welfare of the crows?" Lily asked.

Margaret's lips thinned into a polite smile. "Last winter was unusually mild, which has led to an explosion in their numbers. The knock-on effect is that we've lost more livestock than ever before." Her smile took on a pained slant. "I've lost count of the number of lambs that have been killed. It's absolutely heart-breaking."

"I sympathise, really I do," said Hazel. "But I'm afraid the answer's still no. It's not just about the crows." She chose her words with care. "Lily and I came here for peace and quiet. Not to listen to guns going off."

"Well then, how about this? We–" Margaret interrupted herself with a cough. "Excuse me, I think I've got a frog in my throat. What was I saying?" She fiddled with the silver crucifix dangling from her neck. "Ah yes, we can use air-rifles to cull the crows. They're almost completely silent."

"That sounds like a reasonable compromise–"

"But we're still not going to change our mind," Lily broke in, afraid her mum was about to do that very thing. "We don't want you killing crows or anything else on our land."

"But you're ok with them killing lambs?" Despite her calm tone, Margaret's eyes sparkled with annoyance.

"Obviously we'd rather they didn't kill any more of your lambs," said Hazel. "But to be blunt, I don't see how it's our problem if they do."

Margaret shook her head in disappointment. "It's a real shame. I'd so hoped we could resolve this without having to resort to legal proceedings."

Hazel frowned. "How are we legally responsible for what crows do?"

In a matter-of-fact tone, Margaret reeled out what was clearly a memorised quote. "A property owner can be held responsible for damage or injury caused by a wild animal, if it can be proven they were negligent in preventing the incident."

"Go ahead, take us to court," Lily challenged her. "You'll lose. Just like you did last time."

"Last time?" Margaret's confusion quickly shifted to realisation. "Oh, you're referring to the old boundary dispute." Her voice lightened as if she was pleased the topic had been brought up. "I've been saying to Rupert for ages that we should look into contesting the boundary. Maybe now's the time to do so. I really think we'd have a strong case."

Hazel leaned forwards, her gaze direct, her voice steady. "If you think you can intimidate us into–"

She was cut off by a sharp cough from Margaret. A dribble of chocolate leaked from Margaret's mouth. She sipped her tea, but it came spluttering straight back out. Her eyes bulged as a coughing fit seized her. Tea slopped from the mug onto her lap.

Lily and Hazel exchanged a glance. There was an *Oh my god, what have I done?* look in Lily's eyes. "Do you want some water, Mrs Chapman?"

Margaret nodded, coughing too violently to speak.

Lily hurriedly fetched a glass of water. Margaret put it to her lips, but once again a hacking cough prevented her from swallowing. Red splotches speckled her cheeks. Her belly quaked as if its inhabitant was thrashing around in pain. Lurching to her feet, she managed to gasp out, "I can't breathe!"

She threw back her head. Her mouth stretched wide open. A geyser of tea and chunks of Rocky Road spouted from it. Hazel dodged out of the line of fire as the vomit arched across the room and splattered over the sofa.

There was a stunned silence. Margaret swayed on her feet, panting, her eyes glazed and heavy-lidded. Gently, Hazel took her by the arm and guided her towards the armchair.

Margaret shook her off. "I'm fine now." Her slurred voice indicated otherwise. "It's just morning sickness. I thought I was over it, but…" She looked at the vomit with a sort of dazed disgust. "I'm sorry, I'll pay for any…"

"Don't worry about it," said Hazel.

Margaret gazed around herself as if wondering where she was. "I… I'll go." She turned to the door, slightly hunched over, hands clasped under her belly as if it were made of stone.

"Are you sure you're up to driving?"

"Yes, I'm… Thank you… Thank you for the…" Margaret trailed off, losing track of her words.

Lily rushed to open the front door and stepped aside for Margaret to pass. Margaret's face glowed a ghastly greenish-white in the moonlight. "I'll…" she began, but thought better of what she was saying and adjusted it to, "*someone* will be in touch."

She shuffled towards the bulky outline of her 4x4.

"God, for a second there, I thought she was about to choke to death right in front of us," Lily whispered.

Hazel subjected her to a narrow-eyed look. "Did you do something to the Rocky Road?"

"No." Lily's tone was indignant.

"Are you sure you didn't put pepper or something like that on it?"

"I wouldn't do that to someone, no matter how horrible they are." Lily went into the kitchen and picked up the bag of Rocky Road. She held it at arm's length as if it was infectious waste. "If anyone spiked this stuff, it was Huge-O."

"Well I ate some and I was fine."

"You were probably just lucky. I bet that fat-ass put some *magical*," Lily made an inverted commas sign with her fingers, "herbs in it."

"Don't call him a fat-ass."

"Why not? That's what he is. Anyway, why do you care what I call him?"

"You know how much I hate name calling." Glancing around at the sound of the 4x4 starting up, Hazel added, "And any other kind of bullying."

"I'm not a bully."

"I know you're not, but everything that's happened this past nine or ten months is... well, it's bound to change you. I just..." Hazel struggled to find the right words. She looked at Lily as if appealing for help. "I don't want you to become someone you're not."

Lily thought about the barely recognisable creature her dad had transformed into over the last months of his life. Was she destined to become like him? *No way, I'll never let that happen,* she silently vowed.

Hazel summoned up a smile tinged with melancholy. "Come on, you can help me clean the sofa."

Lily wrinkled her nose. "Do I have to?"

"Yes you do. You're lucky I'm not making you do it on your own."

Hazel filled the washing-up bowl with hot water. Lily scrutinised the Rocky Road, crumbling it between her fingers. It looked like any other Rocky Road. With a sudden movement, she threw it in the bin and followed her mum to the living room. They set about mopping up the vomit with soapy tea towels.

"This smells worse than those dried flowers," Lily whined. She flung open the window and gulped down fresh air.

Hazel couldn't help but chuckle at her dramatics. She wafted a hand towards the doorway. "Go. I'll finish cleaning this."

Flashing her mum a grateful glance, Lily made a speedy exit from the room. After washing her hands at the kitchen sink, she cast a fretful look out of the rear window. She opened the backdoor to check Sam's bowl – the jellied chunks were untouched.

"Still no sign of him?"

Lily turned at her mum's question. "No."

Hazel went outside and emptied a bowlful of murky water down the drain. Lily's lips drew back in disgust as her mum picked lumps of Rocky Road out of the grate. Hazel exhaled wearily. "What a day." She washed her hands and shook them dry. "Right, what do you fancy to eat?"

Lily shot her an incredulous look. "You must be joking. No way can I eat anything right now."

"Not even for the sake of Sam?"

Lily sighed. "Ok, but I can't manage anything much."

Hazel set about heating a pan of soup and slicing a loaf of bread.

"Was Mrs Chapman serious about taking legal action?" Lily asked.

"I don't know. Let's not talk about that anymore tonight."

They ate their soup. Hazel dumped the pots on the drainer. "The washing-up can wait till tomorrow. I'm off to bed."

"I'm going to stay up for a while in case Sam comes back."

"Don't be too late in bed. We might have to be up early to search for him." Hazel gave Lily a peck on the cheek. "Goodnight, sweetie."

"Night, Mum."

Hazel went into the hallway. Wearing an impish smile, she poked her head around the doorframe. "By the way, Margaret would have deserved it if you had put pepper on her Rocky Road."

Lily mirrored her smile. "Too right she would." Her lips flattened as her gaze returned to the garden. "Where are you, you stupid dog?" There was no anger in her voice. Only concern.

16

Lily sat on the backdoor step, staring into the night. Despite the cool air, a sheen of sweat glistened on her forehead. Her stomach was whirling like a washing machine. Her mind was going round and round, too, tumbling from thought to thought. Where was Sam? Were the Chapmans bluffing? And always at the centre of it all, there was Tom. Why couldn't she stop thinking about him? Was she lovesick? Is that what this was?

She searched up 'lovesickness symptoms' on her phone – insomnia, headaches, loss of appetite, nausea, dizziness, intrusive and obsessive thoughts, sweating.

She wiped the back of her hand across her forehead. God, this was insane. It was like having some sort of weird addiction.

Gazing up at the endless expanse of space, she let her mind drift. She closed her eyes, murmuring yearningly, "Tom, Tom–"

She was interrupted by a growl.

Her eyes snapped open. A dog was standing in front of her, almost close enough to reach out and touch. It was an emaciated black thing with ears like tatty cloths. A reddish discharge crusted its eyes. Its front left leg ended at the knee joint in a gnarled stump.

As the dog's jowls drew back from its chipped brown teeth, Lily tensed in readiness to spring up and slam the door shut.

Pity mingled with her fear as its eyes wandered off in opposite directions to each other. The poor creature couldn't even see straight. It wasn't wearing a collar. Was it a stray? It certainly looked like it had been living rough for a long time.

Another growl rumbled from the dog as Lily nudged Sam's bowl towards it. The dog sniffed suspiciously at the bowl's contents. A black-spotted tongue unfurled to lick the chunks of meat. The dog's wariness disappeared and it set upon the food ravenously.

The bowl was soon empty and licked clean. The dog focused its red eyes on Lily again. It glanced towards the trees as if reacting to a sound her ears weren't sensitive enough to detect. Its tail stiffened, arching over its back like a scorpion's stinger.

Lily's breath caught in her throat. There was something impossibly familiar about the dog. A name formed in her mind, but she couldn't bring herself to say it. Her gaze fell to the dog's only front paw. The middle one of its five black claws was missing.

Lily suddenly felt paralysed. All she could do was stare at the dog with a mixture of wonder and dread.

With awkward hopping movements, the mangy-looking animal turned and ambled across the lawn. Lily watched until the darkness swallowed it up. Then, as if released from an invisible grip, she rose and closed the door.

She went into the living room and shone her phone at a bronze plaque bearing the name that was burning on her lips – 'Doubting Tom'. Her gaze traced the crescent of the hound's tapering tail, the straight line of his back, the proudly upright head.

Had he just paid her a visit in the flesh?

She shook her head. "Don't be stupid." Apart from the obvious impossibility of a dog living for hundreds of years, Doubting Tom had four legs.

But what about the broken claw? a voice in her mind persisted.

"It's just a coincidence."

She returned to the backdoor. The garden was deserted. After refilling Sam's bowl, she blew out the candles and headed upstairs. She came to a stop at the 'Hear no evil. See no evil. Speak no evil' tapestry. She thought about the ears, eyeballs and tongue the crow had brought to the garden.

"Just a coincidence," she repeated. A sardonic smile flickered on her lips. Oh yes, just another coincidence to add to the ever-growing list.

She went into her room and flopped onto the bed, too tired to brush her teeth or even to undress. Almost at once, she fell into a sleep as black as Doubting Tom's fur.

17

Lily was awakened by the wind whooshing through the trees. The room was bathed in the soft glow of the rising sun. She sprang off the bed and ran downstairs. A wave of birdsong broke over her as she opened the backdoor. There was something frantic about the way the birds seemed to be vying to out-sing one another.

Her eyes widened hopefully as she saw that the dog food was gone. The bowl was splotched with blood-streaked slobber.

"Sam," she called out, advancing barefoot across the dewy lawn. "Sa–"

Lily's voice died as she noticed a dark shape dangling from the lower branches of a tree. The crow was strung up by its neck. A noose bit deep into its downy under-feathers. With its wings crossed behind its back, it swayed in the wind like a hypnotist's watch.

Her gaze shifted to another crow strung to a neighbouring tree. She turned in a full circle, counting with growing horror, "One, two, three, four, five, six..." She trailed off into a queasy swallow. Many more dark shapes remained to be counted. They surrounded the cottage like an army laying siege to a castle.

Lily glared into the forest, wondering if Jude was gleefully watching her reaction from a nearby hiding place.

"Oh my god!"

She turned at her mum's exclamation. Hazel's hands were

clasped to her mouth. Her eyes were as round as a full moon.

"The Chapmans did this," Lily said without a trace of doubt.

"Did you see them?"

"No, but who else would it be? You realise what this is, don't you? It's a message. They're letting us know this is their land and they can do whatever they want here."

Hazel frowned briefly, then gave a hard nod. "Ok, if that's the way they want it, that's the way they'll get it." She went back into the house and fetched a bin liner and scissors.

She handed the bag to Lily. They made their way around the garden, cutting down and bagging the crows. "They're bullies." Hazel's words whistled through her teeth. She was pale with rage. "That's all they are. Just rich bullies who can't deal with being told no."

"What are you going to do?" Lily's question was tinged with concern. She couldn't remember the last time she'd seen her mum so angry.

Hazel grabbed a crow by the neck. Her knuckles whitened as if she was imagining it was one of the Chapmans, then she flung it into the bag. She cut down the remaining crows. There were twenty-two in all. Lily kept expecting to see the white-winged crow, but it wasn't amongst their number.

Hazel tossed the bag into the boot of her car and got behind the steering-wheel. "You need to stay here in case Sam comes back," she said as Lily opened the front passenger door.

"You're going to Chapman Hall, aren't you?"

Hazel's voice softened at Lily's apprehensive tone. "I'm only going to talk to them." She started the engine. "I won't be long."

Lily chewed her lips as she watched the car pull away. She went to the back garden and busied herself with chopping wood. She swung the axe with all her strength, taking out her anger on the logs. As if feeding off her emotions, the wind rose

133

to a mournful moan.

She kept chopping until her arms were as heavy as lead. Leaning on the axe handle, she stared into the trees. They shook their branches as if urging her to get back to work. A feeling grew in her that she was being watched. Her eyes probed the gloom beneath the canopy. There was nothing to see, but the feeling continued to intensify.

"I'm not scared of you, Jude," she shouted.

Except for the rustling and creaking of the trees, her words were met with silence. She gathered up an armful of firewood. Trying to seem as if she didn't have a care in the world, she sauntered to the kitchen. As soon as she was inside, though, she locked the backdoor and hurried to do the same to the front door.

After lighting the stove, she filled the kettle and put it on the hotplate. She drummed her fingers on the work surface as she waited for the water to boil. God, how did anyone ever get anything done before electricity?

The kettle finally began to whistle. Lily picked it up, but flinched and dropped it at a knock on the front door. She ran to peer out of the front window. Her heart pounded even harder than it already was doing as she laid eyes on the bespectacled, mop-haired boy.

Tom had found a faded t-shirt to go with his frayed shorts. The wind whipped his hair around his face as he called, "Lily?"

His lilting Hampshire accent made her scalp tingle. Running a hand through her hair, she headed to the door. Her trembling fingers fumbled the key into the lock.

Tom greeted her with a smile that revealed a row of crooked lower teeth. "Hi."

Lily opened her mouth, but couldn't seem to find her voice. A flush of heat rose into her face.

"Sorry for surprising you like this, Lily," Tom continued. "I was just passing by and… well, I wanted to see you."

"You wanted to see *me*?" Lily made it sound as if such a thing was beyond her comprehension.

A playful glint shone in Tom's eyes. "That's not so strange, is it?"

"I… err, no."

His gaze moved over the paintings of gingerbread biscuits that garlanded the door. "And I wanted to see the cottage."

"Oh."

Tom eyed Lily intently as if trying to work out whether her crestfallen tone was genuine. "It's ok me being here, isn't it? I can come back another time if–"

"No!" she interrupted, then clamped her lips together, mortified by her revealingly strong reaction.

There was an awkward silence.

Sweat prickled Lily's forehead from straining to think of something to say. All she could come up with was, "It's windy, isn't it?" *Yes, and you're a total idiot,* she told herself.

"I love it when it's like this." Tom lifted his face to let the wind sweep back his hair. "This is Boreas. The wind of death and change."

Lily frowned faintly. 'Death and change', that pretty much summed up her life. "How come you know all this stuff?"

Tom shrugged. "It's just what I'm into. I like anything to do with nature and magic. It makes me feel…" He faltered, then looked at his malformed hand and found some sort of explanation. "Imagine if you could shapeshift into something totally different." He peered at Lily shyly from under his fringe. "Don't you think that would be the most incredible thing ever?"

His words transported her back to the months in Fulham following her dad's death – that powerless sense of being trapped by her past, her name, her face. "Yes."

"What would you change into?"

Lily thought for a moment before lifting her eyes to the sky. "I'd be a bird. I can't think of anything better than being able to fly away to wherever I want."

"Me neither." Looking skywards too, Tom sighed as if imagining himself soaring into the clouds. He lowered his gaze to Lily. "Maybe we can fly away together."

Another silence passed between them. The static-like sensation prickled the crown of Lily's head once more.

Tom broke eye contact to look at the purple flowers. "Mandrakes are used to make flying potions."

"Mandrakes?" Lily echoed. "Oh, is that what they are?"

"Have you seen them in the moonlight?"

"Yes, they glow."

"That's why they're called Devil's Candles. I bet they look amazing."

Lily smiled, glad for the opportunity to make a light-hearted comment. "Yeah, amazingly creepy. If it was up to me, I'd dig them all up."

Tom shot her a cautioning look. "Whatever you do, don't do that. The screams of an uprooted mandrake are supposed to kill anyone that hears them."

"I'd better get myself some earplugs then."

The flippant remark prompted another scrutinising look from Tom. "Has anyone ever told you that you pull a funny face when you're joking?"

"No."

"Well you do. Your eyes go squinty and you get a little

wrinkle right there." Tom reached out to touch Lily between the eyes. Tingles rippled outwards from the spot. For several seconds, she couldn't move, couldn't speak, couldn't even breathe. It was as if his finger had penetrated her skull and blown a fuse in her brain. Then, barely aware of what she was doing, she leaned in to kiss him.

His lips felt hard at first, but swiftly softened. An intoxicatingly sweet taste flooded Lily's mouth as if he was made of honey. She tried to put her arms around his waist, but he stepped away from her.

Lily's cheeks stung as if she'd been slapped. "I'm sorry. I... I don't know why..." She took a second to steady her flustered voice. "I've never done anything like that before."

She held her breath as she awaited Tom's response. His eyes were agonisingly unreadable. A giddy rush of relief swept through her when he asked, "So are you going to invite me in?"

With a dazed nod, she stepped aside. Tom entered the hallway, peering around, taking in every detail. He ran his hands over the walls as if feeling for something invisible to the naked eye. His fingertips traced out a shape on the crooked beam above the front door. "Oh wow, look at this!"

Moving in for a closer look, Lily saw that a letter was etched into the beam. "'W'. Does that stand for witch?"

"It isn't a W, it's two Vs," Tom corrected. "It stands for virgin of virgins. It's supposed to evoke the protection of the Virgin Mary against witchcraft."

"I wonder who put it there?"

"Who knows? Maybe it was one of Mary's accusers. Or maybe it was Mary herself. Wouldn't that be ironic – a woman accused of being a witch who was herself scared of witches?"

Tom went into the living room and perused the portraits. At the sight of the most recent one, he asked, "Where's Sam?"

With worry shining in her eyes, Lily shrugged. "He ran away."

"Oh no. What happened?" Tom shook his head as she recounted the previous day's events. He wagged a finger at her. "I told you that you shouldn't have called Doubting Tom."

An unconvincing laugh escaped Lily as she thought about the three-legged dog that had come to the cottage in the night like a phantom. "Give me a break. That's just a load of nonsense."

"You can think what you like, but I was taught that no good ever comes from meddling with things you don't understand."

"Maybe you're right, but it's too late now to change what I did."

Tom tilted his head as if he wasn't sure that was true. "I'll go look for Sam."

An anxious, almost panicky feeling seized Lily as he turned to leave. "Don't–" she began, but caught herself.

"Don't what?"

She lowered her eyes, then gave him a somewhat shamefaced glance. "Don't you want to finish looking around the house first?"

Tom smiled. "I don't suppose a few minutes will make any difference. Sam's clever. He knows how to look after himself."

With Lily following close behind, he left the room. *Sorry Sam,* she mouthed silently as they climbed the stairs. Tom gave the tapestry a once-over.

"That was here when we moved in," said Lily.

"It's the Rule of Three. Whatever you do unto others will be revisited upon you threefold." Tom pointed at the trio of women, his finger moving from bottom to top. "The maiden, mother and crone will make sure of that."

"Are they witches?"

"It depends what you believe. There's an old saying, *bad things come in threes*. You know, like when one death in a family is quickly followed by two more."

Lily hugged her arms across her chest as a sudden shivery feeling flowed through her. "What do you believe?"

Tom mulled the question over momentarily. "I believe certain numbers hold power over us. Three's an important number in witchcraft. That's why this year's such a special anniversary. On Wednesday, it'll be three-hundred-and-thirty-three years since Mary's death."

"It'll also be my sixteenth birthday."

Tom let out an amused, thoughtful *huh*. "That's a weird coincidence."

Coincidence. Lily frowned. Was there a more annoying word in the English language?

"Are you having a party?" Tom asked.

"With who? You're the only person I know around here besides my mum."

"Then the two of us should do something to celebrate."

Lily's stomach fluttered at the prospect of what that 'something' might be as Tom took her hand and drew her into her mum's bedroom.

The closed curtains and unmade bed hinted at her mum's rushed departure.

Tom's eyes roamed around the room and settled on the moss pressings. "That moss only grows around here."

"The only place I've seen it is the cottage's roof. Do you know what it's called?"

"No, but it's a natural antiseptic. People came from all over to be treated with it by Mary. One man testified at her trial that she made his wound disappear in the blink of an eye."

"Oh my god, how evil can you get?"

Tom chuckled at Lily's sarcasm.

"I wish she'd made the Chapmans disappear," she continued with a bitter edge to her voice.

Tom's smile faded. He let go of Lily's hand.

Something squeezed inside her chest. Had she upset him somehow? "What's wrong?"

He dipped his chin, looking at her over his glasses. Slowly, almost fearfully, he lifted his malformed hand to stroke her cheek. The three nubbins of flesh were as soft as ripe berries. On a sudden compulsion, she kissed them one after another.

A visible tremor ran through Tom. Lily raised her face to his. As their lips brushed against each other, a soft moan escaped him. The sound reminded Lily of the lovers in her dream. She wanted to feel what they felt. Oh god, she wanted it so much...

She exhaled a frustrated breath as Tom drew away from her again. This time, he was the one that stammered. "I'm sorry. I... we shouldn't be doing this."

"Why not?"

"What if your mum comes back?"

"She won't."

Lily's eyes gleamed with longing. Tom ran his tongue over his lips uncertainly. Their gazes remained locked together for a few seconds, then he turned to do a quick shuffle down the stairs. He came to a halt outside the porch and took a deep breath like a drunk trying to sober up.

Lily followed and watched him from the doorway, not knowing once again what to say.

Tom's breath snagged in his throat as he spotted something at the edge of the clearing.

Lily's heart sank when she saw what he was looking at – an upside-down crow was bobbing around behind a veil of leaves.

Tom approached the bird and stroked its sleek feathers as tenderly as he had Lily's cheek. When he drew back his hand, flakes of dried blood fell from his fingertips.

"I thought we'd found them all," said Lily.

"There were more?"

"Yes. Twenty-two more."

"Twenty-two." Tom's voice was heavy with sadness. "Who did this?"

"I think it was Jude."

Tom nodded as if to say, *Of course it was.* Glaring in the direction of Chapman Hall, he called out, "Ever mind the Rule of Three! Three times your acts shall return to thee. This lesson well thou must learn. Thou only gets what thee dost earn."

As his words echoed off into the forest, he released the crow from its noose. Cradling it as if it could still feel pain, he approached the nearest flowerbed. He dug a hole with his hands, gently laid the bird in it and pushed the soil back into place.

His face pinched into a scowl that made him look years older. "I really hope the Rule of Three is real and Jude gets what's coming to him."

With a nod, Lily indicated she felt the same way.

Tom rose to his feet. "I'd better go and look for Sam."

"When will I see you again?"

He found a smile for Lily. "Soon." With that, he headed into the trees.

18

An avenue of tall beech trees climbed gently towards the head of the valley. On either side, sheep-grazed fields rolled away to meet the forest. The avenue ended at open wrought-iron gates set in a stone wall.

The car juddered over a cattle-grid and crunched along a gravel driveway. After passing between manicured lawns, Hazel pulled up alongside a mud-spattered Land Rover. She got out of the car, eyeing Chapman Hall's tall sash-windows, towering chimneys and weathered exterior. A flagpole rose proudly from the highest point of the roof. Its flag fluttered in the wind, displaying a coat of arms with a helmet and shield wreathed in green leaves and red berries.

Hazel retrieved the bag of dead crows and approached an imposingly large door set within a pillared porch.

Echoing clunks rang out as she rapped an iron knocker against the door. The barking of what sounded like several dogs came from inside the house.

"Quiet!" a deep voice commanded.

The barking stopped and the door creaked open. Rupert was framed in the doorway with a pair of bright-eyed Border Collies at his ankles. Dark bags under his eyes suggested he hadn't had much sleep. He subjected Hazel to a stare of undisguised dislike.

"What do you want?" His brusque voice was equally bereft of any pretence at civility.

Hazel responded by upending the bin liner. The crow carcasses landed on the doorstep with a series of soft thuds. Rupert gave them an indifferent glance. He met Hazel's accusing gaze briefly before taking a flat-cap and jacket from a coat stand.

"Come with me." Pulling the cap down over his salt-and-pepper hair, he stepped past Hazel.

"Where to?"

Rupert didn't bother to reply. With the dogs at his heels, he strode towards a cross-beamed door in a brick wall that branched off from the house. Hazel followed somewhat hesitantly. Glancing to either side, she entered an expansive walled-garden. White magnolia petals drifted on the light breeze that managed to penetrate the high walls. The air was infused with the sweet perfume of roses, lavender and wisteria.

Rupert advanced briskly along a gravel path bordered by well-tended rows of flowers, herbs, vegetables and fruit plants.

A bow-legged man with a face like a leather sack was hoeing the rich, dark soil. He tipped his cap at Rupert.

Hazel gave the gardener a polite smile. Without returning the courtesy, he resumed working the soil. She frowned at his bent back and quickened her pace.

She caught up with Rupert as he opened a door in the opposite wall. A sweet-sour scent of grass, dirt and droppings wafted through the doorway. Hens pecked around her ankles as he led her across a hay-strewn yard. Whining and trembling, the Border Collies jumped up at metal railings that enclosed an open-sided barn.

"Sit," Rupert instructed them. They promptly obeyed.

As Hazel saw what the barn contained, her wariness transformed into slack-jawed shock. Rows of lambs were laid out on a bed of hay. Their eye sockets were black holes. Their ears were torn stubs. Dried blood caked their mouths. Their throats had been cut almost to the point of decapitation. Flies swarmed around the carcasses, feasting on blood and excrement.

"Twenty-three," Rupert said in a flat, exhausted tone. "Yesterday I lost twenty-three lambs."

"I'm sorry to hear that, but it doesn't give you the right to string up dead crows outside my house."

Rupert squinted sidelong at Hazel as if to ask, *What are you talking about?* Then a spark of realisation came into his eyes and he gave a sighing shake of his head.

"Oh, I see," said Hazel, reading his reaction. "Your son did it without your knowledge. Where is he? I want to talk to him."

"I don't know. And even if I did, I wouldn't let you talk to him."

"Well tell him from me, if anything like this happens again, I'll–"

"You'll do what?" Rupert turned the full force of his hostile blue gaze on Hazel. With a sudden movement, he leaned in so close that his hot breath made her blink. "What was in that cake you gave my wife?"

Hazel retreated a step. "It was Rocky Road, and I couldn't tell you exactly what was in it. I didn't make it."

"Then who did?"

"Why does it matter?"

"It matters because Margaret's not been able to keep anything down since then. It's like she's been poisoned."

Hazel frowned. "Are you accusing me of poisoning your wife?"

Rupert answered with a meaningful silence.

Hazel shook her head as if to say, *I've had enough of this.* "I'm only going to tell you one more time, Mr Chapman. Stay off my property or I'll call the police."

"I'm the one that should call the police." Rupert bent over the railings and picked up a dead lamb by the legs. Multiple chunks of flesh were missing from its hindquarters. "What does that look like to you?"

"It looks like something took a bite out of it."

Rupert put down the lamb, opened a neighbouring pen and kicked some hay out of the way.

Hazel sucked in a horrified gasp. "No, no, no!" she cried, lurching forwards. She shoved aside more hay, exposing a tangle of bandaged black legs. Pellet holes peppered Sam's body. His amber eyes stared into nothingness.

As Hazel pushed her fingers through his thick fur, a sob forced its way between her lips. She silenced it with a harsh noise in her throat. "Did Jude do this?"

"No, I did." Rupert exuded self-righteousness. "This is your own fault. You left me with no other option."

Hazel clenched her teeth in impotent fury. "We both know why you did this."

Rupert shook his head as if saddened by her accusation. "You don't belong here. You should go back to Fulham."

Fulham. Hazel reacted to the word with a revealing silence.

"That's right, Mrs Knight," Rupert continued. "The whole of Midwood knows who you really are."

Hazel glared at him for a moment, then spoke in a carefully controlled voice. "My surname is Wylde."

Before he could say anything else, she turned and slid her hands under Sam. As she rose to her feet, his body sagged in her arms like a bag of compost.

Avoiding any further eye contact, Hazel strode towards

the walled garden. The bow-legged gardener squinted at her through a haze of cigarette smoke. He was dwarfed by the muscular man now standing next to him. Toby Spencer's landing strip of a chin jutted towards Hazel as he took a drag on his own cigarette.

She briefly met the butcher's impassive gaze as she passed him. Fury flared across her features as laughter erupted behind her. She bit down on an impulse to demand to know what was so funny, telling herself, *Don't give them the satisfaction of getting a reaction.*

It quickly became apparent what they found so amusing. The Border Collies sprinted past Hazel and jumped up to nip at Sam.

"Get down! Go away!" Hazel shouted, to no effect.

She darted a look over her shoulder. Rupert was watching from the barnyard. All it would take was a word to call the dogs to heel, but he remained conspicuously silent.

"Ok, if that's how you want to play it," she muttered. As one of the collies snapped at Sam's tail, she lashed a foot into its chest. Both dogs skittered away, whimpering and growling.

Hazel braced herself against a gust of wind as she emerged onto the driveway. The hollow sound of knuckles rapping on glass drew her gaze to an eerie figure in a first-floor window. Margaret was shrouded in what appeared to be a white nightgown. Her hair was a tangled mess. She was clutching the silver crucifix that hung around her neck.

Even at that distance, Hazel could feel Margaret's eyes drilling into her. Hazel lifted Sam's carcass high as if to say, *Look what your husband's done.* Margaret didn't display any visible reaction.

Hazel placed Sam on a blanket in the car boot, then got behind the steering wheel. The feeling of being stared at pursued her through the gateposts and along the tree-lined driveway. It didn't fade until a bend in the valley hid Chapman Hall from view.

A lump formed in Hazel's throat as her thoughts turned to Lily. What should she tell her about Sam? Perhaps it would be best to say nothing at all. She shook her head, knowing it wasn't an option. Sooner or later, Lily was bound to find out what had happened. Susan Cooper or some other local bigmouth would see to that.

Hazel heaved a sigh, consoling herself with the thought that at least this way she would be right there to pick up the pieces.

19

L ily stared out of the kitchen window. Why was her mum taking so long? With each passing minute, a sense of foreboding grew in her.

There's an old saying, bad things come in threes. Like when one death in a family is quickly followed by two more.

Tom's words kept replaying in her mind. She tried to silence them by focusing on her phone. She typed 'mandrakes' into the search box. 'Mandrakes are a perennial herb in the nightshade family…'. She skipped past the botanical description to 'Throughout history, mandrakes have been associated with the occult. Their parsnip-like roots have an eerily humanoid shape. According to folklore, the only safe way to uproot a mandrake is by tethering a starved black dog to it on a moonlit night. Place a piece of meat just out of reach so that the hungry animal runs towards it, thus uprooting the mandrake.'

Lily thought about the bony three-legged dog that had devoured Sam's food. Had it even been real? Maybe she'd dreamt it. She turned to look in the bin. No, it hadn't been a dream. The empty dog food cans proved that.

She resumed reading 'Mandrakes possess potent hallucinogenic and narcotic properties. Medieval witches were said to use them for flying potions and lucky charms as well as for healing, fertility and love spells. If ingested in high enough doses, the juice from the roots can cause narcosis and fatal respiratory failure.'

Lily looked up 'narcosis'. "A state of drug-induced stupor," she read aloud. "Symptoms include paralysis, headaches, dizziness, confusion, nausea, loss of appetite, rapid heart rate, euphoria–"

She broke off at the rumble of an engine. Relief swept over her as her mum's car came into sight. She dashed out of the house.

Hazel emerged from the car, meeting Lily's gaze with mournful eyes.

The sense of foreboding flared up again. "What is it, Mum? What's happened?"

Hazel opened then closed her mouth, seemingly at a loss for words. She popped the car boot. Her gaze shifted back to Lily. Swallowing hard at the thought of what it might contain, Lily approached the boot. She froze as if turned to stone by the sight of Sam. After a moment, she ever so slowly reached out to touch him. She shuddered at the feel of his cold, stiff body. Tears flooded her eyes. "How? Why?"

In reply, Hazel drew her into a tight embrace and held her silently.

Lily's shoulder quaked. For a while, all she could do was cry. When she finally pulled away from her mum, her eyes radiated grief and fury in equal measure. "Jude did this, didn't he?"

"No, his dad did it. He says Sam was attacking his lambs."

"*Jude,*" Lily repeated, not seeming to hear her mum. "I'm going to show that... that..." She faltered as if there was no insult sufficient to express her hatred.

"I don't want there to be any retaliation. It'll only make things worse."

Lily spread her hands. "So we're just going to let him get away with this?"

"I'm sorry, Lily, but what else can we do?"

Lily chewed over her mum's apologetically pragmatic words.

Her gaze slid towards the little mound of soil where the crow was buried. "Tom was right."

"Who's Tom?"

"He's a boy I met a few days ago."

"Met where?"

"It doesn't matter. What matters is he was right." Lily's voice dropped to a fatalistic murmur. "This isn't the end of it. Someone else we love is going to die."

Hazel frowned. "What on earth are you talking about?"

"It's the Rule of Three."

"The rule of what?"

Instead of answering, Lily stroked Sam's silky ears. She bent to lift him into her arms. Her slender frame stooped under his weight, she made her way to the back garden.

Hazel pursed her lips as if realising it would be best to hold off on further questions for the time being.

Lily set Sam down at the far edge of the lawn and fetched a spade from the shed. She thrust it into the grass and levered up a rectangle of turf. After ten or fifteen minutes of digging, she paused to wipe sweat from her eyes and examine a blister on her palm.

"I'll take over," Hazel offered.

With a stubborn shake of her head, Lily gritted her teeth and resumed digging. By the time the hole was deep enough, the spade's handle was smeared with blood. She lifted Sam again, hugged him for a moment, then eased him into the grave.

Lily and Hazel stared down at Sam, neither of them seeming to know what to say. No more tears found their way into Lily's eyes. She felt as if she'd been wrung dry.

"Goodbye Sam," said Hazel.

Prompted by the simple farewell, Lily shovelled soil into the hole. When it was full, she stamped the turf back into place.

Hazel heaved a sigh. "Perhaps I was wrong after all. Perhaps we shouldn't have come to live–"

"No," Lily interrupted fiercely. "This is our home and no one's going to make us leave it."

As if to put an exclamation mark on her assertion, Lily stabbed the spade into the ground. It trembled upright behind her as she strode to the kitchen. She splashed water on her face at the sink.

Hazel trailed after her with Sam's bowl.

"Put that back where you got it from," said Lily.

"Why? What would be the point?"

Lily took the bowl from her mum. She emptied a can of dog food into it before returning it to the doorstep.

"What's going on, Lily?" Hazel's voice was tinged with confusion and concern. "What aren't you telling me?"

"Do you really want to know?"

"Of course I do."

Lily tilted her head doubtfully. She placed her hands in succession over her ears, eyes and mouth. "Isn't that what we do in this family? We ignore what's happening until it's too late?" The words were more of an allegation than a question.

Hazel compressed her lips as if stifling a sharp response.

Lily nodded, taking the silence as proof that she was right. She stalked up to her room, threw herself onto the bed and closed her eyes. As she caught a whiff of Sam's musky scent on the sheets, tears threatened to overwhelm her again.

Visualising Jude's arrogant face, she muttered through her teeth, "Ever mind the Rule of Three. Three times your acts shall return to thee. This lesson well thou must learn. Thou only gets what thee dost earn."

20

Lily's eyes snapped open. For an instant, she didn't know where she was. The moonlight shining through the window eased away her disorientation. Her face crumpled as the events of the day came rushing back. She groped for her phone. It was nearly midnight. She'd slept the entire day through. Something similar had happened after her dad's death. For weeks on end, she'd slept eighteen hours a day like a hibernating animal. It was as if her body had shutdown to protect itself.

There was a sandwich on the bedside table. The sight of it made her realise she wasn't remotely hungry.

"Loss of appetite," she murmured, thinking about the crossover between the symptoms of lovesickness and narcosis. She mentally scrolled through the others that she'd experienced since coming to the cottage – *headaches, dizziness, nausea.*

So which was it? Was she lovesick? Or could this be mandrake narcosis? Perhaps this place was poisoning her. She moved around the room, sniffing the furnishings. There was no hint of the cidery aroma that had previously pervaded the cottage.

It occurred to her that if something in the cottage was making her ill, then surely her mum would be affected too. But Mum was fine. Or at least she appeared to be. She could always be putting up a front to avoid causing concern.

Isn't that what we do in this family? We ignore what's

happening until it's too late?

Lily cringed at the unfairness of what she'd said earlier. Mum hadn't ignored Dad's drinking, she'd simply been powerless to do anything about it.

Telling herself she would apologise first thing in the morning, Lily lay back and closed her eyes. She drifted off into a dream about Sam. He was chasing lambs on Chapman Hill. His sharp teeth flashed as he ripped out the throat of one. He moved on to savage another and another, leaving the slopes littered with their corpses.

A scream from outside yanked Lily awake. It sounded as if Sam was indeed tearing a lamb limb-from-limb. As the scream rose to an eardrum-shattering volume, she wondered whether this was just another part of the dream. Pressing her hands to her ears, she rose to look out of the window. With the suddenness of a television being muted, the screaming stopped.

There was nothing to be seen, except for the mandrakes shimmering serenely in the moonlight.

What could have made such a high-pitched sound? A fox? An owl? Lily's thoughts turned once again to the three-legged dog. Had the poor creature been howling in pain? Or perhaps crying for more food?

She left the room. Her mum's bedroom door was ajar. Shining her phone through the gap, she was astonished to see that her mum was fast asleep.

She went downstairs. A heaviness settled in her chest at the sight of Sam's unoccupied basket. An almost empty bottle of Emily's homemade wine on the table hinted at why the scream hadn't woken her mum.

Lily cracked open the backdoor. Sam's bowl was gone. Had her three-legged visitor moved it? She edged outside, sweeping her phone's torch back and forth. Its pale beam came to a stop on a flowerbed.

Her eyebrows pinching together, she squatted down and put her hand into a hole that went up to her elbow. Had a mandrake been uprooted? Her frown intensified. A few metres away lay Sam's overturned food bowl. She moved to pick it up. Its interior gleamed as if it had been licked clean.

She eyed the encircling darkness. "Tom?" Her voice wavered as if she wasn't sure who – or what – she was calling to. She opened her mouth to repeat the name, but some instinct stopped her from doing so. She retreated a few steps, then turned to hurry into the kitchen and lock the door.

She didn't feel like going back to bed. Instead, she curled up on the sofa. As she lay listening to the silence, she found herself hankering after the white noise of Fulham – buses rumbling along Munster Road, planes coming in to land at Heathrow, trains clanking towards Central London. Sounds that made her feel connected to the world. Sighing, she closed her eyes and gave herself over once more to the ethereal stillness of the forest.

21

L ily was entombed in earthy darkness. Her hair was being yanked so viciously that it felt like it was being torn out by the roots. She screamed, fighting with all her strength to remain where she was. But she was losing the tug-of-war. With each powerful pull, the unseen force lifted her a little further towards... Towards what?

Light exploded against her eyes. She lay blinking for a moment before rising from the sofa. She shuffled to the kitchen and spotted her mum through the rear window. Barefooted, she went outside and crossed the lawn. Yesterday's wind had blown itself out. Except for a few ribbons of cloud, the sky was clear.

Hazel was staring at Sam's grave. She turned as Lily drew near. "Did you do this?"

Lily's eyebrows lifted. The grave was decorated with stones that formed three spiralling loops. She dropped to her haunches and ran a finger along the stones. One spiral led to another, that led to another, that led to another in an endless circuit. "No, it wasn't me."

"Then who was it?"

Lily shrugged. "Maybe it was Hugo. This looks like the sort of thing he'd do."

"Or maybe it was your friend Tom." When she was met with silence, Hazel pointed to Lily's forehead. "What's going on in there?"

"I…" Lily faltered. How could she put into words something she herself didn't understand? A sigh of frustration escaped her.

Hazel's voice softened. "It's ok, we don't have to talk about this right now. Let's get some breakfast. You must be hungry."

Lily realised her mum was right – her stomach felt hollow. She gave her a grateful little smile. "I'm sorry for what I said yesterday, Mum. I didn't mean it."

Hazel returned Lily's smile. "I know you didn't."

They headed into the house. Lily went for a shower. Upon returning downstairs, she found a bacon sandwich waiting for her. When her stomach accepted the first tentative mouthful without complaint, she tucked into the rest of the sandwich. Hazel watched closely, making sure every last crumb was consumed.

"You don't need to worry about me, Mum," said Lily.

"I know, but that's what mums do. You'll find out when you have a family of your own."

Peter, Peter, pumpkin-eater, had a wife and couldn't keep her. He put her in a pumpkin shell, and there he kept her very well.

The singsong words reverberated in Lily's mind like a warning. "I don't know if I ever want to get married, never mind have children."

A fleeting wince crossed Hazel's face. "Please don't be like that, Lily." There was a trace of guilt in her voice. "I couldn't bear it if you ended up childless and alone because of what happened."

Better that than I end up killing my husband, thought Lily. She lowered her gaze, fearing her mum would read her eyes.

Hazel took a deep breath, then let it go as if clearing her head. "It looks like it's going to be a lovely day. Do you want to help me with the gardening?"

Lily gave an ambivalent shrug. "I suppose I might as well. There's nothing else to do around here."

Hazel chuckled. "I know. It's wonderful, isn't it?"

Lily set to work with a push-along mower, whilst Hazel planted runner beans and erected wigwams of bamboo canes for their shoots to twine around.

The mower ground to a halt as Lily glimpsed movement amongst the trees. Four men entered the garden. Toby Spencer was lumbering along beside a man whose almost equally towering height surely marked him out as Carl Spencer. Behind them, a bow-legged, nut-brown old man was being towed across the lawn by two Border Collies. A few steps ahead, like a general leading his troops into battle, marched Rupert Chapman.

"Mum," Lily called out apprehensively.

Hazel looked up from her task, wiping her forehead with the back of her hand. Her eyes narrowed at the sight of Rupert. The dark circles under his eyes were even more pronounced. Instead of his usual *Lord of the Manor* swagger, he walked with tense, hurried strides.

"I warned you what would happen if you trespassed on my property again," said Hazel, taking out her phone and starting to dial 999.

"Please, Ms *Wylde*, we're not here to cause trouble." Rupert emphasised the surname as if to prove he meant what he said. "We're looking for Jude. Have you seen him?"

Hazel lowered her phone, but didn't return it to her pocket. "No."

Tugging at his beard, Rupert turned to Lily. "What about you?"

She shook her head. His gaze lingered on her as if he was trying to decide whether he believed her.

"When did you last see him?" Hazel asked.

"Yesterday evening." Rupert gestured towards Chapman Hill. "He went to check on the sheep in the top field, but he didn't come home."

"Have you been up there?"

"Of course we bloody well have," the bow-legged man put in gruffly as if the question insulted his intelligence.

Hazel cast an uneasy glance at him. "Look, I understand you're worried about Jude. I'd be frantic if Lily went missing. But I'm not going to be spoken to like that in my own garden."

Rupert raised a hand in apology. "The thing is, it's just not like Jude to go AWOL."

Hazel's eyes softened sympathetically. "Could he have stayed over at a friend's house?"

"I've phoned around his friends. They haven't seen him either." Rupert looked at Lily again. "Can you think of anywhere he might be?"

She fidgeted nervously, thinking about the scream that had disturbed her sleep. What if it really had been the sound of someone being torn limb from limb? Should she mention it? Another question popped into her mind – what about Tom? What if he was somehow involved in Jude's disappearance? Just the thought of saying something that could get him in trouble made her palms sweat and her stomach churn.

"Well?" pressed Rupert.

"Why would Lily know where Jude is?" Hazel asked brusquely enough to suggest her patience was wearing thin. "Let's stop beating about the bush. You're here because you think Lily's done something in revenge for you killing Sam. Well I can assure you that whatever's happened to your son has nothing to do with my daughter."

"Yeah, well you would say that, wouldn't you?" the old

gardener pointed out.

"True," Hazel conceded. "But that doesn't change the fact that Lily was in bed all day yesterday."

"Know that for certain, do you?"

"Yes." Hazel folded her arms, signalling the end of the conversation.

Rupert proffered a business card with 'Chapman Hall Farm' and a phone number on it. "Please call me if you see Jude."

"I will. Good luck finding him."

Mustering up a strained smile, Rupert made an obvious effort to sound like his usual confident self. "Oh I'm sure he'll turn up."

"He's probably shacked up with some girl," chimed in the massive figure at Toby's side. His Hampshire accent was so thick that the words rolled into one another. He winked at Lily. "We all know what it's like to lose your head over a pretty girl."

He looked at her in a way that seemed to suggest he had X-ray vision. She was irritated to feel herself blushing.

The man broke into a toothy grin, clearly getting a kick out of her reaction. "I wouldn't be surprised if Jude came here last night to sneak a peek at you. I know I would have if I were his age."

"Carl." Toby's voice rumbled with disapproval.

The slightly shorter man shot him a sharp look, but said nothing else.

Rupert appeared to be oblivious to the exchange. His eyes were focused on the cottage as if trying to see through its walls.

"I'm sorry we couldn't be of help," said Hazel. Not receiving any response, she added pointedly, "We've got a lot to do, so if you don't mind–"

"Margaret still can't keep anything down," Rupert interrupted. He aimed his piercing blue eyes at Hazel. "Doctor Hughes is coming over to the house later today."

The other men exchanged glances behind Rupert's back. Carl whispered something to Toby, who replied with a nod.

"What did you say?" Lily demanded to know, determined to show she wasn't intimidated.

The smirk that teased Carl's lips suggested he wasn't fooled for a second by her boldness. "I said Doctor Hughes won't be any help."

"And why's that?"

Instead of replying, Carl casually lit a cigarette and blew smoke towards Lily. Resisting an urge to cough, she looked him in the eye. Behind Carl, she noticed the bow-legged old man extending his index and little finger like horns. He surreptitiously directed the horns towards her and flicked his wrist downwards. She shifted her gaze to his grizzled face. Before she could ask what he was doing, her mum said, "Well give Margaret my best. I hope she feels better soon."

Rupert frowned, tugging his beard as if he suspected he was being played for a fool. A flock of crows croaked as they flew overhead. The Border Collies began to whine and pull at their leads, prompting Rupert to turn on his heel and wordlessly walk away.

The gardener and Toby followed him. Carl lingered long enough to blow Lily a kiss. She scrunched her nose as if she'd caught a whiff of something unpleasant. Grinning, he ambled after his companions.

"Ugh, what a disgusting pig," Lily said loudly enough for him to hear.

"Keep your voice down," snapped Hazel.

"You realise they didn't just come here looking for Jude?

They came looking for a fight."

"So let's not give them an excuse to start one."

Lily pointed to the bow-legged man. "I wonder who he is."

"I think he's a gardener at Chapman Hall."

"Well whoever he is, he made a weird hand sign at me." Lily imitated the horns gesture. She searched up 'horns hand sign' on her phone. "It's supposed to ward off the Evil Eye. You know what that means, don't you?" She paused as if for dramatic effect. "They think we're witches."

Hazel burst into laughter.

"This isn't funny, Mum."

"Sorry, Lily, but witches? How am I meant to take that seriously?"

"Well here's something you should definitely take seriously. I get the feeling Mr Chapman blames us for his wife's illness."

Hazel's laughter died. "Unfortunately, I think you're right."

"So what are we going to do about it?"

"I'll tell you what we're going to do – keep a low profile and wait for this to blow over."

Lily snorted. "I wonder if anyone ever said that to Mary."

"This isn't the seventeenth century, Lily. I don't think we need to worry about being burnt at the stake."

Arching an eyebrow, Lily responded with a wry remark of her own. "Are you sure this isn't the seventeenth century? We don't have electricity. My phone's almost out of charge."

"Mine too."

"So if those idiots come back and things turn nasty, we might not be able to call the police. In which case, we'll be totally screwed."

"That's not going to happen. Believe me, Lily, a week or two from now this will all be ancient history."

"A week or two?" Lily repeated as if wondering whether she'd misheard. "The Chapmans have held this grudge for hundreds of years." She made a sweeping gesture at the forest. "They're never going to let it go until all of this is theirs. So unless you're willing to give it to them–"

"Over my dead body!" spat Hazel. "That's the only way they're getting their hands on our land." She covered her mouth, seemingly caught off guard by the intensity of her emotions. "Sorry, Lily, I didn't mean that. It's just that I've worked so hard for this. I'll be damned if I'm going to let anyone take it from me."

Both of them were silent for a moment as if mulling over how to prevent that from happening.

"Right," Hazel exclaimed with a purposeful clap. "Come on, this garden won't do itself." She squatted down to resume planting runner beans.

Lily remained where she was, head tilted downwards in thought. "Doctor Hughes. Hughes. Hughes..." she murmured. Where had she heard that name before?

Thomas Hughes was Midwood's rector.

A vertigo-like sensation washed over her as she recalled Tom's words. She mentally scrolled through the names – Hughes, Cooper, Spencer, Chapman. So all the descendants of Mary's accusers were still in Midwood.

As Lily envisioned them scheming to take the cottage's land, she repeated her mum's avowal, "Over my dead body."

22

Hazel wandered amongst the fruit trees. Their branches were laden with green damsons, plums, apples and pears. Her mouth watered as she thought about the endless pies and jams she could make once the fruit ripened. As her thoughts returned to Rupert Chapman, her lips formed a grim line.

"You won't take my happiness from me." Her tone was steely with resolve. "This is my will. So mote it–"

"I've finished mowing the lawn."

With a start, Hazel turned and gave Lily a somewhat shamefaced smile. "Do you want some lunch?"

Lily replied with a sullen shrug.

Hazel reached out as if to wipe the pout off her daughter's lips. "If the wind changes, your face will be stuck like that."

"There's about as much chance of that happening as there is of the forest spirits dealing with the Chapmans for us."

Hazel chuckled at the well-deserved comeback. She fell silent as a piercing caw rang out. The white-winged crow swooped in from the direction of Chapman Hill, extending its feet to land on the lawn. As it strutted towards them, its eyes glinted in the sun like black gems. It stopped a few metres away and shook its wings as if to get their full attention.

"Hello there," said Hazel. "Are you trying to tell us something?"

Lily let out an exasperated breath. "It can't understand you. It's just a crow."

The crow dipped its head and dropped something from its beak. Cawing again, it spread its wings and broke into a run. It took flight, skimming past Lily so closely that its claws brushed her head.

"Watch out! You nearly hit me!" she shouted after it. Clearing the treetops, the crow wheeled back towards Chapman Hill.

"It can't understand you. It's just a crow," Hazel said dryly.

Lily rolled a sidelong glance at her before stepping forwards to see what the crow had dropped.

"What delightful little present has it left for us this time?" Hazel asked.

A glistening splat of pinkish-red flesh with a white sphere at its centre was nestled amidst the blades of freshly cut grass. "It looks like another eyeball."

"Oh how thoughtful. I'm running low on eyeballs for my potions."

Lily smiled at the droll remark. The next instant, though, her smile vanished and she recoiled as if the eye had winked at her. She jabbed a finger towards it. "*That* isn't a sheep's eye."

Hazel leaned in to have a look for herself. The eyeball was as intact as if it had been surgically removed. A light blue iris encircled the pupil. "I think you're right. Could it be a cow's eye?"

"No way. Cows' eyes are massive. That thing's the same size as a human eye."

A frown crept across Hazel's forehead. "What colour are Jude's eyes?"

Lily pictured him – rosy cheeks, plump lips, button nose. He had a face like an evil cherub. But what about his eyes? What colour eyes did he–

She jolted out of her thoughts with a gasp. "Oh my god, it *is* one of Jude's eyes! Oh my god! Oh my god! When Mr Chapman finds out about this, he probably will burn us at the stake."

"For what? We can't control what a crow does."

"It doesn't matter. Just think about how this looks. Oh god, we're so screwed!"

"Calm down," Hazel firmly told Lily. "We don't even know if it is Jude's eye. Can sheep have blue eyes?"

Lily typed the question into her phone. The answer eased some of the anxiety from her face. "They can, but it's very rare."

Hazel spread her hands as if to say, *Well there you go.*

Lily shaded her eyes to look for the crow, but it had vanished into the blue. "We have to find out where it got the eye from."

"How are we supposed to do that? It could have brought it here from miles away." Hazel motioned to the eyeball. "I think it would be best to get rid of that and not breathe a word about this to anyone."

She fetched a trowel. Like a criminal disposing of evidence, she cast a quick look around to make sure they were alone before scooping up the eyeball and hurrying to the kitchen. She opened the stove and made to throw the eyeball into it.

"Wait," said Lily. "If it is Jude's eye, maybe it can be reattached."

Hazel fixed her with an unblinking look. "You're not listening to me, Lily. No one can ever know about this. Is that understood?"

Lily chewed her lips for a moment, then nodded.

Hazel tipped the eyeball onto the glowing embers. It bubbled and sizzled as flames reduced it to a watery goo.

Lily cringed as if it was painful to watch. She suddenly turned and strode out of the backdoor.

"Where are you going?" Hazel called after her.

"Where do you think?"

"I don't want you wandering around in the forest. Not while Rupert and his goons are hanging around."

"Sorry, Mum, but I have to find out where it came from."

Hazel sighed, knowing that further argument would be pointless. She threw a bottle of water and the first aid kit into a rucksack and hurried after Lily. "You're so bloody headstrong."

"I wonder where I get that from?"

Hazel couldn't hold back a crooked smile. She pointed a few metres to the right of the embracing old oaks. "I think the crow went that way."

"No it didn't." A note of foreboding entered Lily's voice. "It could have almost been following the path to the clearing."

"What clearing?"

"The one where Huge-O and his fellow freaks meet up. I told you about it, remember?"

"Yes, Lily, and I've told you multiple times how I feel about name–"

"Can we save the lecture for later, please?"

With that, Lily set off at a fast pace. She didn't slow down until she came to the fallen tree. She tilted an ear skywards. An ominous feeling settled in the pit of her stomach as snatches of croaks penetrated the canopy. "Do you hear that?"

"It sounds like crows."

"It sounds like *lots* of crows."

Lily redoubled her pace. The cawing built in waves. By the time she reached the avenue of thorny trees, it had swelled to a tsunami. What looked to be hundreds of black shapes were swirling above the clearing.

Lily and her mum exchanged a glance, then both broke into a run. They bobbed and weaved to avoid the clawing branches. The clamour of caws beat against their ears as if a mob was baying for blood. As Lily entered the clearing, she pulled up so abruptly that her mum crashed into her.

They fell to their knees like pilgrims at a shrine. Every last vestige of colour deserted Lily's face. She blinked as if trying to dispel a mirage.

A dozen crows were dotted around the grass. Jude was sprawled across the mound of ash at its centre. His limbs were flung out at odd angles. His clothes were smeared with bird droppings and blood.

It wasn't these things, though, that made Lily wonder whether she was trapped in a nightmare. It was the empty holes and ragged stumps where Jude's eyes and ears should have been. And even more than that, it was the pink strip of tongue jutting out of his mouth, clasped in the beak of the white-winged crow.

Jude's head jerked around as the beak sawed back and forth. Flapping its wings for leverage, the crow snipped off a medallion of flesh.

Hazel sprang up and sprinted forwards, waving her arms. "Get out of here!"

The crows took flight. They were absorbed into the swirling flock, which then broke apart, scattering in all directions like a routed army. Their guttural cries quickly faded into the distance.

Lily edged towards Jude as if afraid he might jump up and attack her. A shotgun and a leather pouch lay on the grass beside him. Half-a-dozen red cartridges had spilled out of the pouch.

Hazel stared dazedly at the blood streaming from what remained of Jude's tongue.

"Is he dead?" Lily asked in a tiny voice.

"I don't know."

Hazel squatted down to feel for a pulse in Jude's wrist. "Jesus!" she gasped as his hand twitched. A bubble of blood inflated from his lips as he exhaled a gurgling moan.

Lily shuddered at the tormented sound. She clutched her stomach as if she might vomit. "What do we do? What do we–"

Hazel cut her off with a sharp, "Shh." She unslung the rucksack. "Jude, can you hear me? It's Hazel Wylde."

Another pitiful moan trembled from him. His limbs spasmed feebly.

Hazel took out the water and first aid kit. "Try to lie still, Jude. I need to stop the bleeding." She dampened a cotton wool pad. Her gaze flitted between the injuries as if she didn't know where to begin.

"How... how did this happen?" Lily stammered.

"That doesn't matter right now." Holding Jude's head steady, Hazel pressed the cotton wool to his tongue. Blood instantly soaked through it. She glanced up at Lily. "Have you got a signal?"

Lily checked her phone. "No."

"Get back to the cottage and call for an ambulance." Hazel handed Rupert's business card to Lily. "And let Mr Chapman know what's going on."

Lily gulped at the prospect of explaining the situation to him. "What should I say?"

Hazel squinted at Jude as if wondering how aware he was of what was happening. "Just tell him Jude's hurt, but alive."

She resumed trying to stem the bleeding. Lily wrenched her

eyes from the gruesome scene and ran out of the clearing. As she pounded along the path, she thought about the mutilated lamb Jude had put out of its misery. Wouldn't that be the most merciful thing to do with Jude? What sort of life would he have if he survived?

She looked up at the blue ribbon of sky, sensing rather than seeing something pass overhead. Was it the white-winged crow taking Jude's severed tongue to the cottage? Her stomach clenched at the thought.

The garden came into view like a light at the end of a tunnel. Wary as a woodland creature, Lily crept to the edge of the lawn. Her intuition had been right! The crow was strutting to and fro by the backdoor like a guard on patrol. As it turned its head towards her, she flattened herself on the ground. She lay motionless, barely daring to breathe. At the sound of flapping, she lifted her head. The crow's wings flashed like white-tipped waves as it flew away. She waited until it disappeared from sight before venturing forth.

She clasped her arms across her stomach as she neared the cottage. Jude's tongue awaited her on the doorstep, glistening like a rasher of bacon.

She wondered with ghoulish curiosity what it would feel like to be eaten alive. Had Jude tried to fight off the crows? Or had he been incapable of doing so for some reason?

Mandrakes possess potent hallucinogenic and narcotic properties, she recited in her head. *The juice from the roots can cause narcosis. Symptoms include paralysis.*

Was it Jude she'd heard screaming in the garden last night? Perhaps, like her, he'd mistaken the mandrake berries for gooseberries. She nodded as if to persuade herself of the possibility. Yes, it was just a horrible accident. Nothing more.

She snatched up the tongue and hurried inside to open the stove. Jude's eyeball had been burned to nothingness. She hesitated to consign his tongue to the same fate.

No one can ever know about this. Is that understood?

Her mum's words kept playing on a loop in her head until, with a sudden movement, she made to throw the tongue into the fire. It clung to her palm like a leech. Squirming with revulsion, she shook it loose. Her throat spasmed at the acrid aroma of burning flesh. She slammed the stove shut, flung open the backdoor and cleared the stench from her nostrils with a deep breath. Then she took out her phone and dialled 999. After telling the emergency operator where to send the ambulance, she hung up and stared at the business card. A long moment passed before she dialled the number on it. She closed her eyes as she waited for Rupert to pick up.

23

T he stretcher swayed as the paramedics threaded their way down the narrow path. Four straps and a neck brace held Jude in place. His head was so heavily bandaged that only his nose was visible. A cylinder attached to the stretcher fed him oxygen through a tube taped under his nostrils. He lay as motionless as a corpse, but Rupert was speaking to him as if he was very much alive.

"It's not far now, son." Rupert sounded hollowed out by shock. "Just hold on, Jude. We're almost there. We'll be–" A sob choked off his words. He looked around himself like someone struggling to get their bearings.

Is this really happening?

Lily read the question in his glazed eyes. She looked down as his gaze passed over her.

"Keep talking to him, Mr Chapman," urged a paramedic.

Hauling in a shaky breath, Rupert found his husk of a voice. "We'll be at the hospital soon, Jude. The doctors there will... They'll..."

His words collapsed into a whimper so desolate that it brought tears to Lily's eyes. She wiped them away with the back of her hand.

"Keep it together, Lily," her mum cautioned softly from behind her. Hazel's face was devoid of pity. She eyed Rupert with a sort of calculating detachment. *What next?* was the only question in her eyes. *What next?*

A policeman was waiting at the edge of the garden. He stood aside to let them pass before following along. Several more constables were milling around at the front of the house, together with the old gardener and the Spencer brothers. Two police cars and a van marked 'FORENSICS' were crammed into the gravelled area. Rupert's Land Rover was parked alongside an ambulance on the lawn.

Lily glanced furtively at the hole where a mandrake appeared to have been uprooted. *What if you're right about Jude eating the berries? The police might think we poisoned him.* Her heart pounded at the possibility.

A feeling of being watched stole over Lily. Her gaze met Carl's shrewd eyes. He was perched on the Land Rover's bonnet, staring at her through a haze of cigarette smoke. He didn't look upset. Quite the opposite, in fact. The twinkle in his eyes seemed to suggest he was enjoying the spectacle. In contrast, the grizzled gardener was peering through his fingers like a frightened child. As usual, Toby was as expressionless as a paving slab. He was whittling a stick with a penknife.

The paramedics loaded Jude into the ambulance. Rupert climbed onboard and sat down beside the stretcher. He rested a hand on Jude's chest as if feeling for a heartbeat.

"Shall I tell Mrs Chapman to meet you at the hospital?" the gardener asked in a choked-up voice.

Rupert's lips worked as if he was searching for an answer, but nothing came.

"Poor Mrs Chapman," Lily murmured, speaking more to herself than anyone else.

Suddenly, Rupert's gaze was fixed on her. His eyes burned with hatred. "You... you..." He managed to say only one word, but it was filled with enough malice to make Lily tremble. She let out a low breath of relief as a paramedic closed the rear doors.

Its siren blaring into life, the ambulance pulled away.

"Bob Cooper." The name scraped out like a knife being drawn across a whetstone.

Lily and Hazel turned to the old gardener.

"Bob Cooper," he repeated, leaning in so close that his tobacco breath made Lily wrinkle her nose. "That's my name and I'm not afraid who knows it."

"Why would you be?" Hazel asked.

Bob spread his dirt-ingrained hands as if to say, *You tell me.* He hawked and spat on the grass before jerking his chin in the ambulance's direction. "I've known that boy since he was in nappies."

"So?" Lily threw the word out like a challenge.

"So I suppose we'll see what we see." Bob nodded sagely as if his cryptic reply contained some pearl of wisdom. He doffed his flat-cap, then turned to approach his companions.

The three men exchanged hushed words. Carl let out a booming laugh that clashed against the solemn atmosphere, drawing curious glances from the police. Scowling at him, Bob clambered into the Land Rover. The brothers got in after him. Bob revved the engine into life and accelerated away sharply enough to chew up the lawn. Hazel and Lily shielded their eyes as the rear tyres spat chunks of turf at them.

Lily did a poor imitation of Bob's raspy voice. "*So I suppose we'll see what we see.* What does that even mean?"

Hazel heaved a sigh that suggested she'd rather not think about what it might mean. She suddenly struck her thigh with a clenched fist. "Why are they doing this to us?"

"Because they're sad little idiots with nothing better to do." Lily squinted skywards as a black speck glided over the garden. "Crows hold grudges, you know."

"Are you saying they were taking revenge? Do you really

173

think that's possible?"

Lily arched an eyebrow at her mum's sceptical tone. "If people can be reincarnated as crows, then surely just about anything's possible."

"Ok, point taken, but tell me this – how did they make Jude lie still while they pecked him to bits?"

Lily pictured Jude gobbling mandrake berries while spying on her. Another image took shape in her mind – him screaming as Tom forced the berries down his throat. "Maybe he fell over in the dark and knocked himself out."

Hazel mulled over the possibility. "I suppose it must have been something like that."

Lily uneasily watched a forensic team put on all-in-one plastic suits. What would happen if they found Tom's hair or fingerprints at the coven's meeting place? Would he be arrested? She might never see him again. Anxiety bubbled up inside her at the thought.

She silently repeated her mum's words, *Keep it together, Lily. Keep it together.*

Hazel prodded a foot at the wheel ruts left behind by the Land Rover. "Look what they've done to the lawn."

"That Bob Cooper gives me the creeps. I bet you he's Susan Cooper's husband or brother or something."

"He's probably her husband *and* her brother."

Lily narrowed her eyes at her mum, wondering whether she was joking. Hazel offered up a mirthless smile.

A woman whose slate grey hair matched her trouser suit approached them. "I'm Detective Sergeant Nicola Edwards. I'm afraid I'm going to need statements from both of you."

"We're happy to help in any way we can," said Hazel.

"I'm just hoping you can shed some light on how Jude

Chapman ended up like…" the sergeant faltered, seemingly at a loss for words to describe what she'd seen.

"I'm sorry, but I'm really not sure what we can tell you."

"How about we start with your surname? I understand you changed it recently."

"What's that got to do with this?" Lily asked with a guarded edge.

Sergeant Edwards focused her steady brown eyes on her. "Let me be the judge of what's relevant."

"Why don't we go inside?" Hazel suggested. "I could do with a cup of tea. Or something stronger."

The sergeant motioned for her to lead the way.

As they headed towards the cottage, Lily remarked to her mum, "Well changing our name was a total waste of time. We might as well go back to the old one."

"No." Hazel's voice had a ring of finality. "There's no going back."

24

L ily was dancing all night long. Dancing in robes. Dancing in the nude. Dancing around a bonfire. Dancing around Jude. Dancing hand-in-hand with her mum, with her dad, with Tom, with the coven. Round and round, faster and faster they went, like children playing Ring o' Roses. Dark forms slunk in and out of the firelight. Black dogs of every size and shape. Some of them walking upright. Crows provided the music, singing in human voices, "Peter, Peter pumpkin eater. Peter, Peter pumpkin eater…"

Moans mingled with the singing. Gasps, groans, whimpers, grunts, growls. The firelight flickered on a writhing mass. Limbs intertwining like vines. Bodies running together like melted wax. Dogs mounting people mounting dogs mounting people…

Laughing, slurping, begging, howling, sobbing, screaming…

On and on and on…

Lily awoke to the pale light of dawn with a bitter scum coating her tongue. She peeled herself off damp sheets and staggered to the bathroom. After rinsing the foul taste from her mouth, she stood under the shower for a long time, scrubbing herself as if she couldn't get clean. By the time she was done, her skin was sunburn-red.

She gathered her hair into a dripping pony tail and dabbed concealer on the dark smudges under her eyes.

"Lily," her mum called from the neighbouring room. Lily

went to her.

Hazel was lying in bed, shrouded by the patchwork quilt. She spoke through a yawn. "You're awake early. Did you have a bad night?"

"Uh-huh."

"Me too. I kept having nightmares about yesterday."

As Lily's own nightmares whispered through her mind, she was glad for the gloom that hid her queasily ashamed expression. "I don't think I'll ever be able to get Jude's face out of my head."

Her words were followed by a silence that seemed to fill the room. Hazel clapped as if to shoo it away. "You know the best way to take your mind off something horrible, don't you?"

"No."

"It's to eat pancakes. Lots of them."

A small smile found its way onto Lily's lips. "Is that scientifically proven?"

"Of course. Look it up if you don't believe me." Hazel flung off the quilt and swished open the curtains. "I'll do the pancake mix. You light the stove."

Lily watched her throw on a sweatshirt and shorts. "How can you have so much energy this early?"

Hazel swept a hand at the scene beyond the window. Lines of candyfloss clouds were splitting the sky. Dew glistened on the trees. Everything looked brand new. "How can you *not* have lots of energy when you live in such a beautiful place?"

Lily's eyes narrowed slightly. Was her mum putting on an act? Or was she in a state of denial? Did she really not see that living here was going to be practically impossible now?

Hazel gave Lily a peck on the cheek. "Nothing worth it is ever easy, Lily."

"Nothing's easy full stop," Lily muttered to herself, watching her mum head for the stairs. "Not if you're us."

Lily stared at the empty landing for a moment, then sighed and shook her head as if giving up on a puzzle. She returned to her bedroom and put on the first clothes that came to hand before going down to the kitchen.

Hazel was whisking milk, flour and eggs to a smooth batter. Lily opened the backdoor. The smell of cut grass still lingered outside. She drank it in like a tonic. She had to admit her mum was right – you couldn't help but feel energised by this place.

She scanned the trees and sky. The white-winged crow was nowhere to be seen. Indeed, there were no crows whatsoever. It was like they were keeping a low profile for fear of retribution from the Chapmans.

Lily set about chopping wood. It was a relief to focus solely on swinging the axe. She was almost disappointed when her mum called out of the door, "That's enough firewood." Hazel gave a smiling shake of her head. "I never thought I'd see you chopping wood so enthusiastically."

Yeah, well I never thought I'd see someone being eaten by crows, Lily bit down on the temptation to reply.

She filled a basket with firewood, carried it to the Rayburn, then went through the now familiar daily ritual of opening the chimney vent, emptying the ash pan and lighting the fire.

When the hotplates had heated up, Hazel poured the batter into a frying pan. She made a pot of coffee to go with the pancakes.

As Lily ate, her eyes kept straying towards the path to the coven's meeting place. Questions were running riot through her head. Was Jude still alive? Was he conscious? Had he spoken? *Could* he speak?

As if confessing a shameful secret, she murmured, "The crow brought Jude's tongue here."

Hazel didn't seem surprised. "What did you do with it?"

"I burnt it."

"You did the right thing."

"Did I?"

"Listen to me, Lily. We have nothing to feel bad about. That boy brought this upon himself."

Lily heaved a sigh. "I suppose so."

"Do you want another pancake?"

Lily frowned at the obvious attempt to change the subject.

"Don't give me that look, Lily. Would you rather I'd told Rupert about our crow friend?"

After only the briefest hesitation, Lily shook her head. Her gaze wandered back to the path.

Hazel rose to clear the table. "Are you going to sit there moping? Or are you going to help?"

Sighing again, Lily took her plate to the sink. "So much for the pancakes taking my mind off Jude."

"Well I know something that'll definitely do the trick – hard work. And luckily for you, there are plenty of jobs that need doing." Hazel ticked them off on her fingers. "There's gardening, sweeping, dusting. But for starters, you can do the washing up."

Lily let her mum know what she thought about the list of chores with a loud burp.

Hazel laughed. "It makes me so proud to see I raised such a lady."

When the crockery was sparkling on the drainer, Hazel pointed to the lines of grass cuttings the mower had left in its wake. "That needs raking up."

Lily fetched a rake from the shed and set to it. A trail of

flattened grass showed where the police had tramped back and forth. She vigorously raked it out of existence. She looked at the hole in the flowerbed. The police had shown no interest in the mandrakes. There was a tiny part of her that wished they had done. She hated keeping secrets. It made her feel paranoid. And she knew only too well how destructive paranoia could be.

As the image of Tom force-feeding Jude mandrake berries came to her again, she kicked soil into the hole. To hell with paranoia. For Tom, she would keep any secret. She chewed on her lower lip, both thrilled and troubled by her feelings.

By the time she was finished raking, the sun had swung around from behind Chapman Hill to the front of the cottage. She stopped dead in the act of scooping up a pile of cuttings. She stared at the front door for several rapid heartbeats, then jerked upright to hurry over to it.

A cross about a metre tall and half-a-metre wide had been gouged into the wood. Lily's mind flashed back to Toby Spencer whittling a stick to a sharp point. She cast a probing look at the trees as if afraid he might be lurking nearby, then shouted, "Mum!"

Hazel's worried face appeared at the kitchen window. "Is everything ok?"

Lily pointed at the door. "You tell me."

Hazel craned her neck to look at the crudely etched crucifix. A twitch in her cheek betrayed her struggle to keep her emotions under control. "No big deal. We can fix this easily enough with some sandpaper and varnish."

"Forget sandpaper and varnish. We need to call the police."

Hazel shook her head. "If we do that, *everything* will have to come out. Can you imagine if the local newspaper got hold of the story?"

Lily cringed at the thought of it. She could see the headline now – *Neighbours claim Killer Widow is a Witch*. "So what do we do? Wait until they get bored of carving crosses into doors and decide to carve them into us instead?"

"That's not going to happen." Hazel flicked a hand dismissively at the crucifix. "An empty threat. That's all that is."

"What if it's not?"

Hazel frowned, then her lips stretched into a thin smile. "Why don't we ask Susan Cooper what she thinks?"

"Is that a joke?"

Hazel raised an eyebrow as if to say, *What do you reckon?* She plucked her car keys from a hook on the wall.

"Where are you going?" Lily asked.

"I just told you – the general store. Are you coming?"

Lily trailed after her mum towards the car. "This is a bad idea."

"Is it? I don't know anywhere else around here that sells DIY products. And while we're in Midwood, we can pop into the butchers. I fancy lamb chops for dinner."

"Ok, now I *know* you're joking."

Hazel's smile climbed higher on one side. "Come on, let's go give the village something else to gossip about."

25

As the car turned onto the main road, Lily pressed a hand against her stomach. The swirling, churning sensation was back.

"Are you ok?" Hazel asked.

"My stomach's still not right."

"We'll get you something to settle it down."

Lily doubted whether the general store – or for that matter, any shop – sold anything that would settle her stomach.

Sunlight trickled through the trees. The trickle turned into a flood as the car reached the outskirts of Midwood. Lily eyed the wisteria-clad cottages. Something about their quaintness grated on her nerves.

"I'm starting to really dislike this place," she muttered. "It's just too… perfect."

Hazel chuckled, nodding to show that she knew what Lily meant. Her amusement shifted to concern as Lily exclaimed, "Stop the car."

"Are you going to be sick?"

"Just pull over, will you?"

Hazel braked in front of the square-towered church. Lily got out and approached a familiar figure splayed across the bench by the graveyard's entrance. Rolls of velvet-encased flesh bulged between the bench's slats. Hugo's hands were resting on the summit of his belly. He looked listlessly at Lily.

"Nice hair," he remarked with a sniff.

She lifted a hand to the white streak, suddenly aware that it was the first time she'd been out in public without her hat. The realisation made her feel strangely naked. "Have you heard about Jude Chapman?"

"No."

"Really?"

Hugo snuffled again at Lily's doubting tone. "Yes, really."

"For someone who spends their life spying on the village, you don't know much about what goes on around here."

The pointed remark didn't penetrate Hugo's indifference. "I don't spy. I simply watch." There was no rancour in his reply. It was a straightforward statement of fact. "And besides, the villagers rarely talk to me."

Lily snorted softly. "I wonder why?"

"Because I'm a witch."

Lily rolled her eyes at Hugo's lack of irony. She turned away, muttering under her breath, "More like because they think you're a joke."

"It's a rocky road, isn't it? Life, that is."

Lily stopped mid-step and narrowed her eyes at Hugo. Was he trying to get a rise out of her? His glistening little eyes gave no hint as to what was going on behind them. There was something infuriating about his big, bland face. She felt like slapping him just to provoke a reaction.

Compressing her lips against the impulse, she strode back to the car.

"What did you say to him?" Hazel asked.

"Nothing worth repeating." Lily exhaled an impatient breath. "Can we please just get to the shop? I don't want to spend a minute more than I have to in this boring village."

As the car accelerated away from the church, Hugo's parting remark pecked at Lily. "He thinks he's so clever. Well he can stick his words of wisdom up his fat ass."

"Hey, there's no need for–" Hazel started to admonish, but her voice died as she caught sight of Toby Spencer. The butcher was smoking a cigarette outside his shop. His white-and-blue striped apron was splotched with blood. In the neighbouring window, Susan Cooper was staring into space from behind the counter.

"She looks like she's dying of boredom," Hazel commented.

"We should be so lucky." Lily's voice was laced with acerbic amusement. "She's got to be related to that creep of a gardener. They both look like wrinkly old gnomes."

"Try not to annoy her. This is the only general store for miles around."

As they got out of the car, Toby scrutinised them with eyes as impenetrable as stones. Lily flashed him a big, overtly fake smile. "Hi, Mr Spencer."

Keeping his gaze fixed on her, Toby dropped his half-smoked cigarette and ground it out under his heel.

"And definitely don't antagonise that neanderthal," Hazel whispered out of the side of her mouth.

"You were the one going on about popping into the butchers."

"Yes well, I think we'll give that a miss."

The bell tinkled as Hazel entered the store. Susan lifted her chin from her hand and peered over the till.

"Morning," said Hazel.

"Morning." Susan's voice was flat. Aloof. Her eyes pursued Hazel and Lily along the aisles as if she suspected they were shoplifters.

At the feel of Susan's stare burning into her back, Lily started to lift a hand to her white streak again. With an annoyed shake of her head, she stopped herself. She reached out to grip a broom handle. "I'll break this over her head if she doesn't stop staring at us like that."

Disapproval and amusement mingled in Hazel's eyes. "The local paper would love that." She traced a headline in the air. "Suspected witch attacks shopkeeper with broomstick."

Lily couldn't help but chuckle at the thought of it.

Hazel perused the small selection of wood varnishes. She picked out the colour that best matched the front door. "It's not exactly the same, but it'll do for now."

She put the tin in a basket, along with a paint brush and sandpaper. They added bread, milk and stomach salts, then went to the till. Hazel summoned a polite smile.

Susan responded with a flick of her platinum-blonde hair. Avoiding eye contact, she scanned and bagged the basket's contents.

Hazel paid her. "Thanks. Bye."

"Bye. Have a nice day," Susan replied in an insincere monotone.

Pursing her lips, Hazel followed Lily to the door. She paused and turned to Susan. "Oh, I almost forgot." She held out a hand. "I thought you might want this back."

Susan looked bemusedly at Hazel's empty palm. "Erm... I don't see anything."

"Really? I'm amazed considering the size of it." Hazel flicked her wrist as if throwing a frisbee. "Here, catch. It's your nose. I found it in our business."

Susan's face reddened under her caked-on makeup. "I suppose you think that's funny, do you? And what about Jude Chapman? Do you think what happened to him is funny too?"

Hazel's voice was suddenly serious. "What I think is that certain people in this village should stay out of matters that don't concern them."

"And certain *other* people should learn where they're not wanted." Susan jabbed a long fingernail at Hazel. "Why don't you just go back to Fulham? Oh I know why – because you're not wanted there either."

The women eyeballed each other for a moment, then Hazel turned and marched to the car. She flung the shopping into the boot, slammed it shut and ducked into the driver's seat.

"Don't say a word," she warned Lily.

Lily put up her palms as if to say, *I'm not that daft.*

Hazel closed her eyes, drawing in a slow breath through her nostrils. Her eyelids sprang apart at a screech of tyres. A Range Rover jolted to a stop centimetres from the front bumper.

"Jesus," Lily gasped, pressing a hand to her pounding heart.

A nightmarish figure emerged from the Range Rover. Margaret was barely recognisable as the 'glowing' mother-to-be who'd called at the cottage. Except for her pregnant belly, the weight had melted off her as if she was stricken by some kind of wasting disease. Her maternity dress hung like a sack from her sharp shoulders. Her sallow skin seemed to be stretched to within a millimetre of breaking point over her high cheekbones. She staggered towards the car, hunched over as if she was carrying a breezeblock.

"Stay in the car," Hazel told Lily.

"Be careful," Lily cautioned as her mum got back out. "She looks crazy."

Keeping the door between herself and Margaret, Hazel demanded to know, "What do you think you're doing? You almost hit us."

"He's alive." Margaret's voice rasped out as if she'd been lost for days in a desert.

"Who's–" Hazel broke off, realising who Margaret meant. "Has he said anything?"

"Said anything?" A shrill laugh burst from Margaret's ashen lips. "The doctors think–" She faltered, her face contorting, her fingers digging deep into her belly. Her throat spasmed as if she was trying to keep down some vile medicine.

Hazel's nose wrinkled as Margaret spat out a mouthful of brown sludge.

Wiping a hand across her lips, Margaret continued, "They think Jude might be braindead."

"I'm sorry to hear that."

"Are you?" The words sounded more like an accusation than a question. Margaret moved a step closer.

Hazel raised a hand, palm outwards. "Look, Margaret, I don't know what you think–"

More laughter scraped from Margaret's throat. "I'll show you what I think."

"Watch out!" Lily yelled as Margaret lunged forwards.

Something glinted in Margaret's hand as she struck at Hazel's chest. Hazel recoiled, swatting Margaret's hand as if it was a wasp. Lily dived across the driver's seat and thrust the car door into Margaret.

The breath whistled from the heavily pregnant woman's lips. She doubled over, bracing a hand against the pavement.

"Mum, are you ok?" Lily asked anxiously.

Hazel peered down at an oval-shaped mole in her cleavage. A white scratch marred its smooth brown surface. "I think so."

With a grunt of effort, Margaret hauled herself upright. A strange, triumphant glee shone in her eyes as she raised her hand. A silver pin glinted between her thumb and forefinger.

Turning to the small crowd of onlookers that had gathered, she displayed the pin like it was evidence for a court. "You all saw what I did." Her eyes scanned back and forth as if seeking a friendly face. They landed on Susan. "I scratched her, but she doesn't bleed. Surely you know what this means?"

Susan rapidly made the sign of the cross on her chest. A couple of other onlookers followed suit.

"I know." Toby's baritone rumbled from his shop doorway.

"So do I," an almost identical voice seconded from behind Hazel. She twisted her head in Carl's direction. He was leaning against the rear end of the car as if to block any retreat. His usual smirk was playing on his lips.

Keeping an eye on the burly publican, Hazel started to duck into the car.

Margaret grabbed Hazel's arm, booming out like a fire-and-brimstone preacher, "Thou shalt not suffer a witch to live!"

"Let go of me!" Hazel demanded.

"I suggest you do as she says, Mrs Chapman," Carl advised, stepping forwards.

Margaret's knuckles paled. "Whosoever lieth with a beast shall surely be put to death."

"By the will of God, may it be so." Carl's voice dropped to a whisper meant only for Margaret and Hazel's ears. "But this isn't the time or place." He glanced at the crowd. "Some of these people are *outsiders*."

Margaret's eyes darted between him and Hazel, then she peeled her fingers away one by one.

Carl made a shooing motion at Hazel as if to say, *You can go now*. His smirk widened as anger flared in her eyes. The next instant, though, it was wiped off his face as Margaret swayed on her feet. He just barely had time to catch her as her legs gave way.

A collective gasp issued from the crowd. Hazel's mouth gaped in horror. Blood was soaking through the front of Margaret's skirt.

"Toby, give me a hand here," Carl shouted, struggling to keep her from slipping through his grasp like limp spaghetti.

His brother lumbered forwards. Between them, they lifted Margaret and carried her towards the butchers shop.

Hazel surveyed the gathered faces. Their expressions ranged from astonishment to concern. Several were regarding her with distinctly unfriendly eyes. She turned away from their stares to get into the car. It took a few attempts for her trembling hand to shift the gearstick into reverse. She did a U-turn and sped towards the forest.

"Mum, what just happened back there?" Lily sounded dazed. "Where was all that blood coming from?"

Hazel didn't reply. Her lips wobbled as if she was fighting back tears. A short distance beyond the edge of the village, she pulled over and rested her forehead on the steering-wheel.

Lily twisted around to make sure they weren't being pursued. The road was clear. "Do you..." She hesitated, almost too afraid to ask the question in her mind. "Do you think she was having a miscarriage?"

Hazel remained silent for a moment before answering grimly, "God help us if she was."

26

S weat coursed down Hazel's face as the sandpaper swished from side to side. The lower half of the crucifix had been rubbed out of existence. She wiped sawdust from her eyes.

"I shouldn't have pushed the door into her," said Lily, staring at the driveway.

"You were defending me."

"I know, but still..." Lily trailed off into pensive silence. At any moment, she expected Rupert Chapman to roll up in his Land Rover and get out with his shotgun in hand. "God, I hope the baby's ok."

Hazel's forehead furrowed as if she was thinking the same thing. She resumed sanding the door, going at it like she was up against a deadline.

Heaving a sigh, Lily looked at her phone. After tapping at the screen for a moment, she said, "It's called 'pricking'."

"What is?"

"What Mrs Chapman did to you." Lily read out the text on-screen. "Pricking involved scratching suspected witches with needles and pins. If a pricked mole or birthmark didn't bleed, it was proof that the accused had been suckled dry by the Devil."

"Oh well then, that proves beyond a doubt that I'm a witch."

Lily smiled faintly at the sardonic remark. Her lips contracted into a tense line as her gaze returned to the sandy driveway. "Do you think we should go away for a few days?"

"No." Hazel's tone was as immovable as Chapman Hill. "It's your birthday in two days and we're going to celebrate it right here."

"It's just a birthday. What does it matter where we are?"

"This is our home and no one's going to make us leave it. That's what you said and you were right." A bittersweet smile flickered on Hazel's lips. "Besides, it's not *just a birthday*. It's your sixteenth. Your coming-of-age."

"My coming-of-age for what?"

"Well, sixteen is the age of consent, which means you could start a family if you wanted to."

Lily pulled an appalled face. "We've already been through this. I told you, I don't–"

"I know, I know," Hazel broke in with a laugh. "I'm not saying you *should* start a family. And anyway, you kind of need a man for that."

"Oh really. I didn't know that." Lily's tone was dripping with sarcasm. "Can we change the conversation, please?"

"Fine by me, so long as I don't have to hear any more about the Chapmans."

Lily tried to think of something else to talk about, but all she could see in her mind's eye was Margaret bleeding as if she'd been 'pricked' by a thousand pins. She sighed, reflecting that at least Jude's mutilated face had been dislodged from the forefront of her mind.

"If you want something to do, go and make me a cup of tea," Hazel suggested.

Lily responded with a bow. "Your wish is my command, oh great and mighty magister."

"Magi-what?"

Lily imitated Hugo's pedantic, nasal voice. "In layman's terms, the magister is the head of a coven."

"Oh leave poor Hugo alone. Besides, didn't he say a magister is a man?"

Lily tapped at her phone again. "A female leader of a coven is called the magistra."

"Well this magistra is thirsty. So do as she says before she puts a spell on you."

Giving an unamused eye-roll, Lily headed for the kitchen. As she waited for the kettle to boil, she kept shooting uneasy glances out of the front window. When she returned to the hallway with a steaming mug, her mum was varnishing the door.

Hazel stepped back to cast an appraising eye over her handiwork. She gave a satisfied nod. "There, good as new."

"I'll be more interested to see what it looks like tomorrow morning," Lily said meaningfully.

Hazel's face set into a stubborn frown. "If they vandalise the door again, I'll fix it again. And I'll keep on fixing it for as long as needs be. We'll see who gets tired of this first."

Lily puffed her cheeks at the thought of waking morning after morning to find the cross carved anew. "I'm already tired of it."

"If it makes you feel better, I'll have an alarm fitted."

Lily scrunched her nose as if her mum had told a bad joke. "What good would an alarm do us without electricity?"

Not giving her mum a chance to reply, Lily turned and trudged to the living-room. She lay on the sofa, scanning the dog portraits, saying their names like a roll call. "Trickster, Midget, Roly, Sweetmeat, Lucky..." A lump formed in her throat when she came to Sam. He would have done a better job than any alarm. If he was here, no one would get near the cottage without him barking.

She scowled as her thoughts turned to the Chapmans again. "You got what you deserved," she muttered. She reprimanded herself with a sharp shake of her head. No, Jude didn't deserve to suffer so horrifically. And Margaret's baby deserved a chance to live. Closing her eyes, she repeated to herself like a prayer, "Please let it live. Please let it live."

"Please let what live?"

Lily's eyes snapped open. "Tom!"

The lanky, curly-haired boy entered the room, stooping to avoid banging his head on the doorframe. His smoky eyes peered down at Lily, magnified to owlish proportions by his glasses.

"How did you get in here?" she asked. "Did you speak to my mum?"

"Yes, we had a lovely chat."

Lily's stomach twisted with jealousy at the thought of her mum and Tom having a 'lovely chat'. "Really?"

Tom's lips curved into an impish smile. "No. I've never even met your mum."

Lily felt herself reddening. "That's not funny."

"Sorry. I couldn't resist."

She rose to look out of the window. The front garden was deserted. She hurried to the kitchen and spotted her mum pottering in the greenhouse.

Lily grabbed Tom's hand and pulled him towards the front door. She pointed to a clump of buddleias at the edge of the lawn. "Wait for me over there. And stay out of sight."

As fast as his shambling gait permitted, Tom headed for the bushes. Lily returned to the kitchen and called out of the backdoor, "I'm going for a walk. I won't be long."

Before her mum could respond, she closed the door and ran to the front garden.

"Psst," Tom hissed, poking his head through a cascade of butterfly-infested purple flowers.

This time, he took her hand and drew her into the trees. He led her to a nearby sun-splashed glade with a stream flowing through it. They sat silently on the grass, holding hands and watching reddish water bubble over iron-stained pebbles.

"You didn't answer my question," Tom said eventually. "What do you hope lives?"

As if she'd been caught doing something inappropriate, Lily withdrew her hand from his. The water suddenly reminded her of the blood soaking through Margaret's skirt. "Mrs Chapman's baby."

"Is there something wrong with it?"

Lily shrugged. She picked a daisy, threw it into the stream and watched it float away. "Mrs Chapman thinks my mum and me are witches."

Tom didn't seem surprised. "And are you?"

Lily frowned. "What sort of question's that?"

"It wouldn't bother me if you were."

Lily snorted as if the conversation was too ridiculous to continue.

Tom lay back and stared at the patchwork of blue shimmering through the trees. He lifted his malformed hand and moved its single finger as if drawing circles on the sky. Lily was struck by how perfect the finger was – long, straight, smooth. Watching it made her feel like she'd swallowed a mouthful of butterflies. Round and round floated the finger. The fluttering intensified. Round and round... So beautiful. So flawless. Round and round...

Lily suddenly couldn't restrain herself from seizing Tom's

hand and pulling it towards her. She closed her lips around his finger and sucked hungrily. A sweet-saltiness flooded her mouth. She let out a, "Mmm," as if it was the most delicious thing she'd ever tasted.

She released his finger and dived forwards to crash her lips into his. Her tongue probed its way into his mouth's warm, wet interior. A moan seeped from her as she pressed herself against his wiry frame. Her heart pounding wildly, she groped at his shorts. He took a firm hold of her hand and moved it away from his groin. She drew her head back, flushed with embarrassment. "What's wrong?"

"Nothing. It's just... well, you're underage."

"Underage?" Lily echoed. "Is this another joke? I'm sixteen in two days."

"So there's not long to wait."

Frustration flashed in Lily's eyes. *I don't want to wait,* she felt like yelling. *I want to know right now why sex is such a big deal.*

Turning her back on Tom, she tore up a handful of daisies and hurled them at the water.

"I'm sorry, Lily, I just want our first time to be..." Tom hesitated awkwardly before saying, "special."

Lily snorted. "Who says we'll have a 'first time'?" Her frustration gave way to a mischievous gleam. "I might just find someone else to be my first. That guy who runs the village pub was eyeing me up."

Tom's eyes swelled in outrage. "You mean Carl Spencer?"

"That's him. I bet he knows *exactly* what to do." Lily hugged herself as if imagining Carl's arms around her. "Oh Carl, Carl–"

"Stop that!" Tom grabbed a stick and sprang to his feet. "If that scumbag lays so much as a finger on you, I'll... I'll..." He whacked a tree trunk to illustrate what he'd do.

Lily gave an exaggerated flinch, then burst into laughter.

Tom frowned at her. "You're having me on?"

"Of course I am." Lily shuddered. "I'd rather die than let *him* touch me."

Tom plonked himself back down beside her, looking more relieved than anything else. They sat in silence again, close together, but not quite touching.

After a minute or two, Tom smiled as if he'd had a funny thought. "I know what I'm going to give you for your birthday."

Lily slid him a sidelong look. "Oh yeah, what's that?"

"I can't tell you that. It would ruin the surprise."

Lily suddenly sounded tired. "I think I'm done with surprises."

"Don't worry, you'll love this one. Trust me."

Lily's lips twisted into a smile that looked more like a grimace. "I'm not very good at trusting people."

"Me neither." Tom frowned at his malformed hand as if he suspected it of some treachery. "But I trust you."

"You don't know me. Not really."

"Yes I do."

"Ok, so what's my surname?"

Tom tilted his head like a quizzical dog. "Is that a trick question? It's Wylde."

"It is now, but it used to be–"

"I don't care what it used to be or why you changed it, just so long as we can be friends."

Tom's words were almost enough to bring tears to Lily's eyes. Marvelling at his knack for saying precisely what she needed to hear, she leaned in to kiss him on the cheek. "Alright, I'll trust you."

"Lily! Lily!"

She jumped up as her name rang through the forest. "That's my mum. I have to go."

Tom caught hold of her hand. "Two days."

The butterflies in Lily's stomach surged back to life as she looked into his tormentingly big eyes. "Two days," she repeated, then she pulled her hand free and ran towards the cottage.

27

For the third time in the space of an hour, Lily went around the ground floor checking the external doors were locked and peering out of the windows. There was no one to be seen in the pale light given off by the moonlit mandrakes. Nor was there anything to be heard from outside, except for the occasional hoot of an owl or eerily babylike cry of a fox.

A whirring, clicking noise drew Lily's gaze to the ceiling. She made her way up to her mum's bedroom.

Hazel stopped working the sewing machine's treadle and looked up from feeding fabric through the needle. "All perimeters secured?"

Lily frowned. "I don't understand why you're not freaking out."

"Because if this past year's taught me anything, it's that life's too short to worry about things I can't control. If I see a mob of pitchfork-wielding villagers heading our way, *then* I'll start freaking out."

Lily's gaze strayed to the window as if to make sure that no such mob was outside. "I wish I knew whether Mrs Chapman and her baby are ok."

Hazel surveyed the dark smudges under Lily's eyes. "Why don't you go to bed?"

"I don't feel like sleeping."

"What you mean is, you're too scared to sleep."

Lily threw her mum an indignant glance. "I'm not scared. I just think we should..." She shrugged. "I don't know, come up with a plan or something."

"A plan? We're not at war."

Lily raised an eyebrow as if to say, *Are you sure about that*? "Well we can't just do nothing."

"I'm not doing nothing. I'm making your birthday present."

Lily eyed the black material draped over the sewing machine table. "So that's your plan, is it?"

"My plan is to get on with my life and try to be happy."

"Or to put it another way, you're going to pretend nothing's wrong. Just like you did with dad." Lily regretted the words the instant they left her mouth. She added quickly, "Sorry, Mum, I shouldn't have said that."

Hazel sighed. "Don't apologise if you don't mean it, Lily."

"But I do mean it."

"Then stop bringing everything back to your dad. It's no good for either of us."

Lily remained silent as if faced with an impossible choice.

"I'd better get on with this if I'm going to finish it in time for your birthday," said Hazel. She refocused on the sewing machine and resumed pumping the treadle.

Lily watched her guide the fabric through the bobbing needle. "What are you making?"

"Ah, you'll have to wait and see."

Lily rolled her eyes. "Oh great, another surprise."

"Ouch!" Hazel snatched her hand away from the machine. A spot of blood glistened on her fingertip.

"So you do bleed when pricked."

A faint smile crossed Hazel's lips at the wry observation.

"Everyone bleeds, Lily." She sucked away the blood, then returned to her task. Lily looked on for a moment longer before leaving the room.

"Bed. Sleep. Do you hear me?" Hazel called after her.

Lily stared down the stairs, fighting a compulsion to check the doors yet again. With a wrench of her shoulders, she turned to go into the bathroom. She scrutinised herself in the mirror. A few pale spots were splotched around her mouth. She prodded them. They felt warm to the touch. What were they? An allergic reaction?

She frowned as another possibility occurred to her – could they have been caused by kissing Tom? Maybe she'd caught something from him.

She scrupulously cleansed her face, then went to her bedroom and looked out of the window. Not a whisper of wind stirred the trees. It was as if the forest was frozen in anticipation of... Of what?

She lit a candle and lay down, but didn't close her eyes. Her body was so tense that she could barely feel the mattress beneath her. The sewing machine droned on and on, playing a relentless, hypnotic tune.

Whirr, click, whirr, click...

Her eyelids grew heavy. They bobbed up and down like the machine's needle for a while, then stayed down.

At once, she found herself back in the forest glade with Tom. The stream was as dark as menstrual blood. Tom was lying naked on the grass, coated from head-to-toe in red as if he'd bathed in the water.

Revulsion and desire burned through Lily. There was something deliciously disgusting about the thought of running her tongue over his glistening skin. As she approached him, he raised a hand, palm outwards.

"Two days," he said flatly.

Her eyes snapped open. An echo of Tom's voice seemed to follow her out of sleep.

Two days. Two days...

She sat up woozily. The candle had burned out. The cottage was wrapped in silence. She stiffened suddenly, ears straining. Her heart skipped a beat at the sound of a low rasp like a knife scraping across wood.

Trembling with equal measures of anger and fear, Lily groped for her phone and turned on its torch. "We'll see what the police have to say when I send them a photo of you idiots."

She tiptoed down the stairs, wincing at every creak. A faint sooty smell tickled her nostrils as she entered the living room. She peeked between the curtains. Her forehead puckered. The window was off the latch. Had Mum left it like that? How could she be so careless?

After quickly dropping the latch back into place, she craned her neck to peer at the front door. There was no one to be seen. She wasn't sure whether to be relieved or disappointed.

She slunk to the front door. As warily as a rabbit emerging from its burrow, she poked her head outside. The cool night air caressed her skin as she ran her fingers across the door's exterior. The varnish was intact. So what had made the scratching sounds?

Her heart lurched at a strangled cry from upstairs. She ran to her mum's bedroom, half-expecting to find her fighting off Rupert or one of his goons.

Hazel was flailing around on the bed as if she was, indeed, being assaulted, but there was nobody else in the room. Her eyes were shut and her jaw hung slack. Crying out again, she clawed at her stomach as if trying to tear it open.

Lily grabbed her mum's wrists and pinned them to the

mattress. "Mum, wake up!"

Hazel's eyelids fluttered apart. "Wha... what's going on?"

"You were having a nightmare."

"My stomach's killing me. Get–" Hazel clenched her teeth as a spasm shook her. "Get me some paracetamol, will you?"

Lily hurriedly fetched the tablets from the bathroom cabinet. Hazel held out a clammy palm for them. "I must be coming down with whatever you've had." She rocked forwards, her breath whistling between her lips. "Christ, this reminds me of going into labour."

"Do you want me to call a doctor?"

"No. I'll be fine when the tablets kick in." Hazel wafted a hand towards the door. "Go back to bed."

Lily stared at her mum's pained face, debating whether to tell her about the scratching. She quickly decided against doing so. Her mum didn't need anything else to stress over. Lily started to turn to away, but paused as an afterthought struck her. "Did you open the living room window after I went to bed?"

"No. Why?"

"It was off the latch. Oh well, I must have left it like that." Lily's tone was casual, but inside she was as tight as a racquet string. All the downstairs windows had been properly closed. She was certain of it. "Just shout if you need anything."

Hazel mustered a grimacing smile. "I will."

Lily went to the top of the stairs. She peered down into the darkness, working up her courage. All her senses on red alert, she crept to the living room for a closer look at the window frame. She drew in a soft gasp. The wood was dented and chipped as if the window had been forced open.

She swept her phone's torchlight around the room. No one was lurking in the shadows. Striving to breathe as quietly as possible, she padded through to the kitchen. It was empty too. Her gaze came to rest on the pantry door. As she edged towards it, she caught a muffled sob from overhead.

She raced upstairs again. Her mum was doubled over with a corner of the patchwork quilt stuffed into her mouth.

Hazel's jaw muscles bulged as she bit down on the quilt. Sweat was pouring from her, pasting her long black hair to her face.

Lily touched her mum's forehead. "Oh my god, Mum, you feel like you're on fire. You need a doctor."

Hazel shook her head, twisting her hands into her hair like she was wringing out a dishcloth. She spat out the quilt. Stretching her mouth as wide open as it would go, she shoved her fingers down her throat as if trying to make herself vomit.

"What are you doing?" Lily exclaimed. "Stop it! You'll hurt yourself."

Hazel pushed her fingers deeper. Lily yanked at the halfway inserted hand. Hazel's other hand shot out like a piston into Lily's chest. Lily staggered backwards, tripping over her own feet and falling. Sparks flashed in her vision as her head thudded into the wall.

Gagging soundlessly, Hazel pulled a stringy, hairball-like thing out of her mouth. Flinging it aside, she clambered off the bed and frantically examined Lily's head.

Lily cringed away from her mum's slimy fingers. "I'm fine."

With a sob of relief, Hazel slumped back against the bed. "I'm so sorry, Lily. I didn't mean to push you over. You believe me, don't you?"

Lily's mind was suddenly back in Fulham, back in the moment of finding out her dad was dead.

I had to do it, Lily. He was going to kill me. Look at me, Lily. Tell me you believe me. Tell me, Lily. Please, tell me. Please, please...

Just like when her mum made that desperate plea, Lily answered with a subdued, "I believe you." Her gaze fell away from the uncomfortably familiar gratitude in her mum's eyes to the black, hairball-like thing. Her forehead creased. "Have you been eating your hair?"

"What? No, of course–" Another spasm stole Hazel's voice. "Oh god, it's starting again. Help me to the bathroom."

Leaning heavily on Lily, Hazel staggered to the bathroom. She sank to her knees in front of the toilet.

Lily looked apprehensively at her mum's green-tinged face. "What if you've been poisoned? What if there was something on that needle Mrs Chapman scratched you with?"

"Don't be silly."

"That woman's nuts. Who knows what she's capable of? And there are poisonous plants around here. Our garden's full of them."

"You mean Emily's purple flowers?"

"They're mandrakes."

Hazel's lips twitched into a smile. "I should've known they were something like that. How did you find–"

"*Shh,*" Lily interrupted. She tilted her head like a listening dog. "Do you hear that?"

"Hear what?"

"That scratching."

Hazel listened for a moment. "Yes, I hear it. It's coming from downstairs. It sounds like mice."

With an unconvinced, "Hmm," Lily padded to the landing.

"Wait, Lily. Maybe you shouldn't go down there. What if it's *them?*" The way Hazel hissed out the last word made it clear who she meant.

"Then I'm going to catch them at it."

"And do what?"

Lily tapped her phone's camera lens meaningfully before pressing a finger to her lips. Hazel tried to stand, but crumpled to the floor once again.

As Lily crept downstairs, her heart pounded so loudly that she feared it would reveal her presence. Upon reaching the hallway, she turned her head this way and that, trying to locate the scratching sound. It was like some creature was burrowing under the house.

She entered the kitchen. The scratching got louder as she neared the rear window. She parted the curtains a finger's width. At first, she saw nothing. Then her eyes picked out a vague black form at the foot of the door.

Doubting Tom.

The name tingled through her mind. She switched on her phone's torch. The three-legged dog was scrabbling at the door with its hind legs. Twisting its head, it squinted up at her. Its eyes were almost completely crusted over with reddish discharge. It was skinnier than ever. The knuckles of its spine jutted out like saw teeth.

A jolt of pity ran through Lily. Forgetting her caution, she went into the pantry. One final can of dog food remained. She peeled off its lid and emptied its contents into a bowl.

She cracked open the backdoor just enough to allow entry to the dog's snuffling nose. "You'd better be good," she warned. "Or I won't feed you again."

Drool streamed between the dog's chipped teeth as Lily set down the bowl. She opened the door wider. The dog made as if to thrust its nose into the bowl, but then its skin-and-bone body was sliding past her bare legs. She shrank away from its coarse fur. "Hey, get back here."

Ignoring her, the dog hobbled into the hallway. She hurried after it, wrinkling her nose at the pungent, mouldy aroma left in its wake. It shambled to the living room fireplace and prodded its nose at the logs.

"Stop that," Lily snapped as, jerking its head up and down, the dog flicked a log out of the grate.

A hoarse shout came from above. "What's going on down there?"

"I just dropped something, that's all," Lily called back.

The dog rolled its eyes at the ceiling.

"That's my mum," Lily told it. "If she comes down here, you'll be in big trouble."

The dog unconcernedly resumed gouging its nose into the contents of the grate. Lily expelled an exasperated breath as a mini-landslide of coal and kindling spilled onto the hearth rug. The dog bit into a layer of screwed up newspaper, ragging it loose and flinging it all over. Seemingly exhausted by its efforts, it tottered backwards and sank to the floor.

"Look at the mess you've made," Lily sighed, picking lumps of coal off the rug. A gleam in the hearth caught her eye. She leaned in to investigate what it was. A teardrop-shaped glass bottle was lodged beneath the grate. She wiggled it free and turned it in the torchlight. A cluster of pins and a black ball of something were steeping in urine coloured liquid. She showed the bottle to the dog. "Were you looking for this?"

Flattening its torn ears against its face, the dog shuffled away from her on its belly.

The bottle's stubby neck was sealed with a protruding cork. Lily twisted at it. There was a squeak as it began to loosen, then it shot through her fingers like a champagne cork and ricocheted off the ceiling. She reeled backwards, squeezing her eyes shut as the bottle exploded. A hail of glass and pins pelted her face. Her breath whistled through her teeth as she hit the floor.

The dog scuttled to her side and licked her face with its sandpapery tongue. She almost retched at its rotten-egg breath.

Feet thundered down the stairs. "Lily!" Hazel cried out as she ran into the room. She pulled up at the sight of the dog, then waved her arms. "Get away from her!"

The dog obligingly limped to the other end of the room and dropped onto its haunches.

Hazel squatted down at Lily's side. "What happened? Oh my god, are those pins in your face?"

Lily felt at her cheeks. She winced as her fingers brushed against a pin embedded like shrapnel dangerously close to one of her eyes.

"Stay still," Hazel urged. She set about carefully extracting half-a-dozen pins and splinters of glass from Lily's face. Then she grabbed a cloth from the kitchen to clean the shallow wounds. "What's this yellow stuff that's all over you?"

"It came from the bottle."

"What bottle?"

"The one that went off like a bomb in my face. It was hidden in the fireplace."

"You're lucky you weren't blinded. How did you even find it?"

"I didn't." Lily glanced at the dog. "He did. I think it was a witch ball."

"A what?"

"They're supposed to protect you from spells. Huge-O sells them on his website."

"Oh yes, I remember. But how on earth did it end up in the fireplace?"

Lily's gaze returned to the dog. "Maybe you should ask him."

Hazel eyed the mangy-looking animal. "And just who is your new friend?"

"He's been coming around for the last few nights. I fed him what was left of Sam's food."

"He's in an even sorrier state than Sam was when we found him."

As if to illustrate Hazel's words, the dog darted out his tongue to lick away the discharge that was seeping from his eyes.

Lily noticed the little black ball on the floor nearby. She prodded it. "What does this remind you of?"

Hazel picked it up and separated it into glistening strands. "Was this in the bottle?"

"Uh-huh. I bet one of those idiots snook into the house and took it from your hairbrush." Lily shook her head. "It's ironic, isn't it? Mrs Chapman thinks we're witches, but she's the one using magic."

"This isn't magic. It's nothing but a load of superstitious nonsense."

Lily gave her mum an appraising look. "How are you feeling?"

Hazel thought for a moment. "Now that you ask, I feel a lot better. But that's just a…" She lapsed into uncertain silence.

"Just a what? A coincidence?" Lily jerked her chin at the dog. "And is it a coincidence that, as soon as you got ill, he turned up and led me to the bottle?"

"What are you saying? That he's my guardian angel or something?"

Lily's blood-flecked brow wrinkled. "Or something… So now will you call the police?"

"And tell them what exactly?"

"That someone broke in and…" Lily trailed off, finishing the sentence in her head – *and put a bottle in our fireplace.* She stifled a laugh at the ludicrousness of it.

Hazel motioned to the dog. "Anyway, why would we need the police when we've got our new guard dog here to protect us?"

"Guard dog? Are you kidding? He can barely walk."

Hazel spoke directly to the dog. "You can bark and scare people away, can't you, old feller? I wonder what your name is?"

"Don't you know?" Lily's tone suggested the answer was obvious.

Hazel threw her a quizzical glance. Something beyond Lily's shoulder drew her eyes. She stared at a faded portrait of a tatty-eared hound. Her gaze shifted to the three-legged dog, then back to the portrait. She opened her mouth and snapped it shut as if reluctant to say what she was thinking.

"Try it," Lily suggested, seemingly reading her mum's mind.

"Have you tried it?"

Lily let slip a nervous laugh. "God no."

Hazel looked at the dog. It stared back as if awaiting a command. Her lips parted slowly, but then the words came out like they'd been yanked from her. "Doubting Tom?"

For a few seconds, the dog didn't respond. Then, with arthritic slowness, it rose and tottered towards Hazel. She exchanged a wide-eyed look with Lily before repeating in a hushed tone, "Doubting Tom?"

The dog's whip-thin tail stiffened, arching over its back.

Her voice barely audible, Hazel murmured one more time, "Doubting Tom?"

The dog ambled past her. Hazel and Lily followed it into the kitchen. It stopped by the backdoor and lowered its head to lick the jelly off the dog food.

"Poor thing," said Hazel. "It can't eat properly with all those broken teeth."

She fetched a fork from a drawer. The dog emitted a low growl as she reached towards its food.

"I'm just going to mash it up for you," she told it.

Her soft tone soothed the animal into silence. It lifted its head to allow her to mash the chunks of meat. "There you go." She straightened and stepped away from the bowl.

The dog set about gobbling up every last morsel. It gave Lily a hopeful look. She spread her hands. "Sorry, that was the last can."

As if it understood, the dog turned to hop out of the backdoor. Lily and Hazel watched it hobble away into the darkness.

Lily lowered her voice as if she didn't want anyone to overhear. "So what do you think?"

"About what?"

"Is it *you-know-who?*"

Hazel remained tellingly silent. She stooped to take a handful of cloths from a drawer. "We'd better get that mess cleaned up."

"Don't change the subject."

"What do you want me to say? I don't have an answer for you. At least, not one that makes any sense." Hazel headed for the living room. "Bring the dustpan and brush."

Lily's gaze returned to the garden. "Thank you, whatever your name is," she called into the echoing night before closing and locking the door.

28

L ily sat yawning at the kitchen table. Her wet hair was dripping on the flagstones. Even after a long shower and several black coffees, she was still fuzzy-headed.

Hazel came into the kitchen looking as fresh as the morning sky. "Considering the hellish night we had, I feel surprisingly ok."

"Lucky you," Lily muttered. "I feel half-dead."

"You should get yourself outside. Look at the trees. Listen to the birds. Let the forest work its magic."

Lily exhaled sharply. "I don't want *magic*. I just want to eat my breakfast and look at rubbish on my phone and... and... I want to be left alone! Why can't the Chapmans just leave us alone?"

"I'm sure they will do once they realise we're not going to simply give up and run away." Hazel gave Lily a look that was part-apology, part-appeal. "But until then, we need to sit tight and keep our heads down. Can you do that for me, Lily?"

Lily sucked in her lips and chewed the request over briefly before giving a less-than-enthusiastic nod.

Hazel rubbed Lily's shoulder. "We'll get through this together. Just like we always do." Her nostrils flaring, she cast a frustrated glance at the living room. They'd cleaned every inch of the room, scrubbing the floor, furniture, walls and even the ceiling, but a faint smell like old wee lingered. "Come on, let's go for a walk. We could both do with some fresh air."

They headed out of the front door. As they entered the shadow-strewn forest, Lily's gaze darted around. She half expected the Chapmans to ambush them from behind a tree.

She frowned, irritated by her own nervousness. "Did you know that tomorrow it will be three-hundred-and-thirty-three years since Mary's death?"

"No."

"*Three-hundred-and-thirty-three years*," Lily emphasised, glaring in the direction of Chapman Hall. "That's how long they've been persecuting us."

"'Us'? What do you mean by 'us'?"

Lily shrugged, lowering her gaze and kicking at fallen leaves. The wind rose suddenly, hissing in the treetops.

"The forest sounds angry," said Hazel.

Lily let out a little snort. "Maybe the trees don't like the Chapmans either."

"Can we please stop talking about the Chapmans?" Hazel spread her arms. "Let's just enjoy where we are."

Lily's eyes probed the surrounding trees. "How am I supposed to enjoy it when they could be watching us right now?" Her lips curled resentfully. "God, I hate them for making me feel this way. Perhaps we *should* become witches. We could do a deal with the Devil and have him scare them away."

"They're already scared of us."

"Yeah, well they're obviously not scared enough. We need to make them so terrified they won't dare mess with us."

Hazel gave a sceptical shake of her head. "Fear can make people do terrible things."

Lily knew from the haunted look in her mum's eyes what she was referring to. "You mean dad?"

Hazel was silent for a moment before answering, "Your dad

was so scared of being alone that he drove me to leave him. He made his worst fear come true. And so will the Chapmans, if we let them." Her shoulders sagged as if the conversation had sapped her energy. "We've walked far enough. Let's go back."

They retraced their steps in silence, together but alone with their thoughts.

Hazel's nostrils flared as she entered the kitchen. "It smells like something died in here." She stalked around the ground floor, flinging open every window. "I know what'll get rid of it." She rifled through the kitchen cupboards for a pair of round cake tins and a mixing bowl. "Nothing smells better than a cake in the oven. I'm going to make a chocolate birthday cake and tomorrow we're going to stuff our faces until we're as fat as Hugo."

Lily chuckled. "It would have to be the biggest cake in the entire world."

Hazel fetched eggs, flour and sugar from the pantry, along with a dusty bottle labelled 'Gooseberry wine'. She uncorked the bottle, filled two wine glasses and gave one to Lily.

Lily eyed the amber liquid dubiously. Its colour reminded her of the whisky her dad had swilled back by the bucketful.

"Don't worry," Hazel said with a perceptive smile. "One glass won't do you any harm."

Lily took a tentative sip. The sweet liquid slid down her throat and immediately set to work on unknotting her stomach. "Wow, this is actually nice."

She kept raising her glass to her lips as she watched her mum whisking together the ingredients. Before she knew it, the glass was empty. "Can I have more?"

Hazel poured her another glass. "Don't drink this one so fast."

Lily waited for her mum to turn away, then took a greedy

gulp. A pleasant sense of disconnection settled over her. A floaty feeling of being outside her own body. It reminded her of dreaming about flying up Chapman Hill and looking down on the intertwined figures. The wine's warmth seemed to pool in her groin.

Two days, Tom whispered in her ear.

"One day," she corrected him.

Hazel turned to her. "What did you say?"

Lily blinked out of her daydream. Heat rose into her face. "Nothing."

Hazel glanced at Lily's empty glass. "That's your last one for today. We don't want you hungover for your birthday party."

"What birthday party? I'd hardly call the two of us eating cake a party."

"You can invite your friend Tom, if you want."

At the mention of his name, a luridly vivid image of him thrusting between her thighs overwhelmed Lily's consciousness. Fresh waves of heat flowed through her. She lowered her eyes as if to conceal her thoughts. "I feel dizzy. I'm going to lie down."

Hazel stepped forwards to cup Lily's face with floury hands. "I just want your birthday to be special. I know it's a cliché, but I really do want it to be the first day of the rest of your life. Tomorrow is for letting go of the past and being happy again."

A slanted smile tugged at Lily's lips. "And they all lived happily ever after."

"Why not? Why can't we have the fairytale ending?"

"Because they don't exist."

Hazel smiled too, cocking her head as if to say, *We'll see about that.*

How can you be so naïve? The question sprang up in Lily's

mind, but she didn't ask it out loud. She yearned to be alone with her fantasies of Tom. She drew away from her mum, went upstairs and flopped onto her bed. A warm breeze whispered through the open window.

Shh, shh, shh, murmured the trees.

Were they talking to each other? Maybe the forest spirits were trying to soothe her off to sleep. A smile played on her face, then faded as she repeated quietly, "They don't exist."

29

A familiar *whirr, click, whirr, click* roused Lily from sleep. The room was shrouded in hazy, violet light. She winced as she sat up. She had a pounding headache and a parched mouth. Was this a hangover? No wonder Dad used to be so grumpy in the mornings.

"Dad," she murmured. Without warning, a flood of grief washed over her. "I miss you so much."

She didn't mean the stranger who'd met such an awful end. She meant the man who'd read her bedtime stories, taught her to ride a bike, helped with her homework, hugged her, kissed her, teased her, encouraged her...

She would have given anything to have *that* man back.

Lily buried her face in a pillow to stifle her sobs. Gradually, they subsided. She rose and headed to the bathroom. The landing was suffused with the aroma of baking. Candlelight slunk under her mum's bedroom door. At the sink, she swilled down painkillers and splashed cold water on her puffy eyes.

When will it stop? she asked herself in the mirror. *When will the pain go away?*

She looked at the stripe of white hair. In an instant, her grief curdled into hate. She snatched up a soap dish and hit the mirror, splintering her reflection into a kaleidoscope of distorted images.

She retreated a step. The face in the mirror didn't belong to her anymore. Someone else was looking at her from the other side of the cracked glass. Someone so ugly it made her feel sick. She whirled around as her mum entered the bathroom.

Hazel frowned as she saw the broken mirror. "How did that happen?"

"I... I..." Lily stammered. Avoiding her mum's gaze, she dodged past her and ran downstairs. A cake coated in chocolate gleamed under a glass dome on the kitchen table. Her stomach grumbled, but not with hunger. A cloying, sickeningly sweet scent permeated the air. She clutched her stomach with one hand, bracing the other against the table.

"What is it, Lily? What's wrong?" her mum asked, coming up behind her. "Have you still not shaken off your stomach bug?"

"It's not a stomach bug." Lily spoke through a swallow. She swept a hand at the room. "I think it's this place. Something in the air or the water or... or... I don't know what, but it's making us ill."

Hazel wrinkled her forehead doubtfully. "The air here's the cleanest we've ever breathed. And as for the water, I had the old lead pipes replaced with copper ones."

"Well there's something," Lily insisted. She cast her eyes around as if searching for what that 'something' might be. "Maybe it's the mandrakes."

"I don't see how it could be, but if they bother you that much I'll get rid of them. In fact, I'll do it right now." Hazel started towards the backdoor.

"No!" Lily stepped in front of her. "It's dangerous to dig–" She cut herself off, realising how ridiculous her next words would sound. Uprooted mandrakes could no more kill with a scream than witches could with spells.

"Don't worry, I'll wear gloves. I'm well aware the roots are poisonous."

"It's not just that." Lily looked out of the window. A crescent moon was dangling crookedly in the darkening sky. Its perfect curve made her think of Dead Woman's Ditch. Only a few hours from now, it would be the anniversary of Mary's death. And what better way was there to mark that anniversary than by burning another witch or two? "What if *they're* out there?"

"There's no one out there, Lily."

"They're going to come after us. I know it."

Hazel's voice softened reassuringly. "No one's coming after us. And if they are crazy enough to try anything, I'll call the police."

"We're miles from the nearest police station. By the time the police get here, those psychos could have burned us at the stake."

"Now you're just being melodramatic."

"No I'm not. Mrs Chapman wants us dead. You know I'm right. Nothing would make her happier than seeing us burn." Lily imagined what such a death would be like – the crackle of rising flames, the stink of burning hair, the sizzle of cooking flesh. "Oh god, I think I'm going to be sick."

"Come on, let's get you to the bathroom."

As her mum ushered her upstairs, Lily said, "I don't want to be here anymore."

"We've already talked about this, Lily. Blackmoss Cottage is our home now." Hazel's tone was gentle but resolute.

"*Blackmoss.*" Lily's eyes widened as if something had occurred to her. She veered towards her mum's bedroom.

"Hey, I don't want you going in there right now."

Ignoring her mum, Lily skirted around the bed and lifted the framed moss pressings from the chimney breast. "What if it's this that's making us ill?"

Hazel positioned herself between Lily and the sewing machine. "Moss is harmless."

"Is it? This stuff's already growing back on the roof. What if it gives off spores or something?"

"Well it didn't stop Emily from living to a ripe old age. Give me that."

Hazel took hold of the frame, but Lily didn't let go. They stood locked in a brief tug-of-war, then Hazel lost her grip. The frame clattered against the cast-iron fireplace, coming apart at the corners.

Hazel expelled a sharp breath. "You're really testing my patience, Lily."

Lily lowered her eyes contritely. She squinted at the frame. "Hey look, there's something sticking out of this." She pulled a rolled-up piece of yellowish-brown material from the hollow frame. It crackled like old leather as she unfurled it. Concentric circles of black writing surrounded a drawing of a horned dog and a stick figure with leaves sprouting from its head. A snake was coiled around the dog's neck and the figure's legs. A crescent moon smiled down at the bizarre trio.

Lily rotated the sheet, reading out the spidery writing. "White Breath. When the Moon is but a few days old, take a root of the mandragora out of the ground. Dry it by the fire, make thereof a powder and mix in a pinch of powdered Witch's Moss. Blow this into the nostrils with the quill of a white crow that has been wetted with blood from the severed left leg of a black dog. This will cause man or woman to do your bidding even unto death."

Hazel leaned in to read the passage for herself.

"You realise what this means, don't you?" said Lily. "Mary *was* a witch."

"Assuming she wrote this."

"It looks old enough."

Hazel rubbed the sheet with her thumb. "This isn't paper. It feels more like... skin."

A shudder ran through Lily. "What type of skin?"

"Well I doubt it's human."

"Perhaps it's pig skin. Mary's husband kept pigs."

Hazel traced a finger over the simplistic drawing. "I wonder what this symbolises."

Lily's big brown eyes travelled around the room. "*I wonder* if any more spells are hidden around here."

As Lily's gaze neared the sewing machine, Hazel shooed her towards the door. "Come on. Out. I told you, I don't want you in here."

Lily homed in on the 'Hear no evil. See no evil. Speak no evil.' tapestry.

"Don't you dare damage that," Hazel warned as Lily set about examining it.

Lily probed at the tightly woven fibres, tugging on any loose threads. She clicked her tongue disappointedly. "There's nothing here." She frowned in thought, then exclaimed, "The dog paintings. You could hide a whole spell book in them."

With Hazel close behind, Lily raced to the living room. "Which one first?" she wondered, scanning the portraits. "Trickster, King, Lucky..." She lingered on a wiry terrier with pointed ears and a stubby tail. "Lovelee." She separated the name into two syllables as if testing how they sounded. "Love Lee."

"Some of these paintings are hundreds of years old," said Hazel. "I won't have you pulling them apart."

"I promise I'll be careful. Please, Mum, it'll take my mind off feeling sick and... and everything else."

Hazel sighed, knowing she was fighting a losing battle. "I want the paintings put back exactly where they came from. Do you hear me?"

Lily nodded. She removed Lovelee's portrait from its hook. The canvas was sealed in by a backing board edged with brown tape. She peeled away a loose strip of tape, revealing several lines of faint writing. She let out a triumphant hiss. "Listen to this." Running a finger beneath the writing, she read out, "Lovelee's Liquor. Take a lock of the desired party's hair and put it in wine. Let it steep three days and three nights. Draw blood from your ring finger and put three drops in the wine. Also put in nine drops of the juice of the mandragora berry. Stir well then strain out the hair. Introduce a little of the liquor into the drink of the desired party. From this day on and for as long as you will it, they shall love you above all else."

"A love potion," Hazel stated the obvious. "I might try that one. If there are any men around here worth having, that is."

"This isn't funny, Mum. The Chapmans were right all along." Lily grimaced as if it pained her to say it.

Hazel tapped the recipe for 'Lovelee's Liquor'. "When was this written?"

Lily turned the painting over to look at its bronze plaque. "1821."

"No. That's when the painting was done. For all we know, this writing might only be hours old. It could be the work of the same person who put the bottle in the fireplace."

"Why would they do that?"

Hazel shrugged. "Maybe they're trying to set us up."

An uneasy silence stretched away from her words. Lily flinched as her phone vibrated. She snatched it out of her jeans back pocket. A number she didn't recognise flashed up.

"Who is it?" Hazel asked.

"I don't know." Lily put the phone to her ear. "Hello?"

"They're coming," said a nasal voice.

Lily's heart jumped. "Who's coming?"

The caller sniffed as if trying to smell her through the phone. "Don't be scared, Lily. Gil won't let them hurt you."

"Gil? Who's Gil?"

"He's one of us."

"Hugo? Is that you?"

There was no reply. The caller had hung up. Her eyes swirling with doubt and dread, Lily looked at her mum.

"Is someone coming here?" Hazel asked.

"That's what he said."

Hazel frowned. "Are you sure it was Hugo? Could it have been a wrong number?"

"It wasn't a wrong number. I think it was a warning."

"A warning?" Hazel echoed, turning towards the window at the murmur of an engine.

Lily darted across the room and cupped her eyes against the pane. The twilight had deepened to semidarkness. The forest was as still as a painting.

"See anything?" Hazel asked.

"No." With a quick intake of breath, Lily corrected herself, "Yes. Headlights."

Ice-white halogen beams cut through the gloom. The engine noise grew louder. "That sounds like more than one vehicle," said Hazel, joining Lily at the window.

Light flooded the garden as a 4x4 pulled into view. It was closely followed by another. Then another.

Lily turned to her mum with eyes like big, black pools. "Call the police!"

Hazel was already taking out her phone. She dialled and pressed it to her ear. "I need the police." A breathless edge betrayed her anxiety. "There are intruders on my property."

30

At the clunk of car doors closing, Lily's attention snapped back to the window. Although the engines had fallen silent, the headlights were still shining. Two figures were silhouetted in front of the foremost vehicle. Lily couldn't see their faces, but she recognised the dishevelled outline of Margaret's hair.

Five more figures joined them. The hulking profiles of the Spencer brothers were unmistakable. As too were Bob Cooper's bandy legs. Margaret marched forwards with one hand thrust out in front of her. A black book was clutched in her bony fingers.

As the others followed, their faces took shape. Lily wasn't surprised to see Rupert alongside Bob. Toby and Carl strode in lockstep behind them. Bringing up the rear were Susan and a bald, beanpole of a man dressed like an undertaker.

Lily's stomach shrivelled as she looked into Margaret's eyes. They burned with a righteous fury hot enough to consume everything in its path.

Lily ducked out of sight, pulling her mum down alongside her. "Oh God, they're coming for us! What do we do?"

"The police..." Panic threatened to snatch away Hazel's voice. She fought to keep her composure. "The police are on their way."

"Hazel and Lily Wylde!" Margaret's voice was as harsh as a knife scraping across porcelain. "Come out here!"

Hazel put a finger to her lips.

"We know you're in there," Rupert shouted. "We're not leaving until you speak to us."

Lily peeked over the window ledge. The group had fanned out to either side of Margaret.

"Come out, come out wherever you are," Carl taunted.

A brief silence ensued. The group exchanged uncertain glances. Margaret flicked her wrist at Toby. The granite-faced butcher lumbered forwards and began pounding on the front door. With each clubbing blow, the entire house seemed to tremble.

"He's going to break the door down," gasped Lily.

"No he isn't. No he isn't," Hazel said repeatedly as if trying to convince herself of her own words. "The door's too strong."

Bang! Bang!

Lily flinched at each impact. Anger surged up her throat, filling her mouth, prising her lips apart. Suddenly, she was springing upright and words were exploding from her. "Leave us alone!"

Carl flung a triumphant jeer at her. "There's the little witch."

Toby halted his assault and turned to Margaret like a soldier awaiting further orders. She beckoned him back into line. "Hazel and Lily Wylde, come out here," she repeated, her manner oddly formal as if she was following a predetermined procedure.

Lily's eyes darted from side to side, searching for potential escape routes. "Let's make a run for it."

Hazel shook her head. "They'll catch us. They know the forest a lot better than we do."

"But if we stay here, we'll die." Lily clutched her mum's arm. "I don't want to die, Mum."

"You're not going to die." Swallowing her own fear, Hazel placed her palms on either side of Lily's face. "We just need to hold on until the police get here. Ok?"

Lily sucked in a shaky breath. "Ok."

A murmur of conversation drew their gazes back to the garden. The group was gathered around Margaret. She was gesticulating towards the sky as if invoking a higher power.

The Spencer brothers broke away, heading around opposite sides of the house.

"The backdoor," Lily hissed.

"It's locked."

Despite her mum's assurance, Lily raced to the kitchen and tried the door. It was, indeed, locked. She recoiled as Carl's grinning face materialised at the window.

He tippy-tapped his fingers against the glass. "Little witch, little witch, let me in."

"We've called the police," Lily retorted. "They'll be here any minute."

Carl giggled like a boy getting a kick out of tormenting an insect. "Do you know what a police scanner is? No one's coming to save you."

"You're lying!"

"Am I?" Carl sounded amused and intrigued. "Or has someone else been telling porky pies?"

Hazel stalked past Lily. "Don't talk to my daughter."

"Uh-oh, here comes mummy witch. Watch out, Toby, she might turn us into toads."

"Why would I need to do that? You already are one."

Carl bared his teeth, then darted his tongue out like a toad catching a fly.

Turning her back on him, Hazel took hold of Lily's hand and drew her away from the window.

"The police *are* coming, aren't they?" Lily asked.

"Of course they are. That moron's just messing with your head."

Carl's singsong voice pursued them into the hallway. "Little witch, little witch…"

"Shut up!" Lily yelled.

Carl's singing degenerated into a rasp of laughter.

Lily opened her mouth to shout something else, but Hazel interjected, "Don't. You're only giving him what he wants."

Hazel's fingers tightened around Lily's hand as Margaret's weirdly euphoric voice rang out. "Hear this, you who feel so secure in your wickedness. Ruin shall fall upon you. All your charms and enchantments will not protect you from it. You too shall know what it is to lose that which you love most."

"*Lose that which you love most,*" Lily repeated in a tremulous whisper. "Do you think she means her baby?"

Hazel's gaze fell to the floor. It was evident from her twitching forehead that she was grappling with an internal debate. Her lips tightened into a hard line. "Whatever she means, it doesn't give her the right to do this."

Holding her chin high, she returned to the living room window and locked eyes with Margaret.

"Ruin shall rain down on you, Hazel Wylde!" Margaret shouted, gesturing towards the sky as if imploring it to fall on Hazel's head. "Do you hear me?"

"I hear you," Hazel muttered.

Margaret shook the black book at her. "And I will strike her children dead. Then all will know that I am He who searches hearts and minds, and I will repay all of you according to your deeds."

"*Hear this*, Margaret Chapman!" Hazel shot back with a wrath that almost rivalled Margaret's. "If you hurt my child, I'll kill you." Her gaze scoured the group. "That goes for all of you."

Susan shrank away from Hazel's glare.

Margaret advanced, holding the book like a shield. "We do not fear you, daughter of Lilith, for we are here on God's business." She turned to Susan. "Behold! I have given you the authority to tread on snakes and scorpions and crush them. Nothing will harm you."

Susan's wide eyes bounced between Margaret and Hazel as if she didn't know who she was more afraid of.

Lily joined her mum at the window. "How long has it been since you called the police?"

"About five minutes."

Lily groaned. "It feels more like five hours."

They both flinched as a heavy impact rattled the backdoor. At the same instant, Margaret swivelled around to spit more fire-and-brimstone at them. "Murderers, liars, unbelievers, those who practice witchcraft – their fate is in the fiery lake of burning sulphur!"

Bang! Bang!

"No one can save you from the flames!"

Bang!

"I can't take much more of this," Lily cried, throwing herself onto the sofa and pulling a cushion down over her ears.

"They're just trying to scare us," said Hazel. "But we don't scare easily, do we?" When Lily didn't respond, Hazel peeled away the cushion and reiterated, "We don't scare easily, do we?"

"No we don't." Lily's voice was almost inaudible.

"Say it again."

Lily repeated the words with a touch more conviction.

"Again," Hazel commanded like a drill sergeant, lifting Lily to her feet.

"No we don't.

"Again."

"No we don't. No we don't!" With each repetition, the mantra grew louder. Lily threw her arms around as if mimicking Margaret's frantic gesticulations. "This is our home. No one can tell us what to do in our own home."

"No one," Hazel echoed, catching hold of Lily's hands.

Jigging in a circle, they chanted, "No one. No one."

They leaned back, counterbalancing each other, spinning faster and faster, giddy with wild, careless energy. Their voices ricocheted off the walls. "No one. No one."

Suddenly, they lost their grip on each other and careered to the floor. "Jesus," Lily gasped. "I think we're even crazier than they are."

Hazel looked towards the window. "It's gone very quiet out there."

A glimmer of hope flickered in Lily's eyes. "Maybe they've given up and gone away."

Hazel pursed her lips doubtfully.

Lily stood up to peer outside and found herself looking into Margaret's haggard face again.

Margaret beseechingly held out her hands. "Child, do not be deceived. The wages of sin are death. The sorcerers, idolators, adulterers and fornicators will be cast into everlasting fire."

Lily sank back down onto the sofa as Margaret continued to sermonise, "And the smoke of their torment shall ascendeth for ever and ever. Those who worship the beast shall have no rest day nor night."

Lily slumped lower as if she was being beaten into submission by the strident voice. "I'm almost tempted to go out there just to shut her up."

Perhaps sensing her words were having some effect, Margaret softened her tone. "Child, you still have time to choose the right path. Open the door. Let me in and I'll–"

"You'll what?" Hazel interrupted, rising to meet Margaret's stare. "You'll save her soul?"

"I shall try to."

"And I shall stop you."

Margaret turned to her companions, flourishing her hands like an actor playing to an enrapt audience. "See! She begins to reveal her true face. She would stop us from saving her daughter's soul, but only so that she herself can sell it to Satan." She stabbed an accusing finger at Hazel. "What has the evil one promised you?" With a shudder of ecstatic revulsion, she groped her milk-filled breasts. "Pleasure beyond all imagining? Perversions of every kind? Sodomy? Bestiality? Incest?"

"Don't project your sick fantasies onto me," Hazel retorted.

An ugly approximation of laughter rasped from Margaret. "See her slippery tongue. The words that slide off it mean nothing. All she cares about is her own pleasure. She'd throw her child into the fire to satisfy her unnatural desires."

Lily shivered as Margaret's voice grated on her nerves. "God, I hate that woman. I wish someone would throw her into a fire."

Hazel smiled grimly. "The oven's pretty big. I think she'd fit in it."

"She's gone totally mad."

Hazel nodded. "And she's somehow persuaded these people to follow her into her madness."

Lily sprang up. "Mrs Chapman's sick," she shouted, sweeping her gaze over the figures behind Margaret. "Can't you see that?" Her voice thickened. "I already know how it feels to lose someone you really, *really* love. It's like... like the world before was just a big lie and nothing makes sense anymore. And it hurts so much you'll do anything to make it stop. So you look for someone to blame. But sometimes there is no one to blame. Sometimes bad things... they just happen."

"No they don't," Margaret countered. "Bad things are God's way of testing us. All are called according to His purpose." She motioned to her companions. "We have been called as warriors to wage the good war and share in the suffering of Christ. And we will either defeat this evil or be enslaved by it."

"Don't listen to her," Lily implored. "Go home."

As if considering doing just that, Susan glanced towards the driveway.

"That's the Devil's way," the bald man told her in a rich baritone that didn't match his gangly frame. "The easy way."

Cowed by his cautionary words, Susan hung her head.

Rupert strode to his wife's side. "This is your last chance. Come out or we'll force our way in."

Hazel made a *stay-put* hand gesture to Lily.

"The Lord God is merciful," said Margaret. "Throw yourself at His feet and beg for forgiveness. Repent and you shall be saved."

"Repent!" Bob chorused.

At the backdoor, Carl took up the chant. "Repent! Repent!"

Their voices stopped all at once. There was a silence, like the instant after a flash of lightning. Then all hell broke loose.

31

Lily screamed as a crash of breaking glass came from the kitchen.

Hazel sprinted out of the living room, snatching up the poker as she passed the fireplace. Toby was reaching a sausage-fingered hand between jagged teeth of glass to unhook the window latch. The poker arced downwards and skinned his knuckles. With a grunt, he jerked away from the window.

Carl took his place. His lips split into a leering grin. "Repent, witch. Repent and I'll go easy on you."

"Mum! Mum!"

The sound of the living room window shattering drowned out Lily's panic-stricken cry. Hazel whirled around to race back to her. They almost collided with each other in the hallway.

Lily grabbed her mum's hand and pulled her upstairs. "We can lock ourselves in the bathroom."

Carl's taunting voice pursued them. "I'm coming for you, little witch."

Hazel frowned at the bolt on the bathroom door. "This won't hold. We need to barricade ourselves in somewhere."

She darted into her bedroom. As soon as Lily was inside too, Hazel closed the door and turned to drag at the wardrobe.

Lily's heart pounded in time to a series of bangs and smashes from downstairs. "Oh my god, they're inside the house!"

"Help me with this."

Lily squeezed behind the wardrobe and heaved herself against it. The sturdy old thing scraped across the floorboards.

Feet thudded up the stairs.

"Move!" Lily screamed at the wardrobe, pushing so hard it felt as if her head would explode.

The bedroom door opened a few centimetres before clunking into the wardrobe. "Little witch, little witch, are you in there?" Carl crooned through the gap.

"Why are you doing this to us?" Lily yelled, bracing herself against the wardrobe alongside her mum.

"Because God told me to, of course."

"Liar!"

Carl chuckled. "Ooh, that hurts my feelings."

"Shut up." Lily pounded a fist against the wardrobe. "You stupid, ignorant–"

"Don't waste your breath on him," Hazel interrupted.

The wardrobe wobbled as the door thunked into it again. Hazel and Lily pushed back, quivering with strain. For several seconds, they held their own. Then, slowly but inexorably, the gap between door and frame widened. A beam of dazzling light streamed into the room. Through the glare, Lily saw the combined bulk of Carl and Toby leaning against the door. Bob was shining a torch at their broad backs.

"That's it, lads, go on," he encouraged.

Lily kept on pushing, knowing it was futile, just hoping she could gain enough time for the police to get there.

Hazel stabbed the poker at Toby. This time, he caught hold of it and wrenched it from her grasp. His dead-eyed, bovine gaze remained on her as he tossed the poker aside. He set one of his massive shoulders against the door. With a final heave, the brothers burst into the bedroom.

Her chest heaving, Hazel shepherded Lily behind her and retreated around the bed. Carl advanced, matching her steps. He ran his tongue over his lips as if anticipating a meal.

Lily darted a desperate look at the window, wondering, *What if I jump? Would I hurt myself?*

As if reading her thoughts, Toby bounded across the bed to the window.

Hazel backed into a corner, her eyes flicking between the brothers. She snatched up a perfume bottle from the dressing-table and hurled it at Carl. He grinned as it bounced off his chest.

Lily grabbed a hairbrush. "Stay away."

"Or what?" scoffed Bob, rocking into the room on his bowed legs.

"Or you'll go to prison."

Bob gave an unconcerned shrug. "Then I'll go to prison. I'm alright with that." He rolled his eyes upwards. "Just so long as there's a place for me up there."

"You're crazy! You're totally–" Lily choked off into a despairing sob.

From somewhere, Hazel found a soothing voice. "Listen to me, Lily, it's going to be ok."

"Yeah, Lily, listen to her," Carl sniggered. "Mum knows best."

Hazel looked him straight in the eye. "I won't tell you again. Don't talk to my daughter."

Carl and Bob exchanged a glance, then erupted into laughter.

Margaret's sharp voice flew up the stairs, slicing through their amusement. "This is no place for laughter. We're here to carry out God's justice. But there can be no justice without evidence." As if reading from an instruction manual, she continued in a flat tone, "The accused's house should be searched as thoroughly as possible, in all holes and corners and chests, top and bottom. And if she's a noted witch, then without doubt, unless she has previously hidden them, there will be found various instruments of witchcraft."

Her words prompted Toby to bend down and hook his fingers under the iron bedframe. He effortlessly lifted the bed on its side. The only thing beneath it was dust. Following his lead, Carl began rifling through the wardrobe and Bob stooped to search the bedside table. A groan escaped Hazel as the gardener removed a lustrous wooden box from the top drawer.

He turned the key and eased open the lid as if afraid it might be booby trapped. "What in God's name…"

"Well, well, what have we got here?" Carl moved in for a closer look at the iron circlet. He touched its saw-like teeth. "Christ, it's sharp!" He snatched his hand away and sucked a dot of blood from his fingertip. His leering face turned to Hazel. "What is this? Some sort of kinky sex toy? Do you get off on pain, eh?"

"Don't talk to her like that," said Toby, his voice as devoid of emotion as his face.

Carl squinted at him in annoyance. "Why shouldn't I? Because her ladyship says we're not allowed to have any fun? I don't take orders from her."

"Neither do I. I take my orders from God." There was no snarkiness in Toby's reply. It was a simple statement of fact. He held up his dinner plate-sized hands. "God has trained these hands for war. And with them I will destroy the works of the Devil."

Lily sagged against her mum and breathed into her ear, "They really are going to kill us."

"Shh," Hazel soothed, wrapping an arm around Lily's shoulders.

"Mrs Chapman," Bob called out of the door. "We've found... something."

An expectant hush ensued, then footsteps slowly climbed the stairs. The room's occupants looked at the doorway as if awaiting the star of the show's arrival onstage.

Margaret shuffled into view with Rupert supporting her by the elbow. His waxed jacket was draped over her stooped shoulders. A hospital gown shrouded her wasted body. She half-turned to whisper something to him. The gown was open at the back, exposing thighs smeared with a mixture of dry and wet blood.

Rupert backed away into the shadows, wearing the blank expression of someone adrift in a sea of shock.

With a tremor of effort, Margaret drew herself up to her full height and turned to face Hazel.

Hazel didn't flinch from her gaze. Ten seconds passed. Twenty. Neither woman blinked.

Bob stepped into Margaret's line of sight. Her eyes widened as she saw the neck ring. "Do you realise what this is?" As if handling a priceless artefact, she carefully lifted the circlet off its bed of red velvet. "It's a witch's collar. It could be the very same..." She paused, then resumed with conviction, "No, it *is* the very same collar Walter had made to fit Mary's neck." Her gaze returned to Hazel. "Where did you get this?"

Hazel pressed her lips together.

"I don't suppose it matters," said Margaret. "What matters is that it's back in the hands of its rightful owners."

"Shall I see if it fits her?" Carl eagerly inquired.

Margaret treated him to a look of faint distaste. "Have you searched them?"

"No."

"Then do so."

"With pleasure."

Grinning wolfishly, Carl approached Hazel and Lily. At a glance from Margaret, Toby closed in on them too.

"Mum, what do we do? What do we do?" Lily's words tumbled out in a panicked rush.

"Don't do anything." Hazel's tone was tinged with fatalism.

Carl pushed his lips out in mock-disappointment. "Aww, come on now ladies, it's no fun if you don't put up a fight."

"*Fun!*" Margaret shrieked as if the word was an obscenity. "There is a time for fun, but that time is not now." She thrust the book out like it was proof of her authority. Gold lettering gleamed on its cover – 'Malleus Maleficarum'. "Now is the time to seek. Seek and you will find."

Carl gave a bow. "Your wish is my command." His tongue slithered between his lips as he looked Lily up and down. "I'll do the little witch first."

Toby placed the flat of his palm on his brother's chest. "I'll do it."

One of Carl's eyes ticked at the outer corner. He stared at Toby for a moment before stepping back and sweeping a hand towards Lily. "Go for it."

Toby's gaze shifted to Hazel. An unspoken communication seemed to pass between them, then Hazel removed her arm from Lily's shoulders.

Lily pressed herself back against the wall, trembling all over.

Toby showed her his palms as if to say, *I'm not going to hurt you.*

"Get on with it then," Carl snapped. "We haven't got all night."

Looming over Lily like Chapman Hill loomed over the forest, Toby set about frisking her. Hazel watched his every move, her jaw clenched in impotent fury. He removed Lily's phone from her back pocket and proffered it to Margaret.

She wafted it away uninterestedly. "Every part of her body."

"You want me to strip search her?" Toby's voice betrayed a trace of hesitancy.

Margaret opened the book and leafed through it to the required page. "They are in the habit of hiding some superstitious object in their clothes or in their hair, or even in the most secret parts of their bodies."

Lily shook her head rapidly. "No. No way." She threw a look at her mum that cried out, *Help!*

Hazel stared back with anguished eyes.

As Toby reached for Lily again, she jerked her chin up and screamed at him as loud as she could. His emotionless façade shattered under the auditory assault. His features scrunching into a lumpy grimace, he backed away from her.

He came to a halt as Margaret prodded him in the back. "Strip her," she commanded.

"No."

Her mouth worked mutely as if she couldn't comprehend his disobedience. He turned and plucked the book from her hands. Tracing a finger along the text, he read out in a slow monotone, "Let the accused be stripped by honest women of good reputation."

Margaret gave him a razor-thin smile. "My apologies, Mr Spencer. You're right, this task must fall to me."

She took back the book and clapped it shut. Her lips curled downwards in revulsion as she eyed Lily and Hazel. Steeling herself with a deep breath, she advanced a step. She swayed to a stop, groping at the air as if searching for something to prevent her from falling over.

Rupert darted forwards to catch hold of her.

238

Bob grabbed the dressing-table stool. "Here, your ladyship."

"Please, God, give me the strength to do what needs to be done," Margaret murmured, reaching for the crucifix around her neck.

Rupert guided her to the stool. "You're not the only woman here who can 'do what needs to be done', Margaret."

Catching his meaning, Bob said, "I'll fetch Susan." He hurried from the room and clumped down the stairs.

Carl gestured towards Hazel with his thumb. "I'll search her pockets."

He stepped in so close that their groins were almost touching. She recognised only too well the sour alcoholic odour of his breath. She stiffened as he teased his fingers into the pockets of her jeans. Smirking at her reaction, he pulled out her phone and the scrap of parchment.

Lily lurched forwards to try to snatch the parchment from him. "You planted that!"

Carl whipped it out of her reach, grabbed her by the throat and held her at arm's length. He chuckled as she futilely tried to break free from his grip.

"Let go of her," Hazel demanded, inserting herself between the two of them. He dealt her a swift back-handed slap across the face. She staggered sideways, blood welling from a split lip.

With a strangled scream, Lily raked her fingernails along Carl's extended arm. He raised a fist as if to hammer her into the floorboards, bellowing, "You little–" He broke off as Toby caught hold of his wrist. The brothers eyeballed each other.

"That's enough," Margaret snapped. She cupped a hand to her ear. "Can't you hear? The Devil's laughing at you right now."

The room was silent for a moment as if they were all listening for the laughter. Carl uncurled his fist. Toby let go of him and ushered Lily to her mum.

"Are you ok?" Lily asked her.

Hazel nodded, pressing the tip of her tongue to her split lip.

Margaret pointed to the parchment. "Let me see that."

Carl passed it to her. As she read the spidery writing, a blend of fascination and disgust flickered across her face. She held aloft the parchment. "This is the Devil's work."

"That thing's got nothing to do with us," Lily protested. She looked at Rupert with imploringly wide eyes. "You have to believe me. I'm telling the truth."

His eyes alternated between her and Hazel, shining with contempt. "There's no truth in either of you. Everything about you is a lie, even your surname – *Wylde.* Who knows what your real name is?"

"It's Knight."

"Is it? Was the man your mum killed even your dad?"

"What... What do you..." Lily stammered as if the question had short-circuited her brain.

Hazel shot Rupert a glare that suggested she wanted to do to him what the white-winged crow had done to Jude. "Don't listen to him, Lily. Don't listen to any of them."

Bob reappeared in the doorway. He curled his fingers into horns and flicked them towards Hazel. "Watch out, your lordship. She's giving you the evil eye."

Rupert stiffened as if bracing himself against a blow.

"The godly have nothing to fear from the evil eye," said Margaret. "No harm shall come to the godly." Her gaze glided towards Hazel. "But the wicked shall have their fill of trouble."

"You're the wicked ones!" Lily retorted. "Not us. You! This is about revenge, nothing else."

Rupert gave a pitying shake of his head. "We're not here for vengeance, Lily. We're here to help you."

"How can this be helping me? How? How?" Lily's voice teetered on the edge of hysteria. "My dad's dead. And now you're going to kill my mum. Well you might as well kill me too. Dying can't be any worse than this!"

"It's not up to any of us here to decide whether you live or die," said Margaret. "Only God can make that decision. And He demands evidence."

Carl pointed at the parchment. "What do you call that?"

"It's a start, but we need irrefutable proof that they've given themselves completely to the Devil in return for everything they desire."

Carl jerked his thumb at Hazel again. "She killed her husband." He spread his hands. "And the Devil gave her all this. That seems obvious to me."

"'Seems' isn't good enough, Mr Spencer. One day you will be called before the highest Judge to give a strict account of your actions. What will you say to Him?"

Carl lifted his gaze to the ceiling as if picturing the scene. His Adam's apple bobbed. "Ok, so what else does He need from us?"

Margaret mulled over the question for a moment. A frown of realisation crossed her face. "Why isn't Ms Cooper with you?" she asked Bob.

He sheepishly rubbed at the back of his grizzled neck. "I'm sorry, your ladyship, but she wouldn't come upstairs."

"Why not?" Rupert asked.

"Because she's *weak*." Margaret spat out the word like it was a lump of gristle. "That's why not. She doesn't have the stomach for the Lord's work." She gestured to Hazel and Lily. "Bring them downstairs." She started to turn towards the landing, but paused as if an afterthought had come to mind. Her eyes glinted within their hollows as she looked at Hazel. "Put the iron collar on her."

Carl's grin returned. "Yes, your ladyship."

With her head lowered and her feet dragging, Margaret left the room. A trail of red droplets on the floorboards marked her path. Rupert followed closely, arms outstretched like a parent ready to catch an unsteady toddler.

"She looks like she's about to drop dead," Lily murmured to her mum with a twisted sort of hope in her voice.

Bob scowled as he caught her whisper. "You'd better watch your mouth."

Lily stiffened and lowered her gaze.

Carl patted the gardener's rounded back. "You'll have to excuse old Bob. His family's been looking after the Chapmans for ooh... well, forever. He's very protective of his lord and ladyship."

"We look after them that look after us," Bob said solemnly. Metal squeaked against metal as he pulled a pin from the clasp of the witch's collar. Hazel shrank away as he approached her with the open collar. "I'd stay still, if I were you," he advised. "Or this thing will cut you to shreds."

Hazel stretched her neck to its full length as Bob closed the serrated choker around it and reinserted the pin.

"Well, well, look at that," said Carl. "It fits like it was made for you."

Hazel twisted her head towards him to fire back a retort, but grimaced as the iron teeth bit into her jaw.

Laughter shook Carl's shoulders. He fell silent as Margaret's rebuking voice penetrated the floorboards. "Where's your faith, Ms Cooper?" she demanded to know. "He commands the winds and the water, and they obey Him. Who are you to ignore His call? Do you think you know better than Him? Do you?"

"What's the matter, Carl?" Hazel hissed through her teeth.

"Are you afraid her ladyship will hear you laughing?"

Locking eyes with her, he pulled a penknife from his jeans pocket and opened out the blade. Hazel blinked as he sliced the air around her face.

"You didn't bleed when you were pricked, but what if I cut off your tongue?" he wondered. "Would you bleed then?"

A rumble like distant thunder vibrated in Toby's throat.

"Don't worry, Toby," said Carl. "I won't harm a hair on her pretty head. Not until her ladyship gives the go-ahead." He leant in close to Hazel. His lips brushed her ear. "And she will give the go-ahead."

In one quick motion, she angled her head away from him and rose onto her tiptoes. With a yelp like a kicked dog, he sprang backwards. Pinpricks of blood welled from where the collar's teeth had cut into his jaw. His eyes bulged. His knuckles paled on the penknife's handle.

Heedless of the collar biting into the nape of her neck, Hazel lifted her chin and awaited his retaliation.

He pressed his palms together with the knife between them. "Please, God, make me the instrument of your wrath against this... this whore of Satan."

Hazel's defiant expression gave way to a pleading one as she turned to Toby. "You can put a stop to this, Toby. You're not like your brother. I can see in your eyes that you don't want to hurt us."

The giant butcher stared at her as if she was speaking a foreign language.

Carl chortled. "You've got more chance of Mary rising from the grave to save you than of him listening to you." He tore a strip from a bedsheet. Hazel noted with a small measure of satisfaction that he took care not to get too close as he threaded the material through a ring on the iron collar. She winced as he gave the improvised lead a tug.

"Walkies," he said, drawing a guffaw from Bob.

"You're worse than Mrs Chapman," said Lily, her voice trembling between anger and tears. "She's crazy, but you... you're just a psycho."

Carl's lips twisted into a snarling grin. "I'm whatever God needs me to be."

He led Hazel towards the doorway. She stuck by his heels so that the lead hung slack. Lily and Bob fell into line behind them.

"Wait," said Toby, picking up a bundle of black material from the sewing machine table. It unfurled to reveal what looked like a hooded shawl.

"Oh my, is that what I think it is?" Carl asked.

"It looks a bit witchy to me," said Bob.

"It's a hoodie I made for Lily's..." Hazel began, but trailed off into a resigned sigh. "What's the point? You people only see what you want to see."

"The evidence is certainly piling up," Carl commented with a gleeful sneer. He pulled the lead taut again.

32

Hazel grimaced, but not because of the collar. The 'Hear no evil. See no evil. Speak no evil.' tapestry had been slashed into ribbons. As Carl tugged her down the stairs, the collar forced her to keep her head level and feel her way forward with her feet.

A dismayed gasp escaped her at the bottom of the stairs. It looked like a tornado had ripped through the living room. Stuffing bulged from the sofa's torn cushions. The piano had been gutted. The portraits were piled on the rug in a jumble of broken wood, shattered glass and shredded canvas. Margaret, Rupert and the lanky, bald man were scrutinising fragments of canvas and backing board.

Susan was on the opposite side of the room, staring at the floor like a reprimanded school girl. She flicked a glance at Hazel and Lily, then lowered her gaze again.

The bald man lifted his head. His shiny pate made a dull clunk as it hit a roof beam. He didn't appear to notice the impact. His eyes burned with the same fanatical fire as Margaret's.

Toby showed them the black garment. "The girl's mum made it for her birthday."

The bald man's eyes drilled into Lily. "When's your birthday?"

She averted her gaze from his, clamping her lips together. Margaret hooked a finger under her chin and lifted it. "You will speak to us, child. Before this night's over, you will tell us everything we want to know."

Lily squeezed her eyes shut, pressing her hands to her ears. "Go away, go away, go away," she kept repeating as if she could make Margaret vanish by sheer force of will.

"It's her birthday tomorrow," said Hazel, looking at Margaret's finger as if she wanted to snap it off.

"How old will she be?"

"Sixteen."

Margaret nodded as if something suddenly made sense. She pointed at the hooded garment. "This is her initiation robe. Tomorrow she gives herself to the Devil."

"You're out of your goddamned–" Hazel began, but Margaret silenced her with a sharp slap on the cheek. Hazel's face jerked sideways. She let out a low cry as the collar sawed into her neck.

Margaret's eyes spat fire. "Keep the Lord's name out of your mouth!"

A wild laugh burst from Hazel. "You're right, Margaret. Tonight at the witching hour, I'm going to give my daughter to the Devil as payment for him crippling your son and killing your unborn baby. So you can stop this madness right now, because I confess." She thrust her face towards Margaret. "I'm a witch!"

Rupert made to push Hazel away, but Margaret raised a hand to stop him. Keeping her gaze fixed on Hazel, she tapped the leather-bound book. "Do you know what this is?"

"No. Should I?"

"Yes, if you want to know your enemy. This is the Malleus Maleficarum. The Hammer of Witches." A condescending smile played across Margaret's lips. "Think of it as a dummy's guide to prosecuting witches. There's a right and a wrong way to do it. There are procedures to be followed before judgement and sentencing can be carried out. A confession isn't enough. The confessor could be lying to protect a loved one. Or they might be insane."

"Someone's insane here, but it's not my mum," Lily retorted.

Margaret gave her a pitying look. "You love your mum, don't you?" She lowered her voice as if letting Lily in on a shameful secret. "But she doesn't love you. A witch cannot love. All witchcraft is born of lust. The only thing witches care about is indulging their filthy delights."

Filthy delights. An image formed in Lily's mind – a tableau of bodies coiled around each other like snakes, groping, thrusting, licking, biting…

Her lips thinned into a defiant smile. "That sounds like fun to me."

"Do you call having sexual intercourse with demons *fun?*" Margaret shuddered as if visualising that very thing. "And what about the deformed offspring that are born of such depravity? They must endure a life of constant pain. Is that what you mean by fun?"

Lily found herself picturing the bobbles of flesh where Tom's fingers should have been, the way he shuffled and limped as if his ankles were shackled. Did he know these people? Was he perhaps even helping them in some way?

No, he wouldn't do that, she told herself. Closing her eyes tightly, she resumed chanting, "Go away, go away…"

"We're not going anywhere, little witch," Carl gloated. "But you and your mum will be going somewhere very soon. We have all the evidence we need now."

"What evidence?" countered Hazel. "A hoodie? Some silly spells you planted when you broke in here the other night?"

The bald man held up a sheet of paper with 'eggs, caster

sugar, butter, self-raising flour, chocolate, baking powder, milk,' written on it in black biro. "This is your handwriting, is it not?"

"Yes. So what?"

The man displayed one of the backing boards to Hazel. Black writing adorned it too. "The handwriting on both is identical." Lowering his stern blue eyes, he read out, "Clay Corpse. If you desire to do someone serious harm, make a clay likeness of them. Take a lock of their hair or a few of their fingernail clippings and place them inside the doll. Take also an item of the person's clothing with which to clothe the doll. Say to the doll 'In the name of the Devil and all the other devils, I baptise you' and then say the name of the person you wish to hex. Then say–"

Hazel cut him off with a scornful laugh. "Wow, how convenient that all this *evidence* was just waiting to be found by you."

Lily opened her eyes and craned her neck to see the 'Clay Corpse' spell. She turned to her mum with knitted eyebrows. "It *does* look like your writing."

"They must have copied it from the shopping list. This is just another mind game, Lily. Don't let–"

"Give me the book," Toby interrupted, holding out a hand to Margaret.

She clutched the book to her chest.

"What do you want it for?" Rupert asked.

Without affording him a glance, Toby flexed his huge hand. "Give it to me."

Holding his gaze as if to say, *I trust you*, Margaret handed over the book. He opened it and slowly turned the pages.

"What the hell are you looking for?" Carl demanded to know. "It's getting late. We need to get this thing done."

Ignoring him, Toby continued to thumb through the stiff, age-yellowed pages.

Hazel and Lily exchanged a faintly hopeful glance. Had some sliver of doubt pierced Toby's mind? With a twinge of satisfaction, Lily noted Margaret was wringing her hands as if tormented by the same question.

Toby lingered over a page. He nodded as if a hunch had been confirmed, then read out, "She was further asked in whose name they did this, and answered, in the name of the Devil and all the other devils."

His impenetrable gaze rose to Margaret.

A momentary silence settled over the room as if his audience hadn't grasped the significance of the quote. Then Lily parroted in triumphant realisation, "*In the name of the Devil and all the other devils.* Those are the same words from the spell. Why would my mum use those words? She'd never even heard of the Malleus Mal-whatever-it-is before today. Neither of us had."

"Can I see that?" Susan asked. Timidly avoiding eye contact with Margaret, she approached Toby. She squinted at the book, then at the 'Clay Corpse' spell. Finally, she plucked up the courage to meet Margaret's gaze. "You *did* write this spell, didn't you?"

Margaret rolled her eyes away from Susan. Her aloof expression suggested she wouldn't deign to respond to such an absurd accusation.

"Who the bloody hell do you think you are?" Bob barked at Susan with such ferocity that she stiffened like a startled rabbit. "I ought to box your ears for talking to Mrs Chapman like that."

"But... But..." she stammered, motioning to the book and the spell.

"But nothing." Bob jabbed a dirt-ingrained finger at Hazel.

"That woman is a lying whore."

In turn, Lily pointed at Margaret. "She's the lying–" Bob shut her up with a smack on the side of the head.

Hazel jerked up a hand to return the favour. She staggered and struggled to remain upright as Carl yanked her lead.

Lily rubbed her head, glaring at Bob as he warned her, "There's a lot more where that came from, so you just keep your trap shut and listen to what I have to say. Who knows, you might even learn something. I've been around long enough to know a liar when I see one. And your mother's the biggest liar I've ever met. I'm not the only one who sees her for what she really is. Your father saw it too. And it cost him his life."

Shaking her head, Lily made to cover her ears again. Bob pulled down her hands. "Before this is over and done with, girl, you'll have to make a choice. Will you give yourself to God or the Devil?"

"The enemy has his eye on you, Lily Wylde," the bald man put in. "He has his eye on *all* of us." A shiver ran through his spindly frame. "I can feel him looking for a way in. All he needs is the tiniest chink of doubt. My ancestor–"

"We don't have time for a history lesson," Carl interrupted.

"There is always time for the word of God," said Margaret. "Please continue, Doctor."

Doctor. Lily darted her mum a meaningful glance. Surely the bald man was Dr Hughes? His next words confirmed her suspicion.

"As I was saying, my ancestor, the Rector Thomas Hughes, learnt that lesson the hard way. Three months after Mary's death, he was found hanging in his church. His suicide brought shame on my family."

"It wasn't suicide," said Bob. "It was witchcraft."

"Maybe. Or maybe he became the very thing Mary said he

was – a Doubting Thomas – and now his soul burns in Hell." Dr Hughes's voice vibrated with resolve. "I will not suffer the same fate."

"Examine yourselves whether ye be in the faith!" Margaret exclaimed. She pointed at Susan. "Are you with God?"

"Yes." Susan's gaze swept over her companions. As if trying to convince them that she meant it, she repeated with emphasis, "*Yes!*"

"Then show Him how much you love Him."

The challenge drew a little sob of capitulation from Susan. "How? Tell me what I must do."

Margaret's finger shifted to Hazel and Lily. "Strip them."

Lily clasped her hands across her chest at the prospect.

Margaret took the cloth lead from Carl. "Toby, you stay here. The rest of you leave the room."

Her instructions wiped the seedy grin off Carl's face. Casting an envious scowl at his brother, he scuffed his feet towards the hallway. Bob and Dr Hughes followed him.

"I'll be just outside the door," Rupert assured Margaret before he, too, left the room.

"Eyes on the floor," Margaret instructed Toby.

He stared at his feet.

"It would be easier if you undressed yourselves," Susan told Hazel and Lily.

Hazel subjected her to a steady stare. "Why should we make things easier for you?"

Susan blinked, breaking eye contact. She reached out, but her hand stopped halfway to Hazel's blouse, seemingly caught between fear and shame.

"God is waiting for you to show your love," Margaret reminded her.

With a quick movement, Susan fumbled at the buttons of Hazel's blouse and jeans. Hazel held herself rigid to prevent the collar from biting into her. Margaret aimed a torch at Hazel's bare midriff. The light picked out a cluster of silvery stretch marks. Susan unhooked the clasp of Hazel's bra. Margaret focused the beam on Hazel's breasts. Networks of bluish veins spread outwards from her pink nipples and slightly darker areolae.

"What are we looking for?" Susan asked.

"Instruments of witchcraft." Leaning in to scrutinise Hazel's right nipple, Margaret added, "Unusual marks."

Susan pulled Hazel's jeans and underwear down around her ankles. She cursorily examined Hazel's pale skin, dark pubic hair and brownish-pink labia, clearly eager to get the task over with. "I don't see anything unusual."

"Then look more closely. The suspect must be searched like the house – in all holes and corners, top and..." Margaret trailed off, her nose almost touching Hazel's nipple. "What's that?" She pointed to a small growth that sprouted from below the nipple. The red twizzle of skin was a centimetre or so long and thickened into a bulb at the end.

"It looks like a skin tag," said Susan.

"It's from breastfeeding," Hazel told them.

Margaret's eyes narrowed. "Breastfeeding who?"

"Who do you bloody well think?" Hazel bent to pull up her jeans.

"Did you hear me give you permission to get dressed?" Margaret snapped.

Hazel shot her a glare, then heaved a sigh, moving swiftly from anger to resignation. She straightened, leaving her jeans around her ankles.

At a gesture from Margaret, Susan set about examining

Hazel's back. She briefly parted Hazel's buttocks before continuing on down to her feet. Looking up at Margaret, she shook her head.

"Are you done?" Hazel asked.

"For now," Margaret said with a begrudging edge.

As Hazel pulled her clothes back into place, Susan approached Lily.

Lily retreated, putting her hands out to keep Susan at bay.

"The sooner you let me examine you, the sooner this will all be over," Susan said like a nurse reassuring an anxious patient.

With a sudden burst of movement, Lily dodged past her. Finding her way to the broken window blocked by Toby, she veered towards the fireplace. She ducked to peer up the chimney in the frantic hope that she would be able to squeeze into it. At the sound of rapidly approaching footsteps, she snatched up a lump of coal, spun around and hurled it with all her might. Susan screamed as the missile hit her in the face.

Lily reached for another piece of coal, but Toby's arms enfolded her in a bear hug and lifted her off the floor.

"Let go!" she cried out, thrashing around.

Pressing his lips against her ear, Toby said so quietly that only she could hear, "I won't let them hurt you."

There was something about his voice – a sort of awkward sincerity – that made her go limp. She sagged against his arms, breathing hard. He lowered her onto the sofa.

"What's going on in there?" Rupert shouted through the door.

"Everything's under control," Margaret replied. "Don't come in here."

Susan dabbed a tissue at a cut on the bridge of her nose. She turned to Margaret with tears of mascara running down her cheeks. "Is it bad?"

"It's nothing." Margaret wafted her towards Lily.

Eyeing Lily warily, Susan bent to examine her. Lily closed her eyes and lay trembling as Susan's clammy fingers explored her body. The shopkeeper worked her way downwards from Lily's scalp, checking behind her ears, prodding at any freckles and moles, peering under her breasts and between her thighs and buttocks.

She pointed at Lily's right calf. "Have a look at this."

Margaret stooped to scrutinise a cluster of three circular brown moles. "How long have you had these?" she asked Lily.

"All her life," Hazel answered for her.

Margaret stared at the moles for a moment longer as if memorising their position before saying to Susan, "Tell the others to come back in."

With relief written all over her face, Susan hurried to the door.

Lily quickly got dressed as the four men trooped into the room. She sat up straight, hugging her arms across herself once more, eyes fixed on her lap. Hazel moved towards her, but Margaret gave the lead a warning tug.

Bob frowned at Susan's swollen nose. "What happened to you?"

In reply, she cast an aggrieved glance at Lily.

Chuckling, Carl pointed out five parallel scratches on his wrist. "The little witch gave me a keepsake too."

Rupert rushed to Margaret's side. She rested her forehead on his shoulder for several breaths as if gathering her strength, then lifted her gaunt face to Bob. "Fetch the dog."

With a nod, he turned to clump from the room.

"What dog?" Lily asked, her head snapping up. "Do you

mean Sam?" Her stomach clenched as she pictured Bob digging up Sam's body. "Please, I'll tell you whatever you want, just don't–"

Margaret raised her voice over Lily's. "God will hear your confession when the time comes."

"My daughter has nothing to confess," Hazel retorted. "I've done plenty I'm not proud of, but Lily's completely innocent."

"No one is completely innocent. You changed your surname to conceal your identity. Lily went along with the deception."

"We just wanted to start a new life. You'd have done the same if you were us." Hazel's gaze raked over her accusers, challenging them to say otherwise.

"We wouldn't have killed anybody in the first place," said Carl.

Hazel fixed him with a penetrating stare. "But isn't that why you're here – to kill us?"

"Kill?" Susan piped up in a wavering voice. "No one said anything about killing anyone."

Hazel's gaze slid across to her. "Are you really that naïve?" She motioned to Margaret and Rupert. "They came here to murder us."

Susan's eyes gaped at Margaret for confirmation or denial of Hazel's words. When she received neither, she gave a rapid shake of her head. "I can't be part of this."

"You're already part of it, Susan," Carl stated. "There's no backing out now. So pack in your whining. It's giving me a headache." He scowled at Hazel. "And you... one more word and I'll slap you into next week."

"Let her speak," said Margaret. "The mouths of fools are their ruin. They trap themselves with their own lips."

Hazel gave a soft snort. "I think you're talking about yourself again."

All eyes turned towards the doorway as Bob's heavy boots tramped back into the house. He appeared with Sam's body in his arms. The sight wrenched a sob from Lily.

Silver duct tape was wrapped around the dead dog's jaw. Bob dumped the body at Rupert's feet, scattering soil across the floor.

"Why have you taped his mouth shut?" Hazel asked with a mocking curl of her lips. "Are you afraid he might turn into a zombie?"

Carl snickered. Margaret silenced him with a sharp glance.

"Last night I was woken by screaming from the barn," said Bob. He focused on Lily like he was trying to draw her into his story. "Have you ever heard sheep screaming? It sounds like someone in the worst pain in the world. I ran to the barn as fast as my old legs could carry me. When I got there, it was as quiet as a graveyard." An uncharacteristic tremor crept into his voice. "Three sheep and seven lambs were dead. They'd been torn to pieces. And when I say torn to pieces, I mean exactly that. I couldn't tell which bits belonged to which animal. No dog could have done that to them."

"No normal dog," Dr Hughes corrected, prompting Susan to edge away from the corpse.

"Oh, so obviously it was Sam," said Lily.

Bob nodded, seemingly oblivious to her sarcasm. "One ewe was still alive but in a bad way. Her udder had been drained dry. Something had suckled on her so hard that she was bleeding from her teats." He shook his head. "In all my years, I've never seen the like."

Rupert pointed at the corpse. "Open it up."

Bob took out a Stanley knife and knelt down stiffly.

"No!" Lily cried, lunging to try to snatch away the knife. Toby caught hold of her. She futilely fought against his grip as Bob placed the knife against the dead dog's belly. With a sound like scissors cutting cloth, the blade travelled across the pinkish-grey skin. There was a *pfft* like air leaking from a burst tyre. A putrid stench filled the room.

Lily screwed up her face and retched.

Bob reached into the gaping incision and pulled out a purplish sack-like organ. He sliced it open and what looked to be several litres of milk spilled over the floor. Rupert retreated from the incoming tide of white liquid, drawing Margaret with him. Susan gasped and crossed herself. Dr Hughes's lips moved as if in silent prayer.

"You put that inside him," Lily yelled.

"And just how did I do that?" asked Bob.

"I don't know, but you... you..." Sobs overcame Lily's stammering voice. Strings of vomit dangled from her chin as Toby lowered her onto the sofa. She buried her face in a cushion.

Heedless of the iron teeth biting into her, Hazel bent to wrap her arms around Lily.

"How often did Sam suckle on you, Hazel?" Margaret asked. When she didn't get an answer, she gave the lead another tug. "Was he gentle? Or did he make you bleed too?"

Tensing against the pain, Hazel peered up at Margaret. "Listen to yourself. Don't you realise how crazy you sound?" She looked at Toby. "You can't seriously believe Sam was my familiar."

He turned his gaze away from her wide, teary eyes.

Carl grabbed the lead from Margaret and yanked it. Hazel fell backwards, clutching at the iron collar. "I know your game, witch," he growled. "I told you, you're wasting your time trying to turn Toby to your side."

"We must now weigh the evidence before us," Margaret

declared with an urgency that suggested she wasn't convinced Carl was right. She pointed at Hazel. "By her own actions and body, she offers this proof – she is a liar and a killer, she didn't bleed when I pricked her, she has an extra teat from which a familiar might suckle." Her finger moved to the collection of spells and the hooded garment. "She was in possession of instruments of witchcraft." As if announcing the coup de grâce, she finished with a flourish of her hands towards Lily. "And her daughter bears the mark of The Unholy Trinity." She glanced at Susan. "Show them."

Lily's head jolted up. "Touch me and I'll bite your fingers off," she warned, baring her teeth as Susan reached for her. Susan swiftly drew back her hand. Glaring at the others, Lily pulled up her jeans leg to display the little constellation of brown moles.

"See!" Margaret's voice rose exultantly. "Satan, The Antichrist and The False Prophet. Lies, hatred and evil."

"Toby, look at me," Hazel implored. "Please look at me."

The big man met her gaze.

Carl made to yank the lead again. Before he could do so, Hazel seized the slack and yanked it herself. The strip of cloth slipped through his grip. She beseechingly opened her arms towards Toby. "Yes, I've told lies. Haven't we all? But we get a second chance. Right? We just have to own up to our mistakes and ask for forgiveness." With shame flooding her dark eyes, she turned to Lily. "I'm so sorry."

Carl strode towards Hazel, but Margaret thrust out an arm to bar his way.

Trembling in anticipation of the answer, Lily asked, "For what?"

"Your..." Hazel faltered. She composed herself with a deep breath. "Your dad was right. I was having an affair."

Lily's mouth hung open in stunned silence for a moment,

then she found a faint voice. "With who?"

"It doesn't matter."

In a heartbeat, Lily flipped from shock to rage. "Yes it does! Who was it? Tell me!"

"It was a friend. It... I..." Hazel stumbled over her words, struggling to explain. "I just needed someone to talk to. I didn't mean for anything else to happen."

Lily's voice dropped to a cutting whisper. "Are you saying it was Dad's fault?"

"I loved your dad, but it all got too much – the drinking, the jealousy."

Lily motioned to Dr Hughes. "So just like with his ancestor, you ended up becoming what you were accused of being. Is that how it is?"

"I... I suppose so." Hazel's gaze returned to Toby. "If you want to kill me for that, go ahead. But don't kid yourself that you're doing this for God. You're doing this for yourself."

"If a woman is found lying with the husband of another woman, both of them shall die," Margaret said matter-of-factly.

Hazel kept her eyes fixed on Toby. "She can try to justify it all she wants, but murder is murder."

Thrusting out the Malleus Maleficarum, Margaret intoned as if God was speaking through her, "Fallen, fallen is Babylon the great! She has become a dwelling place for demons, a haunt for every unclean spirit."

"Amen!" Carl exclaimed like a fanatical fan egging on their idol.

The tendons in Margaret's neck stood out as she somehow raised the pitch of her speech even higher. "And I heard a voice from heaven saying, 'Come out of her, my people, lest you share in her sins, and–'" All of a sudden, her voice failed and her eyes rolled back.

"Margaret!" Rupert cried as she collapsed against him. A rose of blood bloomed through the hospital gown at groin level.

"Lay her down," Dr Hughes instructed, darting forwards to help Rupert lower Margaret onto the rug and prop her head on a cushion.

The doctor took her pulse. After feeling around under her gown and rubbing the blood between his fingers, he regarded her gravely. "You should be in hospital, Margaret."

"No," she breathed, shaking her head.

"But–" began Rupert.

"*No.*" Margaret's voice was low but forceful. "I just need some water."

"I'll get it," Susan offered, dashing towards the doorway like someone fleeing a burning building.

"Put half a teaspoon of salt and eight teaspoons of sugar in it," Dr Hughes called after her.

"And don't get lost on your way to the kitchen," Carl added pointedly. He snatched the lead back from Hazel and wound it around his hand. He made as if to yank it, but didn't do so. His smirk resurfaced as Hazel flinched.

Susan clattered around in the kitchen before returning with a glass of water. She tilted it against Margaret's pale lips. Margaret's eyes fluttered open. She took a shuddering breath and, with Rupert's help, clambered to her feet.

"Hallelujah, she has risen. It's a miracle." Hazel said dryly.

"Hallelujah," Margaret echoed without irony. "For God's judgements are true and just and He has judged the great prostitute." Her voice cranked up to a hoarse shout. "Hallelujah! She will burn and the smoke from her will go up forever and ever."

Rupert joined in. "Amen. Hallelujah!"

Carl, Bob and Dr Hughes took up the chant with gusto. Carl nudged his brother. Toby looked at him with a dull flicker in his eyes. A rumble grew in Toby's chest as Carl kept nudging him. Opening his mouth as wide as a lion's, Toby roared, "Amen. Hallelujah!"

Margaret flung her arms around like a demented orchestra conductor as the chant shook the air. She made a slashing motion. The room fell silent in an instant. All eyes stared expectantly at her.

"Let the sentence be carried immediately." Margaret pointed at Hazel and Lily. "Let them be placed on high in full view of the world." She opened the Malleus Maleficarum and read from it. "So that all good men may be warned and safeguarded and evil-doers may be discovered and punished. So that justice shall be meted out to those who do evil, and thus in all things God shall be glorified, to whom be all honour, praise and glory."

"Let's take them to Dead Woman's Ditch," Carl suggested, almost breathless with eagerness.

Rupert shook his head. "My wife's not well enough to–"

"God will give me the strength I need," Margaret cut in. "Through Him, all things are possible."

Rupert looked at her unwavering expression for a moment before turning to Carl. "Tie their hands."

Carl glanced around for something to use as bindings. His gaze landed on the curtains. He took out his penknife and began cutting them into strips.

"Toby, Bob, fetch what we need from the cars," Rupert instructed.

The two men left the room.

"Susan, Gil, gather up the evidence."

Gil. The name caught Lily's attention. The snuffling voice from the phone echoed back to her – *Gil won't let you come to any harm.* So Dr Hughes was Gil. Did that mean he was... Was what? Some sort of undercover witch? She looked at him, hoping for a sign that she was right, but he didn't meet her gaze.

She glanced at her mum, wondering if she'd picked up on the name.

Hazel was staring at the floor, her shoulders sagging as if she'd had the stuffing kicked out of her. She looked utterly defeated.

Lily's heart ached at the sight, but then her thoughts turned to her dad. Her mind conjured up an image of him slumped in his armchair, consumed by paranoia. Only he hadn't been paranoid. He'd had good reason to want to put his wife in a pumpkin shell.

A liar... Guilty as sin... Should be locked up... Slept with half of Fulham... I hope her husband's ghost haunts her...

Lily shook with rage as she recalled fragments of comments from underneath the newspaper article about her dad's death. "They were right about you," she spat at her mum. "I bet you *have* slept with half of Fulham."

Hazel flinched as if each word was a needle piercing her skin.

"And I bet you killed Dad deliberately," Lily continued, almost choking on her anger. "You did, didn't you? Tell me the truth."

Hazel looked at her with eyes that begged for understanding. "That's what I'm doing, Lily. If I'm going to die tonight, I want you to know who I really am."

"And who's that?"

"I–" Hazel winced as Carl twisted her arms behind her back and set about binding them. "I tried to make it work with your dad, but he just kept pushing and pushing me."

"Oh boo-hoo, poor you," Carl sneered. "You sound like my ex-wife. Nothing's ever her fault either. There's always someone else to blame. God, when I think about what I put up with from that woman..." He trailed off with a shake of his head.

"Careful, Carl, don't let her ladyship hear you taking the Lord's name in vain."

He grinned at Hazel's taunt. "Oh I'm going to enjoy shutting you up once and for all."

Susan used Lily's birthday present to bundle up the pieces of backing board and brown tape from the ruined paintings. As Gil heaved the dead dog onto his shoulder, strings of entrails slithered from its yawning abdominal cavity. He headed for the door with them trailing behind him.

Lily pinched her nostrils, gagging again.

"You think this is bad?" said Carl. "You should smell burning human flesh. I used to be a volunteer firefighter. My first week, I pulled an old dear out of a house fire. She looked like a lump of charcoal with a face. And the smell! Whoo! I've never smelt anything so–"

"Please, Carl," Susan interrupted, swallowing queasily.

He gave a snort of laughter. "Let's just say the stink of it stays with you." After tying Lily's wrists together, he inspected his handiwork and nodded in approval. As if they were about to head out for a night on the tiles, he rubbed his hands together in gleeful anticipation. "Right, ladies, let's get this show on the road."

33

C arl pushed Lily and Hazel out of the backdoor. Susan was the final person to leave the cottage. She started to close the door, but Margaret said, "Leave it. Let the night air clean out the stench of witchcraft."

Leaning on Rupert, Margaret shuffled along the garden path. Gil plodded ahead of them, stooped under Sam's dead weight. His black suit blended in with the darkness, making it seem as if his hairless head was floating in midair.

Toby and Bob approached from the vehicles, wearing head torches and carrying a jerry can in each hand. A coil of rope was slung over Toby's shoulder.

"It doesn't seem real," Lily murmured as if she was expecting to wake up at any second.

"Unfortunately for you, little witch, it's very real," said Carl.

Hazel glared at him. "You're loving this, aren't you?"

He smirked. "I am but God's humble servant."

"What made you like this?" Hazel's voice was tauntingly soft. "Did your ex run off with another man? Is that why you hate women so much?"

Carl's grin faltered. "Keep talking. It only makes me look forward even more to watching you burn."

"The Moon's riding high tonight," Margaret observed, peering up at the perfect crescent. "We must finish our task before the witching hour."

She quickened her pace, forcing Rupert to do likewise. They overtook Gil, following the garden path to the embracing oak trees.

With a sweeping motion, Carl signalled for Susan to go next. "After you."

"What's wrong?" she bristled. "Don't you trust me?"

Carl placed a hand over his heart in mock hurt. "How could you think such a thing, Susan? I just want to make sure you don't accidentally wander off or anything." He put an insinuating emphasis on 'accidentally'.

Susan gave him a sarcastic smile of appreciation. Hanging her head as if she was the one being led to her execution, she trudged after Gil and the Chapmans.

Carl whipped the ends of the cloth leads at Lily and Hazel.

Hazel looked daggers at him before starting forwards. Lily trailed after her, dragging her feet like a sleepwalker. As grim-faced as pallbearers, Toby and Bob took up their positions at the rear of the bizarre procession.

Lily glanced at the rectangular hole from which Sam had been exhumed. "So let me get this straight. Sam rose from the grave like some sort of vampire dog. But a vampire dog that drinks milk, not blood. And when he was full, he came back here and reburied himself. Do you realise how dumb that sounds?"

"Labradors are good diggers," Bob said with deadpan seriousness.

Lily's lips curled contemptuously. "You really are as stupid as you look."

"Maybe I am." Bob's tone was indifferent. "But what does that make you?"

The question wiped the smirk off Lily's face. She walked on in glowering silence. They passed beneath the archway of intertwining branches. The narrow path rose into dense darkness. They hadn't gone far before Rupert called them to a halt. Margaret braced her hands against her knees, shoulders hitching as she struggled to catch her breath.

"I could carry you, Mrs Chapman," Toby offered.

She shook her head and gestured to the stars winking through the leaves. "*He* will carry me."

With that, she straightened to resume her march.

"Why are you here, Toby?" Hazel asked.

"He's here for the same reason as all of us – because he's a good Christian," Carl answered for his brother.

Toby remained silent, but his head torch bobbed as if he was nodding in agreement.

"Good Christians don't go around burning people," said Lily.

"Good Christians do whatever God needs us to do," Bob countered.

"We are His living sacrifices," Margaret piped up breathlessly. "His purifying fire lives within..." She faltered, fighting for oxygen.

"Please, my love, save your breath for the climb," Rupert urged.

There was a strange yearning in Margaret's voice as she continued, "I offer myself, O Lord. Unworthy as I am, use me as the instrument of your divine retribution. Then, if it pleases thee, receive me into the arms of thy mercy, into the blessed rest of everlasting–"

"Please, Margaret, it scares me to hear you talking like this," Rupert cut her off.

"Whoever loves their life will lose it, but whoever hates their life will keep it for eternity," said Gil.

Margaret nodded and exclaimed exultantly, "Amen!" As if

spurred on by the promise of an awaiting eternity, she strode uphill with a renewed spring in her step.

"Let's hope she gets her wish before we reach Dead Woman's Ditch," Hazel whispered to Lily.

"Don't talk to me," Lily muttered.

Hazel grimaced as if the iron collar had bitten into her. "Everything I've ever done, I did out of love for you."

Lily shot her an incredulous glare. "Oh really? You had an affair out of love for me, did you? You killed Dad out of love for me?"

"He was strangling me, so I hit him. What else was I supposed to do?"

Lily's features contorted into a mask of resentment. "It would have been better if you'd let him strangle you."

"You don't mean that."

"Don't I? As far as I'm concerned, you're not my mum. You're..." Lily scoured her mind for words to convey the depth of her anger and despair. "You're dead to me now."

"She'll be dead for real soon enough," said Carl. "Both of you will."

With a scream of unbridled rage, Hazel pivoted and lashed a foot at him. He dodged the kick, then shoved her. She staggered into Susan, who in turn stumbled to one knee and cried out in pain.

"Will you stop bloody well provoking them?" Susan snapped, rubbing her knee. She straightened gingerly and limped on her way.

"You should listen to Ms Cooper," Gil advised. "The witches are a lot more dangerous than they look."

"I think I can handle them," Carl scoffed.

"Perhaps, but the Devil is a master of mind games. We must

be on our guard against his wiles."

Frowning pensively, Carl prodded Lily and Hazel into motion. Up ahead, Margaret was clambering over the fallen tree. As if being towed by an invisible rope, she ascended the path with rapid, stuttering steps. Rupert scurried along at her heels like a faithful hound.

"Wow, look at God carrying her," Lily remarked sardonically. "He's going really fast."

"That's hilarious. You should be on–" Carl began to retort, but broke off as Gil made a disapproving noise.

They proceeded in silence, except for an occasional pained little moan from Susan and the dry wheeze of Bob's breathing. Rupert and Margaret stopped to wait for them at the avenue of thorny trees.

"Blackthorn," Margaret told them. Her tone implied the information was of great significance.

"The dark crone of the woods," said Gil, eyeing the spiky branches as if afraid they might come alive and lash out at him. "It's said that a rod of blackthorn pointed at a pregnant woman will cause her to miscarry."

Pressing a hand to her stomach, Margaret briefly closed her eyes.

Gil turned to Hazel. "Is that how you did it? Is that how you killed the baby?"

"Yes, that's right. I used my blackthorn wand to make Margaret miscarry." Hazel's reply was bone-dry.

Gil nodded, seemingly accepting the words at face value. "We should take some blackthorn for the fire," he said to the others. "It will help to burn the Devil out of them."

"I'll get it," said Bob, taking a Swiss Army knife and a pair of leather gardening gloves from his pockets. "A scratch from them thorns can go bad in no time." He opened out the penknife's small saw blade and set to work on cutting off a branch.

A faint whoosh of air drew Lily's eyes to the darkness overhead. Was it the wind in the treetops? Or was it something else? Perhaps a bird flapping by? Her thoughts turned to the white-winged crow. The image of the bird's downturned beak severing Jude's tongue replayed in her mind. She noticed Rupert staring at her. His haunted expression seemed to suggest that her thoughts were visible on the surface of her eyes.

With a vigorous shake of his head, he turned to Margaret. "I can't do it." He pointed towards the far end of the avenue. "I can't go to *that* place."

"You *can* and you *will*." Margaret's words were as unyielding as iron. Rupert sagged beneath the weight of them. Now it was her turn to cup a supportive hand under his elbow. She ushered him along the avenue, thrusting out her chin as if daring the trees to try to stop her. The others followed, taking care to avoid the thorns. Bob bundled up the firewood in his jacket and laboured along at the back of the line.

Sweat dribbled down Lily's face. The air in the avenue was a warm soup flavoured with the almondy scent of the blackthorn's white blossom. She kept glancing skywards, expecting, even hoping to catch a glimpse of white-tipped wings. She visualised Margaret suffering the same fate as Jude. A smile twisted her lips as more crows invaded her imagination, descending upon her captors like vengeful spirits – stabbing, ripping, feasting. "Die," she muttered. "Die."

"What did you say?" Hazel asked.

Lily blinked like someone emerging from a trance. Shame flooded in and washed away her smile. What was the matter with her? How could she think such things? She gave a hard shake of her head. "I'll never become what they say I am."

"Quiet," Carl snapped. He froze as a heart-rending wail tore through the night.

Margaret choked on her grief and collapsed at the clearing's edge, convulsing like she was having an epileptic fit. With an alarmed gasp, Rupert bent to hold her still.

"Don't touch her," Gil instructed. He dropped the dead dog and squatted down to manoeuvre Margaret carefully onto her side. Saliva foamed through her clenched teeth.

"He's here," rasped Bob. "The Devil's here."

"Where?" Susan asked, her eyes gaping as if she expected to see a horned red face staring back at her from the darkness.

Carl snorted derisively at the question, but his eyes were almost as wide as hers.

Margaret's convulsions stopped as abruptly as they'd started. She reared up and lunged at the air, wielding the Malleus Maleficarum like a duellist fending off an imaginary opponent. "Satan!" she cried. "I come against thee in the name of the living God as an executor of divine justice."

She staggered to the circle of ashes at the clearing's centre. Rupert followed as if wading through mud. The grass around the ashes was stained with dried blood. A keening sound, like an animal in pain, built in Margaret's throat.

Rupert put a hand on her shoulder, but she shrugged him off and turned to point a trembling finger at Sam's corpse. "Burn it."

Gil dragged the carcass onto the ashes. Toby screwed the cap off a jerry can and sloshed petrol over the mutilated remains. The others formed a loose circle around the clearing's perimeter.

Toby struck a match, drawing an anguished, "Please don't," from Lily.

He paused in mid-motion to look at her.

"Do it," Margaret commanded.

Toby touched the match to the corpse. The petrol whooshed into flame. Lily turned away from the sight, but she couldn't block out the sizzle of Sam's flesh. Her throat contracted as the sulphuric stench of burning fur hit her. She battled against the urge to retch. She wouldn't give these psychos the satisfaction of seeing her throw up again.

Margaret beckoned Bob forwards. She took several sticks of blackthorn from him and held them over the flames. Sparks floated up into the sky as the wood caught fire. She strode around the clearing. Her voice rang out like a funeral knell. "All uncleanness is purified. All harm is repelled. No pestilent spirit may abide here."

Watching Margaret wave the glowing sticks, Lily was reminded of the night she spied on Hugo and his coven. "How is this any different?" she asked herself. She raised her voice to shout over Margaret. "How are you any different to witches?"

Margaret thrust the sticks towards Lily and Hazel. "Every word the Devil puts into their mouths to try to weaken our resolve only makes us more determined." She held the Malleus Maleficarum aloft. "For as the book tells us, it is by reason of the Devil's works that faith is made strong."

She threw the sticks onto the burning carcass. Lily made the mistake of looking at Sam. Her throat spasmed again as flames licked his bubbling skin. Bitter saliva flooded her mouth. She lurched towards Margaret and spat it into her face.

Carl yanked Lily's lead hard enough to lay her out flat on her back. Bob lifted a boot to stamp on her.

"No," said Margaret. She pointed to the spittle running down her face. "I shall wear this like a badge of honour."

Straining to get air into her winded lungs, Lily stared at the crescent moon. A tremor of laughter built in her throat as Hugo's nasal, self-important voice echoed back to her.

Soak in the lunar energy. Can you feel it supercharging your body and mind?

"Yes!" she cried out. "I can feel it."

"Feel what?" Carl asked. "Who are you talking to?"

Lily closed her eyes, writhing and moaning as if ghostly hands were caressing her.

"Get up," said Margaret.

Ignoring her, Lily gasped and bucked her hips. "Satan, I can feel you. Take me. I'm yours."

"Stop that!"

Pausing mid-thrust, Lily flashed a provocative smirk at Margaret. "Why? This is what you came to see, isn't it?"

"Lily–" Hazel began in a warning tone.

Lily silenced her with a scowl. "Shut up, whore." Sliding her tongue around her lips, she eyed the other onlookers. "Touch me. Do whatever you want to me. Use me for your *filthy delights*."

Her gaze stopped on Carl. He returned her stare with a mesmerised intensity. "I know you want me, Carl." She rolled onto her side and wiggled her fingers. "Untie me and I'll do anything you want. Anything at all."

"Careful, little witch." There was a thickness in his voice. "You might just get your way."

Margaret stalked forwards and whipped her palm into Carl's face. He bared his teeth as if he was thinking about hitting her back. His features slackened into a sort of confused grimace as she stroked his cheek tenderly. She opened the book. Her gaze circling between Carl, Lily and the text, she read out, "It is commanded that all wizards and charmers are to be destroyed. Also, the soul which goeth to wizards and soothsayers to commit fornication with them, I will set my face against that soul and destroy it out of the midst of my people."

Silence trailed after the words, disturbed only by the hiss and crackle of the flames. Carl lowered his head as if to receive a blessing. "Let's finish this."

Margaret laid a hand on the thinning hair at his crown. She gestured with the book towards Chapman Hill. "Yes, let us continue to the final place."

34

At the head of the procession, Rupert cut a path through the undergrowth with a stick. Margaret trudged along behind him as if she was wearing concrete boots. Her burst of manic energy appeared to have been spent. Even from several metres away, Lily could hear her laboured breathing.

"Poor Sam," Lily murmured, glancing back down the slope. Slivers of flame flickered through the trees.

"Poor Sam," echoed Hazel.

Lily glared at her. "Don't pretend you care."

"I loved Sam."

"You loved that he took my mind off Dad. Otherwise I might have asked more questions and found out what a lying, cheating slut you are."

Anger flared in Hazel's eyes. "You don't have a clue what you're talking about."

"Why? Because I'm only a child? Well I won't be one for much longer."

Hazel's voice softened into a sigh. "You're right." She glanced at the Moon. "In about an hour, you're going to be sixteen."

"In about an hour, I'm going to be dead."

"No you're not. I'd never let that happen."

Lily gave a derisive snort. "What are you going to do? Sell your soul to save our lives?"

"She hasn't got a soul to sell," said Carl.

"Mr Spencer," Gil said in a cautioning tone.

"I'm just saying, she's got nothing the Devil wants."

"Are you sure about that?" Gil gave Lily a meaningful glance.

Her lips curled into a sneer. "I hope the Devil does exist." She raised her voice loud enough to echo off the trees. "I hope you all burn in Hell."

Susan winced as if envisioning such a fate. She stopped and clutched her knee. "I don't think I can go any further."

"Yes you can," said Gil. "I'll help you."

"Thank you, Dr Hughes, but I... I..." Susan stammered as he slid an arm around her midriff. "No... It's... I'd rather..." She lapsed into despondent silence as he coaxed her onwards.

"Don't worry, Susan," said Carl, his voice dripping with disingenuous concern. "We won't let you miss the grand finale."

"Stop winding her up," rasped Bob. "And you, Susan, remember who you are. You're a Cooper. Don't embarrass our name."

"You're a Cooper," Susan parroted to herself, sounding unsure if that was a good thing.

As the trees thinned out, the slope steepened. Margaret halted again to catch her breath. In the pale haze of moonbeams that illuminated the forest floor, she looked like a reanimated corpse.

"What are the bets, eh Toby?" Carl whispered out of the side of his mouth. "Is she going to make it?"

Toby greeted the question with his customary stony stare.

Carl gave a smirking nod. "Uh-huh. That's what I think too. It's fifty-fifty at best."

"One of these days, Carl, someone's going to wipe that grin

off your face," said Bob.

"And who's that someone going to be, eh you old fart? You?"

Muttering under his breath, Bob set down his jerry cans and rolled himself a cigarette.

"Careful you don't blow yourself up," Carl sneered.

Bob hawked and spat on the ground. "Keep on like that and see what happens."

Gil watched the rancorous exchange with troubled eyes. He turned to Rupert and Margaret. "We have to keep moving."

"My wife needs to rest," said Rupert.

Margaret shook her head. "Dr Hughes is right." She eyed the encircling trees. "There is evil at work here. A dark presence is trying to keep us from our righteous work."

Setting her face into a grimace of determination, she strode onwards. The others marched after her, their faces a medley of fear, excitement, exhaustion and resignation.

They emerged from the forest onto the flank of Chapman Hill. As a breeze blew across the hillside, the grass rippled like a black sea. A mournful bleating was carried on the wind.

Rupert's eyes darted anxiously towards Chapman Hall. "The sheep sound worried."

"That's not your sheep," Lily said in a taunting tone. "That's the Devil messing with you."

Margaret nodded as if the veracity of Lily's words was self-evident. "The Devil at times works to deceive by an illusion of the senses."

"Just as he mixes truth with his lies," added Gil. "Trust nothing you see or hear."

"In that case, how can you trust what Mrs Chapman says?" Lily pointed out. "How do you know she's not the Devil in disguise?" She looked at Toby with eyes as big as a begging dog's. "None of this makes sense. Why can't you see that?"

He stared past her, focused only on the climb.

Bob spoke through his cigarette. "He's not listening to you. None of us are. So you might as well keep your trap shut."

"He's right," said Hazel. "You can't reason with insanity. Your dad taught me that."

Lily turned an icy stare on her mum. "My dad wasn't insane. And if he was, it was your fault."

Carl rolled his eyes as if to say, *Here we go again.* He glanced at his brother. "They bicker more than we do. Maybe we should just let them go at each other. They might save us the job of burning them."

"That sounds like a good idea," Susan said with a twisted kind of hope.

Chuckling, Carl motioned with his head towards the shopkeeper. "Don't get on the wrong side of this one."

"I suggest we limit conversation strictly to essential matters," said Gil.

"And I suggest you stop telling us what to do, Doctor," Carl snarled. "We're not your patients." He narrowed his eyes. "Why are you even here? I've never once seen you in church."

"My family stopped going to church the day they refused to bury Thomas Hughes in consecrated ground. But we never stopped believing. We never stopped following His word."

Carl jutted his square jaw at Gil. "I suppose we'll find out soon enough whether that's true. And if it's not..." He left the words hanging like a threat.

Gil blinked away from his stare. "You must go faster," he urged Margaret.

Mouth agape, breathing raggedly, she quickened her pace. Rupert pressed his palms against her back, struggling for breath himself as he pushed her onwards.

The twinkling lights of Midwood appeared from behind the treetops. "Help!" Lily instinctively cried out at the sight. "Help us!"

"Go ahead, shout all you want," said Carl. "No one can hear you."

Lily continued to call for help at the top of her lungs. One after another, her cries faded away into the night.

Susan covered her ears with her hands. "I can't stand the sound of her voice."

"We're almost there," Gil told her. "It'll all be over soon."

The terrain levelled out abruptly. Margaret snatched Rupert's torch from him and aimed it at Dead Woman's Ditch. Lily was struck silent by the sight. The torchlight traversed the grass bank to its entrance and sought out the rowan tree. The bare branches cast a web of shadows on the steep cutting at the rear of the enclosure. Not a single crow was roosting in the ancient tree. The place appeared to be deserted.

Lily sagged as if all the fight had suddenly gone out of her. Somehow, some part of her had expected Tom to be waiting at the tree to rescue her from this madness. "No one's coming," she murmured, feeling so alone it was like she was already dead.

35

"Ok, Margaret, point made," said Hazel. "You can have the cottage's land. Hell, you can have the cottage too. We'll leave tonight. You'll never see us again."

Without affording her a glance, Margaret entered the enclosure.

"Do you hear me?" Hazel called after her. "You win."

Once more, the words fell on deaf ears. Margaret crossed the shallow depression, bowing her head like someone approaching an altar.

"I don't think she's interested in what you're offering," said Carl, flicking the leads at Hazel and Lily.

Lily wobbled forwards on rubbery legs. As she passed through the earthwork's entrance, she half-collapsed, half-threw herself to the ground. She dug her fingers into the grass as if she was clinging to a cliff.

Toby dropped his jerry cans and lumbered to her side.

"Don't touch her," said Gil. He looked at the bright white moon. "The witching hour is almost upon us. At this time of night, they can bewitch you with a touch or even a look."

Toby's inscrutable eyes lingered on the doctor for a moment, then he bent to take hold of Lily's shoulders.

Carl kicked his brother's hands away from her. "Are you going soft in the head?"

A deep rumble emanated from Toby's chest as he squared up

to Carl. His fingers flexed as if he was thinking about crushing his brother's skull with his bare hands.

"I'm only looking out for you, Toby." Carl's voice was as gentle as that of someone soothing an angry gorilla. "These witches are trying to turn you against us."

"Listen to your brother," Bob urged. "We have to stick together."

The rumbling died down. Toby stepped around Carl to retrieve the jerry cans. Carl released an audible breath of relief. He jabbed a boot into Lily's ribs. "On your feet."

She shook her head stubbornly.

"Have it your own way." Carl headed towards the rowan tree, dragging Lily along by the lead. She cried out as her arms were yanked up at an awkward angle behind her back.

"You won't get away with this," Hazel shouted. "I promise you that."

Carl snorted. "What are you going to do? Summon the Devil to shove a hot poker up my arse?"

"I don't need the Devil to deal with you."

Carl turned and stepped in as close to Hazel as he could without actually touching her. He spoke into her ear like a lover whispering sweet-nothings. "Go on then. Do your worst. I dare you."

In response, she jerked her chin around and kissed him full on the lips. He flinched away from her, his eyes goggling. For a second, his lips twitched as if he wasn't sure what to do with them. Then he thrust his face towards her, kissing her so hard that their teeth clacked together. His tongue probed her mouth. His arms encircled her waist and crushed her to him.

"Stop that," Margaret demanded.

Carl spread his lips wider as if he was trying to eat Hazel's face.

Margaret's voice rose to a screech. "Someone stop them!"

Bob stepped forward and swung one of his jerry cans in a haymaker arc. It thudded into Carl's head, sending him staggering away from Hazel. Clenching his fists, Carl roared, "You old–"

Bob swung the second can. It bounced off the other side of Carl's head. His body stiffened and he toppled to the ground like a felled tree. As his fingers uncurled from the leads, Lily cried, "Run!"

She scrambled to her feet, but Gil grabbed her lead and pulled hard enough to dump her on her backside.

"Go, get out of here!" Lily exhorted her mum.

Hazel didn't move. There was a look of tired fatalism in her eyes. Rupert picked up her lead and drew her towards the tree.

Lily cast a confused glare at Gil. Whose side was he on? Had Hugo – or whoever had phoned to warn them – been referring to someone else?

Toby knelt down to cradle his brother's head. Blood streamed from Carl's hairline. Toby pressed his sleeve to a gash on Carl's scalp.

"I had to do it," Bob said in an apologetic tone.

Carl groaned and his eyelids flickered as consciousness seeped back in.

"You see?" Margaret exclaimed. "You see how easy it is to be seduced by the wiles of the Devil?" She pointed at Carl. "Tie him up."

Toby withdrew a gleaming butcher's knife from a sheath on his belt. He unslung the rope from his shoulder and cut off a length of it.

"W…what are you doing?" Carl slurred as Toby rolled him onto his stomach.

As expertly as a chef trussing a chicken, Toby tied his brother's wrists and ankles.

Carl's eyes snapped open. "What the hell? Untie me!"

Toby stepped backwards as his brother thrashed around and kicked out.

Carl glared up at him. "Toby, I swear to Christ, if you don't–"

"Give it a bloody rest, Carl," Bob interrupted. "You've got no one to blame for this but yourself."

Carl turned his enraged eyes to the gardener. "I'll get you back for this, Bob. You're going to regret hitting me." Veins bulged on his neck as he strained against his bonds and bellowed like a castrated bull.

"The Devil has entered into him," Margaret declared. She shook her fist at Carl. "Depart, O Satan, from him." She flipped through the book and read out, "Accursed Devil, hear thy doom, and give honour to the living God, that thou depart with thy works from this servant–"

"Oh drop the act, Margaret," Hazel broke in, her voice oozing contempt. Her gaze raked over the others. "The same goes for the rest of you. You're not doing this for God." She motioned to Carl with her eyes. "And he's not possessed by the Devil. He's just a sicko who enjoys hurting women."

"She's right," said Susan. "The entire village knows he's a wife beater."

"That slut got what was coming to her," Carl hissed. His eyes spat hate at Hazel. "Now it's your turn."

With sudden decisiveness, Susan shook her head. "I'm not going to help him get his kicks. I won't have any more part in this." She threw down the bundle of 'evidence' and set off limping towards the enclosure's entrance.

"God is watching you, Susan Cooper," Margaret shouted.

Susan darted her a glance that was somehow both timid and

determined. "Then He'll see that I've done nothing wrong."

"Nothing wrong? You're guilty of cowardice. And the cowardly shall be consigned to hellfire along with the sexually immoral." Margaret pointed at Susan and Carl. "Both of you will suffer the second death in eternal Hell."

Her face quivering like a soft pudding, Susan looked at Bob. "So you're really going to do this, Uncle Bob? You're really going to burn these poor–"

She gasped as, without warning, the old gardener charged at her. His fingers, thick and callused from a lifetime of physical labour, closed around her throat. She tried frantically to prise them away, her eyes bulging halfway out of her head.

"Look, all you doubters and unbelievers," Margaret cried out exultantly. "His winnowing fork is in His hand, and He will clear His threshing floor and gather His wheat into the barn, but the chaff He will burn with unquenchable fire."

Gurgling like a blocked drainpipe, Susan sank to the ground. Her tongue protruded further and further as Bob's fingers dug deeper into her flesh. "You're no Cooper!" he roared, his face centimetres from hers.

"That's enough," said Rupert. The words were both a plea and a command.

Bob didn't appear to hear. His features contorting into a wrinkled mask of rage, he slammed Susan into the ground so violently that there was a crunch like ice breaking. As if a tap had been turned off, the gurgling stopped.

"I said that's enough, Bob!"

Bob jerked his head up, seemingly startled by his own name. He let go of Susan, blinking as if he'd woken from a deep sleep. Rupert ran over to them, forcing Hazel to scurry along at his heels. He pressed his fingertips to Susan's throat. "I can't find a pulse."

"She'll be fine," Bob wheezed.

Rupert looked at the old gardener, his face torn between horror and sympathy. "I don't think she will be."

Bob bent to tap his niece's cheek. "Susan, open your eyes."

Her eyes remained shut. Her jaw hung slack. There wasn't a flicker of movement anywhere in her body.

"What have you done, you stupid old sod?" said Carl.

"I was only trying to make her see sense." Bob lifted one of Susan's eyelids. Her eye was webbed with burst blood vessels. "Susan, wake up. Susan, Susan..." His voice petered out. He let the eyelid drop.

"You know where murderers end up, don't you, Mr Cooper?" Hazel said with a distinct note of grim relish in her voice. She looked at Margaret. "Tell him."

There was a brief silence, then Margaret spoke reluctantly. "Murderers will be cast into everlasting fire and the smoke of their torment shall ascendeth up for ever and ever."

Bob let out a croaky wail as if he could already feel the flames licking at his feet. He scooped up Susan and hugged her to his chest, sobbing, "I'm sorry. I'm sorry."

"We have to act *now*," Gil insisted, his eyes darting around as if he expected to be attacked from all sides at any moment. "Otherwise there'll be none of us left alive to do what must be done."

He hauled Lily to her feet and shoved her against the tree. She winced as the knobbly bark dug into her spine. He slung her lead around the trunk and looped it through the knot at her wrists. "Bring the other witch here."

Rupert pulled Hazel towards the tree.

Margaret beckoned to Toby. "Bring the rope, petrol and firewood."

He stared at her. Seconds passed. He didn't move.

"Do as she says, Toby," urged Carl.

"No, don't do as I say," Margaret contradicted him. "Do as God says, for it is He who commands you."

Toby slowly bent to retrieve the rope.

"Hurry," Gil implored as the big man plodded over to the jerry cans. "Midnight is here. Evil is amongst us."

Toby's pace didn't alter. He picked up two cans in one hand and the bundle of blackthorn in the other.

Rupert pressed Hazel against the tree. Blood welled from under the iron collar as she twisted her head towards Lily. She dredged up a sad smile. "Happy birthday."

Lily pointedly looked away from her.

Rupert threaded Hazel's lead behind Lily's back. Lily let out a low gasp as her restraints almost slipped over her knuckles. How had that happened? She glanced at Gil. Had he loosened them?

There was no time to wonder about it now. This was her chance to make a run for it. But what about her mum? Could she leave her behind? Even as the question loomed large in Lily's mind, she knew it wasn't an option. It didn't matter what her mum had done. They were either going to escape together or die together.

She cast a furtive glance at Rupert, who was adjusting her mum's bonds. With a wiggle of her wrists, Lily worked her hands free. She whipped them from behind her back and shoved him as hard as she could. He staggered sideways and fell to one knee. She wrenched at her mum's lead. It started to uncoil from the tree trunk, then snagged on something. Cold fingers closed around Lily's wrist. Sharp nails stabbed into her flesh.

"You're not going anywhere but Hell," Margaret hissed.

Lily tried to yank her arm free. Margaret held on with a strength that belied her emaciated frame. She thrust the Malleus Maleficarum into Lily's face. A white flash briefly blinded Lily as her head snapped back against the tree. A branch swam into focus. She flung up her hand and caught hold of it. With a scream of exertion, she broke away from Margaret. She hauled herself upwards, feet scrabbling against the tree trunk. The book slammed into her spine. She flinched, but managed to keep hold of the branch. A small shower of berries rained down as she launched herself at a higher branch.

Rupert clambered to his feet and made a grab for Lily, but his fingers only brushed her heels. With frenetic haste, she climbed through a lattice of branches. She cried out as one snapped under her weight and almost sent her plummeting back to earth. She paused to get her bearings. The top of the tree was five or six metres away. Her way was blocked by the bulbous growth of twigs that enveloped the tree trunk like a massive nest. To get past it, she would have to risk venturing out onto thinner branches.

Her heart lurched as her mum yelled, "Lily, watch out! He's coming after you!"

Peering down, she saw Rupert hoisting himself into the tree. He glared up at her, his eyes reflecting the moonlight. She grabbed a cluster of berries and flung them at him. He blinked as the blood-red missiles pelted his face. She shakily resumed her climb. The branches creaked and bent precariously as she angled away from the tightknit mass of twigs.

"Careful," Hazel shouted. "Don't put all your weight on one branch at—"

"Silence witch," snapped Margaret. She seized a blackthorn branch from Toby and began whipping Hazel with it.

Hazel lowered her face against the flurry of blows as far as the collar permitted. Blood flowed from scratches on her forehead.

"You're the one going to Hell!" Lily yelled at Margaret. "You sad, evil excuse for a human being."

"I am but the hand of God," Margaret stated between gasps, lowering the branch and leaning on it like a walking stick.

Lily's gaze darted back to Rupert. He was catching up with her. His clenched teeth gleamed through his beard. Despite the fear urging her to go faster, she forced herself to take the time to feel for solid branches. The higher she climbed, the heavier her arms became. Her hands were slick with sweat. She felt her fingers uncurling.

Soak in the lunar energy, she found herself thinking, this time with no trace of irony. *Feel it supercharging your body.*

She raised her face to the Moon, sucked in a deep breath, then pushed onwards. Her head emerged through the uppermost branches. Gasping for breath, she straddled a branch and peered all around. Dead Woman's Ditch was an island in an ocean of darkness. The strongest feeling overcame her that if she dived from the treetop, she wouldn't plunge to the ground, instead she would swoop down the hillside as gracefully as a crow.

A *crack* like a gun going off came from below. Rupert was attempting to follow her route to the treetop, but a branch had given way beneath his bulkier frame. His feet dangled in midair for a few seconds before finding purchase on another branch. He edged back to the tree trunk and started snapping off handfuls of twigs to clear a path through the nestlike growth.

A loud caw rang out. A small black head emerged from the tangle of twigs, followed by a feathered body. Fluttering its white-tipped wings to maintain its balance, the crow stabbed its beak at Rupert's face. As the knifelike beak plunged into his left eye, his scream shattered the night. He reeled backwards, arms windmilling. For a heartbeat, he seemed to be freeze-framed in the air, then he was tumbling head-over-heels through the branches.

With another guttural caw, the crow retreated into the tunnel of twigs from which it had appeared.

"Rupert, where are you?" Margaret cried out.

A groan was the only reply. Margaret shrieked as Toby aimed his head torch at the lower branches. Rupert was hanging upside down. His arms swung gently back and forth two or three metres above the ground. His right leg was snared in a narrow gap between two thick branches. The leg was folded forwards ninety degrees at the knee. A bloody shard of bone was protruding like a spear tip from a tear in his trousers.

Rising onto her tiptoes, Margaret stretched a hand towards Rupert. At the merest touch of her fingertips, another scream erupted from him. Blood was pouring from his injured eye. Margaret blinked as it splattered her face.

She whirled to Toby and Gil. "Get him down!"

"I'll hold him steady. You see if you can free his leg," Gil suggested to Toby.

"Don't touch me," wailed Rupert.

"Have strength, Rupert," said Margaret. "God is with you."

He gritted his teeth as Gil took hold of his arms. Toby hooked his fingers over the lower of the two branches and pulled. As the branch bent downwards, Rupert's broken leg flopped about like a dying fish. "Stop!" he howled, flailing his hands into Gil's face. "You're tearing my leg off!"

Gil ducked away from him.

Toby carefully let the branch rise back to its natural position. "The branch is too strong," he told Margaret. "I need a saw."

She shot a glance at Bob. "His penknife has a saw."

Toby was already striding towards the old gardener.

"Don't help her, Toby," Lily called to him. "She's just using you to do her dirty work."

He paid her no attention.

"Your forked tongue won't save you," Margaret retorted. "We all saw you summon your familiar."

Lily's face scrunched in confusion. *Summon your familiar? What familiar?* A tingle ran over her scalp as she glanced at the thatch of twigs that housed the white-winged crow.

Toby searched Bob's pockets. Seemingly oblivious to everything around him, Bob continued to sob into Susan's hair.

Lily's gaze darted to the enclosure's entrance. Something – maybe a movement, maybe just a shadow – had caught her eye. Her heart skipped. There it was again! A shadowy shape flitted across the gap. Had Tom come to save her after all?

Tom, she silently called out to him. *Tom, Tom…*

All eyes turned towards the entrance as a growl floated between the grass banks. The shadowy shape solidified into a familiar form. Lily's face didn't reveal any surprise as the three-legged dog hobbled into view. Following the appearance made by the white-winged crow, she would hardly have batted an eyelid if the dog had walked in upright on its hind legs.

36

Margaret's mouth dropped open, but only a strange strangled sound came out.

"Save us!" cried Gil, falling to his knees.

Lily wondered whether his appeal was directed at God or the dog.

"Toby, untie me," Carl shouted, struggling against his bonds.

Toby moved away from Bob, positioning himself between the dog and the tree. The bony animal eyeballed him. Returning its stare, he advanced a step. The dog held its ground. Its jowls lifted, exposing curved brown teeth. Metal scraped against leather as Toby unsheathed his knife. They faced off, each seemingly waiting for the other to make the first move.

"Margaret," Rupert said in a weak whisper.

Something gleamed in his hand. He dropped the object at Margaret's feet. Hazel inhaled sharply. It was a lighter. Margaret's forehead furrowed. She found her voice. "What do you want me to do with that?"

"Finish it," Rupert croaked.

A horrified realisation dawned on Margaret's face. She gave a hard shake of her head. "No, no, I can't."

"You can. You *must*."

Margaret closed her eyes. "Please God help me. Tell me what to do."

"God isn't here, my love."

Rupert's words reignited the fanatical fire in Margaret's eyes. "God is *everywhere*," she admonished. She lifted her face to the starry sky. "Lord, forgive my selfishness. I hear you and I will obey. On this hill which you have shown me, I will give my husband to you as a burnt offering. I will not fail you, O Lord!"

With that, she put down the Malleus Maleficarum, unscrewed the cap from a jerry can and turned to Hazel.

"Get away from me," Hazel shouted, kicking out. Her foot clanged into the can, sloshing petrol over both women.

Her stick-thin arms shaking, Margaret lifted the can overhead and upended it. Hazel squeezed her eyes shut as she was drenched in petrol. Choking on its sickly-sweet fumes, she continued to kick blindly at Margaret.

"Toby, help!" Lily cried. "You said you wouldn't let them hurt us."

Toby didn't move a muscle. He appeared to be locked in a staring contest with the dog.

Margaret cast aside the can, then picked up the lighter and a blackthorn branch. She sparked a flame into life and held it and the branch aloft. Blood dribbled down her wrist as she squeezed the branch, driving its thorns into her palm. Her voice filled the enclosure, reverberating like a violin strung too tight. "I have the flame and the wood." She met Rupert's remaining eye. "And…" she faltered, but quickly recovered herself, "I'm ready."

"I'm ready too, my love," said Rupert, spreading his arms like Jesus on the cross. "Send me to Him!"

Margaret looked at Hazel. "Now is the time to confess, witch. Confess and renounce your sins before you meet your maker."

Hazel raised her chin defiantly. "Go to hell."

Margaret nodded as if that was the response she'd expected

or, perhaps, prayed for. "The evil enemy of mankind, who is Satan and the Devil, is in your heart, Hazel Wylde. Since you are determined to keep him there, your punishment shall be the death of your body in this world and of your soul in the next."

The flame wobbled as Margaret lowered it towards Hazel.

Lily started scrambling down through the branches, not looking where she was putting her feet. Her only thought was to get to Margaret. She slipped, fell the length of her legs and landed with bone-jarring force on a branch.

"Stay there, Lily," Hazel shouted.

Ignoring her, Lily resumed her reckless descent.

The flame continued on its path towards Hazel.

"You can stop now, Margaret."

Margaret paused at the sound of Gil's velvety voice. He unfolded his long body from its kneeling position, holding out his hands as if offering an invisible gift. "You've passed the test, and for that you will be truly blessed. He will multiply your descendants beyond number, like the stars in the sky and the sand on the seashore."

A heartbroken hope filled Margaret's eyes. "I'll be able to have more babies?"

"As many as you want."

"Don't listen to him, Margaret." Rupert's voice crackled with pain. "He's turned away from God."

"I knew it!" Carl exclaimed. "I knew he was a Doubting Thomas."

"I'm no Doubting Thomas," said Gil. "I'm a true believer."

"Yeah, a true believer in Satan."

"Light the fire, Margaret," Rupert implored. "Do it now."

Gil's voice dropped to a tender whisper. "You can still have a life, Margaret. You can still have a family. All you have to do is put down the lighter."

Seemingly considering his words, Margaret was silent for a few breaths. Then, shuddering as if something slimy had touched her, she cried out, "Away with you, Tempter! I will not eat your fruit. I will ascend to Heaven." Her eyes jerked to Hazel. "And you shall be brought down to the lowest depths of the pit!"

With that, she thrust the lighter at Hazel.

At the same instant, Lily landed on Margaret. The two of them crumpled to the ground and rolled about in a chaotic jumble of limbs. One second, Lily was on top, fish-hooking her thumb into Margaret's mouth. The next, Margaret flipped her onto her back and lunged downwards, teeth bared like a rabid animal. Lily screamed as Margaret bit her ear. Margaret ragged Lily's head from side to side, then reared up with a chunk of bloody flesh clasped in her teeth. She spat it into Lily's face and jeered breathlessly, "That's for Jude!"

Hazel cried out as if it was her ear, twisting and straining in a desperate attempt to free herself.

Lily bucked her hips. Margaret fell sideways, landing just out of reach of Hazel's flailing foot. Margaret sparked the lighter into flame again. "Burn!" she spat at Hazel. "Burn! Burn!"

Lily frantically scrambled towards Margaret. Her palm landed on something flat and leathery. She knew at once what it was. She snatched up the Malleus Maleficarum and hurled it at Margaret. It twirled through the air and hit her hand, knocking the lighter into her lap.

Margaret's petrol-soaked gown burst into flame. She sprang to her feet, her eyes seemingly trying to eject themselves from their sockets. The flames whooshed up her sleeves and ignited her hair.

"Margaret! Margaret!" Rupert wailed helplessly as she

staggered around slapping at the flames.

Gil dodged out of her way. Bob's head snapped up as she passed close enough for the flames to stroke his neck. "Your ladyship!" he cried, dropping Susan as if she suddenly meant nothing to him.

Margaret careered towards the dog, arms spread as if to envelop it in a fiery embrace. Rearing up onto its hind legs, it punched her in the chest with its single front paw. The blow spun her around, sending a swirl of flames skywards. She staggered up the embankment, groping at the air like someone feeling their way in the dark.

Bob ran after her, rocking on his crooked legs. "Your ladyship! Your ladyship!" he kept calling out as if they were the only words his panicked brain could generate.

For an eerily motionless instant, Margaret stood rigid on the brow of the grass bank. Then, trailing sparks like a comet, she disappeared down its other side.

Bob pursued her. "Your ladyship! Your ladyship..."

The flicker of the flames faded along with his voice, leaving behind a stupefied stillness. Rupert seemed to stare off into an abyss only he could see.

Lily blinked rapidly as if trying to dispel a hallucination. She rose to pull at the iron collar's pin. A cry of frustration escaped her when it refused to come loose. She whirled around, fists clenched at a touch on her shoulder.

"Let me," said Gil, reaching for the pin.

His voice jolted Rupert back to life. "Traitor!" Rupert yelled, convulsing with grief and rage. "All the torments of Hell await you."

"Better to reign in Hell than serve in Heaven," Gil replied. He smiled at Lily. "Don't you think?"

Her lips formed a cautious line.

Gil tweaked the pin from its clasp. Hazel gasped with relief as the iron collar's hinges squeaked open. Puncture marks dotted her throat like a line showing where to cut. Little rivulets of blood trickled down her chest.

Gil flung the collar aside as if it were a grenade. He turned his attention to untying Hazel's wrists. When her bonds dropped to the ground, she set about rubbing the circulation back into her hands.

"You saved my life," she said to Lily, her eyes shining with pride.

Lily gave a shrug. "What else was I supposed to do? You're my mum."

Hazel placed both hands on her heart as if the simple statement meant more to her than anything.

Rupert's voice scraped out overhead. "Babylon the great, mother of whores and of Earth's abominations." He stabbed a finger at Hazel. "God will repay you double for your deeds."

"And I will repay you triple for yours," she fired back. "Ever mind the Rule of Three! Three times your acts shall return to thee. This lesson well thou must learn. Thou only gets what thee dost earn."

"So mote it be," Gil intoned.

"So mote it be," a host of voices joined in from the darkness outside the enclosure.

37

With a creeping horror, Lily looked from her mum to Gil and back. "You're... You're..." she stammered, struggling to process the full significance of what's she'd heard.

"I'm a witch." Hazel's tone was matter-of-fact. "As have been all the women in our family, all the way back to Mary."

Lily swayed like someone on shifting sands. "So who... what am I?"

"You are my firstborn daughter," Hazel stated as if that was the only thing that mattered.

"And what..." Lily could barely bring herself to ask the question. "What about my dad? What was he to you?"

"He was exactly what he needed to be."

"What does that mean?"

"It means you are of your father, the Devil," Rupert interjected hoarsely. "And the lusts of your father, it is your will to–"

His words transformed into screams as Gil reached up and pulled one of his arms like it was a bell rope.

As Rupert trailed off into gasping sobs, Hazel told Lily, "It means everything has happened as it was meant to happen. I had no choice in the matter and neither do you. You're sixteen now, Lily. It's time to accept what you are."

Tears spilling from her eyes, Lily glared at her mum. "I'll tell you what *you* are – you're a murderer. You did something to my dad – drugged him or... something. You drove him mad. Why? Why did you do it?"

"Because I didn't need him anymore."

Lily's face went slack at the chillingly frank admission.

"You want the truth," Hazel continued. "Well here it is. I used your father to give me a healthy daughter. I used him to help raise you. And when the time came, I gave him just enough rope to hang himself."

Laughter rasped from Rupert. "Shameless witch. God is laughing at you, for He knows your day is coming." His bloodshot eye traversed the enclosure's perimeter. His voice rose to a croaky shout. "The same goes for all of you deceivers. The moment is near when you shall be repaid in full for your detestable practices."

"And what about you, Rupert?" Hazel asked with calm curiosity. "When will you be repaid for your 'detestable practices'?"

Spreading his arms, Rupert spoke to the air. "I hear you. I surrender myself to your judgement."

A smile played on Hazel's lips. "He thinks that voice he's hearing is God."

Gil chuckled as if she'd said something witty. A bark echoed around the enclosure. He fell silent and turned to the dog. It barked again, jerking its scabby black nose towards Toby. The butcher was cutting his brother's bonds.

Hazel strode towards them. From somewhere secreted on herself, she took out a white feather. Toby looked up from his task. At the same instant, she put the feather's quill to her lips. Her cheeks inflated as she blew a puff of white powder into his face. He clambered to his feet, blinking and wiping his eyes. Hazel dodged away as he lashed out blindly with his knife.

A dry, hacking cough shook Toby's powerful frame. He doubled-over, then dropped to one knee.

"Get up!" Carl bellowed.

"Stay where you are," countered Hazel.

Toby trembled as if he was caught between two opposing forces. He started to rise, then slumped forwards.

Like a priest laying on hands, Hazel pressed her palms on his broad back. "Lie down."

He sank onto his belly.

"Good boy," Hazel said as if praising an obedient dog.

He didn't resist as she took his knife from him. Her gaze shifted to Carl. He sprang up like a jack-in-the-box, rapidly shuffled his tied feet towards the enclosure's entrance, overbalanced and pitched forwards onto his face. He rolled over with blood running from his nostrils.

"I'll give you anything you want," he pleaded as Hazel approached. "Just don't hurt me."

She side-stepped as he kicked out at her. The knife blade darted towards him. "Oh God, no, no–" He was rendered mute with astonishment as she sawed at the rope around his ankles.

"Silly boy." Amusement tinkled Hazel's voice. "I'm not going to hurt you."

The severed rope dropped from Carl's ankles. Confusion swirled in his eyes as Hazel freed his wrists. She straightened. He rose to tower over her. She gestured towards the entrance. "Go, if you want to."

His eyes narrowed as if he suspected a trick. "Just like that, you're letting me go?"

Hazel nodded. "You have nothing we want."

"You want me to keep my mouth shut about this, don't you? I could go to the police."

"Feel free to do so." Hazel gestured to herself and Lily. "We've done nothing wrong." She titled an eyebrow at Carl. "Can you say the same?"

His tongue darted uncertainly between his lips. He glanced at the entrance as if he was thinking about making a run for it. His gaze shifted to the dog. It was licking a sore on its front paw. It didn't look up as Carl took several tentative steps towards the gap in the grass bank.

"How can you leave your brother behind?" Lily called after him.

Carl paused. Toby was lying motionless, his breath shuddering out in quick spurts. Carl looked at Hazel. "Can I take Toby–"

"No," she cut him off.

There was something almost comically pitiful about the sudden mass of tics and twitches that overtook Carl's face. His eyes fleetingly spewed hate at Hazel before submissively dropping to his feet. Head hanging like a broken puppet's, he resumed walking towards the entrance. He gave the dog a wide berth.

"Coward," Lily shouted at his back.

"The cowardly will be cast into the lake that burns with fire and sulphur," Rupert cried out.

"Oh shut up," Lily snapped.

"Burns and burns forever and–"

"Shut up!"

Lily bent to snatch up a blackthorn branch. She made as if to bludgeon Rupert into silence. He crossed his arms over his chest and bowed his head like a worshiper receiving Holy Communion. Lily froze midmotion. An intense pressure suddenly seemed to permeate the air. An itch grew between her shoulder blades.

Turning, she saw that her mum, Gil and even the dog were watching her intently. Meeting her mum's gaze, she dropped the stick. "I told you, I'll never become what they say I am."

Hazel's face gave no indication of her thoughts. She glanced up at the sickle moon. After waiting for a cloud to pass across it, she nodded as if satisfied everything was as it should be. She lifted her hands and clapped twice.

The sharp sound echoed off into expectant silence. The air pressed in on Lily, squeezing her chest, making it difficult to get a full breath. She gave a slight start as a low, dark shape appeared in the enclosure's entrance. At first, she thought it was another dog. But as the shape advanced, she saw that it was someone in a hooded black robe. The figure's enormous belly dragged across the grass as it crawled backwards on its hands and knees.

An obvious name sprang to Lily's mind – Hugo.

Another robed figure crawled backwards into view. And another, and another, until nine of them were lined up behind the dog. Gil joined the end of the queue.

The dog rolled its eyes towards them, lifting its tail erect. The first figure turned to crawl forwards. Lily's suspicion was confirmed as Hugo's round red face emerged from his hood. Her stomach gave a convulsive twist as he puckered his lips and ever so tenderly kissed the dog's anus.

Rupert's voice rang out like a clap of thunder. "Shame on you!"

As Hugo crawled onwards, the next witch in line repeated the ritual. Hugo heaved his corpulent frame into a kneeling position in front of Hazel and kissed the back of her hand.

A jolt of realisation struck Lily. She shot her mum a razor-sharp look. "You're the magistra."

"The title passes down through the women of our family," Hugo informed her, using the tree to clamber to his feet.

"Our family?" echoed Lily, struggling once again to wrap her head around what she was being told. "And you're what to me?"

Hugo's thick lips curved into a curiously gentle smile. "I'm your uncle."

"Hugo's my older brother," Hazel elaborated.

"Uncle? Brother?" Lily murmured as if trying to decipher some cryptic code. A splutter of involuntary laughter burst from her. She clapped a hand over her mouth and swallowed her laughter before pointing to the other witches. "I suppose they're my family too, are they?"

"In a way, yes they are," said Hazel, extending her hand again as another robed figure drew near.

A pair of vaguely familiar keen blue eyes peered out from under the hood. Lily struggled to place who they belonged to. Was it... Yes, it was the policewoman who'd taken her statement about Jude. What was her name? Nicola something-or-other.

Nicola kissed Hazel's knuckles before rising to stand beside Hugo.

"Shame! Shame!" Rupert kept booming out the word as, one by one, the rest of the figures kissed the dog's behind and Hazel's hand. Their hoods shadowed faces both old and young, male and female. Lily didn't recognise any more of them.

When the last in line had performed the arse-kissing ritual, Hazel turned and walked backwards to the dog.

"Don't do it, Mum," Lily implored. "Please don't do it."

Hazel smiled and mouthed, "It's ok."

She bowed to press her lips to the dog's anus. As if she was kissing a lover, she kept them there for a long moment. The dog lifted its face towards the Moon, letting out a soft whine that crawled over Lily's skin like hundreds of spiders.

At last, Hazel straightened, approached Lily and laid a hand on her shoulder. "It's time."

"Time for what?"

Hazel's gaze slid meaningfully towards the dog, then back to Lily.

Once more, realisation hit Lily like a stone thrown from the darkness. Grimacing, she shook her head as if attempting to detach it from her body.

"It's your birth right," said Hazel.

"I don't want it."

"It doesn't matter what you want." Hazel motioned to her fellow witches. "Try to imagine they're not here. Imagine it's just you, me and Doubting Tom."

"That's not Doubting Tom." Sounding like she was trying to convince herself, Lily added, "It can't be."

"There are many Doubting Toms in the world, Lily. All this one wants from you is one thing." Hazel made a narrow gap between her thumb and forefinger. "Just one little thing and he'll be your best friend for life. There's no one more loyal than him. No one more caring or giving."

Tears trembled on Lily's eyelashes. "I can't do it."

"Yes you can. Besides, there's no point resisting." Hazel ran a finger along the white stripe in Lily's hair. "His mark is already upon you. Whether or not you like it, you belong to him."

"No I don't." Lily's voice quivered, but didn't give out. "I belong to me."

Hazel smiled, seemingly pleased by Lily's defiance. Her gaze swept over the onlookers. "Blessed are the strong."

"Blessed are the strong," they chorused. "For they shall inherit the Earth."

Their voices made Lily's ears buzz as if a bee was trapped

inside her skull.

Hazel gently placed her palms on Lily's cheeks. "Only the strong get to enjoy every pleasure life has to offer. After everything you've been through, Lily, don't you think you deserve to enjoy yourself?"

Her words etched a deep crease into Lily's forehead. "Yes but... but..."

"But what? What are you so afraid of?"

Lily jerked away from her mum's hands. "You! I'm afraid of you."

"It saddens me to hear that, but it changes nothing. You're going to do this, Lily. And believe me, if you do it of your own free will, it will be all the sweeter."

"Sweeter for who?"

"For all of us."

Lily eyed the dog. It stared back, tongue lolling, drool dangling from its jowls. With its usual shuffling movements, it turned to present its rear end to her. *Sweeter.* The word seemed to echo tauntingly in her ears. A shudder of visceral disgust ran through her. "I won't do it. I'm not like you."

Hazel took a patient breath. "I know you think I'm evil, but... Well you tell me, who's the truly evil one here? Me, who just wants to protect my family?" She pointed to Rupert. "Or him, who was going to burn us alive?"

"You're both as bad as each other."

Hazel's jaw twitched as if she was struggling to hold back her emotions. "*Three-hundred-and-thirty-three!*" She hurled the number at Lily like an insult. "For three-hundred-and-thirty-three years, the Chapmans have blackened our name, murdered us and stolen our land. And what did we ever do to deserve it?"

"You sold your soul to Satan," Rupert retorted.

"And what about your soul, Rupert? Who have you sold your soul to?"

"My soul belongs to God. If I have done wrong, He will forgive me."

Hazel gave him a lopsided look. "Are you sure of that?"

"I will accept His judgement, whatever it may be."

A smirk danced on Hazel's lips. "It's not the false god's judgement you should be worried about. For three centuries we have waited and now the moment is here. Tonight we will put right all the wrongs you have done."

"Do what you will. I'm not afraid of you."

"All in good time." Hazel's voice was calm but firm as if she was dealing with an impatient child. "You'll get your chance to prove your worth soon enough."

Her gaze returned to Lily. She opened her mouth to speak, but Rupert beat her to it. "Don't listen to her. She would murder the entire world to save herself."

"He's wrong." Hazel leaned in to whisper to Lily. "I would murder the entire world to save you."

Lily recoiled as if her mum had some contagious disease. "I don't want you to murder anyone for me. And I *don't* want to join your coven. All I want..." A sob shook her shoulders. "All I want is my dad back."

Something akin to jealousy flashed in Hazel's eyes. "Well you can't have him back. He's dead." With relish, she spelled out each letter. "D...E...A–"

As the dog barked again, she broke off and cast it a questioning look. A spark of comprehension flickered in her eyes. "Maybe..." she faltered as if hesitant to reveal her thoughts. Another bark from the dog prompted her to continue, "Maybe there is a way for you to have him back."

"I can have my dad back?" Lily's voice quivered with the

same pitiful, empty hope as Margaret's had.

Hazel stroked her chin, seemingly mulling over the question. She looked at Hugo as if seeking his opinion.

He nodded. "It can be done." He glanced uneasily at the dog. "But you must not make Doubting Tom wait any longer, Lily. He doesn't like to wait for anyone. Not even a future magistra."

There was none of the usual snuffling condescension in his voice. It was a simple, stark statement.

Lily thought about her dad, how he used to tell her inappropriate jokes, take her to fast-food restaurants, let her stay up past her bedtime... The list of things she'd loved him for went on and on. "How..." Her mouth was so dry she could barely get her words out. "How can it be done?"

"First things first," said Hazel, sweeping a hand towards the dog.

Lily's nose wrinkled. Doubting Tom's anus looked like an open wound. *Could I?* she asked herself queasily. *Could I actually do it?*

"It's a trick," Rupert slurred, sounding as if was he on the brink of losing consciousness. "Satan will take your soul and give nothing in return."

"Wrong," said Hugo, reverting to his pedantic, nasal tone. "Unlike your god, who expects everything for nothing, our master's generosity is without measure."

"Listen to your uncle," Hazel urged. "If you worship the true god of gods, it will all be yours. Everything you dream about. Everything you wish for. *He* is the only one who can give it to you."

Tears of longing slid down Lily's cheeks as she closed her eyes and pictured her dad's face as it was on his wedding photos – smiling, clear-eyed, full of excitement for the future. He seemed as far away as the Moon, yet somehow so close that she could almost reach out and touch him.

You can do this, she told herself. But when she opened her eyes and saw the dog, her face crumpled once more into hopeless disgust.

Hazel took hold of Lily's chin and turned it towards her. "Don't look at him. Don't even think about him. Just listen to my voice and do as I say. Take a step backwards."

Lily hesitated for a moment more. Then she stepped back as slowly as if she was approaching the rim of a bottomless pit.

"You're doing good, keep going," Hazel encouraged.

Lily retreated another step and another…

She caught sight of Rupert. Blood was oozing from his pierced eyeball. His other eye was glassy and unfocused. His mouth gaped like he was silently screaming. "Is he dead?"

Gil reached up to feel for a pulse in Rupert's wrist. "He's passed out. I'll try to bring him around."

"No, don't," said Hazel. "I don't want him ruining Lily's moment. Just make sure he doesn't die."

Gil retrieved one of the cloth leads and set about bandaging Rupert's injured eye with it.

Hazel continued guiding Lily towards the dog. The other witches looked on as avidly as a church congregation. Hugo held up the 'hoodie' Hazel had made as if to say to Lily, *This will soon be yours.*

Lily's breathing quickened as Susan's corpse came into view. Susan's features were as shapeless as melted cheese. Burst blood vessels had transformed her eyes into black mirrors.

"Keep looking at me, Lily," said Hazel, her voice reassuringly soft. "You're almost there."

You're almost there. Lily trembled at the words.

Hazel squeezed Lily's hands as if transferring strength to

her. "You can close your eyes if you want."

Lily shut her eyes as tightly as possible. She visualised her dad again, picturing him holding her hand, stroking her knuckles. Back and forth went his thumb. Steady. Soothing.

She felt herself being turned around. Her mum pressed down on her shoulders. Slowly, inexorably, Lily bent at the knees.

"Resist!" a voice cried out so piercingly that it paralysed Lily. Rupert had regained consciousness. "For the love of God, resist!"

Lily tried to focus on nothing but her dad's thumb feathering its way back and forth, back and forth...

"For the love of your father, do it," Hazel countered.

The words wrenched Lily into motion. Her knees came to rest on the grass. Her mum guided her forwards.

Imagining her dad's face in front of her, Lily pursed her lips to give him a peck on the cheek. A musty, fishy, faintly metallic stench invaded her nostrils, shattering the carefully constructed illusion. She jolted her head back.

"Oh no you don't," said Hazel, giving her a shove.

Bile bubbled up Lily's throat as the putrid smell attacked her even more savagely. Opening her eyes, she found herself staring almost point-blank at the dog's winking anus. With something between a retch and a scream, she twisted away from her mum and fell onto her front. She crawled towards the enclosure's entrance, her back arching as she dry-heaved.

Rupert let out a triumphant shriek.

Clicking her tongue in disappointment, Hazel strode after Lily. "Why do you always have to make things more difficult than they need to be?"

"She's wilful, just like you," said Hugo.

The dog gave another high-pitched bark, scuffing at the grass with one of its hind legs.

Hazel's voice vibrated with urgency. "Ok then, Lily, the hard way it is."

She grabbed Lily's chin and pulled her head up. Lily saw the white feather, but didn't even have time to close her eyes before a plume of powder hit her in the face.

38

L ily's nostrils felt as if they were on fire. She fell onto her face, snorting and spitting. The fiery sensation raced down her throat, scorching away the nausea. She tried to wipe off the powder, but her arms felt as rigid and heavy as tree trunks. Her mum rolled her over.

Lily gave a strangled gasp. Shafts of light as silver as the Moon were radiating from her mum.

Smiling like some benevolent goddess, Hazel reached down to clean Lily's face with her sleeve. The other witches closed in. They seemed as tall as trees that encircled the cottage.

Go away, Lily strained to shout. All she managed was a guttural groan.

Gently, the witches stripped her, lifted her and carried her towards the dog. The new moon seemed to leer down at her naked body. The witches turned her over. She found herself staring at a pair of feet – human feet – one of which had no toes. Her gaze glided over skinny legs, a forest of dark pubic hair, a veiny erect penis.

She felt nothing at the sight. No disgust. No arousal. It was as if her emotions had been scooped out like a boiled egg.

A wiry abdomen slid into view, a scrawny neck, a sharp jawline, downturned lips, a beaky nose, grey eyes...

Tom, she exclaimed, unsure whether she'd said it out loud or merely in her head.

"Hi Lily." He smiled, reaching up to stroke her face with the nubs of his partially formed fingers.

A static-like tingle ran through her at his touch. She pushed some words past her swollen tongue. "Are you really here?"

"Yes, I'm really here. Kiss me."

As the witches lowered Lily towards Tom, she saw that his jaw was dotted with blonde stubble. The coarse hairs prickled her as he planted a hard kiss on her slack lips. He rammed his tongue so far into her mouth that she choked on it. Flecks of spittle sprayed his face as he drew away from her.

The witches flipped her over again and set her down beside him. Torchlight dazzled her. People swam in and out of focus – her mum, Uncle Hugo, an old woman with a whippet-like face, a man with ratty whiskers.

"I want my dad," Lily heard herself saying in a voice as hollow as the rowan tree.

"He's on his way," her mum assured her. "He'll be here soon."

Tom loomed into view, haloed by orange light. He eagerly parted her thighs and slid between them. His pubic hair rubbed against hers. An intense stretching sensation assaulted her groin. His tongue poking out in concentration, he thrust his hips at her.

Out of nowhere, a giggle escaped Lily.

"Try to relax," said Hugo. "You'll enjoy it more."

"Ok, Uncle *Huge-O*."

Lily's laughter grew louder as bemusement rippled over Hugo's face.

"Tell her to be quiet, Dad," Tom whined, slowing to a stop. "I can't do *it* if she's not quiet."

"Dad?" Lily parroted. "So you're my cousin?" As if she'd never heard anything so ludicrous, another bout of strangely toneless laughter shook her.

Tom's face reddened. "Stop laughing!"

"No." Hazel's voice rang out authoritatively. "Let there be laughter." She swept a hand at her fellow witches. "Laugh, dance, embrace. Take whatever pleasure you want."

At her words, the onlookers erupted into forced-sounding laughter. They shed their robes, revealing bodies of all varieties – smooth, wrinkled, chubby, slim, toned, saggy...

Lily lapsed into a sort of awed silence at the sight of Hugo's belly. The vast expanse of hairless flesh hung down almost to his knees, concealing his genitals. Deep stretch marks mapped out its surface. With surprising nimbleness, he rose onto tiptoes and danced around her and Tom. The other witches followed his lead, keeping their backs turned to each other.

Their prancing movements became increasingly frantic, leaving shimmering trails across Lily's vision. Suddenly, the witches converged into one groping, squeezing, licking, slurping mass. Their laughter changed to grunts and moans.

Tom began to move his hips again, pounding away faster and harder, faster and harder...

A sense of dislocation overtook Lily. Every impact seemed to knock her body a little further out of sync with her mind.

"Lily, Lily," Tom chanted, his buttocks going up and down like a jackhammer.

"Lily, Lily," echoed the coven.

Her gaze drifted to the rowan tree. Rupert's intact eye was closed. His lips were moving as if in silent prayer. As she took in his bloodied face and broken leg, she once again felt nothing – no anger, no sympathy. He could hang there until he rotted for all she cared.

Her eyes wandered back to the witches. They were coiling around each other like eels in a bucket. It was difficult to tell where one body started and another ended. She caught glimpses of her uncle and the policewoman and... Was that Toby? And who was that he was thrusting away on top of? Was it... Yes, it was Susan's naked corpse.

Still, she felt nothing. Just a vast emptiness.

Her gaze fell on her mum, who was watching over the proceedings as closely as a mother hen with her brood.

Another impact jolted Lily. Her vision blanked out for a split second, then she found herself staring down at her own expressionless face. It dawned on her that she wasn't in her body anymore. She was floating above it like a balloon on a string.

Am I dead? she wondered. The possibility didn't seem so bad. At least it had been painless. And it would wipe the smug look off her mum's face. It would almost be worth it just to see that.

Hazel turned away from Lily and Tom to approach the tree. A powerful sense of déjà vu washed over Lily as she saw that it was now thronged with crows. Dozens of them were perched wing-to-wing on the branches, jostling and pecking at their neighbours.

"Rupert, Rupert," Hazel cooed as if rousing him from a nap.

His eye blinked open.

She motioned to the scene of debauchery. "Do you like what you see?"

Rupert's beard split into a righteous snarl. "Unclean spirit, you will not tempt me." He made the sign of the cross at her. "In the name of God, I reject the power of Satan. Be gone! Get thee behind me!"

Hazel's eyes sparkled with amusement. "There's someone I want you to meet. Someone who's been waiting a long, long time for this."

She squatted down, poked her head into the hollow tree trunk and called out, "Mary. Mary. Mary."

An eerily paralysing silence descended over the enclosure. The witches lay like a heap of corpses. The crows looked on like little statues. Even the air seemed to be frozen in place.

Then Lily heard it – a scrabbling like an animal digging for roots, barely audible at first, but gradually getting louder as if something was clawing its way up the burrow.

Hazel glanced at Rupert. "She's coming."

His lips trembled, then his words rattled out like a dying man's. "Our Father, who art in heaven, hallowed be thy name. Thy kingdom come. Thy..." He faltered as a dry wheeze issued from the hollow.

"Come, Mary," Hazel encouraged softly. "Come see what we've brought you. Come see how much you're loved."

The wheezing intensified as if the tree was struggling for breath.

"Thy will... Thy will..." Rupert stammered.

Hazel gave him some encouragement too. "Speak up, Rupert. Let her hear your voice. Let her know her enemy is here."

"Thy will be done!" he obliged. "On earth as it is in heaven. Give us this day our daily bread. And forgive us–"

"No!" Hazel snarled as if he'd offended her. "We do not forgive. Vengeance is *ours*."

"And *we* shall repay it, sister," Hugo added from amidst the jumble of sweaty bodies.

"Many times over, brother."

A collective gasp filled the enclosure. "Behold!" Hazel proclaimed, spreading her arms. "The hour cometh, yea, is now come!"

Slowly, ever so slowly, a pair of hands emerged from the hollow. Their fingers were as twisted and knobbly as the tree's branches. Their long nails were curled like wood shavings.

Lily's ears buzzed. The pressure was suddenly back in her groin, stretching, throbbing.

"Forgive those who trespass against us." Rupert's words spilled out in a horrified cascade. "And... And..." He faltered again as arms as brittle-looking as rotten twigs edged into view. A withered head with a wispy covering of ash-grey hair materialised from the darkness.

"Oh God! Oh Lord!" Rupert gasped. "Lead us not into evil."

"You mean lead us not into temptation," Hazel corrected. She reached for the gnarled hands. "Let me help you, Mary."

Like a midwife easing a newborn into the world, Hazel drew the mummified-looking creature out of the tree. A groan rasped from Mary's lipless, toothless mouth as Hazel helped her to sit up. Tatters of scaly skin flaked from Mary's hunched back. Her jutting spine creaked like a branch in the wind.

A bark rang out. Hugo lurched from amongst his fellow witches as if they'd prodded him with a spike. He bounced forwards on his belly like a walrus. A three-legged shape ambled out of the hole he'd left.

Mary's milky eyes widened in recognition.

The dog hobbled towards her, wagging its tail. It nuzzled her, unfurling its tongue to lick her face.

"My prince," Mary said in a voice like the rustle of dead leaves.

The pressure inside Lily ratcheted up to a stabbing pain. She realised she was descending towards the last place she wanted to be – her own body. Tom was moving more slowly between her thighs now. With each rhythmic thrust, sweat overflowed from a pool in the small of his back.

"Our prince!" the coven chorused. "We praise and honour thee."

Rupert lifted up his voice in opposition. "Deliver us from

evil!"

Mary's jaw clicked as she whispered something to Doubting Tom. He backed away from her, pawed at the air below Rupert and emitted a soft whine.

"Yes, my prince," Hazel said as if she understood the dog's language. She beckoned over her shoulder. "Gil."

The doctor extracted himself from beneath several of his fellow witches and scurried to the tree.

Hazel pointed to Rupert. "Take off his shirt."

Gil tore apart the buttons. Fleshy, almost feminine nipples protruded from Rupert's greying chest hair. Hazel smiled as if she liked what she saw. Gil yanked the shirt sleeves over Rupert's hands. Rupert's lungs heaved in agony as his broken leg bobbed up and down. Spatters of blood flicked from the open fracture. Doubting Tom stuck out his tongue as if trying to catch raindrops on it.

"For thine… is…" Rupert said in a weak, stumbling voice.

Doubting Tom's ribs rippled against his scabrous fur as he rose onto his hind legs.

"Lift him up," said Hazel.

Carefully, reverently, Gil clasped the dog's shoulders and hoisted him overhead.

"The kingdom, the power…" Rupert gasped as he came face-to-face with Doubting Tom.

The dog's tongue darted out to slide under the makeshift bandage and probe at Rupert's eye.

"And the… And…" Rupert's voice degenerated into sobs as the long, black-spotted tongue slithered over his face and neck, leaving behind a snail-trail of saliva. With a sudden hungry movement, Doubting Tom latched on to one of Rupert's nipples.

The sobs became screams as the dog's teeth sheared through the bullet of flesh. Blood spurted from the little stump that remained. The dog lapped it up like cream.

"The glory!" Rupert shrieked, wrapping his arms around Doubting Tom and embracing him tightly.

The grotesque slurping sounds made by the dog sent something akin to a shudder through Lily. Her body was within touching distance. The nearer she got to it, the more her nerve endings came back to life. Soon she would be reconnected with all of its suffering.

Lower and lower she descended like a coffin being consigned to the grave. Suddenly, as if a switch had been flipped, she was no longer looking down at herself. She was looking up at Tom.

His pupils were glassy and dilated. Breathing like he'd run a marathon, he gave one final quivering thrust. Lily gasped, feeling as if she was being pumped full of ice water. He collapsed onto her chest and lay there twitching. She tried to push him off, but her arms still refused to work properly.

A tortured moan issued from Rupert's white lips. He was so pale it looked as if there was no blood left in him. "For ever and ever..." he breathed, trailing off into unconsciousness. His arms dropped away from the dog. His eyes rolled back into his head.

"That's enough for now, Gil," said Hazel.

Gil gently lowered Doubting Tom to the ground.

The dog flopped down like a distended leech. His belly pushed out from between his ribcage as he breathed with sedated slowness.

Gil pressed a thumb to Rupert's bleeding nipple like he was plugging a leaky pipe. Hazel beckoned to the other witches. "Bring my daughter."

The naked figures disentangled themselves from each other.

Tom shook himself out of his stupor. His eyes were sunken with fatigue. Crow's feet radiated from their outer corners. It was as if a mask of makeup had been removed from his face. Lily wondered how old he was. He didn't look like a teenager anymore. He looked like someone in their twenties. Maybe even older.

She winced as he heaved himself from between her legs. He grasped her wrists and pulled her into a sitting position. Her head lolled forwards and she saw that her thighs were smeared with blood.

"I'm too knackered to carry her," he grumbled.

A bearish figure shambled towards Lily. Toby's thick biceps swelled as he lifted her into his arms. A low moan whistled from her as her head flopped at an awkward angle.

"Be careful," Tom snapped.

As blank-faced as ever, Toby cradled Lily's head in the crook of his arm.

The coven gathered around the tree. Hugo took up a position beside Hazel again. Toby moved to stand at her opposite shoulder. She reached to give Hugo and Lily's hands a squeeze. "I've never been happier than I am right now."

Tom straggled over to Hazel. "Did I do ok?"

She cupped his face and kissed his forehead. "The seed has been planted in a good soil by great waters, that it might bring out branches, and that it might bear fruit to be a goodly vine."

"Not too goodly, I hope," Hugo quipped.

Laughter rippled through the gathering. The crows erupted into a cacophony of caws as if they, too, were amused.

So slowly that it seemed like the slightest movement was an immense effort, Mary shuffled on her bum to Doubting Tom. She rested a hand on his bloated belly. He lifted his front paw, placing it proprietorially on her shoulder. There was a hairless pink patch of skin with a wart-like growth in his armpit. Mary's black-rimmed mouth puckered. She slumped forwards to latch onto the bobble of flesh. Her throat contracted as she sucked. A substance as white and lumpy as cottage cheese leaked from the corners of her mouth.

Mary's sucking strengthened as if Doubting Tom was pumping fresh vitality into her withered body. With a sudden whimper, he pushed a paw into her chest. She fell away from him, spitting up chunks of the creamy secretion like an overfed baby. Her cloudy eyes focused on Lily. Her barely-there voice whispered, "Come, Lily." She lifted a hand to fondle one of her raisin-like nipples. "Veni, veni, Lily."

Hazel put a hand to her mouth, tearing up as if Lily had been chosen for a high honour. The other witches clapped. The crows shook their wings and filled the night with their croaking song.

"They give praise to you, my daughter," said Hazel.

With every last bit of conviction she could muster, Lily breathed out a single word, "No."

"You can't turn this down, Lily."

"Yes I can."

Hazel leant in close to murmur, "Please don't make me use the White Breath again, Lily. A second dose now might leave you permanently stuck outside of your own body. A spectator of your own life. A living ghost."

"Good."

Hazel sighed. She looked at Toby. "Take her to Mary."

He approached Mary and lowered Lily towards her. Mary's hands trembled upward to cup the back of Lily's head. She guided Lily to her breasts. Lily clamped her lips together, but Mary's shrivelled black nipple wriggled between them as if it had a life of its own.

A stream of cold, slimy liquid spurted into Lily's mouth. She choked as it hit the back of her throat. Her cheeks filled up with the bitter goo.

"Swallow it," said Hazel.

Lily shook her head.

Hazel squatted down at her side. "You never listen to me, Lily." Her voice was sharp with resentment. "The only person you ever listened to was your dad. But he never knew what you needed." She jabbed a finger at herself. "I'm the only one who knows what you need, because I'm the only one who knows how you feel. I've been where you are, Lily. I fought against it too, but…" A wry smile crossed her lips. "Well let's just say the Devil always gets his due."

With that, she pressed a hand under Lily's chin and pinched her nose. She didn't let go until every last drop of the slime had slithered down Lily's throat.

"There you go. That wasn't so bad, was it?" said Hazel, rubbing Lily's back like she was winding a baby.

Lily glared at her with a hatred that no words could have expressed.

Hugo waddled forwards with Lily's birthday present. He put it over her head and drew it down her body. The robe bagged out shapelessly around her hips. Her sweaty hair clung to her face. Tears, spittle and snot glistened on her cheeks.

The coven applauded. "Beauty!" They called out as one. "Beauty!"

"Amen!" Rupert cried out, jolting back to consciousness.

Hazel and Hugo shot a look at each other, then burst into laughter.

"Lift me up to him," Hazel instructed Toby.

Taking hold of her waist, he hoisted her overhead like a ballerina. She took out the white feather again. The rest of the witches joined in laughing as she said solemnly, "By the true God, who redeemed thee with his precious blood, that all the illusions and wickedness of the Devil may depart thee. By him who will purge the earth with fire. I exorcise thee, Rupert Chapman, being weak but reborn in Holy Baptism. Amen."

"Judge them, Lord," Rupert screeched. "Send them to Hell. All of them. Every last one!"

As the final word left his mouth, Hazel blew the white powder into his face. His nostrils flared. Froth burbled between his lips. For several seconds, he squirmed like a worm on a hook. Then his eye glazed over and he went limp.

Hazel produced a second feather, inserted it into one of Rupert's nostrils and blew into it. The slightest of tremors passed through him, then... Nothing.

Lily eyed the treetop. Was Rupert up there, peering down at himself?

A living ghost.

She shuddered at the thought of her mum's words.

"Get him down," Hazel said to Toby. "And don't damage the tree."

He lowered her to the ground, then began to climb the tree. The crows took flight in a chaotic swirl. They fanned out in all directions, their guttural cries ricocheting off the hillside.

Hazel sank to her knees by Doubting Tom, then threw herself facedown on the ground. The other witches followed suit.

The dog sat up, yawning and stretching. His pus-encrusted eyes passed uninterestedly over the prostrate figures. He rose and hobbled to Mary. Her lipless mouth twisted into a semblance of a smile as he licked her face.

Like a drunkard stumbling home after a night of revelry, Doubting Tom turned to meander towards the enclosure's entrance. He paused to cock a leg and urinate on Susan's corpse before swaying between the grass banks.

The witches rose to their feet. Hazel took Mary's hands in hers. They stared at each other for a moment as if in silent communion. With infinite tenderness, Hazel kissed Mary's forehead. Then she beckoned to Gil and Nicola.

They came forwards and slid their hands under Mary's frail body. As carefully as if she was made of glass, they carried her to the tree. As they inserted her back into the hollow, Hazel murmured, "Death, death."

Her fellow witches took up the soft chant. "Death, death."

Lily watched Mary slide from view. The scrabbling started up again. Lily wondered where the burrow led to. A word rang in her mind – Hell.

"Death, death..." The chant faded. Likewise, the scrabbling died away. Silence reigned.

Lily's gaze drifted past the tree to the hazy pink glow crowning the hilltop. She yearned to feel the sun on her face. She felt so cold that she wondered if she would ever be warm again.

She became aware that she was being watched. With a wrench of effort, she turned her head. Every pair of eyes in the enclosure was fixed on her.

"Beauty," the witches hissed like a pack of envious cats.

The circle of naked bodies closed in around Lily, obscuring the dawn sky. They licked their lips. Saliva dribbled down their chins.

They're going to eat me, she thought. She forced out a few hoarse words. "I want to die."

"You can't die, Lily," her mum told her. "You've drunk the elixir of life. Now it's time to share your gift."

Closer they came. Closer and closer, blotting out the light

until it seemed to Lily that she was following Mary down the burrow. Down, down, down, all the way to Hell.

39

Lily's eyelids seemed to be glued together. As she wiped away a gooey, grey discharge, she found herself staring at her bedroom ceiling. Fingers of sunlight were reaching out across the bumpy white plaster. Her stomach felt uncomfortably full. Her mouth tasted like burnt sugar. What was the last thing she'd eaten? She couldn't seem to remember. Pressing a hand to her throbbing forehead, she searched her mind for any memory at all of the previous day. A hazy picture formed of herself drinking gooseberry wine while her mum made a birthday cake. Was that what this was? Was she hungover?

With a groan, she sat up. Her brow furrowed as she caught sight of herself in the dressing-table mirror. Was it her imagination or had her breasts grown overnight? The bulge in her vest was certainly more noticeable. She touched her nipples and winced. They were swollen and sore.

She inhaled sharply as she noticed something even more disturbing. On wobbly legs, she stood up and staggered to the dressing-table to scrutinise her reflection. Bloodshot eyes stared back at her from a pale face. She looked as if she'd been locked in a dark room for months. But that wasn't what troubled her most of all.

She lifted a trembling hand to her hair. There was a second white stripe running parallel to the original streak, like double lines on a road.

"Mum, Mum," she called out, turning to reel across the room

to the landing. Her mum's bedroom door was ajar. The bed was made. Birdsong floated in through the open window. Her gaze lingered on the empty picture hook above the fireplace. Where was the pressing of black moss? Had Mum got rid of it? Or... or...

Her eyebrows knitted as something unseen stirred in her mind.

At the sound of the front door opening, she turned and hurried downstairs. Her mum was lugging bags of groceries into the hallway. A silky scarf was draped around her neck. A quartet of red lines crisscrossed her forehead like whiplash marks.

"Lily!" she exclaimed, dropping the bags. "How long have you been awake?"

"Not long. What happened to your head?"

"Oh it's nothing."

"It doesn't look like nothing."

Hazel wafted her hand dismissively. "Never mind about me. How are you feeling?"

"I'm not sure. How long was I asleep?"

"A long time. We were starting to wonder whether you'd ever wake up."

"'We'? Who's 'we'?"

Instead of answering the question, Hazel took Lily's hand and kissed the back of it. "I'm so happy to see you up and about."

Lily pointed to the new white streak. "Have you seen this? When did this appear?"

Again, Hazel sidestepped the questions. "You must be starving. I'll make you breakfast. What do you fancy? How about pancakes?"

She drew Lily into the kitchen, opened the fridge and made a *ta-da* gesture as a light came on.

Lily frowned as if unsure what to make of the sight. "We have electricity."

Hazel laughed at her statement of the obvious. "We've had it for weeks now."

"Weeks?" Blood was suddenly pounding behind Lily's face. The floor seemed to sway beneath her like the deck of a boat. She gripped the table to keep her balance. "I've been asleep for weeks?"

"Well, yes and no. You've been in and out of sleep."

"I don't understand. Have I been ill?"

"Well, you've..." Hazel searched for the words to explain. "You've not been yourself."

Lily closed her eyes, pinching the bridge of her nose. *Not been yourself.* What did that even mean? If she hadn't been herself, who had she been? The unseen thing stirred again. She could feel it scratching at the surface of her mind.

"Poor darling," said Hazel. "You're as pale as Snow White." She poured a glass of fresh orange juice. "Here, this'll make you feel better."

Lily swallowed a mouthful. As the cold liquid settled in her stomach, Tom's face flashed in front of her like a glimpse of a subliminal image. His eyes were bulging, his teeth were clenched, veins were popping out on his forehead. She flinched, slopping juice over her hand.

"What is it, Lily? What's wrong?"

"I don't know. I think I just had some sort of flashback. I saw Tom. He looked..." Lily trailed off as she felt a strange fluttering in her belly. It was as if dozens of bubbles were bursting inside of her. "He looked angry. I think he might have done something to me."

"Such as?"

"I..." Lily fell silent, reluctant to repeat what the phantoms clawing their way out of her subconscious were whispering to her.

Hazel gave her hand a squeeze. "Whatever it is, you can tell me."

Lily chewed her lips, plucking up her courage, then said quickly, "I think he raped me."

Hazel tilted her head, smiling.

Lily stared at her in stunned silence for a moment. "Did you hear me? I said I was raped."

"Tom loves you."

"What? Why would you say–"

A high-pitched bark from outside interrupted Lily. She looked out of the front window, squinting as if someone was shining a torch in her eyes. A sudden flood of memories overwhelmed her – blood, flames, flesh, pain, laughter, moans, sobs, screams... It was all coming back now, spooling across her mind in a blur of colour and sound like a movie on fast-forward.

The front door clicked open. "I'm back and I have a surprise for you!"

The horrifically familiar voice stole the strength from Lily's legs. She crumpled onto a chair as Hazel replied, "I have a surprise for you too."

Tom entered the kitchen, dressed as usual in shorts and a t-shirt. A chubby black puppy with floppy ears and big, round eyes was cradled in his arms. A broad smile broke out on his face. "Lily!"

"Stay away from me, you rapist!" she retorted.

"Don't talk to your brother like that," admonished Hazel.

"Brother?" Lily echoed. She couldn't have heard right, could she?

"I'm your older brother," said Tom.

Lily swayed on the chair. The room was suddenly spinning like she'd drunk an entire bottle of Emily's gooseberry wine. "How can you be my brother? We're the same age?"

"No you're not," said Hazel. "I had Tom before I met your dad. He's twenty-two."

Lily clasped her hands to her head as if to prevent it from falling off. She couldn't grasp what she was hearing. It was just too horrible. "I don't understand."

"It's really not that complicated, Lily. It's all about the bloodline. You see, Mary's bloodline must be kept as pure as possible. But if it becomes too pure..." Hazel cast a meaningful glance at Tom.

The confusion drained from Lily's face. She subjected her mum to a glare of dazed contempt. "Oh I get it. If we become too inbred, we give birth to freaks like him."

"I'd rather be a freak than a fake," Tom fired back.

Lily threw him an indignant look. "You're calling me a fake? I've never pretended to be something I'm not."

"Are you sure about that? You act like you're oh so virtuous, but I know different." A lecherous smirk lifted Tom's lips. "I felt how much you enjoyed having me inside of you."

Anger flaring in her eyes, Lily hurled her glass at him. It narrowly missed his head, shattering against the wall. His eyes flinched shut as he was showered with orange juice and broken glass.

With a startled yelp, the puppy wriggled from his arms. Its legs splayed in all directions as it hit the flagstones, then it scuttled to Lily and cowered behind her ankles.

"You're going to regret that, Lily," Tom growled, striding

towards her.

Hazel put a hand on his shoulder. He shot her an annoyed glance. His anger dissolved into sullen submission at the warning in her eyes. She looked at the puppy, then at Lily. "The poor thing's scared. Give it a stroke."

Lily reached for the puppy, but hesitated and drew her hand back. Shaking her head as if to say, *I'm not going to fall for that*, she levelled a piercing stare at her mum. "God, I hate you so much."

"Oh stop feeling sorry for yourself," Tom retorted. "What have you got to cry about? You've been handed the world on a plate."

"He's right," said Hazel. "One day, you'll take my place as magistra. And after you, your firstborn daughter will lead the coven, and so on and so on. Our line will continue long after the last of the Chapmans are dead and buried."

Chapmans. At the mention of the name, Lily's mind flashed back to Rupert dangling upside down from the rowan tree. "Is Mr Chapman dead?"

Tom chuckled. "He's much worse than that."

"He's in hospital," said Hazel.

"A prison hospital," Tom elaborated gleefully. "Along with his wife."

Lily's eyes widened. "Mrs Chapman's alive?"

Hazel nodded. "Yes, she's alive."

"Just about," said Tom. "She suffered third-degree burns over ninety percent of her body." His grey eyes glittered with amusement. "Apparently, she spends her days begging to be put out of her misery."

Lily grimaced at the thought of the unbearable pain Margaret must be going through.

"There's no need for that face, Lily," said Hazel. "We've won."

"Won?" she echoed hollowly.

Hazel squatted down and placed her palms on Lily's lap. Lily froze as if a snake was slithering over her. Hazel's dark eyes radiated reassurance. "You should be looking forwards to the future, Lily. To all the pleasures that are to come."

"All the pleasures that are to come," Tom parroted like a churchgoer repeating the benediction.

Yapping as if in agreement, the puppy pawed at Lily's legs.

Hazel smiled. "He likes you. What do you think we should call him?"

"Hey, why does she get to name him when I was the one who–" Tom protested. He subsided into pouting silence once again at a glance from Hazel.

Lily's gaze fell to the puppy. Its head was tilted downwards, but its eyes were peering up at her. It was a look she herself had perfected for manipulating her dad into giving her what she wanted. He'd been a sucker for puppy eyes.

She icily met her mum's gaze. "Do you really think you can buy me with a puppy? I'm not a child."

Tom's smirk returned. "Not anymore you're not. I saw to that."

Rage seized Lily and hauled her to her feet. The sudden movement dumped Hazel onto her backside and sent the puppy skittering into a corner. Lily swung a fist wildly at Tom.

He dodged out of reach, laughing. "Missed again."

Hazel sprang up between them. "That's enough from both of you! We're a family. Let's start acting like it."

"A family?" Lily gave an incredulous snort. "We're not a family. We're a sick joke." She pointed at the puppy. "And as for that *thing*. I'll kill myself before I kiss its arse." She pivoted, deftly dodged around her mum and snatched a carving knife from a block of knives. She pressed the blade against the underside of her wrist. "I mean it, I'll slash my wrists."

Tom's lips crooked up into a sceptical sneer. "She's bluffing."

Lily glared at him as if to say, *Try me.*

"Put the knife down, Lily," Hazel said with a soft plea in her voice.

"Or what? Will you give me another dose of White Breath?"

Hazel shook her head. "No more White Breath. No more arse kissing. From now on, you're free to make your own choices. That's what true strength is, Lily. It's having the freedom to live life on your own terms."

Lily's eyes narrowed. "So I'm free to walk out of this house right now and never come back?"

"Yes, of course you are. But believe me, Lily, it doesn't matter where you go, you can't escape what you are."

Peter, Peter pumpkin eater...

Lily heard her dad's drunken voice as clearly as if he was in the room. She blinked at a sudden sting of tears. "So that's it, is it?" she murmured more to herself than to anyone else. "I'm stuck in a pumpkin shell and there's nothing I can do about it?"

"Pumpkin shell? What are you gibbering about?" Tom asked.

"You're not stuck anywhere," said Hazel.

A shrill laugh escaped Lily. "I'm free to be what I want, but I can't escape what I am." She yanked at her white hair as if trying to tear it out. "How does that even make any sense?"

"It doesn't have to make sense. You just have to accept it."

"No! I'll never accept it. I'll never be like you."

"Yes you will, Lily." Hazel's tone implied that what she said was the absolute truth. "In the end, we all become what we once hated."

Lily shook her head vehemently. "I'd rather die."

"Then do it," Tom challenged. "Kill yourself." He rolled his eyes towards the ceiling. "But don't expect any sympathy from *him*. Suicide is a mortal sin. And you know where sinners go, don't you?"

"Shut up, Tom," snapped Hazel. She summoned up a thin smile for Lily. "I know you think I'm this evil witch, but ask yourself this – why did the Devil become the Devil?" She paused a second before answering her own question. "He was just trying to survive. And that's all I'm doing. And that's all Mary was doing three-hundred-years ago. What's so bad about that? What's wrong with selling your soul in exchange for a future?"

"There's only one thing I'd sell my soul for." Lily pointed the knife towards Hazel and Tom. "To see you both dead!"

Such was the venom in her voice that the puppy whimpered. An idea sparked in Lily's eyes. She darted to the dog and snatched it up by the scruff of the neck. The puppy cried out, waggling its stumpy legs as if trying to run in midair.

"You're hurting him," Tom exclaimed, starting towards Lily. He pulled up abruptly as she shifted the knife blade from her wrist to the dog's throat.

"I'm leaving and neither of you are stopping me."

Hazel heaved a sigh. "As usual, Lily, you haven't listened to a word I've said."

"Yes I have, but all I've heard is lies and more lies. Now open the backdoor."

At a nod from Hazel, Tom moved to do so.

Lily jerked her chin towards the other side of the kitchen. "Go over there. Both of you."

She waited for her mum and Tom to do as she said, then she backed towards the door.

"Think about what you're doing, Lily," said Hazel. "You have no money, nowhere to go." She motioned to herself and Tom. "We're your only family and we love you very much. Don't we, Tom?"

"Yes." His voice was deadpan. "We love you very, very much."

Some of Margaret's words found their way into Lily's mouth. "A witch cannot love."

As Lily retreated out of the door, Hazel raised her hands in entreaty. "Are you really going to throw away everything your ancestors fought for?"

"I didn't ask them to fight for me." Lily cast her gaze over the room. "And I don't want this place."

"What about Chapman Hall? Do you want that?"

"What sort of stupid question is that? We couldn't afford to buy that place in a million years."

"We won't have to buy it if we win the court case. We're suing the Chapmans."

"We're going to take them for everything they've got," Tom said smugly.

Lily's lips curved into a derisive smile. "We all become what we once hated."

"Exactly. So why fight it?" Hazel asked. "Why not just enjoy it?"

The puppy squirmed in fright as Lily practically screamed, "Because I don't want it! I don't want it! How many times do I have to tell you before it gets through your thick skulls? I just want to be left alone."

"Fine, if that's what you really want. But I don't think it is. I think what you really want is to know everything's going to be ok." Hazel's voice was as soothing as warm milk. "Well everything *is* going to be ok, Lily. All the bad stuff's out of the way. It's time to start enjoying–"

"Oh shut up! Just shut up. I..." Lily faltered, her expression suspended somewhere between despair and exhaustion.

"Alright, Lily." Hazel followed her outside. "Just know that we're here for you, whatever you need from us."

"Why won't she listen?" Lily spoke as if addressing an unseen entity. "Why can't she understand that I don't need anything from–"

She broke off as a snuffle came from behind her. A heavy hand landed on her shoulder. With a small scream, she whirled around. She found herself staring into Hugo's piggy little eyes. His breath whistled through his teeth. Face quivering like a pink blancmange, he looked down.

Lily did likewise. A horrified gasp burst from her. The carving knife was buried to the hilt in Hugo's belly. The blade slithered free as he staggered backwards. He collapsed onto his backside with a thud like a sack of potatoes hitting the ground.

"Dad!" Tom cried out, surging past Lily. He dropped to his knees by Hugo. His hands hovered above the dark stain that was spreading across his dad's burgundy robe. "What do I do?"

"Pressure! Put pressure on it!" Hazel told him frantically.

There was a hideous squelch as Tom pressed his hands to the heaving mound of flesh. Hugo let out an equally wet-sounding moan.

Hazel spun Lily around by the arm. "Now look what you've done."

"It... It was an accident," Lily stammered.

Hazel reached for the knife. "Give me that."

At the last second, Lily dodged away from her. She put the knife to the squeaking puppy's throat again. "I'll kill it."

"I'll kill *you!*" Tom exploded.

"No one's going to kill anyone." Hazel's voice rang with

authority.

Tom ground his teeth in frustration. "So you're just going to let her get away with this?" Tears welled in his eyes. "What if Dad dies?"

Hugo's voice trickled out in a thin wheeze. "We take care of our own."

"No matter what," Hazel affirmed. She aimed a hard stare at Lily. "But that doesn't mean this will go unpunished."

Lily retreated from the promise in her mum's eyes.

Hazel took off her scarf, revealing pale red track marks where the iron collar had bitten into her neck. She dropped to her haunches beside Hugo and tried to staunch the bleeding.

Lily flinched as, without warning, the puppy sank its pin-sharp teeth into her arm. In turn, the puppy let out a childlike yowl as the blade nicked its throat.

Tom sprang up as if to charge at Lily. Hazel caught hold of his wrist. "Let her go. She'll be back." She looked at Lily with a certainty that could only be born of experience. "She knows what she is and where she belongs. She just needs time to come to terms with it." Hazel opened her arms as if offering an embrace. "And when she does, we'll be here."

For a brief moment, Lily's eyes betrayed a yearning as deep and dark as the forest. A flicker of movement on the cottage's roof caught her attention. A crow was pecking at the black moss that had already begun to populate the new thatches. As if spurred on by the sight, she turned and ran towards the trees.

40

L ily passed beneath the arms of the embracing oaks. She gripped the puppy under her arm, darting glances over her shoulder. There was no sign of anyone in pursuit. At first, all she focused on was putting some distance between herself and the cottage. When she came to the avenue of blackthorns, she stopped to catch her breath. She stared around herself as wide-eyed as a lost little child. A despairing sob rasped from her throat.

What now? Was she supposed to live in the woods like a wild animal? Or perhaps she should turn herself in to the police for stabbing Hugo. Considering the alternative, neither possibility seemed so bad.

She placed a hand on her stomach as the fluttering sensation started up again. Something weird was going on in there. Did it have anything to do with the vile milk they'd made her drink from Mary's breast? Her forehead wrinkled. Had Mary even been real? Maybe the old hag who'd crawled out of the tree hadn't been Mary at all. Maybe she'd been a member of the coven acting the part. Was it possible? Could it all have been... Been what? A sort of twisted play? A magic trick intended to frighten its audience into doing as they were told?

"Well it didn't work on me," she said to the puppy, stroking its soft ears.

The chubby bundle of fur licked her hand like it wanted to make friends.

"Was it a trick? Or was it real?" A grim smile crossed Lily's face. "Shall we see if we can find out which it was?"

As if frightened by the suggestion, the puppy whimpered and tried to wriggle free. Lily tightened her grip. "What's wrong? Don't you want to meet Mary?"

She set off along the avenue. "You know what you need?" she told the puppy. "A name." She winced as a thorn embedded itself in the sole of her foot. She reached down to pull it out, stared at it thoughtfully for a moment, then looked at the puppy. "Thorn. That's what I'll call you."

As Lily entered the clearing, she tensed in anticipation of seeing Sam's charred remains. The sun-splashed circle contained nothing other than grass, weeds and ash. Maybe whatever was left of Sam had been returned to his grave. Or maybe the crows had feasted on roast dog.

A giggle tainted with hysteria slipped past her lips. "Look, Thorn, this is where the witches come to recharge their crystals."

The puppy squealed as Lily hoisted him overhead and twirled around.

"Peter, Peter pumpkin eater. Peter, Peter pumpkin eater," Lily chanted like an incantation. She staggered dizzily. A puff of ash flew up as she fell to the scorched earth at the clearing's centre. With Thorn trembling against her, she lay staring at the cloud-dotted sky. Several crows passed high overhead, heading towards the hilltop.

Lily sat up. "Looks like they're going to the same place as us, Thorn." As if they were all on their way to a party, she waved to the crows and called out, "See you there!"

She picked her way through the undergrowth, avoiding nettles and brambles. A brisk wind murmured through the trees behind her, speeding her progress.

"Is that the spirits of the forest?" she wondered with a scornful smile. "What do you think, Thorn? Are the forest spirits helping us?"

The puppy's eyes were closed. Tremors were rippling across its sleek coat.

"There's no need to be scared," Lily soothed, mimicking her mum's milky-soft tone. "Everything's going to be alright. All the bad stuff's out of the way." She giggled again. "And if you believe that, you're as stupid as me."

They emerged from the forest. As Lily climbed the hillside, she kept up a running commentary like a tour guide. "You see over there, Thorn, that's where I first met Jude." She pointed to Chapman House's grey façade. "And that's where he lives. Or used to live. I don't know if anyone lives there now." They arrived at the broad grassy shelf occupied by the earthwork. "And this is Dead Woman's Ditch where Mary was put to death."

As they entered the enclosure, Lily's bleak grin faltered. "And this is where Tom raped me." Her fingers contracted on the knife's handle as she thought about select parts of his anatomy that deserved to be chopped off.

Nothing in the enclosure hinted at what had transpired there. There was no blood. No scorch marks. Lily wondered whether other people besides Mary and Susan had died there over the years and left no trace behind. Perhaps the earthwork's mysterious builders had used it as a place of sacrifice. The blood of hundreds might have soaked into its grass. Forgotten victims sacrificed to forgotten gods.

A handful of crows looked on from the rowan tree. Lily eyed the bulbous twiggy growth high up on the tree trunk, wondering if the white-winged crow was lurking within it. Her gaze descended to the hollow at the base of the tree. Part of her was tempted to crawl into it, not to find out if Mary really existed, but to join her in the darkness. Perhaps down there she would finally be left in peace.

Come, Lily, a voice rustled through her mind. *Veni, veni, Lily.*

She shivered, then trudged forwards and sagged against the tree. God, she was so tired. She felt as if *she* was three-hundred-and-thirty-three-years old. She slid to the ground. The puppy was soothingly warm against her stomach.

"What am I doing here, Thorn?" she asked, heaving a sigh.

The puppy's mournfully round eyes peered up at her.

The sun appeared from behind a cloud. The crows fanned their tail feathers, idly sunning themselves. A rustling from overhead drew Lily's gaze. The white-winged crow emerged from its home. Twigs fell on Lily as the crow shook out its wings.

Thorn lifted his head and started yapping.

"Shush," Lily scolded. "That's my friend." She looked askance at the bird. "You *are* my friend, aren't you?"

The crow shuffled along its perch. The other crows sidestepped away from it, cawing as if annoyed. Or perhaps afraid. The black-and-white crow spread its wings and swooped gracefully down to land in front of Lily. It bobbed its head at her.

"What do you want?" she asked.

The crow opened its beak wide like a chick begging for food.

"I don't have anything for you to eat."

The crow croaked as if it disagreed.

The harsh sound set off Thorn's trembling. Lily frowned, then hugged the puppy closer and shook her head. "Uh-uh. No way. You're not having Thorn for breakfast."

Its beak gleaming like jet in the sun, the crow hopped forwards. Lily shielded the puppy's eyes with her hand. "I said *no.*"

The crow took another hop closer. Lily pointed the knife at

it. The bird puffed out its chest against the tip of the blade as if certain she wouldn't harm it. Then it dipped its head to touch one of her knuckles with its downturned beak.

Lily's frown faded as the beak shifted sideways to tap ever-so-gently at the neighbouring knuckle. It moved on to the next knuckle and the next before retracing its path. Stroking. Tapping. Back and forth. Back and forth...

She closed her eyes and suddenly found herself back in Fulham. Back with her dad. His fingers were playing on her knuckles. Steady. Soothing. "Go to sleep," he was murmuring. "Go to sleep. Go to sleep..."

Her eyes snapped open as the crow drew away from her. She stared into its beady eyes as if striving to see what was behind them. An awestruck whisper found its way past her lips. "Dad?"

The crow cocked its head, seemingly trying to understand her.

"Is that you, Dad?" Lily's voice trembled from fear to hope and back. "Are you... in there?"

The crow remained silent.

A flicker of uncertainty crossed Lily's face, then her eyes narrowed as if an idea had occurred to her. Slowly at first, but with increasing speed, she started to chant, "Peter, Peter, pumpkin eater, had a wife and couldn't keep her. He put her in a pumpkin shell, and there he kept her very well. Peter, Peter pumpkin eater had a wife and couldn't keep her..."

As her chanting reached a crescendo, the crow joined in, cawing and strutting around.

"It is you!" Lily jumped to her feet. Holding the puppy up to her face, she exclaimed ecstatically, "It is him!" She laughed as the crow sprang into the air. It circled her head before landing nimbly on a nearby branch.

Lily's smile wavered. Fresh uncertainty glimmered in her eyes. "Did Mum and Uncle Hugo bring you back? Did they actually do what they said they would?"

The questions drew an indecipherable stare from the crow.

"No." Lily's voice quivered with conviction. "That was just another lie to get me to do what they wanted. You chose to come back and protect me, didn't you?" She nodded as if answering for the crow. "I need your help again, Dad. I can't stay with Mum, but I've got nowhere else to go. I don't know what to do." Tears shimmered in her eyes. "If you don't help me, I'll die. I can feel it."

After what felt to Lily like a torturously long moment, the crow extended a wing revealing a pure white feather on the underside.

Confusion briefly lined Lily's face before giving way to horrified comprehension. "You want me to use the White Breath on them? I can't do *that*. There has to be another way."

The crow mutely kept its wing outstretched.

Send them to Hell. All of them. Every last one!

Rupert's final appeal for God to pass sentence on the witches shivered through Lily like a winter wind. She looked up as if expecting to see his 'living ghost' glaring at her from the treetop. A dozen pairs of inscrutable little eyes stared down at her. The crows were grouped together like jurors in a court.

She blinked as the black-and-white crow pushed its wing into her face. The splayed wingtips tickled her nostrils.

She shook her head. "I won't do it." To show she meant what she said, she turned her back on the bird and flung away the knife. It spun through the air and embedded itself in the ground near where she'd lain paralysed with Tom on top of her. She grimaced, recalling the stretching, stabbing pressure as he'd forced himself inside her.

The seed has been planted in a good soil by great waters, that it might bring out branches, and that it might bear fruit to be a goodly vine.

As her mum's celebratory words echoed in her mind, Lily's hand returned to her stomach. Suddenly, it felt like there was an entire bath's worth of bubbles bursting in there. A wave of realisation came crashing down on her. The force of it was so great that she had to cling to the tree to stop herself from falling over.

"No, please god no," she gasped. "I can't be." Her terrified eyes rose to the crow. "But what if I am? What if I'm preg–" Her throat contracted involuntarily around the half-formed word.

Hatred disfigured her face as Tom's grinning mug materialised in her mind. She wanted to punch the smugness out of him. Just keep on punching and punching until he was battered to a bloody pulp.

As if propelled by some external force, her hand jolted up to pluck the white feather from the wing. She flinched away from the crow as it let out a piercing caw. The puppy gave a start, too, and squirmed so frantically that it nearly escaped her clutches.

"Stop it, Thorn," she snapped.

The crow stretched out its other wing and gave it a shake. Two more white feathers seesawed to the ground at Lily's feet.

She looked at the feather in her hand, then at those on the grass. "They deserve everything they've got coming," she muttered. "All I want is to be left alone. But that won't ever happen. Not while they're around."

Scanning the area to make sure no one besides the crows was watching, she scurried to retrieve the knife. Thorn whimpered as Lily pinned him to the ground. She held the blade to his front left leg and peered up at the crow.

"Is this what you want me to do?" she demanded to know as if hoping the decision would be taken out of her hands.

The crow folded its wings back to its body, watching her fixedly.

"I'll do it. Ok, here I go. I'm doing it. Here goes." Lily's words went round in circles as if she was daring herself to take a plunge into unknown depths. "I have to do this. I have to do it. Do it. Do it!"

Her entire body tensed as she pressed down with all her might. Thorn's scream stabbed at her eardrums. Kneeling on the thrashing animal, she sawed back and forth. The blade crunched through ligaments, tendons and bone. Hot, salty blood spurted into her face and mouth. She gagged and spat it out.

The sawing and screaming seemed to go on endlessly. Her forearm was throbbing. Her ears were ringing.

Thorn's mouth was stretched so wide open that his jaw looked dislocated. His bulging eyes seemed to cry out, *Why are you doing this?*

"I'm sorry, Thorn. My..." Lily struggled to push her words past a lump of shame. "My mum was right about me."

Blood pumped spasmodically from a band of flesh encircling a cross-section of bone. A scrap of skin was the only thing holding the leg in place. Almost sobbing with relief, Lily sliced through it.

Thorn had gone deathly still. His eyes were closed. His tongue lolled out of his foam-flecked mouth.

Tears mingled with the blood on Lily's cheeks as she glared at the crow. "Are you happy now?"

Appearing indifferent to her resentful tone, the bird began to groom itself, poking and nibbling at its feathers.

Lily dropped the knife and picked up the white feathers. One by one, she dipped their quills in the bleeding stump as if it was an ink pot.

Thorn spasmed like a corpse being shocked back to life. At the third prod, he jerked to his feet. He staggered around, falling over, flopping about, struggling back up, going in circles.

The crows let loose a string of cackling cries from the treetop.

"Shut up," Lily shouted. "It's not funny."

Thorn collapsed by the entrance to the hollow tree trunk. This time, he didn't get back up. He lay panting, glassy-eyed.

"Please die," Lily murmured. "Please just die."

She flinched as the puppy suddenly slid into the hollow. Had Thorn moved by himself? Or was something pulling him along? Her heart hammering against her ribs, she grabbed the knife and edged forwards to peer into the aperture.

A trail of blood led down the burrow. There was nothing else to be seen and nothing to be heard.

"Mary?" Lily couldn't bring herself to speak above a whisper. "Mary?"

She opened her mouth to repeat the name a third time, but her tongue refused to utter it. Lowering the knife, she backed away from the tree. The crows had fallen silent.

A strange hopelessness dulled her eyes as she looked at the white-winged crow. "I love you, Dad."

The crow inflated its chest and emitted a soft, almost purring call that lifted every hair on Lily's body.

She held up the severed leg on her palm as if offering it in payment. The crow fluttered down to scoop it up with its clawed feet before wheeling towards the clump of twigs that girdled the tree.

Lily watched the crow squeeze itself into its home. Then she turned to make her way back to her own thatched house.

41

At the edge of the garden, Lily paused to hide the three feathers in a small cavity in one of the oak trees. Her mum, Tom and Hugo were nowhere to be seen. She strode to the cottage and opened the backdoor. Bloodstained towels and cloths were strewn across the kitchen floor.

Her eyes widened as a wheezing groan seeped through the ceiling. She was more surprised by the fact that they'd managed to get Hugo upstairs than that they hadn't taken him to hospital.

The kitchen was suffused with a medicinal pine aroma. A bunch of long green stems crowned with clusters of tiny white flowers lay on the work surface. The stems had been mostly stripped of their feather-like leaves. Bits of finely chopped leaves were scattered across a chopping-board. Doubtless, her mum had whipped up some herbal concoction to treat Hugo's wound.

Lily made a mental note to ask what the treatment entailed. She wanted to learn everything her mum had to teach, everything she would need to survive here on her own.

She reached for the tap to wash the blood off her hands and face, but stopped short of turning it on.

"Let them see," she told herself. "Then they'll know not to mess with me."

More groans came from above as she headed for the stairs. The medicinal smell intensified, stinging her nostrils. She hesitated as Tom piped up, "He's getting worse. We have to call an ambulance."

"And what are we supposed to tell them?" Hazel retorted.

"That it was an accident."

Hazel gave an exasperated laugh. "Just how does someone accidentally stab themselves in the stomach?"

"I don't want Dad to die." Tom sounded like a scared little boy.

Something close to sympathy tugged at Lily's heart as she recalled how devastating it had been to watch her dad being taken away in a body bag. With a sharp shake of her head, she cast the feeling aside before entering her mum's bedroom.

Hugo was splayed out on the bed, his chest heaving and rattling. The mattress was sagging almost to the floorboards beneath him. His robe had been cut open. A wad of bandages splotched with blood and dark green stains swathed his belly.

Hazel was stooped over the nearside of the bed. Tom was at the far side. Lily couldn't help but feel a twinge of satisfaction at the sudden start he gave upon seeing her.

Not so smug now, are you? she resisted the urge to say.

Hazel lifted her gaze to Tom, then turned to Lily with an infuriatingly knowing smile. A frown took over at the sight of Lily's blood-spattered cheeks. "Whose blood is that?"

"It's the puppy's."

"What have you done to my dog?" Tom demanded to know.

Lily locked eyes with him. "I killed it."

He opened and closed his mouth, momentarily dumbstruck, then spluttered, "Why?"

Lily arched an eyebrow as if it should have been obvious. "To spite you."

Paling with rage, Tom clenched his fully formed hand into a

fist and stalked around the bed. "I'll–"

"You'll do nothing," Hazel commanded.

Tom halted in mid-step. He looked back and forth between his mother and sister several times, then stamped his foot and stayed put. Hazel's gaze returned to Lily. "It doesn't matter about the puppy. All that matters is that you're back." A note of uncertainty entered her voice. "You *are* back to stay, aren't you?"

"Yes, Mum, I'm back to stay. I know what I am now." Lily spoke in a flat, fatalistic tone.

Her face softening into a smile, Hazel spread her arms. Lily stepped into her embrace. Hazel kissed Lily's forehead and stroked her white-streaked hair. "I knew you'd see sense, Lily. Now all I want is for us to be a happy family."

I just want what we had. I want us to be a happy family.

Lily closed her eyes as the words – almost the last ones her dad had ever spoken – echoed from the darkness of her mind. "We will be." Her voice was so low it was like she was talking to herself. "I was wrong. Fairytale endings do exist."

BOOKS BY THIS AUTHOR

Don't Look Back
(Fenton House Book 1)

What really haunts Fenton House?

After the tragic death of their eleven-year-old son, Adam and Ella are fighting to keep their family from falling apart. Then comes an opportunity that seems too good to be true. They win a competition to live for free in a breathtakingly beautiful mansion on the Cornish Lizard Peninsula. There's just one catch – the house is supposedly haunted.

Mystery has always swirled around Fenton House. In 1920 the house's original owner, reclusive industrialist Walter Lewarne, hanged himself from its highest turret. In 1996, the then inhabitants, George Trehearne, his wife Sofia and their young daughter Heloise disappeared without a trace. Neither mystery was ever solved.

Adam is not the type to believe in ghosts. As far as he's concerned, ghosts are simply memories. Everywhere he looks in their cramped London home he sees his dead son. Despite misgivings, the chance to start afresh is too tempting to pass up. Adam, Ella and their surviving son Henry move into Fenton House. At first, the change of scenery gives them all a new lease of life. But as the house starts to reveal its secrets, they come to suspect that they may not be alone after all...

House Of Mirrors
(Fenton House Book 2)

What will you see?

Two years ago the Piper family fled Fenton House after their dream of a new life turned into an unspeakable nightmare. The house has stood empty ever since, given a wide berth by everyone except ghost hunters and occult fanatics.

Now something is trying to lure the Pipers back to Fenton House. But is that 'something' a malevolent supernatural entity? Or is there a more earthly explanation? Whatever the truth, Adam and Ella Piper are about to discover that their family's future is inextricably bound up with the last place they ever wanted to see again.

The Pipers aren't the only ones whose fate is tied to Fenton House. Three thieves seeking their fortune and a mysterious redheaded woman are also converging on the remote Cornish mansion.

Over the course of a single stormy night, each of them will be forced to confront their true self. How far are they willing to go in pursuit of their deepest, darkest desires? How much are they prepared to give in order to simply survive till dawn?

Mr Moonlight

Close your eyes. He's waiting for you.

There's a darkness lurking under the surface of Julian Harris. Every night in his dreams he becomes a different person, a monster capable of evil beyond comprehension. Sometimes he feels like something is trying to get inside him. Or maybe it's already in him, just waiting for the chance to escape into the waking world.

There's a darkness lurking under the surface of Julian's picture-postcard hometown too. Fifteen years ago, five girls disappeared from the streets of Godthorne. Now it's happening again. A schoolgirl has gone missing, stirring up memories of that terrible time. But the man who abducted those other girls is long dead. Is there a copycat at work? Or is something much, much stranger going on?

Drawn by the same sinister force that haunts his dreams, Julian returns to Godthorne for the first time in years. Finding himself mixed up in the mystery of the missing girl, he realises that to unearth the truth about the present he must confront the ghosts of his past.

Somewhere amidst the sprawling tangle of trees that surrounds Godthorne are the answers he so desperately seeks. But the forest does not relinquish its secrets easily.

The Lost Ones

The truth can be more dangerous than lies.

July 1972

The Ingham household. Upstairs, sisters Rachel and Mary are sleeping peacefully. Downstairs, blood is pooling around the shattered skull of their mother, Joanna, and a figure is creeping up behind their father, Elijah. A hammer comes crashing down again and again...

July 2016

The Jackson household. This is going to be the day when Tom Jackson's hard work finally pays off. He kisses his wife Amanda and their children, Jake and Erin, goodbye and heads out dreaming of a better life for them all. But just hours later he finds himself plunged into a nightmare...

Erin is missing. She was hiking with her mum in Harwood Forest. Amanda turned her back for a moment. That was all it took for Erin to vanish. Has she simply wandered off? Or does the blood-stained rock found where she was last seen point to something sinister? The police and volunteers who set out to search the sprawling forest are determined to find out. Meanwhile, Jake launches an investigation of his own – one that will expose past secrets and present betrayals.

Is Erin's disappearance somehow connected to the unsolved murders of Elijah and Joanna Ingham? Does it have something to do with the ragtag army of eco-warriors besieging Tom's controversial quarry development? Or is it related to the fraught phone call that distracted Amanda at the time of Erin's disappearance?

So many questions. No one seems to have the answers and time is running out. Tom, Amanda and Jake must get to the truth to save Erin, though in doing so they may well end up destroying themselves.

Blood Guilt
(Steel City Thrillers Book 1)

Can you ever really atone for killing someone?

After the death of his son in a freak accident, Detective Harlan Miller's life is spiralling out of control. He's drinking too much. His marriage and career are on the rocks. But things are about to get even worse. A booze-soaked night out and a single wild punch leave a man dead and Harlan facing a manslaughter charge.

Fast-forward four years. Harlan's prison term is up, but life on the outside holds little promise. Divorced, alone, consumed by guilt, he thinks of nothing beyond atoning for the death he caused. But how do you make up for depriving a wife of her husband and two young boys of their father? Then something happens, something terrible, yet something that holds out a twisted kind of hope for Harlan – the dead man's youngest son is abducted.

From that moment Harlan's life has only one purpose – finding the boy. So begins a frantic race against time that leads him to a place darker than anything he experienced as a detective and a stark moral choice that compels him to question the law he once enforced.

Angel Of Death
(Steel City Thrillers Book 2)

They thought she was dead. They were wrong.

Fifteen-year-old Grace Kirby kisses her mum and heads off to school. It's a day like any other day, except that Grace will never return home.

Fifteen years have passed since Grace went missing. In that time, Stephen Baxley has made millions. And now he's lost millions. Suicide seems like the only option. But Stephen has no intention of leaving behind his wife, son and daughter. He wants them all to be together forever, in this world or the next.

Angel is on the brink of suicide too. Then she hears a name on the news that transports her back to a windowless basement. Something terrible happened in that basement. Something Angel has been running from most of her life. But the time for running is over. Now is the time to start fighting back.

At the scene of a fatal shooting, Detective Jim Monahan finds evidence of a sickening crime linked to a missing girl. Then more people start turning up dead. Who is the killer? Are the victims also linked to the girl? Who will be next to die? The answers will test to breaking-point Jim's faith in the law he's spent his life upholding.

Justice For The Damned
(Steel City Thrillers Book 3)

They said there was no serial killer. They lied.

Melinda has been missing for weeks. The police would normally be all over it, but Melinda is a prostitute. Women in that line of work change addresses like they change lipstick. She probably just moved on.

Staci is determined not to let Melinda become just another statistic added to the long list of girls who've gone missing over the years. Staci is also a prostitute – although not for much longer if Detective Reece Geary has anything to do with it. Reece will do anything to win Staci's love. If that means putting his job on the line by launching an unofficial investigation, then so be it.

Detective Jim Monahan is driven by his own dangerous obsession. He's on the trail of a psychopath hiding behind a facade of respectability. Jim's investigation has already taken him down a rabbit hole of corruption and depravity. He's about to discover that the hole goes deeper still. Much, much deeper...

Spider's Web
(Steel City Thrillers Book 4)

It's all connected.

A trip to the cinema turns into a nightmare for Anna and her little sister Jessica, when two men throw thirteen-year-old Jessica into the back of a van and speed away.

The years tick by... Tick, tick... The police fail to find Jessica and her name fades from the public consciousness... Tick, tick... But every time Anna closes her eyes she's back in that terrible moment, lurching towards Jessica, grabbing for her. So close. So agonisingly close... Tick, tick... Now in her thirties, Anna has no career, no relationship, no children. She's consumed by one purpose – finding Jessica, dead or alive.

Detective Jim Monahan has a little black book with forty-two names in it. Jim's determined to put every one of those names behind bars, but his investigation is going nowhere fast. Then a twenty-year-old clue brings Jim and Anna together in search of a shadowy figure known as Spider. Who is Spider? Where is Spider? Does Spider have the answers they want? The only thing Jim and Anna know is that the victims Spider entices into his web have a habit of ending up missing or dead.

Now She's Dead
(Jack Anderson Book 1)

What happens when the watcher becomes the watched?

Jack has it all – a beautiful wife and daughter, a home, a career. Then his wife, Rebecca, plunges to her death from the Sussex coast cliffs. Was it an accident or did she jump? He moves to Manchester with his daughter, Naomi, to start afresh, but things don't go as planned. He didn't think life could get any worse...

Jack sees a woman in a window who is the image of Rebecca. Attraction turns into obsession as he returns to the window night after night. But he isn't the only one watching her...

Jack is about to be drawn into a deadly game. The woman lies dead. The latest victim in a series of savage murders. Someone is going to go down for the crimes. If Jack doesn't find out who the killer is, that 'someone' may well be him.

Who Is She?
(Jack Anderson Book 1)

A woman with no memory. A question no one seems able to answer.

After the death of his wife, Jack is starting to get his life back on track. But things are about to get complicated.

A woman lies in a hospital bed, clinging to life after being shot in the head. She remembers nothing, not even her own name. Who is she? That is the question Jack must answer. All he has to go on is a mysterious facial tattoo.

Damaged kindred spirits, Jack and the nameless woman quickly form a bond. But he can't afford to fall for someone who might put his family at risk. People are dying. Their deaths appear to be connected to the woman. What if she isn't really the victim? What if she's just as bad as the 'Unspeakable Monsters' who put her in hospital?

She Is Gone

(Jack Anderson Book 1)

First she lost her memory. Then she lost her family. Now she wants justice.

On a summer's day in 1998, a savage crime at an isolated Lakeland beauty spot leaves three dead. The case has gone unsolved ever since. The only witness is an amnesiac with a bullet lodged in her brain.

The bullet is a ticking time bomb that could kill Butterfly at any moment. Jack is afraid for her. But should he be afraid of her? She's been suffering from violent mood swings. Sometimes she acts like a completely different person.

Butterfly is obsessed with the case. But how can she hope to succeed where the police have failed? The answer might be locked within the darkest recesses of her damaged mind. Or maybe the driver of the car that's been following her holds the key to the mystery.

Either way, the truth may well cost Butterfly her family, her sanity and her life.

ABOUT THE AUTHOR

Ben Cheetham

Ben is an award-winning writer and Pushcart Prize nominee with a passion for horror and crime fiction. His novels have been widely published around the world. In 2011 he self-published Blood Guilt. The novel went on to reach no.2 in the national eBook download chart, selling well over 150000 copies. In 2012 it was picked up for publication by Head of Zeus. Since then, Head of Zeus has published three more of Ben's novels – 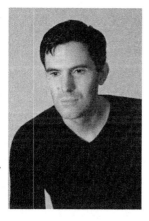 Angel of Death, Justice for the Damned and Spider's Web. In 2016 his novel The Lost Ones was published by Thomas & Mercer.

Ben lives in Sheffield, England, where he spends most of his time shut away in his study racking his brain for the next paragraph, the next sentence, the next word...

If you'd like to learn more about Ben's books or get in touch, you can do so at bencheetham.com

Printed in Great Britain
by Amazon

43278278R00198